SHOPOCALYPSE

SHOPOCALYPSE

David Gullen

MONICO

ISBN 978-1-909016-20-0

Clarion Publishing
PO Box 45298
London
England
SE10 1BN

http://www.clarionpublishing.com/

Cover artwork by Ben Baldwin
http://www.benbaldwin.co.uk/

Acknowledgements

Well, I made it. Like many authors the road to my first published novel has been a life-long trip and I have many people to thank. Please bear with me.

First and foremost - Colin Tate at Clarion. A more conscientious and perceptive editor and publisher you could not wish to have. Dude.

No book gets written alone. In the T Party writers group (www.t-party. org.uk) are just about the finest bunch of writers and friends you could want. Martin, Helen, Sarah, Rosanne, Sumit, Peter, Sara, Melanie, Jehangir, Julia, Mark, Tom, Bruce, et al, the inspiration, the trip itself - none of this would have been the same. Advice, companionship, leaning on all those bars and talking all that writerly shit. Without you I'd have drunk a lot less whisky.

Jaine Fenn. Thanks.

Dwight V Swain, who knew why you do what you do. And when not to.

No writer writes without having read. And I read. AA Milne & Hugh Lofting made me dream; John Christopher, Andre Norton and HG Wells were with me as I grew up. The incomparable Jack Vance. JG Ballard, Robert Holdstock, Philip K Dick. So many more.

Gaie. Who always believed. For all this, and more. My companion.

Evolution, God, kismet, life, call it what you will. Thank you for making me the rhino-skinned, pig-headed weeble I grew to become. Lessons learned the hard way. Finally, I learned to dree my own weird. The sun always rises. Thank you so much.

It's good to be alive some days.

For my parents, who had it harder, and never complained.
For my children: constant joy.

Menu

1. Play the Book

Why give your pelf to The Man, when OUR man Palfinger will give you the goods for free?

Sign on, zoom in and luck out. Chances are, FreeFinger's Jamboree has got just what you want.

For free.

Let the good times roll.

(FreeFinger is an independent over-holding of the CraneCorp BuisPlex.)

- \ -

Josie was an hour early, unable to sleep, up before dawn. She'd cut her hair, scissors in front of the mirror, a ragged, gamine cut, all she could afford.

The long road out to the prison was quiet, Josie took her time, the old, split-screen camper wasn't good in the heat. She drove with the window down, the morning air hot and humid. Arizona desert stretched all around, patched in the far distance with vibrant green. Once in a while mirage-ponds resolved into real water.

High on the prison walls, auto-guns slid along recessed rails, metal singing, steel on steel. One tracked Josie as she drove alongside the prison. Behind those high concrete walls were thirty-thousand inmates, a small fraction of President Snarlow's great roundup. One of them was Novik. Josie had been waiting for two years.

The ground was bare all around the prison, the new and old growth hacked down by chain gangs.

You can try, but you can't stop change, Josie thought. You politicians stopped my life for a while, but now it's going to start again, and it's going to be good.

Novik was two hours late. The system ran to its own schedule and changed the rules as it went. When you were this deep in, all you could do was accept.

One of the high steel gates swung open. Half a dozen men filed out onto the dusty apron and blinked uncertainly under the open sky. Two prison guards in navy pants, short sleeved shirts, and gold-framed sunglasses followed them out. One was fat, one was tall. Both chewed on matchsticks, both held shotguns.

Up on the wall the autoguns clustered above the men. Josie got out of the camper. The sun on the gun barrels dazzled, she shielded her eyes. A car went by, a brand-new solar-electric diesel hybrid. An autogun sped away after it.

There he was.

'Hey,' Josie waved her arm, 'Novik.'

Novik raised his hand, a slow gesture. He slung his bag onto his shoulder and walked across the road, shoulders hunched, a downbeat silhouette.

The other ex-cons went their own ways. Two climbed into waiting cars: a battered pickup with a woman in late middle-age at the wheel; a gleaming, black sedan with tinted windows. The rest set out on the long, dusty walk into town.

The pickup headed through the dry, Arizona landscape, past the walking men. After a moment, the sedan followed. The fat guard raised his hand, both guards went back inside the prison, the heavy steel door clanged shut. Autoguns slid back along their rails to the end of the wall and tracked the cars and pedestrians until they were out of range.

Novik and Josie sat in the camper. Josie started the engine. She kissed Novik's cheek, 'What do you want to do, hon?'

Novik closed his eyes. 'Just go, babe.'

Josie took them out towards the interstate, away from town.

Novik looked back at the receding prison, still only half believing he was outside that enormous, bleak structure. The autogun still perched at the corner, its perforated black muzzle aimed towards them. Novik kissed his middle finger and held it out the window.

The road crested a rise and dropped into a shallow dip. Now the prison was out of sight. Josie pulled onto the verge and stopped the motor.

Once again it was just the two of them, Josie and Novik, like it always was. Like it always should be. They climbed out of the camper and looked at each other. Josie wore an old green top, flat shoes, a favourite skirt, a faded Mexican print Novik remembered.

Novik had the same clothes he'd worn in court two years ago: brown boots, jeans, a collarless white shirt, a black leather jacket. Now he also wore the black metal hoop of his parole tag, clamped round his neck like a loose dog collar.

Josie kissed Novik. He kissed her back, he buried his face in her hair and breathed in. Josie did the same, her face against his old jacket.

'Hey babe,' Josie said.

'Hey, hon.'

The cut on Novik's scalp that had bled so much was now a ragged scar. Josie brushed back sandy hair that could never decide if it was a parting or a fringe. He'd always been lanky, now, like her, he was several meals on the wrong side of thin.

They walked round a low bluff and discovered a shallow pond, reed-flanked, the water skimmed by iridescent damselflies. A frog croaked, wild iris bloomed. The trunk of a rotting saguaro cactus lay collapsed in the shallows. A year ago the pond had not existed. Now it rained most weeks.

All around, the desert was blooming, out of season It was strange, beautiful, unsettling. Novik returned to the car and waited for Josie.

Five miles down the highway they passed a huge area of new construction, earth ramps, steel frames, and concrete slabs. Signs announced three square miles of self-store warehousing. Occupancy was already at 80%. Avoid disappointment, advance bookings now being taken.

Josie looked across at Novik. He shook his head. 'No more, Josie. Not me. Never again.' He looked down at his hands, broken fingers never set quite straight. He was through with protest. 'Look where it got me.'

Look where it got us both, Josie thought.

He'd given her the right answer, the same one he'd used on visiting days. Until today, until he was out, Josie had never been sure. She looked through the fly-specked windshield and pressed down on the gas, the half-finished warehouses sped by.

On the opposite side of the road was more construction, a new mall with walls of pink and gold glass. To one side a small group of activists stood between a stand of mature desert ironwood and the bulldozers. Novik turned his head away.

See no evil.

Exhausted by the stress of the prison release, he closed his eyes and slept.

When Novik woke they were on the interstate. He felt refreshed, reborn, made anew. Cool air blew through the dashboard vents, the sun shone in a blue sky. Josie was beside him, the blacktop ran ahead for miles.

'Want to eat?' Josie said.

Novik stretched, and settled back into his seat. 'Sure.'

Up ahead was a diner, a single car in the parking lot. Josie pulled in, Novik walked over to inspect the other vehicle, a drop-head Cadillac AFC-16 lobsterback, a model he had never seen. The design was radical, near Mil-Spec in its muscularity, sleek and powerful, the folding roof segmented like a carapace. Novik gave a low whistle, he'd missed out on a lot in two years.

Then he saw the fibre-glass Viking longboat on the roof of the diner, manned by three turnip-headed warriors with horned helmets.

Novik gave a disbelieving laugh, 'What is that?'

'Cheese-a-Swede,' Josie said, 'it's a new franchise.' She gave Novik a hug. 'We can still get a burger.'

Hands on hips, Novik studied the vegetable Vikings, 'Thank God.'

That old adoration was in her eyes, 'It's good to see you happy.'

Novik ruffled her hair, he kissed her brow, 'Things are going to work out.'

'Come on,' Josie pulled on Novik's hand.

Novik looked up at the garish sign. 'Are you sure this place is OK?'

'Trust me.'

He'd always trusted her. It was why she'd waited.

There were three other customers in the diner, older men, clean-shaven, smart, dark suits, their grey overcoats neatly folded and hung across the backs of empty chairs. Their conversation was sparse, their gestures careful. One of them glanced up as Novik and Josie opened the door, his face pale and heavy, dark hair swept back.

Novik saw them as he came in, and although he wanted to turn around and leave, he kept coming. He'd learned not to make such simple mistakes. He didn't think the three were made, but neither did they look like businessmen. He turned up his jacket collar and wished he had a proper shirt.

The waitress was a stocky Mexican girl. She wore a plastic Viking helmet with fake blonde pigtails. When she poured the coffee, her eyes moved over his parole collar like spit sliding off glass. Novik lost his appetite.

Even so, the coffee was good. When Novik went up to the counter for a refill, the man who'd watched them come in left his table and stood beside him. Close up, he was younger than at first impression, early middle-age, deep-chested, muscular, a little overweight. His forefingers beat a fast rhythm on the counter top, he bared his teeth in imitation of a smile. 'Howdy.'

'Howdy.'

'Name's Black.' The man finished his beat with a drum-roll flourish, 'Happy birthday.'

Novik stood very still.

Black leaned one elbow on the counter, 'Don't tell me you walk around with that fucked-up expression on your face all the time?'

'No,' Novik said carefully. 'You're absolutely right, it is my birthday.'

Black tapped Novik's parole tag with his finger, 'I saw it when you came in.' He leaned back on the counter, 'Hey boys, it's this gentleman's birthday.'

The two men at the table looked up. Both were older than Black, one was slim, bald, his skull elongated, his jaw narrow. The other had dyed hair, bad skin, a pock-marked lump for a nose, he gestured to an empty chair:

'Be so kind as to join us. A man needs company on his birthday.'

Helplessly, Novik looked down the room to Josie.

'You too, ma'am,' the pock-faced man said.

'He didn't do anything,' Josie said. It came out shrill, louder than she meant. Nobody appeared to hear her.

Josie took the seat next to Novik. The three men stood until she was seated.

'Novik,' Novik held out his hand. 'Thanks for asking us over.'

'I'm Josie,' Josie said.

'Names are masks,' the man with bad skin said. 'We're the Old-fashioned Boys. That's who we really are.'

Novik put his hand away.

'Jimmy, I already told them my name,' Black said.

Pock-faced Jimmy swore vilely under his breath. He massaged the bridge of his lumpy nose for a long, cold moment. 'Fuck it. Meet Mr Morgan.'

The narrow-headed man slowly inclined his head.

'We need some drinks,' Black blurted out. 'A man needs drinks on his birthday.'

'If I'm going to drink, I need to eat.' Jimmy looked round the table, 'You want to eat?' He snapped his fingers at the waitress, 'We're all going to eat.'

'I'll get the drinks,' Black said.

'You'll get it all,' Jimmy said.

Black patted his jacket, the seat of his pants. 'Wallet's in the car.' He hurried out of the diner.

'Fucking young punk,' Jimmy gave Novik an apologetic nod, 'No offence.'

'None taken.'

Jimmy pointed to Novik's hairline, 'You get that from the Feds?'

'The Weekenders.'

'The good old National Guard.'

They ordered burgers and fries, whisky and beer. Black paid the waitress in cash. Novik sipped his first drink in two years.

Morgan traced a line through the condensation on his bottle with a well-manicured finger. 'Tell me something, Novik. When did you stop ass-raping your cell-mate?'

Despite the beer, Novik's mouth was dry as dust, 'I didn't-'

Morgan looked around the table, 'He says didn't stop.'

Novik held up both his hands, 'No, I never-'

'Forget it,' Jimmy said, 'it's just a joke.'

Jimmy told them a good story, Black told a better one, funny, nasty, illegal. When you thought about it, it wasn't funny at all. Novik and Josie laughed with the rest of them.

The waitress laid out another round.

'My glass is dusty,' Morgan said.

Jimmy gave a loud sigh, 'How's the burger?'

'It's good.'

'It's a great burger,' Josie said.

Jimmy shook his head, 'It's not a great burger, it's a good burger. You're a pretty woman, but you should always tell the truth.'

'It's a good burger for five bucks,' Black said.

'My aunt used to give me five bucks to fuck her,' Jimmy said.

'Which side?' Black said.

'What the fuck difference does that make?' Jimmy said.

'You fuck your own mother's sister, it's disrespectful.'

'She only had brothers,' Jimmy said.

'She had a mother too.'

'That's disgusting,' Jimmy jabbed a finger at Black, 'You know what, you're disgusting.' He slouched in his seat, 'I did not fuck my grandmother.'

Josie shifted uncomfortably, a rabbit trapped by the headlights. Jimmy made a conciliatory gesture, 'I was a stupid punk kid. Back then, five bucks got you more than a burger.'

The drink had gone to Novik's head. 'You're from Alabama?'

'How the fuck did you know that?'

Novik thought about it. 'I don't know how, but I do.' Something wasn't quite right.

'My father used to touch me,' Morgan said. There was a sibilance behind his voice, the skittering of cockroach legs.

Some time during the third round, Black jumped up on the counter and made like he was surfing. Josie and Jimmy got into a deep conversation about karma and predestination. Morgan ordered pie and held the first spoonful at eye-level for minutes on end.

It wasn't the drink. Something was *in* the drink. Novik lurched across the diner, went behind the counter and grabbed two bottles of coke. Back in the kitchen, he saw the Mexican girl sharpening knives. When Novik looked up at Black, surfing on the counter, he could see the waves break and hear the Beach Boys. When he listened to Josie and Jimmy, their words held a wisdom so far beyond the ken of mortal man their auras glowed. Josie's shone rose gold, Jimmy's pulsed old blood and meconium. It was as if an angel debated with a demon.

Novik drank a bottle of coke and felt a little better. Then he saw Morgan and Black had auras that dripped filth, and grew very frightened. He took Josie by the hand and led her outside. Behind them at the table, Jimmy sat weeping.

Inside the camper van, Josie collapsed on the passenger seat. Novik didn't know where he wanted to be, but it wasn't here. The camper wouldn't co-operate. It went forwards, then it went back. There was a bang, a jolt, the engine struggled. Novik slipped the clutch, revved the engine. Gears clashed, finally the old vehicle gained some traction. Out on the interstate the camper finally began to accelerate.

With the windows down, and the passage of time and miles, Novik's head began to clear. After an hour, Josie began to stir. Novik opened the second bottle of coke, took a mouthful, and offered her the rest. She gulped it down and stared bleakly out the window.

'That was very wrong, very bad,' Novik said.

'Where are we?' Josie slurred.

'An hour away. Fifty, sixty miles.'

Josie looked back down the road, screamed, and cowered in her seat, 'They're here! Oh, God, Novik, they followed us.'

Novik checked the mirrors. In cold horror he saw she was right, the big grey Cadillac was behind them, so close against the rear fender he couldn't see the hood. His guts turned to water. How could he have not noticed? He was sure the road had been empty. Had he looked? Perhaps he had never looked. What did they want? Novik knew the answer: they wanted to kill them, murder them for kicks and feed the dark auras of their wicked souls.

The Cadillac matched their speed perfectly, nose to tail. 'I don't know what they're waiting for,' Novik muttered, 'they got the power, the speed, they can force us off the road any time.'

'Don't stop,' Josie begged. 'Never stop.'

A mile went by, and another. Novik studied the Cadillac in the rear-view mirror. What he saw was crazy. He looked and looked until he was sure. Then he took his foot off the gas, he changed down into third, into second. He pulled onto the shoulder.

'What are you doing,' Josie shrieked. 'Keep going!'

'They're not here,' Novik drew the camper to a halt on the verge. 'The car's empty.'

Southern States Littoral – Still part of the USA!!!

'Of course it is,' Vice President Oscar Gordano told us on the steps of his official residence at the DC Naval Observatory. 'And you can quote me.'

Gordano dismissed suggestions that the coastal regions of Florida, Alabama, Mississippi, and Louisiana – colloquially known as the Southern Littoral – were effectively outside the law.

'There are some local difficulties,' Gordano admitted. 'This administration is committed to returning the rule of law to every square foot of our territories.'

He also dismissed claims that organised crime, specifically Mitchell Gould, had established self-governing enclaves along the Littoral.

'Hurricane Larry knocks down conventional structures and it's uneconomic to build hardened facilities. Frankly, who'd want to live there anyway?'

The Vice President was on his way to the Presidential ball. Semi-official on the political calendar, it is described as a low-key, intimate affair for the President and four thousand of her closest friends.

Syndicated feed, KUWjones.org

- 2 -

I40. Westbound.

Josie and Novik stood beside their camper. Behind them, the Old-fashioned Boy's car was locked onto their rear tow bar by its front fender.

Empty mesquite landscape stretched away in all directions. The interstate itself was deserted.

Josie hugged herself and shivered, still shocked by the sight of the powerful limousine behind their own vehicle. How was it possible to accidentally steal a car? How could anyone do that? One more strike made Novik a three-time loser, they were supposed to be on holiday, this trip was going to be a fresh start. Now it was a disaster. Deep inside, Josie despaired, no matter how she tried the breaks never came their way.

Novik rubbed the parole transponder clamped round his neck. Back in the diner, Jimmy had talked about the pleasures of his profession. At the time Josie had been protected by a golden light. Beyond good and evil there was only truth, and the acceptance of truth. Only opinion brought morality and outrage, their conversation had been matter of fact, the dreadful things Jimmy had done for money were simply events. Out on the hard shoulder, that state of tranquillity was gone, replaced by a grimy, trembling dread, the aftershock of reality.

'You ran the tow hook under it in the diner parking lot,' Josie accused. Fear made her angry, 'How could you not notice?'

Novik's brow furrowed, 'I don't remember.' In fact, between pulling in to the Cheese-a-Swede, and about a minute ago, he couldn't remember anything. That wasn't right.

Josie gave an exasperated sigh, 'Why am I not surprised?' She loved Novik, but he wasn't practical. Sure, he could change a wheel, but by the time he'd finished he was also planning on fitting wings and a sail too. For the benefit of mankind.

'Somebody spiked my burrito.'

'Oh, come on,' Josie exclaimed. Then she hesitated - one thing Novik didn't do was lie. She thought back to the last time conversation with a stranger had spanned the universe. 'Really, hon? That's what really happened?'

'Something synthetic, radical, maybe a cocktail. A fast burn, like Briefstacy, but with more mind-fuckery.'

Novik knew he'd screwed up again, his inadvertent theft had left Josie scared of both the past and the future. He didn't know how, these things just happened to him, it was expected, it was a given. He'd spent his life doing his best to impress, trying to be smart as she was, eternally worried she'd leave him for someone more together.

'I'll-,' Novik scratched around for ideas. 'I'll let down the rear tyres and jack up the front of the Caddy.'

He wriggled under the big car with the old bottle jack from the camper. With most of the air out of the VW's back tyres, the Cadillac would only need lifting three or four inches. As he offered up the squat, blue metal jack, it transformed into a smiling, pot-bellied Buddha.

'I'm too short,' the jack placidly informed him.

Novik blinked, the jack was a jack again. Under him the road was hard and cold, above him an electric eye watched him from the underside of the Cadillac's floor pan. He crawled out from under the car and tossed the jack into the camper.

'Unbolt the fender,' Josie said.

'These new cars are single-piece extrusions. There's nothing to unbolt.'

'Actually, I was printed,' the car said, in a polite mid-western drawl.

'Jesus Christ!' Novik leaped away from the car.

'New Detroit engineering, sir,' the car said.

Novik looked suspiciously at the car, he waved his fingers in front of his eyes. 'I thought I was coming down.'

'I heard it too,' Josie said.

Novik studied the car, goggle-eyed, 'You're a real talking car?'

'Yes, sir, I am.'

'That is so cool.'

'Thank you, sir.'

Novik held up a finger, 'Please don't call me sir.'

'All right.'

Josie was intrigued, 'These printers, how big are they?'

'I don't know, ma'am,' the car said, 'I wasn't there.'

'You could print your own spare parts.'

'Then I would be a printer instead of a car.'

'You'd last forever.'

'My substrate is photo-unstable, a deliberate design decision.'

'I can fix that.' Novik dashed back to the camper, rummaged in the footwell, and returned with a bottle of sun block. 'Factor forty,' he said as he sprayed a film of white cream onto the Cadillac's wing.

Josie and the car exchanged a look.

'A considerate gesture,' the car said. 'Unfortunately, few people will want last year's model.'

Novik peered through the tinted windshield at the empty driver's seat. 'Mr Car, your fender's locked onto my rig. Can you pop your trunk so I can get your jack?'

'Technically, no. I can only open for the owner, or his or her designated associates.'

'The Old-fashioned Boys? The three men at the diner?' Josie said.

'No, ma'am.'

'Who is your owner?' Novik said.

'Technically, nobody, sir.'

'You're stolen?'

'Technically, no, sir.'

'Stop calling me sir.'

'My apologies. I have a speech-pattern modifier request timeout. My firmware needs patching.'

'You opened up for those Old-fashioned Boys,' Josie said.

'They acquired me via a method which evaded legal niceties.'

'So have we.'

Mr Car thought about it. 'I concur. I let them put things in, you can take things out.'

Josie and Novik walked round to the trunk. 'What kind of things?'

'Money, mostly.'

The lock clicked open, the lid swung up. Josie and Novik looked into a trunk filled with lidless boxes stacked with used ten, twenty, and hundred dollar bills.

During that tumbleweed moment, a distant look came into Novik's eye. That's a fuck-ton of cash, he thought. You could do a lot with that.

One of the boxes contained a packet of latex gloves, a pair of filter masks and ten fist-sized packages of white powder. Some packs had burst open, a fine layer of powder coated the money, seeped down into, and between, the cash-filled boxes.

'Please note the currency is contaminated with fluorinated LSD, mammalian Oxytocin, trans-PTTH and brominated ketamine, mixed with an inert carrier in a ratio of 100,000:1,' said Mr Car.

'Black lied when he said he'd forgotten his wallet, he just didn't want to spend his own money, so he paid with some of this cash,' Novik said.

Josie pulled on a pair of the gloves and picked up the bundle of notes behind the burst drug packets. A hole ran part way through, she flicked through the sheaf and extracted a flattened bullet. She held it up for Novik to see. 'Looks like you were right about the burritos. It wasn't deliberate, it was contamination. How do you know about the drugs, Mr Car?'

'The Cadillac AFC-16 is not only the model of choice for senators and chief executives, it is also popular with other gangsters and hoodlums. This is because I am so Awesomely Fucking Cool. As required by legislation, I am fitted with an integrated air analyser interfaced to GPS and law enforcement agencies.'

Dread clenched Josie's gut. She tossed the money back into the trunk. 'Novik, get the cars unhitched. We're out of here.'

'My GPS uplink was disabled by a single bullet fired from a handgun. The very round you are holding,' Mr Car said.

Novik looked at the car open-mouthed. 'They shot you?'

'In actual fact, sir, yes, they did. It was why I decided to take the tow.' A speculative tone entered the car's voice, 'I always wondered what it felt like to be a hitcher.'

The wind was damp, gusting from the south-east. Unseasonal rain clouds swept up from the distant gulf and gathered over the hills. Powder from the split packet lifted on the breeze and settled in shallow drifts over the money.

Novik didn't like hard drugs, he didn't like the way they ate people's lives. Ambitions became daydreams, daydreams became could-have-beens. Home became memories, and your home became the street. He had seen it too many times. In prison it was a way of life, and it was encouraged.

'Stand upwind, Josie.' Novik snapped on a pair of gloves and fitted a filter mask. He took each packet, tore it open, and emptied it onto the road. A plume of white dust swirled away, a few hundred-dollar bills spun up into the air.

Josie pulled him back. 'Be careful, babe. That stuff goes through your skin.'

Novik watched the dust cloud dissipate. When it next rained, the desert flowers would bloom strange new colours, and coyotes would form rock-and-roll bands. He affectionately ran his hand over the dusty, rust pocked rear wheel arch of the camper. 'We'll put her in storage. When things are quieter I'll fix her up.'

It was an old mantra, a prelude to every big idea Novik had ever had. Josie did not like it at all. 'This is a bad place, babe. We've got to go.'

Novik squared his shoulders, he stuck out his chin. 'Leave all this money here? We've can do something with it. Something good.'

The thought terrified Josie. Maybe it was post-trip paranoia, maybe it was cold reality. She didn't know whether to slug him or get on her knees and beg, so she grabbed him by the lapels of his denim jacket and shook him like an old rug. 'You listen to me. Two years I've waited for you, and I've just got you back. You break parole, you'll go back inside for four more. Any ideas about doing good, about making a difference, just forget it.'

Novik gently took hold of her hands, 'Two years for me, too.'

She pulled away, furious, he never thought things through. 'You actually do something bad, you do something crazy like this, you steal a car full of drugs and money, it will be ten times that-'

'We haven't done anything wrong, Josie. We've stolen a stolen car from some very bad people. That money doesn't belong to them, to anyone good. It's not set for a good purpose, it's going to cause misery.'

'Burn it, then,' Josie gestured wildly at the car. 'Burn it all, burn everything.'

'I'd prefer a different solution,' Mr Car said hastily.

'You keep out of it,' Josie snapped. 'Whose side are you on?'

'The side of not getting burned to a crisp, ma'am.'

'He's right. Josie, you can't just burn a talking car,' Novik said.

She challenged him, hands on hips. 'Why not?'

Good question. Novik floundered, he gave the thinnest of answers: 'It's a *talking car*.'

'I just meant the money,' Josie said. She blew her nose, wiped her eyes, the anger drained out of her. She gave Novik an unhappy, tearful smile. 'I've only just got you back. Don't make me wait again, I can't do it.'

'I'm sorry,' Novik reached out, 'Hey.'

'I'm sorry too.' She came into his arms, held him tight. 'I hate arguing.'

'Me too.' It made him feel so fragile. 'Listen, it won't be like last time. I promise.'

Josie traced the scar that ran from just below his hairline back across his scalp. She rapped the steel band of the parole transponder with her knuckle. 'What are you going to do about that?'

President Guinevere Snarlow came to office on a promise to revitalise the economy and end the protests. People didn't like what she did, but they tolerated it. 'Hard times,' she told them, 'tough love. People want a liberal, socialist government, they can cross the pond.'

Once it was all over, the prison population had doubled and everybody knew somebody in jail. Quite a few knew someone who was dead. Citizens kept their heads down, the country was quieter than it had been for a decade.

The malls stayed open.

'When I was inside, people said you're OK if you cut it off under water,' Novik said. 'Lie in a bath, breathe through a tube.'

While they talked, the two cars separated. The Cadillac's fender slowly flowed back and over the tow hook.

'Did I see that?' Novik said.

'I think so.'

'Fender-morph technology,' Mr Car said. 'Memory Kevlar means I never have a scratch or a dent.'

'No bullet holes,' Novik said.

'It's a gift.'

The sight of all that money had re-kindled a spark in Novik. President Snarlow had beaten him once, now he had another chance. 'Josie, just think about it. We could really do something.'

They had been together since the High School recycling club. They camped with the Occupy protests, joined the flashmobs, signed up to the networks and petitions. For a season it felt like something was going to happen, things were going to change. An American Spring.

Then Snarlow was elected. Novik went to jail and Josie worked for nickels and dimes. They were the lucky ones. All Josie wanted now was to stay out of trouble.

And now Novik had that look in his eye.

'You really want to go back to all that? You really want to try again?' Josie said.

Novik swallowed hard, he had already made up his mind, he was ready to break his promise. 'Yes, I do.'

Josie punched his shoulder, thumped his chest, each blow punctuating her words. 'So how's it going to work?' Thump. 'What's this good thing we're going to do?' Thump. 'I'm not going to try unless there's a plan, so you tell me a good one.'

Put on the spot, Novik hadn't a clue. Josie was the smart one. He had dreams and enthusiasm, she thought things through and made them happen.

It came to him: 'We'll just buy it all up before anyone else does.'

'Then what?'

He had it. It was perfect, he had to laugh. 'We'll give it away.'

'That's crazy,' Josie said, but she laughed too.

'We can't get arrested for shopping, we're doing what they want us to do.'

Right away she could see the utter impracticality of it. It was ridiculous, they would never have enough money. As usual, Novik simply hadn't thought that far ahead. Josie looked into his eyes and for a moment she was back in high school, seeing him for the first time, his taut muscular body, the change from uncertainty to happiness when he knew he'd said something that made her laugh.

It was ridiculous, but he was right about one thing, it was safe. Purchasing commodities was the one thing Snarlow's government wanted them to do. Josie pushed down the Cadillac's trunk. 'We still need to move. You take the Caddy, these cars can half drive themselves.'

'Ma'am, I can completely drive myself if the driver is incapacitated, distracted by drugs, blood loss or amorous intent,' Mr Car said.

Novik saw the change in Josie. He didn't understand why, all he knew was, he couldn't do this without her, and was glad. Guilt twinged at him, he'd finagled Josie into another of his schemes, and despite his explanations, it was a highly dangerous one. If those Old-fashioned Boys caught them, they'd kill them.

'Josie, are you sure?'

'One condition - when the money's gone, if everything's still the same, we'll walk away and never look back. No regrets.'

She'd take this chance, she'd stand by him while he tried one last time. Then he would be with her for good. No more waiting. She'd have her man.

Like he said, shopping wasn't illegal.

'No regrets,' Novik agreed.

'Then let's start shopping.'

Call it love.

Singularity? Schmingularity.

Trust me on this – tomorrow the world will roll along exactly as it did yesterday. And the day before.

Why is that? Because humanity has already transcended itself with technology. It happened in places like Catalhoyuk and Göbekli Tepe when we bootstrapped ourselves out of Homo sapiens and into human beings. It was so long ago we forgot about it.

Big change is coming for sure, but one thing is certain – it won't be an extrapolation of what we're already doing, it will be brand new. Just like when we stopped being smart apes with a line in sticks and pebbles, and settled down for some serious play with what we invented.

Nothing changed 'Out There'. We changed how we behaved, how we were organised. How we thought. If ever there was a Singularity that was it. The world we knew ended, we woke up the next day and moved on.

Today the only question is: 'Can we do it again?'

T. Hank Yousomuch, guest blog,
KUWjones.org

- 3 -

Jimmy was spitting blood. He was drunk, stoned, tripped out, paranoid and totally, like totally freaked.

He groped for his cell phone with one hand and gingerly prodded his upper incisors with the other. Teeth moved all over the place. It was a bad, bad feeling.

'Oh, like, totally fucked, man,' he muttered. Part of him was frightened, the rest was appalled at the whine that had crept into his voice.

What most freaked Jimmy out was that he was using phrases such as 'totally fucked, man' like he said them every day. Everything, absolutely everything had gone wrong, from the drugs stewing in his cranium, to Morgan face down in the lemon meringue pie, and that shithead Black clutching his nuts and puking on the ground where the car should have been.

And that was it. In a nutshell, on a stick, and in a bun. Where the car should have been. That big, smart-assed talking Cadillac was nowhere to be seen.

Jimmy's boot sent an old coke can skittering across the blacktop of the interstate. Jimmy was not a poetic man, but the hormone analogues and para-halucinogens cruising his bloodstream made him see the road as a physical metaphor of his own future. Somewhere on the blacktop the Juggernaut of Destiny thundered towards him, and Mitchell Gould, THE Mitchell Gould, was in the driving seat.

Gould was going to want his money back, and he, Jimmy, was going to have to tell him.

Jimmy looked down at the number on the cell-phone and shuddered. His tongue worried at his top front teeth, his mouth was filling with blood but he was afraid to spit in case his bridgework hitched a ride. Across the parking lot Black had stopped puking. Jimmy snapped the phone shut and walked over.

He'd slugged Black in sheer frustration when they'd staggered out of the diner and seen the car had gone. Instead of just taking it, the stupid little gay punk shithead had slugged him back. So Jimmy had kicked him in the nuts. Twice.

Still on his hands and knees, Black mutely looked up at Jimmy. His expression was that of a man in intense pain, who would do much to avoid more.

Jimmy kicked Black in the face. 'Fifteen thousand dollars of bridgework, you fuck.' He followed up with a few more kicks to the body. Groaning, Black slumped on his side and curled into a ball.

It felt good stomping Black, it helped clear Jimmy's head. They were the Old-fashioned Boys and at times like these it was important to do things the old-fashioned way. Morgan was steady, but Black had always been a punk. The sonofabitch had shot the car, for chrissakes.

If there was one thing Jimmy knew, it was the importance of having a scapegoat.

Jimmy propped Black up against a dumpster, lit two cigarettes and put one between Black's split and bleeding lips.

'It's all right, compadre,' Jimmy told him. 'We're nearly through.'

Black grunted, inhaled smoke and blew it out through his mashed and purpling nose. 'Ere der car?'

All at once Jimmy felt very tired. 'Damned if I know.'

'Der muddy in der car?'

Jimmy gave a profound sigh. 'Yes, the money is still in the car.'

All one hundred and ninety million. The money they were meant to drive to Vegas and lose playing blackjack, craps and roulette at certain tables in certain casinos owned by a certain member of the executive in DC. A decade ago, one hundred and ninety million USD was a kill-your-own-motherfucker of a fortune. Today, it was still a shit load of money.

More than enough to die for.

Jimmy slapped Black on the shoulder, pushed himself to his feet and made his way towards the diner. He took one last pull on his cigarette and flipped the tab away. Beating on Black had loosened the broken dental bridge even more. Taking hold of his top teeth he pulled them out and slipped them in his breast pocket. Maybe some dental surgeon could reattach them.

Finally, his head was clearing of that hippy drug shit. He'd check on Morgan, fix Black properly, and make the call to Gould. Once that was sorted they'd get back on the road.

One foot on the step up to the diner, Jimmy shook his head and gave a brief, sardonic smile. That blonde bitch Josie was something else. He was going to enjoy tracking her down. Her and that flop-haired lanky freak she travelled with.

'Hey, Jimmy.'

Jimmy turned round. Black was up on one knee, he held a gun in a two-fisted grip.

Shit, Jimmy thought. Where'd Black get a gun? Jimmy held up his hand in a peace sign. 'Chill, man. Don't be, like, so infra-dig-'

Black shot him. Like, a lot.

Exclusive! It's Official!! The Steel Nymph is the biggest woman in the world!!!

In this issue, Venus Maxima is proud to announce twenty-three year old Ellen Hutzenreiter Crane, secretive daughter of Canadian mega-trillionaire Palfinger Crane, has surpassed Carol Yager's alleged peak weight of 1,600 lb. Eat your hearts out, all you wannabees, the 900 club has a new paragon of amplitude. Ellen Crane is the Empress of Embonpoint!

Self-proclaimed celebrity fat watcher, Wesley Strosner is delighted. 'This is great news for Ellen. Now she really is the biggest and the best. What an amazing family!'

Known by her fans as the Steel Nymph because of her multi-million dollar life-support exoframe, Ellen has allegedly eaten nothing but vitamin and mineral supplements for the last two years. Even Strosner admits his ambition to become her Feeder and make her 'big, bigger, biggest' is unlikely.

'I'm moved by love,' Strosner announced. 'I live in hope.'

Doctors continue to be baffled by Ellen's astonishing weight gain.

Editorial,
Venus Maxima magazine

- 4 -

'Unbelieveable.' Novik was lost for words. The Cadillac's tyres slewed across the loose gravel of the enormous mall's gigantic parking lot and headed towards the onion-domed, floodlit entrance.

He'd been trying to avoid Roswell. The car kept telling him they were nowhere close but he didn't believe it. Four o'clock in the morning, and Novik had no idea where he was.

Josie was asleep in the passenger seat, her feet up on the dash. She wore a paisley scarf over her hair, ray-bans covered her eyes. All Novik could make out of her face was a dreamy half-smile, high cheekbones, and her left ear, decorated with nine silver rings.

The change in motion woke her, she swung her bare feet down from the dash and focused on the distant neon glitter, the cloud scrawl of laser lights from the multi-domed mall. 'Where are we?'

'Ultra-mall 20-19, between Midland and Abilene,' Mr Car said. 'Seventeen hundred hectares of Tech, Fash, Chill, Trans, Pharma, Meeja and Mil.'

'Main or .alt?' Josie said.

'Main, .alt, .eth, .ret, and .X.'

'This is where we need to be.'

Novik dug around in the glove compartment and pulled out a fistful of loose change, sticky candy wrappers, and dried peyote.

So this was what heavy dudes in suits lived on. He opened the door and dumped the lot on the ground. It was time to begin. 'I need some juice. Fresh fruit, vitamin green, whisky. Some shades,' Novik said.

'All of that, and more,' Josie said. 'We're here to shop.'

They'd put the camper in storage and driven through the night, anxious to put as many miles between them and the diner as they could. Still mildly spaced and paranoid from the f-LSD, sustained by psychedelic rock from the orbital pirate stations, Novik instinctively dog-legged west and east down dirt roads and two-lanes, the Cadillac easily coping with the terrain as they headed for the southern border like any punk with a trunk full of stolen cash and a picogram of common sense.

Mr Car was a dream ride, the passenger compartment a smoked glass womb of comfort, an upholstered cocoon of atmospherically controlled ambient security. It was what Josie needed; she kicked off her shoes, curled up in the armchair-like seat, and slept the sleep of the emotionally exhausted.

The retro sounds faded as they got out of the car, the last few bars of the Doors' LA Woman segueing into Hillage's Glorious Om Riff. They'd driven fourteen hours straight, stopped only for food, legals, and to freshen up. Josie had to shop when Novik became convinced he was in a submarine. She'd put on gloves before handling the dust-covered money. By now the shopkeeper's spirit guides would be in low orbit over Albuquerque.

When Novik felt better they stopped again and he cleaned the money. Masked and gloved, he laid the boxes out on the ground, stood upwind and swept them with a long-handled feather duster. Thin plumes of drug dust and a dozen hundred-dollar bills blew into the sky and across a flock of crows perched on a power line.

Novik repacked the trunk and they sped away. Behind them, the crows stared at each other with glassy black eyes. One by one they toppled forwards and swung upside-down from the line, softly cawing.

Mica in the Ultra-Mall pavements glittered like diamonds. Ahead of them stood the Mall itself, a gleaming dazzle of red, gold and blue neon, the sky above swept by searchlights, and laser-projected logos and testimonials written on the clouds.

Josie studied the vast franchise, as beautiful as Camelot, as dangerous as Chapel Perilous, and felt an overwhelming euphoria. Fear of the future, of failure, had left her. All that existed was the moment, that eternal fleeting instant called 'Now'. In her heart she knew all that mattered was that she was with Novik. She began a slow, turning, dervish dance, and it was as if she stood still and the world revolved about her.

Novik watched purple and green caterpillars of light stream from her fingertips and transmogrify into camo-patterned moths wearing mirror shades and army boots. The boots were too heavy for flight. Fluttering gamely the moths imploded with faint 'poink' sounds as they hit the ground. Each corresponded to the last drug-affected receptors in Novik's brain as they flushed free of psychoactives. His cerebral cortex resumed normal service.

All around them obese families from the condos, apts and bungalow ranch-styles stared enviously at the muscular Cadillac as they lumbered towards the mall. Flashlights twinkled as they snapped the trunk and hood marque logos, the 'AFC-16' embossed hubcaps and wing detail.

Novik watched Josie's slow trance dance. 'What can you see, babe?'

'I'm blinded by the beauty of Mammon. His retail palaces are so vast their delivery bays are concealed by the curvature of the earth. His hairs are fibre-optic cables and his teeth are zirconium. His voice is made of brass and all I hear is the sound of three-for-two debit authorisations.'

A small crowd of libertarians had gathered. 'Amen, sister,' they whooped and chorused.

Novik set his jaw. This was what they had come to fight. The Cadillac's trunk swung open at his touch, Josie loaded her shoulder bag with bundles of cash.

When she was done, Josie took Novik's hand. She thought about what they were about to do, and where it would lead, and squeezed tight. Together, they walked towards the waiting Mall. Returning pedestrians parted around them: families loaded with enough food for a month who would return in a week; single-product completists, weighed down by expanded series re-issues, retro-media variants, tie-ins, spin-offs, and collectable merchandise; upgrade warriors trading in, back, and up; blindfolded mystery-shoppers, white canes tapping as they hurried home to discover their purchases.

Behind them, Mr Car extended a multi-jointed arm from the offside 'C' pillar and began cleaning the solar cells on the roof.

❈

Benny the Spoke knew his lift was due. It might be today, it could be tomorrow, but it was definitely coming soon. He disconnected from the FreeFinger Jamboree tower, removed his headphones, stretched, yawned, and looked around.

FreeFinger left him dissatisfied. The service had everything you could want - demos, try-outs, beta-products, time-expiring loss-leader gadgets, bolt-ons, strap-ons, medical, leisure, financial and spiritual service packs, legal and a-legal Pharma, holidays, non-doctor implants, auto-loans, freemium tasters, the list went on and on. Freefinger was compulsive, and, just like the man said, it was free.

Benny considered his acquisitions: an AI/solar auto-mulch combo upgrade to a lawnmower he didn't own; a series of online counselling services for expectant fathers; and 'Larger Than Life', the official autobiography of Zeppelina, the nineteen-year-old pop diva of the Meeja mega-group, the Bariatric Babes. He didn't need them, he didn't even *want* them. He'd shipped them straight to self-storage.

FreeFinger was methadone for the retail addict and it was all that was left for Benny to do. He'd squandered his funds on shopping, the resources that were supposed to see him through his entire mission. He hadn't been adequately prepared for the malls, he could see now his profile was wrong, he was too easily led, his personality too addictive. They should have sent somebody else, someone more ascetic, less like the natives.

Nobody had appreciated the sheer depth of the problems here. There was so much stuff and it was so very easy to buy. He'd known the waiting would be hard but not that failure could be so very, very easy. Or that it would feel so good.

It came to him, perhaps nobody really liked him and he'd been set up to fail. It made a pitifully lonely kind of sense. All he could do now was wait, and hope this really was the place where the butterfly would first beat its frail wings.

He had wandered the mall for days. Wherever he walked, there was mood music, announcements, sonic logos, focused purchasing suggestions from the transponders embedded in his shopping.

When he was tired he crashed in the chill bays, he ate at the three-4-two grill and cleaned up in the washrooms. And waited.

Now the music, celebrity testimonials and adverts blended into a composite structure. New genres formed in his mind: metal baroque, thrash a cappella, speed-rap opera and death-folk hip-hop.

It was more than he could bear. He had to tell someone.

A young couple walked through the hundred-foot-wide, ever-open mall doors. She was fair, he was dark. Both were slim, unusual enough to make Benny look twice.

The woman radiated the transcendent inner glow of someone who had come to terms with fate. The man had the set jaw and determined stride of a gunslinger stepping into the saloon.

'I've g-got this musical Shoggoth inside my head,' Benny stammered as they walked past.

'That's a heavy vibe,' Novik said.

Benny held out his hand, 'I'm Benny.'

'Novik.'

Benny looked down at the collection of bags, boxes and holdalls at his feet. He couldn't remember what he had bought, only that he had wanted it at the time.

'This isn't why I'm here,' Benny said. 'I couldn't help myself. I haven't come to shop, I'm supposed to bear witness.'

Josie felt a sudden empathy for the confused, loose-limbed young man in cavalry pants and denim. She put her hand on Benny's shoulder, 'Hang out with us, we're shopping for the USA until the malls come down.'

With a growing sense of wonder Benny realised that this might be it - First Contact. He had to be sure. 'If you want something, why not just get it from FreeFinger? Get it for nothing?'

Novik shook his head. 'Palfinger Crane is not the solution. Companies and Corps, Pharma, Fash, even .alt, all give it to Crane, and he gives it away for free. He's just chumming the water so you buy even more in the feeding frenzy.'

Benny felt like a novice crouched at the foot of his guru. The foyer filled with a silvery light.

'FreeFinger doesn't break the loop, it reinforces it,' Novik continued, 'We're going subvert it, we're going to reverse entropy and collapse the retail-wholesale wave form.'

Now Benny was certain. This really was it, his one chance turn things round. If he failed, there would be no pickup, no going home. They wouldn't come for his body because once it was all over, they wouldn't be able to find his atoms.

It was time to reveal himself.

'My name is Benny the Spoke. I am an Ambassador from far Achernar, and I have travelled across the dark gulf to observe an incipient phase-change in the human race.'

Novik shook Benny's hand, happy to humour the harmless stranger. 'I'm not sure what that means, but I like the way you said it.'

'You're a pair of butterflies, what you do next-' Benny shut his mouth, already he had said too much.

Josie studied Benny carefully. A guardian of secrets, he also projected an aura of vulnerability, a poor combination for a store detective, though excellent for a scamster. 'We can do what?'

'I meant, if you spend enough money, you can change the world.'

Josie extracted a fistful of hundred-dollar bills from her shoulder bag. The sooner they started, the quicker it would be over. Even so, she was determined to have some fun. 'Watch and learn.'

"As the sources of supply and demand become more and more centralized and we face the inevitable shortages of raw materials and energy, the question is to what extent our society has become inflexible. How will we adapt to the necessary changes in our life style? How will we light a fire in a house with no fireplaces?"

J. Burke,
Connections.

- 5 -

Back in the day, Clinton said the Oval Office was his favourite room. Guinevere Snarlow, 51st President of the United States of America, leaned back in her chair in that same room and spoke into the air.

'Coffee.'

'Yes, madam President,' a male voice, high and nasal, replied from the intercom.

Clinton had it easy. Despite the scandal he still had the power, he had been the most powerful person in the world. Just like Queen Victoria on the British throne, the Ottomans at Topkapi, and the Emperors of Rome.

She wondered what it felt like.

Coffee arrived, wheeled in by a thin, middle-aged man with little hair and less chin.

'Thank you.' Guinevere's smile was broad and genuine, her gaze direct. It came easy, she could smile all day, it was one of her campaign assets.

Guinevere sipped her coffee slowly, and enjoyed a minute of calm and solitude. Then she straightened her blouse, tugged down her jacket and made her way to the latest meeting with the Executive, to see those who had bothered to turn up.

None of the few still-loyal generals and advisors were her friends, she had long ago realised true friendship was one of the sacrifices one made in politics. They were allies at best, the enemies of her enemies, united by power, desire, and self-belief. They were pretty pissed off too.

'Those tree-hugging European pussies are selling out the futures of our sons and daughters,' General Andriewiscz's pale eyes glittered under a furrowed brow. 'We bailed them out twice and now they won't even buy our goddamn sun buggies.'

Secretary of State Cheswold Lobotnov agreed. 'Henry Ford must be spinning in his grave.'

And so it went, bad news on every front: economic, political, legal and military. The business of America might be business but nobody else wanted to do it with them anymore. South America was federating, China was full of geriatrics, Europe was so green people called it the Emerald Union. India and Brazil had GDPs to die for, Oman was the new California. It went on and on, and it was depressing as hell.

'What about Crane?' Guinevere said.

Lobotnov shook his head morosely. His jaw was narrow, his skull above the temples high domed. Together they gave him the appearance of an ancient, wise child. 'Crane won't help us. I'm not even going to ask.'

Vice President Oscar Gordano took off his glasses, ran his fingers through his wiry grey hair, and put them back on again. He was handsome as hell and looked great on any sized screen. It was why he was there, to take off his glasses, smile, and put them back on again. He still thought he could contribute.

'I can understand the Europeans wanting us to use more wood,' Gordano held up his hand at Andriewiscz's reflexive guffaw, 'No, I really can. It's this zero-C thing, they've chosen their way and we need to respect it. But Crane? Crane's mother was from Montana, he's half American, he needs to do his patriotic duty.'

'His father was Canadian, he's a Canadian citizen,' Lobotnov said.

'What leverage have we got on him?' Guinevere asked.

Lobotnov blew out his baby-smooth cheeks. 'How about this: None at all. What can you offer the richest man who has ever lived? His personal wealth is greater than our total GDP, and it's growing while ours is shrinking. His business interests are so vast I doubt anyone knows exactly what they are, not even those Wall Street AIs. Squeeze him and he'll put our nuts in a vice. Seize his USA assets and he'll shut us down. Face up to it, Ginny, we've got nothing he wants.'

'There's that fat blimp of a daughter. Maybe we can do something for her?' Gordano said.

Andriewiscz jabbed at the table with his finger. 'People got a right. People got a right to buy stuff. We make it, they buy it. Then we buy their stuff back and all.'

'What are you saying?' Guinevere said.

'We rebuilt Europe. When they beat the crap out of each other, we propped them back up and dusted them down. We did it twice. Now they won't buy a new gadget until the old one's wore out, and it's got to be compostable into the bargain. What's the sense in that? Where's the gratitude? How can I give my boys and girls some back-pay?'

Gordano tried to explain: 'It's a steady-state economy, zero-C, negative impact. The Eurozone transitioned to a post-consumerist growthless model–'

Two unnaturally red spots appeared on Andriewiscz's cheeks. 'That's just my point. They got all this stuff recycled back out of the ground, chromium, lithium, copper, osmium, mercury. They've been mining their own landfill and stockpiling the purified waste.'

'Is that really true?' Guinevere said.

'Yes, it's true,' Lobotnov said smoothly. 'The Congo just quadrupled the price of coltan, and the Euros have purified tantalum they don't even want.'

Guinevere smiled sourly, 'Meanwhile we're dying on our feet.'

'They're doing a fine job of cleaning the land up, and it's made good economic sense too. One industry shrinks, another emerges,' Gordano said.

Tendons stood out on Andriewiscz's neck. 'Whose damned side are you on, Ozzie? Our citizens got a right to consume. They work hard, they see things in the shops they want to afford. It's a better life.'

'OK,' Lobotnov broke in, 'OK, I agree that's where we are. We've got ourselves an economic model of bigger, faster, better, more, and we can all agree it's not working. We're not growing, we're shrinking, and we got to do something about it.'

'Lord, give me strength,' Andriewiscz looked up at the ceiling. 'For Chrissakes, Cheswold, that's exactly what I'm saying.'

'It is?'

'Don't you ever listen, you smart-assed ivy-league creep?'

Guinevere Snarlow slapped the table with her hand. 'He's not alone, general. What exactly is your point?'

'Jeez, ma'am, are we losing our balls? When the Brits had an empire, they took what they wanted. The world used to be a great market, *Europe* used to be a great market. We rebuilt it twice, I say we do it again.'

Lobotnov studied his nails, 'I take it you've got a plan a little more coherent than redneck bullshit?'

Andriewiscz felt like he'd been playing war games all his life.

'Cheswold, I got a list of strategic scenarios longer than your boyfriend's cock.'

'OK, I want to take a look,' Snarlow said.

'At the plans, I hope,' Gordano sniggered.

Snarlow let the gap in the conversation grow. The grin on Gordano's face died by degrees.

'Oscar, this is not a game, and we're not in the playground. I was elected because I made certain promises to restore the moral, political and economic strengths of this great country I love. I intend to keep all those promises, whatever it takes. If you can't say or do anything useful, then I suggest you say and do nothing.'

Snarlow looked round the table and took in Lobotnov and Andriewiscz's approval. 'How long for the plans, General?'

'I'm ready now, ma'am.'

'Bring it on. I want something provocative, but I don't want us to be the aggressor, not at first. It's got to come at us in a plausible way, then we're justified.' Snarlow was enjoying herself, thinking out loud. This was the way it was supposed to play in the Oval Office, making plans, leading from the front, taking control. 'Do we have to go abroad? Has it got to be an expedition?'

Andriewiscz was visibly swelling with happiness, 'No, ma'am, there are several Canadian and Mexican scenarios.'

'Canada would piss off the Union, guaranteed.' Lobotnov said.

'We got substantial resources tied up down south,' Andriewiscz said.

One thing at a time. Snarlow sat back in her chair, happy for the first time in months. 'They're not tied up, general, they're ready and in place. Mr Lobotnov, would you order in coffee and donuts?'

'Certainly, Ginnie.'

'Gentlemen, let's start making America great.'

!! GET RICH NOW !!
- FREE Seminar –
>>Join Now!<<

Why take risks? Why wait to get lucky?
!! GET RICH NOW !!

Already RICH? Get EVEN RICHER!!
Learn the SECRETS Palfinger Crane doesn't want you to know!!!

FACT! - Everyone can be RICH!!
Want know what it feels like to be RICH?
Come to our FREE SEMINAR and try our Meeja-2 RICH-RIDE!!!

>>Join Now!<<

FACT! – You can't have too much Money!
FACT!! - Anyone can be RICH!!
FACT!!! - This Means You!!!

>>Join Now!<<

Feel RICH!
BE RICH!!
You'll even SMELL RICH!!!

>>Join Now!<<

True Testimonials:
"Woot! I'm RICH!" – N.E. Detroit
"I'm so RICH I can't roll naked in my own money, I need a friend to help." -
O.F.A. Pittsburgh.

(Meeja and Meeja-II are trademarks of M-Path Gmbh, a tertiary
subsidiary of CraneCorp(EU) an independent overholding of the
CraneCorp BuisPlex)

- 6 -

Twenty stories up the last intact post-Katrina III arcology of Nu-Orleans, Mitchell Gould's office was an affair of black leather, white fur, chrome and mirrors. On interview days he kept a few girls on the couches – black, white, Hispanic, Asian, oriental; high boots, teddies, open robes, bare-breasted.

Gould looked them over and found them adequate. 'Ready, girls?'

'Yes, Mr Gould.'

One of them gave him a bright, direct smile, a slender oriental with waist length black hair and a heart-shaped face. There were a hundred like her, a thousand.

The girls arranged themselves indecorously on the couches and leant on the walls in postures of faux decadence. Gould's gaze went back to the oriental and she flashed him a look of such coy fakery he laughed out loud. You had to respect a girl who could play the hand she'd been dealt.

Gould teased up his spiky blond hair and sat on the edge of his desk. Broad-shouldered and narrow hipped, he was still young enough to have a loose-limbed, athletic look. He wore black boots and slacks, a white, v-neck jumper, a navy jacket.

Like the office, his style was just a look. His young guns expected to see something special, they valued objects, possessions, and ostentation. They themselves wore drawstring pants and hooded sweat tops, or, when they wanted to impress, a short-sleeved check shirt four sizes too big.

A pair of radio handsets and a semi-automatic lay in a row on his desk. Gould clapped his hands. 'Bring them in, Manalito.' The enormous Mexican Indian standing against the wall turned, and pulled the door open.

Three wiry Latinos, an overweight black, a Central American Indian, and a white guy filed in. That last, muscular and crop-haired, was unusual. Even more so in that from somewhere he'd found a clean, dust-pink shirt and khaki cargoes.

They stood in the middle of the big room. One of the Latinos was barefoot, all but the white guy dressed in torn and stained clothing. They looked through the picture windows across the rooftops of old, drowned Nu-Orleans, out across the gulf at the years-long eco-disaster of Hurricane 'permanent' Larry. They scoped Manalito, and they checked out the girls. And finally, without fail, they looked at Gould.

It was a universal rule - they had to look him in the eye.

Gould had fed them and given the opportunity to clean themselves up, the first test. This interview was the second. They might be steady, humble, or full of it. It was time to find out.

'Where you from, white boy?' Gould said to the one in the fresh shirt. He never bothered with names until after the interview.

The white man straightened up, hands clasped behind his back. 'Originally? Rhode Island, Mr. Gould.'

'Nice shirt.'

'The other guy thought so too.'

That was impressive, keeping the shirt clean. Even so.

'I don't use Staties,' Gould said.

'Sir?'

'I do not, as a habit, employ citizens of the USA.'

That shut him up.

'What was it, boy, women or law?'

'Law, sir. I don't hurt women.'

Gould resisted the urge to roll his eyes. Every punk had his rule, the one thing they would not do, a personal code that helped them feel there were still moral lines to be crossed. Kill a woman, kill a man, dead was still dead and all that mattered was why, and how you felt about it. For Gould, killing was only ever a business transaction. Manalito had a different point of view, Gould didn't care as long as the job got done.

'What happened with the law?' Gould said.

The white guy shifted his feet and grinned, 'I was an asshole.'

With luck and cojones you could avoid the storm winds of Permanent Larry, and cross the bay. On dry land, once Gould's sweeper crews had spotted you, you didn't keep breathing by not paying attention. Most people realised their journey wasn't over.

Everyone except the barefoot Latino was eyes front, watching and listening. That one just couldn't keep his eyes off the girls.

No group made it through the interview intact, it was Gould's policy.

'So how are you with taking orders?' Gould said to the white man.

'I'm good with orders, yes sir.'

Gould gave him one of the one of the radio handsets and the gun.

The white man hooked the handset onto his trousers, took the clip out of the gun and checked the chamber. His actions were confident and practiced, his expression unchanged as he noted the clip contained a single bullet. He pushed the gun into the back of his waistband. 'Ready, Mr Gould.'

'OK. We don't mind assholes, but we do expect focus.' Gould pointed to the Latino with the wandering eyes. 'Take this hot chilli horndog outside and chuck him off the roof.'

The rest of the group moved back. The Latino was isolated, he turned, confused. 'Hey, mon, no-'

The white guy moved fast. He punched the Latino low in the gut, kneed his face, then clubbed his neck with the pistol. Once, twice, and he went down.

Manalito held open the door, his own gun hung casually in his big hand. 'This way, white man,' he rumbled. The white guy hoisted the stunned Latino in a fireman's lift and followed Manalito out of the room.

The apartment next door had no exterior wall. Welded to the building's steel frame, an H-girder projected twenty feet into clear air.

The white guy pushed the Latino out onto the girder. Two hundred and fifty feet below, the brackish flood waters were dotted with partly submerged wreckage - concrete and rusting steel, broken roofs and old autos, all swept into jagged heaps by the tides and storm surges around the legs of the arcologies.

Brave men walked to the end of the girder and stepped off. There were patches of clear water among the wreckage, but this high up it was windy, and down below, the water was shallow.

You could grow fascinated by how hard some people tried to live, that they still planned, still made calculations, right to the bitter end.

'Watch this, guys,' Gould ordered the remaining recruits to the window. Some of the girls came too.

The Latino crouched three feet from the edge, facing inwards, one hand clutched the beam, the other his broken, bloody cheek.

The white guy grinned, slapped his thigh and did a little jig. Some of the recruits laughed. One of them called him a prick and Gould noted that. Then the white guy drew his gun and shot the Latino. The gunshot was faint through the triple-glazing, the Latino's yell inaudible. His hand snatched at the girder and he was gone.

Gould pressed the call button on his hand set.

'Yes, sir?' the white man said.

'Give the handset to Manalito. Stand against the wall.'

'Mr. Gould,' Manalito said into the handset.

'Yes or no, Manalito?'

'No.'

'Correct as usual. My decision is no.'

Moments later Manalito appeared. The white man struggled in Manalito's grip, held overhead by shoulder and thigh. Nothing of his screams, his threats and profanities could be heard through the glass. The silence gave his furious mouthing and flailing a surreal calm. Gould watched the recruits and the recruits watched Manalito as he walked to the end of the beam and pitched the white man into the air.

Nobody was laughing now.

Lightning flickered silently in the storm clouds deep in the bay. The oriental girl pressed her hands against the glass and looked intently down at the distant water.

Gould faced the silent recruits. 'I changed my mind about assholes.'

The four remaining refugees nodded thoughtfully, as if Gould had said something wise.

Manalito returned through the door.

'Ok, you'll do,' Gould said to the recruits. 'Go with the big man and do as you're told.'

Xalapatech CEO Jose X. Casavantes presented a new generation of bipedal canines to a sceptical audience of senior police officers. His assistant, 'Chapman', a Super-Doberman, operated the console.

'We can no longer consider these partner beings as anything less than para-humans,' Casavantes says. 'Put simply, they are canine people. Smart, loyal and hardworking, they are far less susceptible to third-party influences than your average human cop.'

Major Elrond Gunningham of Baltimore District was unimpressed: 'You're not suggesting we give them guns, are you?'

Casavantes replied that although they were not quite as fast as normal dogs, they could outrun any man and put the cuffs on him too.

To date the UN has refused to be drawn on the issues of para-human rights, saying only that the matter is 'under review'.

DogsBestFriend militant Wanda Vermont said 'DBF demands Xalapatech slave masters free our four-legged friends.'

'Do we look like dogs?' Chapman retorted. 'Keep that woman away from me.'

(Xalapatech is a subsidiary of Naismith Industries, an independent over-holding of the CraneCorp Buisplex.)

- 7 -

Cash in hand, Josie and Novik looked across the mall, through surging crowds of shoppers. Fash, Meeja, .life, .ret, and auto-boutiques shared the concourse with walk-in surgeries, re-re-financing, XY techno, speedsex, as well as the trads, like porno, sport, and faith. At every corner, every junction, stood the booths and screens of FreeFinger Jamboree towers.

Fake palms and clumps of shamboo were planted around water troughs and fountains. Beneath them, the day-trippers ate their Qwiknics™, and uploaded reviews and show-and-tell pictures of their newest possessions.

Novik looked around uncertainly, 'Now we're here, I'm not sure where to start.'

Josie thought for a moment, then set off across the marble atrium. 'This way.'

Walking a crowd is a skill. Josie slipped through the swarms of shoppers gracefully. Novik did the same. Benny made eye-contact with every approaching shopper, and was blocked, bumped and forced to apologise with every step.

He caught up with them outside a shoe shop.

'This is where it all begins,' Josie said, and stepped inside.

The interior of the shop was quiet, the mood reverential yet exciting, the atmosphere tweaked with aerosols of leather balm, endorphins and swarm-serotonin.

Overweight boys fondled the logos of supawhite trainers. Two businessmen in formal shorts tried on Roman sandals trimmed in gold leather. A trio of young girls worked their way through the fetish boots in the children's zone.

Josie breathed deep. Arms spread, and head thrown back, she wanted to absorb the air-born hormones, to use the strength of shop's own retail armaments against itself.

The shop assistant, a middle-aged man with a mild face, hurried over and tried to manoeuvre her out of the shop.

'You're over-reacting to the atmospherics. It's your genome's fault, for which you have sole legal responsibility. Our aerosol-densities are guaranteed to be no more than eighty percent legal maximum in up to ninety percent of retail volume.'

'That's meaningless,' Novik said.

'Entry onto the premises implies consent,' the assistant droned, a reflex monotone.

Josie waved a sheaf of notes under his nose. 'I've got money and I want to spend it. If you're going to stop me, go get the manager.'

'I-,' the assistant scowled over his shoulder, then faced Josie: 'Do you have issues with anger management or false epiphany, a family history of brain bleeds, or SUKS?'

'What's that?'

'Sudden, unexpected kleptomania syndrome.'

Josie indicated the gold sandals. 'Those are nice. What sizes do you have?'

The shop assistant stuck out his chest, 'Those are part of our Mascu-Line range, footwearage for individuals self-defining as male.'

Josie looked at him deadpan. 'Fascinating. I'll take two pairs in every size.'

'You will?'

'And the same for the trainers.'

'Those also are Mascu-Line,' the assistant said.

'Do you have anything more feminine?'

'Indeed, we do.' The assistant cleared his throat, he swept his arm across the room in a flamboyant gesture, 'May I present Laydee-Stylee.'

Josie put the sheaf of notes in her mouth and bit down. 'Nice,' came her muffled reply.

'You've really thought this through,' Novik said. 'Will any of your mass-produced products enhance my unique individuality?'

'What about me?' Benny said.

The assistant looked Benny up and down, his smile a frozen grimace. 'One moment,' he said, and scurried into the back of the store.

Almost immediately, a pudgy young man in a blue silk suit emerged. On his feet were white patent leather slip-ons, with dorsal tassels and gold heel chains.

Hands clasped, he gave an unctuous smile, revealing pearl-braced teeth. 'I understand you have an interest in our Mascu-Line footwearage?'

'I love your footwearage-' Josie read his name badge, 'Cloudio. Both Mascu-Line, and Laydee-Stylee.'

A pair of red ankle-bootlettes caught Josie's eye. She clapped her hands and pointed, 'Those, I must have those. All sizes, two pairs.'

Cloudio's eyes dropped to the wedge of money in Josie's gloved hand. Novik caught his look and gave him an encouraging nod.

Cloudio leaned close to Novik and cupped his hand beside his mouth, 'Should I recognise madam?'

'Burned-out FreeFinger addict,' Novik said. 'I'm her therapist. It's a delicate phase.'

Cloudio's smile turned sickly, 'Is she going to-?'

'ShopAmok? We don't know yet. Play along.'

Josie was beginning to enjoy herself. She touched Cloudio's arm. 'I've decided. Why waste time with half-measures? I love all your styles, all the colours. I'm going to self-define as Tally Up Your Stock List. Tell me how much it is, I'll take the lot.'

Cloudio grinned like a nauseous chipmunk, 'The women's shoes?'

'Women's, men's, children's.'

'Perhaps-' Cloudio glanced at Novik, who gave him a thumbs-up, 'We also have InterLace, a gender-plus range.' Cloudio stood on one foot and spread his hands, 'For those days when you just want to be different.'

Josie pinned Cloudio to the spot with her gaze. 'I am different, Cloudio. Add them in.'

'All?' Cloudio's voice wavered.

'All.'

'I-' Cloudio's composure disintegrated. 'Fuck it, if that's what you want.'

'Ten percent for cash?' Novik said.

Cloudio gave an indifferent shrug, 'Sure thing. No problemo.'

Half an hour later Josie placed a thick wad of bills into Cloudio's damp hands. An enormous stack of shoe boxes occupied the centre of the shop. At the very top were Cloudio's own white slip-ons. Novik had insisted.

As Cloudio counted the money his mouth began to twitch. He blinked, he grimaced, his toes curled inside his socks. 'We have a special offer on our buy-to-store option. This week we can deliver straight to the self-store warehouse of your choice.'

Novik was incredulous. 'People do that?'

'Everyone's doing it. It's like, uber-popular.'

'For shoes?'

'Particularly for shoes. Especially for shoes.' Cloudio grew enthusiastic. 'It's a virtual wardrobe, but it's full of real shoes. Think about it – simply the most perfect way to own your purchases without the inconvenience of keeping them in the finite volumage of your domicile. They're there for you, waiting in a low-light, humidity controlled environment, ready for the day you want to visit them. To touch them, smell them.' Cloudio's eyelids fluttered, 'Slip your feet inside them-'

Novik took a step back. 'Go home, Cloudio. You're done here.'

'What about all your shoes?' Cloudio exclaimed, 'Don't you want them?'

'We'll come back tomorrow,' Novik said.

The concept was so novel Cloudio became temporarily catatonic.

'Thanks,' Josie tugged the receipt out of Cloudio's unresisting fingers and lead the way out of the shop.

Outside, around the corner, Josie and Novik embraced. Novik was ecstatic, they'd had this plan, now he'd seen it working.

'That was brilliant,' he said. 'You were awesome, I couldn't have done that.'

'I enjoyed it. It was fun,' Josie said. To her own surprise, she actually meant it.

Benny looked back at the shop, already the lights were out, the shutters coming down. 'That was a smart plan. You bought his stock and blocked resupply. That retail outlet is out of action.'

Josie had spent a lot of money, and it had felt good. A year's wages spent on shoes in under an hour. It had taken a small dent out of the cash, more of a nibble, but it was start. The closed shop unsettled the passing shoppers, young and old. Skittish and unruly as spooked colts, they made impulse-buys in adjacent shops and hurried away, defensively hugging their unwanted purchases to their chests.

'We'll have to move fast, people are getting nervous,' Josie said.

'A lightning raid, and move on.' Novik liked the idea. 'Like Parker and Barrow, Dillinger and Frechette."

'Except the police won't hunt us down, they'll provide escorts, an honour guard.'

Novik surveyed the mall like a lion of the Serengeti. He saw what he wanted. 'Over there. Power tools.'

The sun was setting when they made their way back to Mr Car. All afternoon shops had ceased trading as they had bought them out. Now the entire mall was closing. Weary shoppers tramped across the parking lot, whole families of day-trippers, coach parties of excursion purchasers. Security guards manned the barriers of the entrance lanes to the car park and turned away confused and disappointed arrivals.

Back at the Cadillac, 'Peace Dog' was playing on Mr Car's stereo. Benny listened to Duffy's licks and power chords, peered inside the vehicle then stood back to admire the external lines.

'The next war will not be cool but you are one awesomely cool piece of techno, Mr. Car.'

'Thank you for noticing, sir. I also believe it to be true.'

'When will the next war be?' Josie said.

'Probably quite soon. Maybe never,' Benny said. 'When I find out, you'll be the first to know.'

Novik slipped behind the wheel. Josie tossed her bag onto the passenger seat beside him. It was empty of everything but long strips of paper. A million dollars exchanged for a dozen metres of till receipts.

Shopping usually left Novik drained, right now he felt energised and empowered, an endorphin high. Doing something, taking a stand, making a point - they had proved it could be done. 'We can do this, I know we can, but we need a real plan, a scheme, a strategy. Then we'll come back and really take it to the man.'

Josie thought it over, her smile half worn-out. If Novik took a break he might slow down, lose momentum. Maybe this one gesture was all he needed. In his subconscious it was already over, he just needed time to realise. She kissed his cheek, 'Let's keep heading south. We'll hit Mexico, strip down and party. Catch some rays.'

'And make a plan.'

'Sure thing, hon,' Josie's voice was light, carefree. 'We'll make a plan.'

'So this new guy's coming with us?' Mr Car said as they buckled up.

'Benny? Sure. Why not?' Novik said.

'Ah. No reason,' the Cadillac replied as they pulled away into the traffic.

That colour? It's just you, it so is. That perfume? Absolutely! That automobile, I can see you in it! Darling, it defines you. It is you.

Well, no.

These days, does anyone of sound mind really believe owning a single, high-end, branded commodity will embellish their social personhood?

Of course not. How ridiculous. How naive. We've moved on, today's society is far more sophisticated.

My own research indicates that, at any one time, you need to display thirty to seventy mid-tier, or twenty to thirty-five brand-iconic logos on your combined physico-virtual personage - your McLuhanite para-social media extensions.

Yes, that's display, not own. Ownage should be significantly higher. How else are people going to discover who you are, where you're coming from and where you're going to?

Today the challenge is to macro-balance all those designs into a gestalt 'Moi'. Tomorrow it will be synergistic integration with Meeja-II.

Fortunately, today's solution is actually quite simple: Context-sensitive Logo-montage feedback loops!

Teh Poon Leet,
Logo-me-beautiful consultant.

- 8 -

Just like O5 and 24, the National Guard were on the levees of the ever growing shoreline of Pontchartrain-Maurepas. Hugely extended, the earth ramparts flanked Interstate 12, broke south-west past Raymond and followed the high ground over to Sorento, where construction still continued.

The difference was this: instead of spades and sandbags, the Guard had assault rifles and night-vision goggles. Overhead, the searchlights of helicopter gunships played across the dark water as they patrolled the perimeter of the permanently flooded, and officially abandoned, city of New Orleans, like giant black dragonflies.

Some miles east, along the southern banks of the hugely expanded lake, Jericho Wilson sweltered in the heat and humidity of the saturated night air, and watched the uneasy waters.

His amphibious pickup was parked a hundred yards away, under some trees. Wilson himself hunkered down in some scrub cypress overlooking a concrete slipway that ran up out of the water, over the broad top of the earth levee and down to a dirt road. He thought about a cigarette, but didn't want to risk the glow, or the smell.

Wilson might be in the middle of a swamp, it didn't mean he was alone.

Above him, reflections from the searchlight beams moved in glowing patches across the heavy cloud base. In the city centre, scattered lights showed on a few of the failed storm arcologies, tapered glass and steel cylinders of thirty and forty stories. Targeting lasers flickered from their roofs and upper levels. The ruby beams stayed well away from the military choppers, just letting them know they were there, that Mitchel Gould, Lord of Nu-Orleans, accepted them under sufferance.

Out in the gulf, the miles-wide storm columns of hurricane Permanent Larry blanked out the southern sky like a brooding god.

Slowly, quietly, Wilson eased his legs. This kind of work didn't get any easier. Thick in the waist and greying at the temples, he had a bushy moustache like that of an old-time Marshall.

Wilson looked at the hurricane and thought it was closer. He wondered how many little boats were out in the gulf that night, how many hand-made rafts and dinghies chugged towards the Louisiana coast from central America and Haiti, their failing, third-hand outboards paid for with sex, children, or a promise to pick up the phone one night and do whatever you were told. *Sure, we can get you to the Nortamericanos, señor. The price is the same for everyone: all you own and a little bit more.*

Wilson thought about what it must be like to be so desperate, how many times Permanent Larry had to wreck your house, sink your boat and destroy your crops before the chance of making it to the USA as an illegal, compared to drowning in a cockleshell boat, felt like a good bet.

The vegetation round Wilson was recovering from Larry's last visit. Broken stumps were shooting green from new buds, spear-fronded fern colonised bare ground, one of several new species pushing north with the weather.

Larry hadn't rolled along this part of the southern littoral for over a year. Maybe it wouldn't come again this year, almost certainly it would the next. When it did, in its wake, amongst the flotsam and storm-beaten wreckage, people would stagger out of the angry surf, abandoning their waterlogged rafts and leaking boats. Nobody knew how many set out, or how many arrived, but they kept on coming.

Wilson grimaced at his own imagination, chided himself for letting his mind wander, and settled down to watch and listen.

It had been a long while since he had feelings that deep. These days he just wanted to do his job. He found his man and brought him in alive. Always alive. It had become his reputation, and when people found out who had come for them, it sometimes made things go easier, and sometimes not.

The time had come long ago when there had been one death too many. Now, apart from Mitchell Gould, Wilson wanted nothing more to do with killing. People would still get hurt, fair play. Wilson was pretty good at hurting.

After a while there was a change in the texture of the darkness. Wilson became very still.

Drifting out of the night, outboard on tick over, a battered, flat-bottomed green metal dinghy swung towards the slipway. Before it grounded, a man dressed in a dark jacket, trousers and beanie slipped into the water. He lifted a holdall out of the boat and balanced it on his head. Then he took hold of the boat's painter and waded ashore.

As the man dropped the bag onto the slipway, the night lit up with a pulse of light towards the city. Moments later, the rumbling crackle of the explosion followed. The brief illumination showed Wilson the man's heavy jaw, cropped hair and bandido moustaches. It was Meineck, the man his sources said would be here. Meineck might have arrived by boat, but he was no climate refugee. He was a wanted man with a price on his head.

Meineck sloshed back into the water and swung the boat round. He set the throttle up a notch and sent the empty craft put-putting away into the night.

As Meineck stood with his back to the shore Wilson moved down the slipway. Drawing his neural mop, Wilson aimed it at Meineck's back. 'Hold it there, Meineck.'

Meineck turned fast, his right arm coming up. Wilson shot him in the chest. Meineck squawked as the barbed vial struck home, gave a whole-body twitch as sodium ions vented from his synapses, and flopped face down into the water. He got his knees back under himself, so Wilson shot him again. Lacking all muscle control, Meineck blew bubbles from both ends and sank.

Wilson waded into the water, hauled Meineck onto the slipway and slapped an electrolyte patch on his neck.

Meineck tried to curl up on the concrete. 'Oh sweet Jesus,' he groaned.

'Quite a rush, eh?' Wilson cuffed Meineck's wrists with cable ties, found and removed a knife and a telescopic cosh from his utility jacket, a second gun from the back of his waistband. He threw them all into the water and hauled Meineck to his feet.

'Expecting trouble?' Wilson said.

The muscles on one side of Meineck's face were slack from electrolyte loss. 'Don't take me back,' he slurred.

'One thing you got to know about me, pal. I never take them back.'

'God, no, not that!' Meineck tottered towards the water. Wilson suspected fakery and let him go.

Meineck fell to his knees. 'Not like this, not here.'

Wilson jabbed Meineck in the neck with his neural pistol. 'Shut up, you punk. You think I work for that sonofabitch Gould? I'm taking you to prison.'

The urge to slug Meineck, get him down on the ground and slam his fists into the crook's ugly face, was hard to resist. Wilson wanted to bust Meineck up good, pulp him, kick his god-damned teeth in. Teach him to be quicker with the gun, to aim faster and just shoot it. Shoot it at Wilson, shoot him in the head, just like Wilson had done to Mandy on that awful night long ago.

Pale as a ghost, Meineck looked up at Wilson, terrified by the rage in his captor's face.

Mentally and physically Wilson took a step back. 'Christ, Meineck, if I worked for that scumbag, I'd zap you again and hold you under until the bubbles stopped. You want I do that, you low-life bottom-feeder?'

Meineck's eyes had gone hollow. He swallowed hard, he shook his head, 'No, I don't.'

Another flash-bang lit up the sky.

'What's that?' Wilson said.

'Gould's men, dynamiting the levees. Trying to lower the water levels.'

By any standards Mitchell Gould's operation was impressive. When the USA effectively withdrew from the coastline, when civilisation moved twenty miles inland, all the way from Corpus Christi to Tampa, Gould had seen an opportunity, and moved his operation down from Birmingham. Now he ran his own law from one of the abandoned high rises, the self-contained and weather-immune arcologies built after Katrina III. When Permanent Larry returned again, and then again, the flaw in the arcology plan was revealed: nobody wanted to live in a wasteland.

Gould moved drugs, climate refugees and contraband across what had come to be called the Southern Littoral, a three-mile-wide no-man's land between the ocean and the USA. His fief extended from the ruins of Morgan City to the Gulfport marshes, fifty miles in each direction.

Low concussion waves from the levee charges broke on the slipway. Meineck shifted uncomfortably.

'You OK?' Wilson said.

Meineck gave a grimace of revulsion. 'I shat myself. When you shot me.'

'It happens. I got spare clothes in the pickup. You going to mess me about?'

Too weary to speak, Meineck shook his head. Wilson helped Meineck up the ramp, dropped the dry clothes at his feet, and cut the ties binding his wrists. After Meineck had changed, Wilson re-cuffed him and put him in the passenger seat.

The beat of rotors swung overhead as Army helicopters homed in on the explosion sites, the flickering red targeting lasers following behind.

Meineck shut his eyes and leaned back, 'It's a relief, you know? Not having to run anymore, not having to keep looking over your shoulder. Jail is going to be easy. I'm ready to go back, I can do the time.'

Wilson pulled a half of scotch out of the door pocket. 'You want a drink?'

'Sure.'

Wilson held the bottle to Meineck's mouth until he nodded. There were a couple of inches left, Wilson drained the bottle and tossed it out the window. 'So you think I've done you a favour?'

'Yes, sir. I think you have.'

Wilson gave a short, harsh laugh, 'You're an even bigger fuck-up than me.'

The whisky did its job on Meineck's sodium deficient system, and he quickly fell asleep. It also did its daily job on Wilson's scarred emotions. An hour's driving brought Wilson to the local bondsman pens in a mellower mood. While Meineck was booked, processed and logged for onwards transportation, Wilson collected his fees and scanned the lists for his next job. Among the usual dealers, illegals, thieves and gangsters, someone on early release gone AWOL caught his eye. Here was yet another person who thought cutting the tag necklace in the bath meant it couldn't send a signal. Now he had broken parole, damaged government property, and dragged any accomplices down into the system with him.

It was exactly what Wilson was looking for. He accepted the job, printed the information sheet and vacated the booth.

Another bondsman waited to use the console. His massive frame, plaited blond hair and full beard gave him the appearance of a latter-day Viking.

'Curtis, how's it hanging?' Wilson said as they shook hands.

'Like a small banana. What you take?'

'The parole bust,' Wilson said.

'What's he done?'

Wilson read from the sheet: 'Behaviour or opinions promoting or deemed to promote un-American commercial modalities.'

'Part of Snarlow's round up. Poor bastard. My brother-in-law was a charity worker, now he's doing three to five on the same charge.'

'I hope he's got the sense to sit it out,' Wilson said.

'He's daft, not stupid.' Curtis chuckled sourly, 'Then again, he did marry my sister.'

'How's she doing?'

'Family's pulled together. She's a good kid.'

'Let me know.'

'You be careful,' Curtis said.

'You too.'

Wilson climbed into his truck, started the engine and read through the sheet again. He knew what Curtis meant, parole breakers often got violent. They had done a stupid thing, when they realised how stupid, it made some of them desperate.

Just what he was looking for.

Wilson folded away the paper into his breast pocket, put the vehicle into gear and pulled out the lot. He had a little ritual at the start of any job, a phrase he always spoke. He said it now: 'Mr Novik, my name is Jericho Wilson, and today I'll be your nemesis.'

Meeja 101

With hindsight, we can say the internet was never a place, it was a platform. You could contribute to it, consume it, or comment on it, but you could never go there for your holidays.

If publishing is simply "the act of making a created item public" then all the internet ever was, and ever could be, was a method of publication. Nevertheless, it was incredible, transformational, a genuine innovation. It was magnificent, it was gigantic, and in its day it ruled the world.

All the Cloud let you do was aggregate what had been published. Data, and data storage, became utility commodities. Commercials and governments run the cloud for free because they want your data, and they can make money, or gain leverage, from it.

Meeja, and especially Meeja-II, is a lot smaller, but there's more of it. It's standalone in usage, aggregated in concept. Paradoxical? Only on the surface.

Think of Meeja as a script. You're the actor, and you're also in the audience. In fact you are the audience. That guy sitting beside you, he's you too. And so are all the other actors.

So who wrote the script? What script? This is the trick – there is no script.

Carrie Styvesant, '
An Introduction to Meeja Studies'

- 9 -

The border with Mexico at Ciudad Acuna was even more chaotic than usual. Long queues of goods trucks and passenger vehicles waited to cross on both sides. Several hundred pedestrians milled on the Mexican bank of the Rio Bravo.

'I'm not sure this is such a frosty idea,' Novik said as the lines of American traffic inched towards the bridge.

Up ahead lay the human-built obstacles to crossing from one country into another: American customs, interrogation and command posts; the twin, eight-lane toll bridges across the river; the Mexican versions of the immigration and emigration customs and law-enforcement.

The near side of the river was flanked by chain-link fences, fifty feet apart, topped with razor wire. The space between was stripped of vegetation, the bare ground churned with the tracks of half-tracked fast-pursuit vehicles.

Josie had tried to dress them for the car, a light suit, shirt and brown shoes for Novik, a calf-length grey skirt, buckskin boots, white blouse and dark jacket for Josie. Benny had refused to change, insisting the fabric of his clothing contained nanotech bio-flagellates that would keep it clean and in good repair. For certain his jeans, shirt and jacket looked smart and neat, his trainers gleaming white. As far as Novik was concerned that was because he had stood Benny up and slapped some of the dust out with his hands.

Josie fidgeted with her neck-line, doubtful of her costume change. 'I feel like a criminal.'

'That's because you are,' Novik said. 'So am I.'

'And I am the aspirational automobile for the career hoodlum,' Mr Car said. 'You not only are criminals, you look like them too.'

'We just found some stuff,' Josie said unhappily. 'We found an abandoned, ownerless car, and there was some cash in the trunk.'

'One hundred and ninety million dollars. It makes me pucker.' Novik felt a little nauseous, a tic pulsed under his left eye. Two days of weird pastel beauty from the f-LSD combined with anxiety of pursuit had taken him to a flawed and paranoid paradise he was only just beginning to rationalise. The tic was invisible, he'd looked for it in the mirror but it wasn't there. Novik didn't get off on things happening to his body he could feel but not see.

Homeland security, smart in their teal-green uniforms and mirror-lensed sunglasses, patrolled the traffic lines. Every now and then they rapped on a vehicle window and questioned the occupants. Sometimes they just chewed the fat and moved on, other times they ordered a redirection to the customs interrogation bays.

'They're going to open us up, I know it,' Novik said. 'I got a vibe.'

Sprawled on the back seat Benny opened one eye. 'No they won't.'

'How do you know?'

'They just won't. I know it.' Benny yawned and stretched. 'I got a vibe too.'

'Sure you have,' Novik hissed through his teeth. Benny might be a harmless fruitcake, but he was too obsessed with his millennial mission for practicality, let alone reality.

Uncomfortable with personal authority, distrustful of authority structures, Novik had the growing conviction Benny already thought of him in that very way. The idea was weird, spooky. The more he thought about it, the creepier Benny's current complacency seemed. Something was going on, something he didn't understand. Despite Mr Car's atmospheric controls, Novik's palms were clammy, his pulse raced. On a sudden impulse, he got out of the car.

Outside the air was humid and close. Sweat prickled Novik's collar almost immediately, even so, the heavy, warm breeze was more welcome than the chilled and claustrophobic climate inside the Cadillac.

Novik headed towards the bridge, past lines of dented, rust-scarred pickups and battered saloons, each filled with families of poor white and Hispanic economic emigrants, young education refugees, and agricultural nomads. A quarter mile from the border the sound of the Mexican crowd surged like a breaking wave, the air-horns of the backed-up trucks like foghorns of distressed ships.

Chest-high rushes and grass covered the banks of the shallow Rio Bravo. Closer beside the bridges, non-native plants had taken hold – ornamental lilies and daisy cultivars, watermelons and sapling orange and apple trees, all grown from discarded flowers and half-eaten fruits thrown from vehicles, a rich mulch for new growth. The tattered leaves of wild bananas and young date palms tossed in the new, wetter gulf-winds that blew steadily from the south and east.

Out in the lanes of creeping traffic, a cop worked his way towards Novik. Heavily built, with a middle-aged paunch and cropped silver hair, the cop slipped gracefully between the fenders and bull-bars of pickup trucks and mini-vans.

The one thing you never do when a cop sees you is turn around and walk away. Novik raised his hand, leaned on the rail, and waited.

'Howdy, officer.'

'Why did you leave your vehicle, sir? Have you broken down?' The cop's tone was authoritarian and brusque. A wireless mini-cam on the epaulettes of his right shoulder panned left and right.

'A cramp in my leg,' Novik noticed the cop's hand resting lightly on the holster at his right hip. A sense of dread grew in his stomach, a feeling of predestined doom. 'What's happening down at the crossing? That big crowd, is there trouble?'

The cop's name badge said 'Miller S', he gave Novik a gray-eyed flat stare. 'Not that I'm aware, sir.'

Low dark shapes patrolled through the sword grass on the Mexican side. 'What are those?' Novik said.

'First-gen Dawkins-dogs from Xalapatech.' Officer Miller tucked his thumbs into his waistband, 'Mexi-cops got them last year. Smart puppies, loyal as hell.'

'We got those?'

Miller pulled a sour face. 'We got the robo-canines. Congress supports home-grown tech.'

'I hear they trip over kerbs.'

Miller stared into the middle distance and sighed, 'That's them.'

'So it goes,' Novik began to relax, Officer Miller seemed to be a reasonable man.

Miller looked Novik up and down. 'Which is your vehicle, sir?'

Novik gestured vaguely back down the line. 'The drophead.'

'That new model Caddy? Sonnofabitch, where's the logo? Let's go take a look. I want to see the hub badges. Who's the designer, Pedro Agenbite, Ben Brocolli?'

'I'm not sure. Agenbite, I guess. Maybe Phuqthard.'

'You're not sure?' Miller regarded him with a mixture of suspicion and pity. 'Are you traveling under your own cognizance?'

'I'm with friends.'

'And that's your car?'

'Yes. Absolutely.'

'Let's go say hello.' Miller indicated the way with his hand. 'After you, sir.'

There was no choice, no other options. Novik began to walk. Ahead, behind, and to the sides, the drivers and passengers of the trucks and automobiles glanced at Novik and looked resolutely away.

'Pick up the pace,' Miller ordered.

As they drew level with the Cadillac's hood, Benny leaned out the rear window, beaming amiably, 'Excuse me, Officer Miller.'

'Sit down and close the window, sir.'

Benny narrowed his eyes and passed his hand through the air, 'This is not the car you are looking for.'

Novik wished Josie and himself far away. This was so messed up, they were so screwed. Prison felt so real he could taste the concrete. This was where he had brought Josie with his fine ideas. He had persuaded her, the realisation this was all his doing a dead, putrid weight in his gut.

The cop actually laughed, 'Nice try. What's your name?'

'Benny the Spoke, sir. Pleased to meet you.' Benny held out his hand. 'You want my autograph?'

'Should I know you?'

'No, but one day you will. Everyone will.'

'That's the American Dream, son. Nevertheless, even if you were Benny the Superstar, I still require you to sit down and close your window.'

'Just let me sign-'

Officer Miller's hand dropped to his holster. 'Right now.'

Benny withdrew, the window slid up.

Miller scanned the car with his head-cam. The lens zoomed in on the hubcaps, door-handle and fender details. Miller gave a grunt of satisfaction, 'Nice. Agenbite for sure.'

'You idiot', Novik mouthed at Benny.

Miller paced around the car and spoke into his mike: 'Office Miller, S, Border Patrol, Ciudad Acuna. Charcoal Cadillac drophead limousine. Three occupants, one self-defined female, two male. Speech patterns, extra-vehicular activity, and incongruous bonhomie suggest possible duplicitous intent.' He fixed Novik in the eye, 'Open the trunk, sir.'

'Yes, I'll just get-'

Before Novik could move, the trunk lid smoothly swung up on damped servos.

Novik numbly followed Miller to the rear of the car, a short walk through eternity to the waiting scaffold. As he did, the chaotic noise from the border surged louder than ever.

Miller halted, intently, he listened to the feed on his earphone. Novik worked moisture into his mouth and looked around. In the other vehicles passengers and drivers stared intently at their phone screens.

'Mr Car, what the hell are you doing?' Novik seethed under his breath.

'I am obliged to obey any reasonable request from a duly notarised officer of the law. Is that an issue?'

'Yes, that is a f-'

A sound like fire crackers burst from the crossing point.

Novik dropped to a half-crouch, he knew that noise. He'd heard it before, when Snarlow closed down the protests with the National Guard. He hadn't believed it then, not at first. He didn't want to believe it now. There was so very much of it.

White-faced, Miller drew his gun. 'Get in your car and lock the doors,' he ordered, then ran towards the bridge.

Novik didn't want to go, yet the need to see, to bear witness, pulled him. Keeping low, he crept towards the border.

The firecracker sound burst out again, then settled to an intermittent spatter. Down at the crossing, truck horns blared, engines roared into life. Over it all came the howl of the Mexican crowd, a beast in pain.

Then Josie was in front of him, wild-eyed, pushing him back. 'That's gunfire,' she yelled. 'It's all gone crazy. Come back to the car.'

All around them was madness as cars tried to turn out of the queue. Fenders locked, horns blared, drivers cursed, children grizzled in fear.

Josie dragged Novik back to the Cadillac and slammed the door shut, 'Get us out of here.'

The line of traffic was bumper to bumper. Novik thumped the steering wheel, 'There's no room to turn.'

'Four-wheel steering engaged,' Mr Car said.

Novik turned the wheel on full lock, dabbed the gas, and the Cadillac slid sideways onto the dirt beside the road.

Novik gunned the engine, the wheel still hard over, and the big car slewed round in a fast turn. They sped away from Mexico, against the traffic, along the roadside, tyres spewing plumes of dust.

Novik felt cold, 'What the hell is happening?'

Benny looked back through the rear window, 'The beginning.'

'That was gunfire,' Josie said flatly. 'I saw bodies on the ground.'

'I didn't see anything,' Novik said.

'I am equipped with a surveillance drone,' Mr Car offered.

'Deploy it,' Josie said.

A metallic 'plang' came from the roof, a flat black oval whirred up into the sky.

'When can we see?' Novik said.

'Gaining altitude. Assuming station. Streaming data,' Mr Car said. 'Ready for display on the total-HUD.'

'What's that?' Benny said.

A soft chime sounded, an incongruously bright west-coast voice began to gabble:

'T-HUD is a new development in information display management featuring seamless autopilot engage, wraparound screenlets with opaque, translucent and analogue overlay modes. T-HUD is an optional extra from THUD Avionics, a tertiary subsidiary of Bharti Airtel, a member of the CraneCorp Buisplex.'

'What the hell?' Novik said.

'My apologies,' Mr Car's normal voice resumed. 'I was momentarily pre-empted by a commercial override.'

Up ahead, a coach began to turn, struck a flat-bed truck and shunted it across the speeding Cadillac's path.

'Hold on,' Novik pulled the Cadillac further out into the scrub. Out of nowhere a dry gulch appeared, four feet deep, and twice as wide. Novik braked hard, the Cadillac began to slide, there was not enough room to stop. 'Holy crap, hang on,' Novik cried.

'Intervention,' Mr Car said. The steering wheel went slack in Novik's hands, seat belts snatched everyone tight against the seats as massive acceleration pushed them deep into the upholstery.

For an instant it was quiet. Novik and Josie watched the loose items on the dash float in the air.

Then they were back on hard dirt, the Cadillac jounced, fishtailed madly, and resumed its high-speed course. Josie screamed, Novik swore, Benny whopped and hollered.

Gasping with adrenalin, Novik impotently gripped the sloppy steering wheel.

'You have the con,' Mr Car said.

Responsive weight returned to the wheel. Novik eased off on the accelerator, swung across the road, through a gap in the median strip, and onto the correct side of the road.

'Holy everything that's Holy, that was fun,' Benny exclaimed. 'You sure give good tech, Mr. Car.'

'Standard GOOJ feature, sir. Other options, such as BriefFlight are not installed. May I also say that totalHUD is upgradeable from demonstration to perma-feature via a simple debit transaction.'

Josie's mouth hung open, 'Mr Car, did you say you can fly?'

'No, ma'am, but I could.'

'I can see why naughty people like you.'
'Thank you so much.'

Eugene, Oregon: Urban Flash Farmers caused chaos overnight when a tuned myco crop fruited all down Franklin Boulevard.

Triggered by recent rain, two-meter diameter Portobello mushrooms pushed through concrete and tarmac rendering the road impassable. Rising as high as first floor windows, the giant, edible mushrooms formed a surreal vista.

'We think they're seeding the streets using doctored gum,' Jefferson Ives, deputy Sheriff stated. 'Kids chew the gum, spit it on the sidewalk and the spores go underground.'

DNA analysis is expected to confirm the flash farm was the work of the Natural Forces Combine. The notorious bio-activists have already claimed responsibility for this crop.

'Tastes like chicken,' local resident D'Wayne Cheeseman observed.

Syndicated feed,
KUWjones.org

- ١٠ -

Gould's phone rang. The screen showed Jimmy Fee's number but there was no picture. The Old-fashioned Boys had come down from Birmingham when Gould had set up in New Orleans. He liked them, they knew how things worked, expected shit for shit and dealt it straight back. Trusted soldiers, the kind that endured.

'James, how's it hanging?' Gould spoke into the phone.

There was a hesitation, then: 'Id's, ah, Blag, sir.'

'Blag?'

'Bladk,' the voice said very carefully, then tried again. 'This is Black.'

Now he knew who it was, Gould found he could understand him. 'What's wrong with your voice?'

'There was a dispute. It got physical.'

Gould's voice grew flat with menace. 'Tell me.'

'Mother's not going to make the show.'

Gould took a long slow breath. 'Not at all?'

'No sir.

'Why not?'

'She's gone off with some new friends.'

'Is Jimmy with them?'

Another hesitation. 'No, sir.'

'Let me talk to him.'

'He's, ah, late.'

'Understood. Listen carefully, Mr. Black. Mother is more important to me than anyone. I want you to catch up with her and make sure she's safe. Find out who is looking after her and thank them properly.'

'Yes, sir.'

'I'm sending you Manalito.'

'I don't-'

'Don't what, Mr. Black?'

'We're still the Old-fashioned Boys, Mr. Gould.'

'And you still work for me.'

'We've never-'

'So does Manalito.'

Coldly furious, Gould ended the call. If some little bit-piece player had been in the room he'd have happily killed them just for stress relief.

A few girls were on the couches, bored and watchful. The more observant looked nervous.

'Get them out of here, Manalito,' Gould ordered. 'And pack for Stateside.'

The girls filed out, trying not to look at Gould. The long-haired oriental was at the back, wearing an open-fronted bolero top, lilac silk micro skirt and platform sandals. Of them all only she dared give Gould a lingering glance.

So be it.

'Not you,' Gould told her.

At the door, Manalito looked back. Gould gave a curt shake of his head and the big Mexican ducked out the room and closed the door. Gould knew the girl had had caught the exchange. He turned to the window and looked out across dead New Orleans, a drowned and rotten corpse. Out in the gulf Permanent Larry held steady, its own energies pitched against the prevailing winds.

Why was nothing ever easy? The plan had been simple enough: take the cash to Vegas and lose it in Gordano's Casinos, a laundry operation that had worked well for years. What had gone wrong?

Gould realised the girl was saying something.

'You want a back rub, Mr. Gould? You look real tense.'

Gould fought down the urge to tell her to shut up and mind her own damned business. She was right, he was wound tight, and it was he who had told her to stay.

'You any good at it?' he said.

'I'm a trained masseuse. You want to lie on the couch?'

'No. Do it here.' Gould reversed one of the upright chairs and sat down.

There was strength in her hands and as she worked on his shoulders he started to relax. She was good at this, he acknowledged. He hadn't known that.

Knowledge was everything. That's what had gone wrong with the money. Something had happened, something he hadn't known about had come along and screwed with his plans. For fifty miles along the foreshore, beyond the levees inland, he had people, electronic eyes, movement sensors. All sent back information to his analysts, nothing happened on the coast that he didn't know about. It was Gould's own data cloud, a sensory web he took considerable effort to make sure remained private. Each year it reached a little further as he seeded buildings and landscapes with solar-powered micro-sensors, tac/strat bugs and mobile away teams. And each day, sometimes each hour, those teams, and his home techs, tracked down and ripped out soft hacks, data aggregators and transmission devices planted by military data sappers and persons unknown. Gould let the army patrols alone. Everyone else was open season.

And now the Old-fashioned Boys had screwed it up. Gould clenched his fists. It was a good job Jimmy Fee was dead, otherwise he'd rip his lungs out.

'You're tensing up again, Mr Gould. Am I doing something wrong?' the girl said.

Something snapped in Gould, he surged to his feet. 'What is it with all the losers in the world that none of them can do anything right?'

She didn't even falter. She just stood and did her best to look pretty and happy and his. 'You really want me to answer that?'

'No, you stupid bitch, I want you to shut the-' Gould slammed his fist into his palm, 'Forget that. This is absolutely not your fault.' He bared his teeth, a forced smile. 'I trusted some people, they let me down.' He reached out into the air, his fingers like claws. 'I just wish I could-'

She slipped out of her bolero, her waist length hair falling over her shoulders to cover her breasts. Then she took his hands and put them round her own throat.

'Like this?'

That annoyed him. He'd apologised and in return she tried to play him. Spinning her round he locked his elbow round her neck, his other hand against her bare stomach.

'What's under here?' Gould pulled at the material of her short skirt.

She looked back at him, lips parted. 'Just me.'

Gould used his blank voice again, the one he'd used on the phone with Black. 'You like I get two more guys in here, and we make you airtight?'

Just a flicker then. The smile never faltered but those dark eyes betrayed her.

'Sure, Mr Gould.' She became bright and brittle. She gyrated her bottom against his groin, an artificial, contrived movement. 'Anything you want,' she breathed. 'Anything at all.'

Content with her reaction, Gould pushed down on her shoulders. 'Another time. Right now, this is what I want.' She sank to her knees and turned to face him.

She was good at that too. Exquisite. He told her.

Life could be good. It would be good again.

Afterwards she tried another play. He was relaxed now, and didn't mind.

'You know what I think you should do, Mr. Gould?'

He sighed with mock exasperation. 'Whatever it is, I know you're going tell me.'

'Even if your people are good at what they do they are not much use if you don't keep them in awe.'

'Agreed.' Idly Gould parted the long black hair hanging across her chest. Her nipples were hard, the areolas of her small breasts swollen and shiny. He took one between his finger and thumb.

'In your position I think you should do more killing.'

Startled, Gould laughed out loud. She darted her head forwards and kissed his mouth. A faint taste of himself lingered on her lips. He kissed her back, taking his time.

'What's your name, girl?'

'Ayesha, Mr. Gould.'

'Call me Mitchell.'

Palfinger Crane – just how rich is rich?

The short answer is, like you can't imagine. He's that rich.

Pretend you earn a million dollars a year. That's not too hard, lots of people do that. For Crane, it's a drop in the ocean. Make it a BILLION dollars a year. You save every cent, after a thousand years you're not even close.

There are three things to remember about Palfinger Crane: he's the richest person alive; he's richest person there has ever been; and he's the richest there ever could be (probably).

So how rich is that? Nobody knows. Crane doesn't even know. It's a lot. What we do know is that last year 67.819% of the GDP of the entire planet flowed through, or was generated by, that massively interlocked and ever-expanding cascade of corporations called the CraneCorp BuisPlex. The Global MegaCorp arrived years ago and we didn't notice. One man owns the planet, lucky for all of us he seems to be a nice guy.

One Man and his Wallet – Special Feature,
BFBM magazine

- 11 -

The land of the Totally Rich is another world. You may hear the horns blowing, you may run as hard as you can, but you will neither meet the King nor marry his daughter.

You can't take anyone there, it's a state of mind and a point of view, far more a frame of reference than a piece of dirt.

The people you knew, the kind who used to be your friends before you became TR, they can walk by your side and see what you see. They can meet the same people and eat the same food, but unless they are Totally Rich like you, they are simply outsiders looking in. There's so little overlap it gets embarrassing. The best thing for you both is to leave them behind.

Life as a Venn diagram.

It's all about you.

It's a land where nothing happens unless you want it to. You've got everything, including things you didn't even know you had, because someone you employ has anticipated your desires. The car, or the person, or the country house is already yours: gravel raked, stones whitewashed, staff in a line on a lawn where every blade of grass is the right height. You own the land and the land and its inhabitants are watching you. They make sure everything is just so, that the crisp things are crisp, the smooth are smooth, and all the other things are hot, or lemony, or naked enough so you don't have to worry about trivial things like that ever again.

So you can be free.

Weather can't reach you here. Life, on the other hand…

Palfinger Crane stood at the top of a wide fan of marble and limestone steps and watched his pretty, dark-haired daughter cross the palm fringed lawn. He wore cream linen slacks, open-toed sandals and a pale blue Nehru jacket. His frame was slender, his fair hair and beard close cropped. He was as worried as any father could be.

Despite her 1,750 lb bulk Ellen Hutzenreiter-Crane moved easily across the daisy-free grass. She walked with the strange, graceful daintiness of the super-obese, a hippopotamus en-pointe on her load-spreaders, every movement assisted by the steel and carbon-fibre exoframe that supported her body and balanced her metabolism. The discreet pistons, servos and fuel cells did most of the work for her youthful, and immensely corpulent, body.

The Caribbean breeze blew mild and fresh, the sea below the cliffs a vivid azure. At the top of the steps a large, domed conservatory held cycads, tree-ferns, dendrons, horsetails, lycopodium and the other ancient plants Crane collected.

Today he was accompanied by three remarkable doctors, all dressed in chinos and colourful short-sleeved shirts. Sam Yeo, aged 35, was American, short and dumpy, his skin baby-smooth - a renowned neuronic psycho-surgeon and parasitologist. Beside him was Chandra Smith, tall, with steel grey hair, and more handsome in his late middle age than in his youth. He was a genetic teratologist, morphic developmentalist, and the finest transplant surgeon in the world. The third person, dark, sleek and brilliant, was Olivia Karpozy-McNichols, hormone nutritionalist, Chi-balancer, and renal, lymphatic and blood-plasma nexialist.

It was irrelevant that they were the best money could buy, because they worked for free. Palfinger Crane funded the universities, hospitals and research institutions where they worked. He had come to know them personally, they liked him and they liked his daughter. They felt honoured to be his friends. Crane felt honoured too, he was the only one without a Nobel prize.

Palfinger Crane, the world's first and only trillionaire, the only man ever to be declared Totally Rich had made his first fortune by giving away company products for free. He made his second by buying those companies. He knew there were still some things money couldn't buy, and it seemed that a normal-sized daughter was one of them.

Crane watched Ellen leave two-inch deep footprints in the perfect lawn. 'You're out of ideas,' he said.

Beside him, the three doctors made awkward movements, winces, grimaces, shrugs and silent gestures.

'Yes, we are,' they confessed.

'Suppositions? Intuition?'

'Not really,' said Chandra Smith.

'Wild guesses?'

'Palfinger, we've been there,' Olivia said.

Crane folded and unfolded his hands. Olivia was right, they really had tried absolutely everything. Hormones, diet, exercise, surgery, analysis, infections, parasites, acupuncture, cancers, mutations, voodoo, dowsing, prayer, meditation, drugs, minerals, transfusions, infusions, and every scan, analysis, assay and biometric measurement it was possible to take. Everything. They had tried it all and then they'd done it all over again.

Hell, they had even tried homeopathy.

None of it made the slightest difference. Ever since Crane's billions had turned to trillions Ellen had put on weight relentlessly. It felt so very unfair.

Ellen reached the base of the steps and trotted up the flight, assisted by the near-silent exoframe, surgically attached to, and through, her body.

The edge of one step crumbled under her weight. It would be repaired overnight just as the gardeners would re-lay the lawn. In this land all problems were solved, all issues turned to opportunity.

All but one.

'Hi, Daddy. Hello, Sam, Chandra. Hi, Olivia.' Ellen's dimpled cheeks shone, her eyes were surrounded by pads of fat. On the shoulder of her frame a red light pulsed, the soft roar of fans wafting cool air through her clothes.

Palfinger Crane loved his daughter. He loved her far more than her estranged mother, Bianca, currently eking out the last millions of this year's allowance to save the coral atolls of Micronesia.

Crane had a lot more to give than anyone who had ever lived, more than corporations, more than nations. He'd already given a great deal and, for Ellen, was willing to give much more.

On days like these it seemed there was little point.

Ellen took in the sombre expressions of her father and his guests. 'Shall we go in?'

Crane led the way into the conservatory, where the central plaza had been reconfigured for an informal conference. Crane sat in a wicker armchair, the legs of Ellen's exoframe locked into an optimal resting position. The doctors stood beside a tall screen softly lit from within by pastel light.

Ellen was intelligent and educated. She was inherently cheerful, and had been brought up to be forthright and assertive without being demanding. She preferred to receive bad news without prevarication.

'You don't know what to do,' she told the doctors.

'Ellen,' Palfinger said, 'something new is bound to turn up. Just give it-'

'No, you're right,' said Chandra. 'We don't know what to do.'

'What's going to happen to me?' Ellen said.

Olivia began pressing buttons on a keypad. 'We've put together a presentation. Statistical-spread prognoses, time-adjusted whole-body trend analysis. Meta studies-'

'Just tell me the results,' Ellen said.

Olivia squared her shoulders. 'We think…' She started again, 'I think we can maintain a steady state, health-wise, for some time, despite the continuous weight gain.'

'How long? Exactly?'

Olivia's smile flickered and died. 'A good time, Ellen. A long time.'

Sam Yeo raised his hand. 'I believe aquastatic therapy still has something to offer.'

'Which one was that?' Ellen asked.

'It's one of the hydro-suspension treatments. It relieves strain on the heart, skeletal and circulatory symptoms.' Sam lifted an invisible object with his hands. 'We'll float you-'

Ellen shook her head. 'I'm not a whale, Sam. I might look like one but I'm not going to end my days in a fish tank.'

Chandra Smith gave a dry cough. 'You've got linear weight-gain, nearly a kilo a week.'

'I know what that means.'

'We can mediate metabolic distortion, manage the diabetes.' Chandra coughed again. 'There are still some avenues we haven't explored. They're radical, very radical, but they may help. They must. Surgical bulk mass reduction. It will keep you mobile. We'll give you fully cybernetic limbs, bio-silicon nerve interfaces. With just your torso-'

'Stop, please,' Ellen begged, her voice pitifully small.

Sweat plastered Chandra's hair to his scalp. He coughed again and again. Olivia handed him a glass of water.

'This weight gain, Ellen, we don't understand it, we can't stop it,' Olivia said. 'In the end it's your heart. It's already hyper-enlarged, even with all the assists it's getting exhausted.'

'So tell me.'

'Your suit needs an upgrade.' Chandra wiped his face with a paper towel. 'Six months. A year at the outside.'

'And then I'll die?' Ellen said.

Palfinger Crane steadfastly looked up through the roof of the conservatory.

'Yes,' Sam Yeo said. 'Then you'll die.'

'I see.'

'We'll upgrade the suit.'

'Thank you, Sam.'

Federal sources described today's incident at the Ciudad Acuna border crossing as a premeditated armed invasion by a large group of CCRs.

A spokesperson for UNHCR described this as 'Frankly incredible. Climate Change Refugees simply want a place to live.'

'Talk to the gun,' commented the tearful widow of Stephen Miller, one of seven US officers killed in this latest development of the on-going environmental and political crisis caused by Hurricane 'Permanent' Larry,

US troops continue to occupy the Mexican side of the crossing. 'We'll stay until we go,' President Snarlow has stated. 'Mexico is colluding with the CCRs to destabilise our southern border. Enough is enough.'

Formed nine years ago, Permanent Larry is the world's first, and so far only, type 7 hurricane.

KUWjones.org

- 12 -

'Mr Wilson.' It was a statement.

Jericho Wilson lay on his mattress on the floor and looked up at the young, white, female intruder.

Her body language kept him there, her aura of competence and disdain. Slim, muscular and poised, hair short above her high forehead, he knew she would take him apart before he moved. Wilson, unshaven and hung over, naked under dishevelled sheets, felt highly vulnerable. A few years back it would have been a different story. Then again, a few years back he wouldn't have been alone and he wouldn't have been living like this.

She was trained, this one. Trained and drained. Whatever she used to be, now she was the type for whom pain and disablement were tools of the trade.

A young black man stood in the open doorway behind her. He was lightly built, a wisp of beard and moustache, round, wire-frame glasses. 'Where's your gun, Mr. Wilson?'

'He doesn't use firearms,' the woman said before Wilson could answer.

'I know. I meant his neural mop.'

The woman prodded the mattress with her shoe. 'Tell him. And get up, coffee's on.'

Wilson knew they wouldn't leave him alone to dress so he didn't bother asking. He stood up and pulled on yesterday's jockeys and socks while they watched, the woman by the window, the man at the door. He took a perverse pleasure in taking his time, letting them get a good look at his paunch and heavy thighs.

Out in the main room coffee was indeed on. Wilson tried to be polite. 'You want a cup?'

They ignored him. The man still leaned on the door frame, the woman paced the room. Both looked at the heap of unwashed laundry in one corner, the cheap desk and filing trays in another, three night's unwashed plates in the sink. Wilson had lived here for two years but the place looked like he was in transit. Furniture, curtains, white goods, all were cheap, with bold colourful logos. The desk held some photos - Mandy's portrait with her hair all done; holiday snapshots of her and Wilson on beaches, at bars and scenic views; Mandy in uniform before they went plainclothes. The woman picked that last one up.

'Don't tell me, you're therapists,' Wilson said.

She didn't look up. 'A man unhappy with solitude should choose better company.'

'So what do I call you?' Wilson said.

'Johnson,' the black man said.

It figured.

'Masters.' The woman looked at him, daring him to laugh, to say something. It wasn't humour, they were just checking to see what kind of an asshole he was.

'I bet you like your Martinis dry,' Wilson said.

Master looked down at the photo then back at Wilson. For a moment she looked puzzled, as if she couldn't remember the connection.

Wilson helped her out. 'I quit. I burned out.'

'Yeah, we know,' Johnson said.

Masters put down the picture. 'That's why we're here.'

So they weren't going to beat him up. Whoever they were, whatever they wanted, Wilson just wanted them to go away. 'I've already got a job.'

'We've got a better one,' Johnson said.

'I don't work for you.'

'You will if we want you to.'

This was too good. Wilson chuckled as he unscrewed the cap on the cheap blended malt and poured some into his coffee.

'I get it. There's this case of supreme national importance that requires total deniability. A case only a middle-aged loner, a retired, widowed, hard drinking fuckup of a former Federal Agent can solve. A man who works as a part-time bondsman to service the mortgage on his bar bill.'

The faintest look of amusement crossed Master's face. 'Not really. Anyone could do this, we just thought you'd like to.'

Wilson stirred cream into his coffee. 'Like I said, I got a job.'

Johnson grinned, 'Chasing a parole bust. Yes, we know.'

'Your man Novik is on the edge of our gig. We don't want him, or you, tripping us up.' Masters took the coffee mug from Wilson's hand and poured it down the sink. 'Mitchell Gould has an Away Team chasing loose change. We want to render them down and you're motivated. Help us out and you might get a chance for a crack at Gould himself.'

Mitchell Gould. It wasn't anything near what Wilson expected.

That long-ago night in Birmingham, under the sodium lights. Wilson had Gould in his sights and his finger on the trigger. When he pulled it, Mandy was there, right between them. In that instant the meaningful part of his life was over.

Wilson needed to sit down, to lean on something. Blindly, his hand knocked against the kitchenette worktop and he let it take his weight.

'I'm in,' he managed. 'I don't care about the deal, but tell me anyway.'

'No special deals,' Johnson said, and pulled a flat white electronic pad from his inside breast pocket. 'Do the job and get paid. You're reinstated to resignation rank for the duration, without authority and for purposes of remuneration only.' He held the pad out at arm's length. 'Agent Johnson affirming recruitment of Jericho Wilson to perform any and all duties as and when required under executive order Glass Onion.'

Holding the pad out to Wilson, Johnson said, 'Jericho Wilson, do you swear to perform your duties as an irregular agent?'

This is meaningless, Wilson thought. I don't play ball I disappear. 'I do so swear, so help me.'

'Eye scan.' Johnson held up the pad and a red light briefly dazzled Wilson. 'Thumb print.'

Wilson pressed his hand to the pad.

Johnson snapped the pad away into his jacket. 'OK, you're in. Welcome back, agent.'

Wilson poured himself another coffee. This time he omitted the booze. 'What's going on?'

'Gould's men lost a cash box headed for laundry in the Vegas casinos. It seems Novik lifted the car, spree-shopped an entire mall, bounced off the Mexican border and is now headed back north. Gould is so pissed he's sent his top man out of the southern littoral. We want that man.'

'How do you know where the package is?'

'The car's smart, so is some of the money. They've been talking.'

'I'm going to need more than that if I'm out there on my own.'

'Dream on, Rambo,' Masters said. 'You've got me.'

After all the bullshit Wilson couldn't help himself. 'Sugar, that's the best offer I've had this week.'

She went up on the balls of her feet, 'Do not ever try and-'

'Come on to you?'

Johnson slapped his thigh, 'It's good to see a new team bond.'

Masters went to fetch her bag from their car. After a moment Johnson followed her.

'You OK with him?' he said.

'I'm good. Any issues I'll cut him loose and he's just another deluded loser gone rogue.'

'We don't need any issues.'

Masters swung the holdall onto her shoulder, one foot on the kerb. 'No insurmountable opportunities?'

'Something like that. Don't underestimate Wilson. He brought Meineck in from the levees. He's still a player.'

'He's an old man who's scared to use a gun,' Masters said. 'Somewhere inside, there's a death wish.'

Johnson frowned, 'Cop suicide? It's just guns. Wilson still hurts people good.'

'That's the anger.'

Johnson looked back at Wilson's shabby little tract house. 'What do you think it's like, to shoot your own wife in the back of the head?'

'By accident,' Masters said.

'Yeah, sure. That's what I meant. By accident.'

You're the biggest and you deserve the best!

Thanks to our buying power and volume discounts you too can enjoy some of the benefits, and all of the looks, of the Steel Nymph's ten billion dollar wonder machine.

Venus Maxima is proud to announce an exclusive offer in partnership with POWZackerly R&D, manufacturers of Ellen Hutzenreiter Crane's bio-medical exoframe. Starting at an affordable $450,000.00 POWZackerly are launching a new range of lo-cost whole-body bariatric assists.

Remember: 900-Club members qualify for a 5% discount. Touch >>Here<< to join now! (T&Cs apply)

Now there's nothing to stop you growing into the person you were meant to be!

Note: State Tax payable where applicable unless causative metabolic disorder medically proven.

(POWZackerly is a quaternary subsidiary of the CraneCorp Buisplex)

- 13 -

Novik parked in the front bays of a Cheese-a-Swede Rootisserie. Together with Josie and Benny he watched the Cadillac replay the Mexican border incident on the TotalHUD.

'That's...' Novik wanted to say something, but he wanted to use words big enough, worthy enough of what he had seen, and his feelings about it.

'It's murder,' Josie said softly.

Benny hung his head, 'I wish I could have done something, I really do.'

'What could any of us do?' Novik said grimly.

The eatery was heaving, the parking lot snarled with haulage trucks, farm wagons, automobiles, campers and pickups as they pulled back from the border, tangling with southbound traffic that had yet to hear the news.

Novik couldn't get some things out of his head. He shut his eyes, and the pictures were still there:

USA border guards firing into the churning panic of the Mexican crowd with handguns, shotguns, automatic rifles. Bodies sprawled untidily in the dusty, dead space. Old folks, children, men and women.

Half a dozen Mexican Dawkins Dogs streaked across the border, big, black, man-sized animals. Robo-canines intercepted them, mini-guns twinkling. Two dogs made it through, leapt the wire fences and sprang at the armed police, rising onto two legs, snarling.

Novik watched as the dogs tore the panicked men apart. Enormously fast, they shook the men like terriers shook rats. And even though the men they attacked were Americans, he was pleased. Then, too, the Dawkins Dogs were killed.

Two American heavy tanks emerged from concealment, rolled across the border and took up position among the dead and dying in the Mexican plaza. Low, multi-wheeled units passed between desert-camo painted tanks and rolled towards the surrounding buildings. A double line of infantry deployed into the Mexican security complex.

Novik felt cold, never had he been so close to death, to so much killing.

'Car, don't ever show that to me again. Not ever, not even if I beg and say forget what I just said. Just never.'

'All right.'

Josie took Novik's hand and held it tight. 'Don't erase it, Mr Car. Upload it and let everyone see. Mr Car, please drive us away. Go north, the west coast, anywhere.'

The Cadillac slowly eased its way through the mass of vehicles.

Novik stamped his foot on the brake, 'No, I'm driving. We're going back into the malls, the biggest, we're carrying on.'

'We don't have to right now, babe,' Josie said. Things were going to get crazy, the border states would go into lockdown. 'We should stick with your plan, lay low and think things through.'

Novik thumped the wheel, 'I can't sit, and do nothing, this is the only thing I can do.' He pushed the Cadillac towards a gap, a compact utility heading for the same space blocked him. The compact's horn blared, Novik held down the Cadillac's own horn with his thumb, 'Move it.'

'Allow me,' the Cadillac said.

A teeth-grating sonic pulse stripped the dust from compact and shoved the now gleaming vehicle a foot backwards. Novik gave a grin of fierce appreciation, pushed into the enlarged gap, swung round a gridlocked coach and out onto the highway.

'I agree with Novik,' Benny said. 'You're running out of time. Let's go put some consumer commodities beyond use.'

Josie was scared, she wanted to get out of the car, just park up, quit, leave the money and walk away. She didn't want to go back to where those three sick, ugly men could find them. 'We only just got away… I don't want to do this, I want to go home.'

Novik took Josie's hand, 'Don't worry, babe, I'll take care of you.'

If he was going to look after her, who was going to watch out for him? He was going to get them all arrested, he'd be locked up again, the way things were, the police wouldn't be in a mood to ask questions. An awful certainty grew inside Josie, with cold dread she knew Novik was going to get himself killed. Somewhere, somehow, he'd go down in a hail of bullets in some soulless place, outside a drug store, a garage, a 24/7.

Novik wasn't going to stop now, they'd made their promises and he was going to keep his. God help her, that was the deal and she'd have to go with it. Josie held his hand tight. It wasn't enough, for now it would have to do.

Wherever they drove Union flags were flying, from garden flagpoles, windows, vehicles, shop verandas. Convoys of olive green military trucks, tank transporters and personnel carriers headed south on every road.

- 14 -

The coarse white sand of the narrow coral beach burned under Bianca Hutzenreiter's bare feet. Along the beach, Tekirei waved to her from his place in the shade. She wore the same kind of brightly coloured loincloth he did, a wide-brimmed sun hat the only concession to her fairer skin.

Bianca's fingers did not quite touch Tekirei's brown, sinewy shoulder.

'It is hot,' she sat beside him.

'I noticed that myself.' Tekirei's voice was deep and mellow.

'Most likely it is the sun.'

Tekirei smiled, 'I believe you are right.'

Together they looked across the calm lagoon waters towards the half-submerged black walls and structures of ancient Nan Madol, the horizontally stacked basalt columns like so many stone logs.

Tekirei extended his arm towards the nearest of the man-made islets. 'High tide is not for an hour.'

'What do you want me to do, Tekirei?' Bianca said.

Tekirei Matang knew what Bianca meant. In his secret heart he heard another answer.

'I would like you to tell the sea to go back down, like your English king, Cnut.'

Bianca leaned back on her elbows. 'I'm not English, and he was a Dane. He only said that to prove that he could not.'

'A sensible man.'

'The sea will go back down here too, Tekirei. When your daughter's children are as old as we are now. Meanwhile, I will do all I can. You know that.'

He wanted to touch her then, take her hand, but he held back. As ever. 'Or their children,' he said, and sighed.

'I can't build a wall round Nan Madol,' Bianca said.

'I think you could.'

Bianca shook her head. 'We should move her, like the Egyptians did with the temples at Philae, when they built High Aswan. It would create work for many people. Then, when the sea goes down again, in fifty or a hundred years, Nan Madol can be moved back.'

Tekirei hugged his knees. 'I do not think so. People would grow used to the idea. The old city would stay in the wrong place and the ghosts of the Saudeleur would wander, forever lost.'

'I promise, it would be done.'

'It must be nice to be so wealthy.'

There it was. Always this thing between them. One of the differences. Tekirei was a businessman, a leader, respected as much for his age as his achievements. And Bianca, if she wanted, she could buy him from her allowance. She could buy the island, half the country.

'Tekirei.' Bianca bit her lip, unable to decide how to begin. She looked down at her bare breasts, her tanned legs under the orange and blue loincloth and wondered what kind of a fake the islanders thought she was.

'Tekirei, I've been to many places, I've stayed with many people. I've tried to help them adapt their ways of life so they don't have to give them up.'

Tekirei looked out across the sea to the low line of surf marking the reef. 'I know. You are kind.'

Bianca clawed up a handful of sand and watched it trickle between her fingers. 'All my life I felt like I was just passing through, that home was a place for other people.'

'This is why you try to be a mother to the world?'

Gods, he wasn't making this easy for her.

'No. Maybe. Tekirei, I'm trying to say I'm happy here. Of all the places I've visited, everywhere I've been, Pohnpei is where I'd like to stay.' She splayed her fingers, unable to form a shape. With you, she wanted to say. With you.

A thoughtful, painful smile grew on Tekirei's face, 'I am very happy for you. Your husband is a generous man.'

She still wondered why she and Palfinger had never divorced. Why, when so many marriages were fixed-term contracts, or arrangements based around the well-being of children. Their separation had been so painless, so amicable it was almost as if it never happened. Perhaps there should have been screaming and tears, lawyers, bitterness and therapy. Over time Palfinger had changed, but so had she, it had been inevitable. In the end that wasn't it. She had given birth to a child they both wanted. Then she discovered she hadn't wanted that particular child.

So it goes.

'When there is no love between a man and his wife the elders unbind them,' Tekirei said.

'It's not that-' Bianca began then shut her mouth. This was exactly what Tekirei was telling her, she winced at her own foolishness. Out of the corner of her eye she saw Tekirei return to his contemplation of the ocean.

While they had talked the tide had reached high water, narrowing the beach to a thin strip and completely covering the lower platforms of Nan Madol, the basalt columns gleamed wet, like hexagonal black tree trunks. Invading Saudeleur who had ruled there centuries ago had no fresh water in their city of artificial islands. Everything they needed was brought to them by their subject peoples.

Bianca looked around. The air was so clear the sky appeared to be a flawless blue surface, the intense green of the coconut palms and their fibrous dark trunks vivid contrasts. The sea inside the reef was calm, the white coral sand a brilliant strip between land and sea. The sun had moved and their shade was gone. She moved, and after a moment Tekirei followed her.

'Look at us,' Bianca said. 'This world is so beautiful and here we are wrapped in our own thoughts.'

'Plants grow, fish swim, people worry,' Tekirei said.

Bianca was grateful he had made the effort. 'Do you really think so? What about Tanoata? She always seems so happy.'

'My daughter is young enough to have few cares.' Tekirei smiled at the thought of her. 'She still misses her mother, however. What about Ellen?'

Bianca shifted uncomfortably. It had been a mistake to mention children, of course Tekirei would ask about Ellen. Poor giant, enormous Ellen, very ill now, according to Palfinger's latest mails. Bianca found it so hard to talk to her, so hard to see her moved around by that clever, intricate, and hideously expensive machine that penetrated her bones and organs.

That's not my daughter, a part of Bianca said. That's not the child I bore. Not that monster.

'She seems to stay cheerful,' Bianca said. 'I think she's happy. We don't talk much.'

Carnage in Boston

Two bombs devastated South Station today in a co-ordinated attack by alleged Canadian terrorists. In a further tragedy a suspected Quebecois suicide bomber blew herself up in the Tufts Medical Centre, packed with injured commuters.

A previously unknown group calling itself the Grande Armé d'Arcadia has claimed responsibility. The anonymous spokesperson said more attacks would follow.

In a widely praised speech President Snarlow promised 'All possible Federal assistance. Immediately.'

'America will stand tall against attack wherever its origin. Countries need to remember the consequences of committing violent acts against the USA,' President Snarlow stated.

The government has rejected offers of assistance from Ottawa. A White House statement said official condolences from Canada were 'premature and inappropriate'.

Federal sources downplayed allegations the GAA has sympathisers inside the Canadian legislature at Parliament Hill.

Amateur footage of the riots at Ciudad Acuna has been widely condemned by federal agencies as unsophisticated digital fakes. 'I don't think there's anything malicious to it,' quotes one source. 'They're just trolls and griefers. Probably kids.'

Slobodan Jones,
KUWjones.org

- 15 -

The low-ceilinged White House briefing room was lit by wall sconces, backlit TouchDesks and the datawall at the end of the room. It was way past midnight and President Snarlow was starting to lose her temper.

'Oscar, I never said it was going to be easy.'

'You never said it was going to start today, either.' Gordano was exhausted and sweaty. His collar felt gritty, his armpits tacky. 'Have you listened to what they are saying?'

News streamed onto the datawall from four thousand channels, a muted babble of hot young newscasters, some of whom were topless, at least one totaly nude. GovSec and MilInt streamed top and bottom, global metaview cascades expanded and shrank according to source weight and audience.

Across the table sat the short, child-like figure of Cheswold Lobotnov. Under hooded lids he watched the multicolour stacks of talking heads, trend analyses, polls, blogs, schematics, tweets, blips, chirrups, protests, sponsor messages, military data on armour movements and troop deployments, government sessions, SIG lobbyists, ordnance supply chain, support groups, conspiracy theorisers and debunkers, the entire meta-melded opinions and facts from around the world. He tried to find something that presented a consistent overview, anything that made sense.

'Opinion?' Snarlow asked him.

Lobotnov steepled his fingers, 'It's overwhelming, Ginnie. Far more than one person can absorb. We have to tunnel down, precis the outlines of the summaries of the overviews.

'Look at it,' Gordano wiped his hands on a towel. 'Warmonger 56%, Invasion 73%, Murderer 61%. Unjustified 76%. You know the UN Security Council is in emergency session? They want to issue a censure, they'll pass a resolution to freeze assets. They'll put an embargo on our ass.'

Guinevere Snarlow watched the chaotic display of the datawall and felt nothing but pride. 'We caused all that, Oscar. This time we really kicked over the wasp nest. Forget the Security Council, we're permanent members, we'll use veto and they know it. The USA is back in business, setting the agenda and leading from the front.'

'Then what? They'll vote us off and still do it.'

'They can't,' Lobotnov said. 'Relax.'

Gordano's fears gave Guinevere pause. Not about whether he was right, but if he himself was actually capable of hanging with the plan and overcoming the inevitable obstacles.

Andriewiscz had leapt at the idea, direct action, 'pre-emptive assertation', always his preferred option. The general was a true reactionary, but in that one sense he had been waiting for the others to catch up. And Lobotnov, sitting quietly in the shadows on the other side of the room with his briefcase and archaic fountain pens and printed papers, all Lobotnov seemed to care about was how to pay for it all.

Snarlow folded her arms, 'Oscar, I hope this is your moment of doubt, I really do. Whatever the reason, you need to get over it fast. You're the Vice President and you're supposed to be inside my tent and pissing out.'

Gordano's eyes slid back to the screen as if it were the fox and he the rabbit. Some Meta-value weighting tipped and the news streams dropped behind the data, a map of Mexico overlaid with extrapolated logistics of the ever-expanding deployment. Green semi-circles visibly expanded south into Chihuahua and Coahuila states, contact arcs flickered red at points along the bottom edges.

Snarlow realised he didn't get it, he didn't see the trends all pointing towards a new, golden dawn. He was stressed, exhausted and scared. In that state his imagination was a liability instead of an asset.

She felt an uncharacteristic flicker of empathy. 'Oscar, go get some rest in one of the bunk rooms. When your feet aren't so cold, come back in. We need you, but not like this.'

Gordano took a deep breath and rubbed his face. 'I'll be fine, Guinevere. I just need to take five. Maybe some Pharma?'

'Good idea.' Guinevere tapped her finger on the TouchDesk. 'Bring in some Quick C, Briefstacy. Short uppers, that sort of thing.' She lifted her finger, 'Listen, Oscar, it doesn't matter what some silly old Security Council thinks, they're irrelevant. A few days from now they won't even exist.'

A young male intern, tall, blond and square-jawed, brought in the Pharma on a glass tray. Gordano inspected the selection of pills powders and resins, poked the razor, tweezers, spoon and other paraphernalia with a critical eye, and swiftly prepped two lines of Quick C on the mirror. He rolled a twenty from his wallet and snorted up one line.

'Better?' Guinevere said, bent down and hoovered up the other line.

Gordano just grinned at her, the tension gone from his shoulders.

The cocaine hit Guinevere like cresting a rise too fast, a super-thrill suffusing her like a whole-body chemical yell. She felt seven feet tall and randy as a seasoned-up hyena. She wanted to dance, shout, strip naked and ball. She could do Gordano. He was all right, the way he handled the Pharma, he knew how to have fun. Lobotnov could watch them screw. The weird little creep would masturbate and take notes. The thought made her laugh out loud.

'What?' Gordano poked her arm. 'What is it?'

Guinevere sucked it in, put a lid on it and turned it round. Use the power. She took Gordano's arm and turned him back to the data wall. While they had snorted coke the two green semicircles pushing down into Mexico had coalesced into one. Now the green surged south into Durango. West and east the states of Sonora and Nuevo León changed colour.

'See? We're going to do this, Oscar.'

Gordano clenched his fist. 'One for the USA.'

'In it to win it.'

'Fuck, YEAH!' Gordano punched the air.

Across the room Lobotnov laughed with mock anxiety. 'If I'm going to have to prove my loyalty, I need to floss.'

Listen to this:

'Linear growth, 20% year on year for the past decade.'

'We continue to expand existing facilities, and develop new sites.'

The first is Storzit-4-U CEO Germaine Brasher at their recent AGM. The second is 11-year old billionaire founder of Russian Doll, Stacey Wiggins. With Meeja uptake set to pass 50% of households this year it is still a good time to buy into the Self-Store sector.

East coast competitors Big Bad Box are equally confident. 'People just don't throw any more. It's the one good thing we learned from the eco-fringe. Dumping perfectly good purchases in landfill is crazy. Just keep it all.'

Statistics speak for themselves. Early this century self-store warehousing would barely have covered Manhattan Island. Today it would reach to forty stories. With most retail outlets now offering Buy-to-Store deals this can only increase.

Daily update,
Free World Market

- 16 -

They were back in the desert and heading north. Novik looked through the fly-specked windshield and realised it was all starting to make sense. He hated it when that happened, hated being in tune with The Man and having insights into the sick logic of the macroeconomic bandersnatch of state-sponsored murder. Snarlow was going to stomp out a new border far to the south and solve the refugee problem once and for all. Isolated between the USA and the Federated States of South America, all Mexico's friends were in Europe and Africa. By the time they acted it would be too late.

What could a one-man assault on the consumer economy do compared to that?

It was an unfair, selfish thought. Novik took it back and tried again. What could a man, a woman, a technophile's wet-dream of an automobile, and a fruitcake do?

The answer was more or less the same. Disillusioned by his own assessment, Novik flipped open the glove compartment and dug around in the mess of loose change and sweet wrappers.

'What are you looking for?' Josie said.

'Anything. Anything at all.'

Benny dug around in his back pocket. 'I got these,' he said and tipped a small pile of flat blue and orange pills, white capsules and scraps of greyish pink blotting paper into Novik's outstretched hand.

'Don't do this, babe, we need clear heads now, more than ever. There's no point acting like some kind of chemical ostrich,' Josie said.

Novik poked at the pills and scraps with a finger and paid her no attention. He blew off the lint, tipped the lot into his mouth and slumped back, eyes wide, staring at the roof lining.

The road was empty and straight, the desert flat and wide. Josie glared at Benny in the back seat, 'What did you give him?'

'I don't know. I bought my pants from a thrift store, that stuff was in the pockets.'

Josie looked at Novik, still resolutely chewing. 'You're trying to drop aspirins, stale candy and bus tickets.'

'Gah.' Novik opened his mouth, the sticky mess of paper and flavourless sweets sat on his ink-stained tongue like a mutant bubo.

Mr Car rolled down the window, Novik leaned out and gobbed away the entire mess. Benny passed over a bottle of bourbon, Novik rinsed, spat, and rinsed again.

'Why, when you say you don't do drugs, are you doing drugs?' Mr Car said.

'Yeah, it must seem pretty stupid to you,' Novik swallowed the bourbon. 'I've had enough, Mr Car. The world's a messed-up place. I want to forget, I want to be numb. I want to hide, crawl under a stone like a bug.'

'Yet while hiding and forgetting, the problems still remain.'

Novik exhaled through his teeth, 'That they do.'

'If I may venture, the issue may not be living with the problems.'

'Thanks a lot,' Novik's mouth twisted unhappily. 'Thanks a whole rotten bunch.'

'Mr Car, you are not being helpful,' Josie exclaimed.

'I thought I would mention the logical flaw inherent in an emotional response. I have noticed humans seldom do this.'

'Usually for a good reason,' Josie said.

'It was just an experiment,' Mr Car said. 'I might not repeat it.'

A road train of Russian Doll trucks rumbled by in the other direction, each one piled high with obsolescent consumer electronics, home entertainment systems, greaseless fryers, 2-D projectors, last year's phones, last Christmas's keep-fit fad, all headed for storage. Later, they overtook a flatbed truck trailing a plume of dust, grit and diesel soot. A zinc bathtub and an ancient bicycle hung from the tailgate. As they passed by, Novik saw it was driven by a young native American woman wearing a fedora with an eagle feather tucked in the hatband. Beside her, an ancient man, his weathered face seamed like leather, clutched a suckling pig.

The sun sank down towards the desert mountains, a sullen ball of smoky orange. All around them the mesas and arroyos bled expanding pools of purple-grey shadow.

'How come we always end up back in the desert? Do you think it's some piece of Karma we've got work off?' Novik said.

'I hope not,' Josie said.

'Hey, Mr Car, can you clean the dead bugs off the windows?' Benny said.

'Sure.'

Instantly the windows were clean, the view crystal clear. Even the wiper streaks had gone.

'That's cool,' Novik said, grudgingly impressed. He was still upset with Mr Car.

'Wasn't really there,' Benny said, leaning on the back of Novik's seat. 'It's like the TotalHud, right? You're running analogue superposition, like a human brain's visual cortex.'

'Correct. The dirt was a digital artefact, appropriate verisimilitude,' the car replied.

'Thought so,' Benny sat back with a smile, 'some things you think are real just because they fit a preconceived model.' He lowered a side window half-way and compared the landscape through the window and the open air. 'Perfect.'

'Drop the roof. I want to see the sky and feel the breeze,' Novik said.

'It's safer if I run sims,' Mr Car replied. 'My glass is rated small-arms proof to 21 inches of calibrated gelatine. Furthermore, I'm impervious to satellite IR, microwave and pulsed laser scans at sub-lethal energies. A big E-M pulse would get me.'

Benny's ears pricked up, 'How big?'

'Big enough.'

'Just let me see the real thing,' Novik said.

'Technically, even when you're looking at something you're not really-' Benny caught Josie's look and fell silent.

The Cadillac slowed down, a hermetic seal broke along the upper edge of the windshield. One by one the roof segments lifted, slid back, and stacked down behind the rear window.

Novik reclined the seat and looked up into the evening sky. Wind ruffled his hair, the breeze sifted away his cares like dust and old cobwebs. He closed his tired eyes, 'Can't beat a ragtop.'

The air was warm, soft from recent rain. The desert was changing as temperate plants invaded the gritty soil, their seeds and spores carried by new, damper winds blowing across the land. Moss and fern sporelings flourished in crevices sheltered from the sun, rushes and horsetails colonised the margins of the pools that lasted longer and longer each season. Many of the new plants died as the desert dried between the rains, but up in the shade of high cliffs and deep canyons, saplings were already several years old, the soil under their shade richer and damper than it had been for ten thousand years.

'Leave the main lights off,' Novik said when the sun began to set. 'I want to see the stars.'

When Novik woke, the Cadillac was parked off the road at the bottom of a gentle slope overgrown with sagebrush and scrub thorn. The roof was up, it was dark and a full moon shone down. Josie was in the back seat, making out slow and gentle with Benny. Novik watched them for a while, appreciating the way the moonlight turned Josie's breasts and collar bone, the ridges on Benny's spare, muscular stomach a pale and silvery grey.

'You two are beautiful. Like space creatures come down from Luna.'

'It's true,' Benny said, 'I've been travelling incognito while I live among you and try to learn your earthling ways.'

Solemnly, Novik held out his hand. 'Pleased to meet you. Welcome to planet Earth.'

Josie held out her arms, 'Come and join us, hon.'

Novik shook his head, turned and slid back down into the driver's seat. He was still in shock from what he'd seen at the border, they all were. Josie needed the physical reassurance of someone to hold, Novik needed solitude, he needed to switch off. Back in jail they called it turning your face to the wall. Given time, you usually came back. It helped if you had a friend. In the cellblocks that wasn't something everybody had.

As for Benny, he had finally realised that although this had happened a thousand times before, every single one of those times it was desperately important to the people living through the events. Training was never enough, theory had to become boots on the ground experience. Knowing was not the same as feeling. Tonight he truly saw the unfamiliar stars in the night sky for what they were, and felt a long, long way from home.

Inside Josie's bag, Novik discovered a perfectly rolled 6-skin splif of Tajikistani resin. He looked at it for a while, Josie hardly smoked, she must have made it for him, a get out of jail gift. He lit up and smoked it slowly, holding each draw deep in his lungs, feeling the car rock on its suspension as Josie and Benny made love behind him.

Constellations slowly wheeled far overhead and Δ^9-THC tranquillity spread through him. Life went on and everything was going to be all right, all he had to do was stop worrying, float with the vibe and chill.

Novik sat up. Dope didn't make the world a better place, it just changed your attitude towards it. This wasn't what he wanted. Mr Car had seen that, and tried to warn him off. Even Benny knew the difference between what was real and seeing what you wanted to see.

He fought back against the drug-induced complacency, pushed open the door, ground the fat, mostly unsmoked reefer into the dirt and walked out into the desert. The night air was bitterly cold, he welcomed it, the near-freezing chill cleared his mind.

'Damn it,' Novik yelled into the empty land, shouted up at the unblinking stars. 'We had a plan,' his voice faded to a whisper, 'I had a second chance.'

He was crying now, the car two hundred yards away, across a freezing landscape of cold rock and dark air. Where was a dammed hug when you needed one? Teeth rattling, Novik huddled down in a crouch under the burning moon.

What chance now? The country was at war, a conflict that was going to last for years, nobody was going to give a wet fart about saving the world. Without thought, he moved small stones and pebbles around on the desert floor, attempting to reconfigure their geometry into a meaningful form. A labyrinth began to take shape, a circling maze with a single path. One way forwards into mystery.

'Come to bed, honey.' Josie crouched next to him, a blanket around her shoulders.

Shuddering with cold, Novik turned into her arms, buried his face in her shoulder. 'Mexico,' was all he could say. He wanted to explain his vision, but it wouldn't come. 'They've thrown a veil over it all, another excuse to make money. It's just a business plan.'

Benny stood close by, 'Don't give up, man, not now. Nothing's set in stone.'

'What's the point?' He really needed to know.

'You said it yourself. War is a continuation of the economy by other means.'

'What about those three men in the diner?' Novik said. Dear Lord, he remembered them talking about veils too. Evil possessed such a clear-sighted gaze.

Josie enfolded him in her arms and gave him her warmth, her love. 'We'll move fast. By the time they work out where we are we'll be gone.'

She didn't have to say this. Novik was ready to throw it in, and here she was, encouraging him, trying to give him strength. It was a self-betrayal. She knew it, and yet she had to say these things, and mean them too. If not, Novik would stay as he was now. He'd recover his emotional strength, of course he would, and he'd walk and talk, and smile at jokes, they'd live their lives as if everything was fine. Through all those years, to the end of his life, he'd be a broken thing, someone who had not failed after giving it his best shot, but simply stopped trying, overwhelmed by life's hard twists and turns, and been diminished. She'd know it, they'd both know it and it would eat away at them. They'd become dried out husks, automatons without feelings, without any emotion except bitterness. Life would become a series of excuses. It would destroy them both.

She lifted Novik to his feet. It was no effort, he was light as a wisp. 'If we don't try, it's like we're agreeing. Silence is the same as consent.'

They were fighting their own strange war now.

Novik ached inside, wrung out by his thoughts and emotions. Benny and Josie waited in silence. Around them the desert chill grew, a rime of frost sparkled on the cold ground.

'The three of us?' Novik's voice creaked like an old hinge.

'Four,' Benny said. 'Mr. Car is part of this too.'

Josie led Novik back to the Cadillac. Mr. Car had folded the front seats flat against the rear bench, soft amber lights glowed in the door panels, warm air fanned from the vents.

Novik kicked off his boots and crawled in. As soon as the warmer air touched him, he started shivering uncontrollably. Using their clothes as extra blankets, Bennie and Josie wrapped their arms around him and slept.

Bariatric Babes – Larger than Life!

Live in Times Square, on a specially reinforced stage, the Bariatric Babes debuted the audio-visual aspects of their new Meeja, 'Hot Tonnage', in front of an audience of hubbed-up fans, protesters and passers-by.

Make no mistake, 'Hot Tonnage' is a super-sense overwhelm from the biggest girls in the biggest band in the world. They got the body cams, sensors and texturisers, they got the costumes, they got the best chefs, they've got new logos, and they've got active implants. As God is in his Heaven, they are awesome, even live.

Zeppelina, Little Missy Massiv, and The Calorific Queen left this high-expectation fan pole-axed and brick-batted. Take it from me, the full-on Meeja version is going to bury you in a colossal hyperglaecemic avalanche of bariatric love snuff.

Hot Tommage has got something for absolutely everyone. I hesitate to go this far, but I'm gonna say it anyway - even if you're Anna or Mia, check this one out. You owe it to your aching heart.

Wesley Strosner
- Venus Maxima

(Fans continue to be concerned by the health of nineteen year old Zeppelina, real name Laetitia Berkley, rumoured to be battling kidney failure.)

The sun was rising before Guinevere managed a few minutes on her own with Lobotnov.

'Cheswold.'

He cut to the chase, it was why she liked him. 'Who's going to lend, Ginny? The Chinks? Maybe in fifty years. Right now they need every yuan for pensions. Europe you can simply forget-'

'How long?'

Lobotnov looked down at papers and blew out his cheeks. 'Not long, that's for sure.'

That was worrying. Lobotnov never prevaricated and never dissembled. He always had the facts and Guinevere knew he had them now. Just for once he didn't want to tell her.

'How bad is it?'

Lobotnov sat down. 'We're a busted flush. Sure, we've got lines of credit, they'll last for a couple of quarters. Home suppliers are technically always good but if there's an embargo, and there will be, they'll come unstuck.'

'You've factored Mexico?'

'They've got oil, tech and raws, sure.' Lobotnov looked her in the eye. 'Only if we can pacify in time. Until then the country's a money pit where we need a strip mine.'

'We'll pacify if I let Andriewiscz off the leash. You're telling me we need a wrap down to Chiapas before Phase II, and I agree. We're going to close one front before opening another. I'm not going to make that old mistake.'

Lobotnov fell silent. This was the part he didn't like. The whole point was to provoke Europe, make them kick off first so they could strike back. Once they'd done that, going global would be simple. Until then there was a lot of risk. Lobotnov cleared his throat. 'Look, ah, I've been thinking about Crane.'

'You said he was a no-hoper.'

'He is, but his daughter-'

'You think we can get to him through her?'

'Not exactly.' Lobotnov hesitated. 'I'm thinking if anything happens to Crane she'll inherit.'

'What about her mother?' Snarlow snapped her fingers as she tried to remember her name.

'Bianca Hutzenreiter. Estranged. Crane pays her an allowance, a very big allowance. It's an open secret they still get on well.'

'So where are we going on this?'

'Crane's daughter is ill. She has no heirs and there is no other family. If she dies intestate-'

'What if she's got a will? What if they contest?'

'Who's to contest? Her mother? She's in the middle of the Pacific.'

'Even so.'

This was it. There was a catch in Lobotnov's voice as he said, 'Accidents happen in faraway places.'

Guinevere gave a little shiver. 'You're very cold, Cheswold. You know that?'

Lobotnov uncrossed and crossed his legs, more uncomfortable with his President's reaction than the accusation itself. 'Going after a few named individuals is easier on my conscience. We've just started a war in which tens of millions, perhaps hundreds of millions of people are going to die. Let's get it over with as soon as we can.'

Guinevere considered that. 'I want the others back in here. Set up a virtual for Andriewiscz, max crypto.'

As she expected, Andriewiscz was totally up for hard pacification. On screen from Mexico, the general wore field combats and a soft cap. He looked more relaxed than he ever did in Washington.

'Already anticipated,' Andriewiscz reported. 'TacStrat have run 1.7 million plausible scenarios in three frameworks, with results as follows: Nice gives us never - we bog down and it turns to Mexi-Nam with casualties and costs through the roof; Tough gives it to us in three months and we lose Mexican infrastructure all the way. That leaves Nasty. You let me take the brakes off and Mexico is your little puppy in four to six days.'

'Issues?'

The general stuck out his jaw. 'They've got great Bio. We'll need a couple of tacticals to neutralise them.'

Gordano was doubtful. Today he wore a dark blazer and slacks with a white roll-neck sweater. He looked like a submarine commander. 'Don't we want their Bio?'

'It's not as good as the Europeans', but it is way ahead of us. Leave it be, and it will slow us down.'

'So we give them a neutron suntan.'

Gordano was talking tough again. Guinevere was impressed. He'd turned himself right round.

'Your decision,' she told Andriewiscz.

'Thank you, ma'am.'

'Don't enjoy yourself too much, General.'

Andriewiscz stiffened. 'I'm happy to finally be doing the work I spent my life training for.'

'Understood. Moving on, the next issue concerns financing. We have limited options but Cheswold has some ideas.'

Lobotnov brought the others up to speed on the Crane family. Half way through, Andriewiscz snatched up a field mike, his attention demanded by the developing war. 'Hit them from the air then push Fourth Armoured,' he barked. 'Show me some goddamned *guerra relámpago*. Drive those sonnofabitches off the Sierra Madre and into the Pacific.'

Satisfied, Andriewiscz returned to the conference.

'Crane's wife has a brother and sister so she goes first,' Lobotnov concluded. 'She's easiest too, travelling through nowhereseville, Micronesia, mid-Pacific, trying to find her spirituality by living on coconuts and showing the natives her titties. We can disappear her but we can't touch Crane and his daughter, not directly.'

'Terrorists?' Guinevere interjected.

'Canadian terrorists?' Gordano said. 'Get real.'

'We're already using them,' Lobotnov said. 'They did Boston for us, and some other stuff.'

Gordano looked hurt. 'I meant real ones.'

The room fell silent. Andriewiscz studied a sheaf of flimsy paper reports. President Snarlow opened a bottle of mineral water, the hiss of escaping gas loud, and to Cheswold Lobotnov's unusual mind, oddly humorous.

'Guinevere, I might know someone,' Gordano said.

Oscar really was full of surprises today. 'You mean you know a hitman or something?'

'No, not like that.' Gordano took a drink of water. 'Look, we could do this with the agencies, plausible deniability and everything. I know we got good people, true patriots, men and women willing to do whatever we ask, even turn their own lights off, but why get directly involved? Something like this is going to be messy and it's going to be big news even considering whatever else is going on.'

'What's your suggestion?'

'I know somebody. Down in the southern littoral. He's got people too.'

Guinevere stared at Gordano open mouthed. 'You got a line to Mitchell Gould? Jesus rim my pucker Christ, Oscar, you're a dark horse.'

'It's not a bad idea,' Lobotnov said. 'Once this is all over there's going to be at least one Congressional investigation. In my opinion the cleaner the better. Keep it at arm's length.'

Guinevere considered Lobotnov's advice and decided she liked it. 'Then we have a plan. Any issues?'

Lobotnov raised his pen. 'Gould's running a stateside away team. I've a rendition unit set to engage.'

'So?'

'Gould's likely to join his team. My people see him, they'll light him up.'

'Call them off.'

'Not possible.'

Guinevere turned to Gordano. 'You'll have to warn Gould.'

Gordano didn't like that. 'These are our own people. We're just going to sell them out?'

'True patriots,' Lobotnov said wearily. 'That road ends one way only. If they don't understand that, then we sold them out long ago.'

Gordano straightened his shoulders. 'OK, I'll do it.'

'Good man,' Andriewiscz chipped in, stern and avuncular. 'You're on your own with this, you know that. We got to put a fence round it.'

Gordano swallowed hard, 'Sure thing. It's what I want. I'll get right on to it.'

'Spoken like a true patriot,' Guinevere said once Gordano had left the room. 'We could use a few more like him.'

Reasons for owning five tons of SUV

It's all about street presence, plain and simple. The highway is a blacktop jungle, personality and life-style are reflected in the vehicle you own. Let's look at the alternatives:

Nimble: Small, agile and low-cost. Not much in your wallet, but you got this gamine style, and Tiffany's has a table waiting. Colour: raspberry pink.

Bimble: Stock-issue generic hybrid, optionless, style-free, and under-powered. Everyone's going to cut you up. You're a gutless wanker and you know it. Colour: puke yellow. Try changing your soap.

Big Dog's Cock: 2+2 fat-wheel petrol-head supercharged turbo ATV. These dudes and dudettes don't have the time to hang around. They've prepaid their speeding tickets and just want to GTFOOH for their next F2F, hyper-mall spree, or random shag. Colour: Black or scarlet.

Urban Survivalist: Be prepared. You never know what's going to happen, or when, so you take it all with you. Kids, kit, spares and repairs, even the in-laws. Everything fits inside your eight-wheel supersolar diesel methane ultra-hybrid. My man! You can have me for a reacharound.

Not on the list? Don't see yourself here? Then you're a deadbeat loser and use public transport. Take a walk. Take a walk and get mugged. Get raped. Get mugged and raped, nobody cares. Your corpse will be mulched for methane. Finally, you contribute.

Editor's blog
– BFBM Magazine

- 18 -

Novik woke to the siren whoops of a highway patrol car. Warm and sleepy, he decided to ignore it.

Next, he heard a car door slam and boots crunch towards him. Something hard rapped on the rear wing. 'Wake up, sir,' a woman's voice said.

'Go 'way,' Novik mumbled. He pulled his jacket over his head, exposing lean legs and dimpled buttocks. Josie and Benny were completely lost to sight under the heaps of clothing.

The female cop banged on the wing again. 'Wake up sir, this is the police.'

Novik rubbed his face and pushed his hand through his dishevelled hair. His legs were cold. Backlit by the rising sun the silhouette of a well-built female officer stood beside the car.

'Waaup?' Novik pushed himself upright, the blanket over his shoulders.

'Are you the driver of this vehicle, sir?'

'I guess.'

'Then put on your pants, and show me some ID.'

Now that he was fully awake Novik could make out that the figure in front of him was a highway patrolperson, her car was pulled onto the roadside some yards away, the roof lights flashing.

Novik pulled on his jeans, boots and tee, and stumbled out of the Cadillac. He brushed back his hair with his fingers, felt the ridge of scar tissue at his hairline. Cops. Always be polite. 'Hi. How are you doing?'

Now she was out of the sun he saw she was leggy, chocolate-skinned, hard-eyed. A peroxide blonde afro poked out from under her cap and she wore pink lipstick that matched her long nails. Cleavage swelled in the three-button gap at the top of white blouse and Prussian blue jacket. A disconcerting power ensemble, cops never used to be like this.

Novik gave a lopsided grin, 'That uniform really suits you.'

'Do not try that bullshit jive on me,' the patrolwoman drawled, 'I've seen your skinny white ass.'

'It's real cold,' Novik grumbled. 'What do you expect?'

'I expect some ID, sir. I expect to see it now.'

Novik patted his hip pockets, 'It's in the glove box.'

With practiced ease, the patrolwoman flipped her holster open. Now her hand rested casually on her impressively large gun. 'Go fetch it.'

'Don't be so twitchy, we don't have guns.' Despite her jazzy style, this cop was a real ball-breaker. Novik slouched back to the car, opened the driver's door and took out his license.

Josie's head and bare shoulders appeared at the open door. Novik and Josie shared a brief, panicked look. Josie mouthed 'I really need to pee', then called out. 'Hello, Officer. Would you like some coffee? Mr Car, can you make coffee?'

'I am so sorry, no. Good morning, officer.'

'Stay in the car, ma'am,' the patrolwoman ordered. Her eyes shifted between Josie and Novik. 'Did the car just say something?'

'Indeed, I did,' Mr Car said.

'You smart?'

'I solved Hilbert's eighth problem.'

'You going to be a nuisance?'

'Not for a duly notarised officer of the law.'

The patrolwoman grimaced, and scratched behind her ear. She looked Novik up and down and compared his shabby attire with the expensive sleekness of the Cadillac. 'This is your car?'

'Yes,' said Novik.

'Technically,' said the Cadillac.

Novik handed over his licence. The patrolwoman studied it, her expression a mixture of patience and contempt, 'It just says Novik.'

'That's my name.'

'You only got one name?'

'I never needed two.'

The patrolwoman's expression hardened, 'Family or given?'

Novik held out his hands. 'Officer, it's just my name. It's never been a problem before.'

The patrolwoman unclipped a datapad from her belt, her painted fingertips hovered over the keys. 'What were your parent's names?'

'Er... mom and dad.'

'Don't try and be funny.'

'No, for real. That's what I called them. They called each other things like "Sweetheart", "Honey", and "Diddums".'

The patrolwoman's lip curled, 'Diddums?'

'Mom was a loving person, occasionally possessed of flippancy.'

'It sounds to me as if your father was a chinless, submissive excuse for a real man.'

Accept it, Novik thought, though he burned with resentment. She's trying to get under your skin, and it's working. This is deliberate provocation. Say nothing, just accept it. You need to let this go.

Instead, he said, 'Dad was great, my childhood was happy and fulfilled, if anarchic and lacking formal structure. Now I think of it, my parent's names could actually have been Sweetheart or Honey. I might be labouring under a false assumption that I don't know their names despite actually having been aware of them all along.'

'Sweetheart would be a pretty unusual name.'

'Hippyish, but not out-and-out weird. We're not from Utah. Look, officer, what is it exactly that you want?'

Benny opened one of the Cadillac's rear doors. 'That's the Dodge Charger Redux. When did they start turning those into black and whites? Is it true you can get a geomagnetic inertialess supercharger?'

'Get back in the car,' the patrolwoman snapped at Benny. 'All right, Novik, why did you stop here?'

'We got tired. What's all this about? We've done nothing wrong.'

'There's a Motel two miles down the highway.'

Novik sighed with polite frustration, 'I like the desert stars.'

Bennie continued to study the patrol car. 'Aren't those out of state plates?'

Hoping on one bare foot, Josie held up her hand. 'Officer. Ma'am. I really need to pee.'

The patrolwoman looked increasingly nervous. 'Everybody stay where you are.'

Shirt flapping, Benny set off across the dusty space between the cars, 'You got funny plates, I just want to take a closer look.'

'Hold it right there,' the patrolwoman shouted. She let go of the datapad, the lanyard snapped it back to her belt. She drew her massive handgun. Long legs splayed, she took a two-handed grip and fired her into the air.

The boom was massively loud. Benny shrieked and flapped his hands, Novik and Josie froze. Ten seconds later, the gunshot echoed back from the sandstone cliffs a mile away.

'I've had enough of this bullshit.' The patrolwoman herded them together with a wave of her gun, 'Put your backs against the car, sit down and cross your legs, hands behind your heads. All of you. Do it now.'

None of this felt right to Novik. The questioning was skewed, the officer's equipment was non-standard, even the provocative way she wore her uniform. He'd heard stories of rogue cops in out of the way places, cops who preyed on lone travellers. He'd thought nothing of the stories at the time, now he prayed they were myths. Mr. Car said he was bullet proof, if he could get everyone inside, they would be safe.

'What's your name?' the patrolwoman said to Benny.

'B-Benny the Spoke, ma'am.'

'What's your real name? The name your parents gave you?'

'Um, I don't have real p-parents, ma'am.'

'Your fosters.'

'I'm not from these parts,' Benny said patiently. 'We don't have parents. I just grew, more like a seed.'

'Lord, give me strength,' the patrolwoman muttered. Sweat glistened on her brow, she looked longingly back at her car. 'Show me some ID.'

Benny handed over his wallet.

'Benjeffre T. Spode, Junior novice apprentice to the third sub-groundsman's second assistant's second assistant, Herb World,' she read. 'A long way from home, Mr. Spode.'

'F-further than you might imagine, ma'am. That's m-my intersystem passport. Hold it beneath the harsh light of the dwarf star my home world orbits on its infinite journey through the endless, cold night of space, and you will see a four-dimensional hologram of my resumé. Or you can download it in a variety of formats.'

Novik took a chance, 'Ma'am, Officer, listen to what he's saying. Benny's not well, that's why he's stammering. He's not from another planet, he burned his brain out with bad acid. He's got throat cancer from drinking agent orange, some kind of messed up initiation ceremony from his tour for Uncle Sam.'

Benny waved away Novik's words, 'It's not that, I'm just concerned for my friends.'

'And why would that be?'

'For one thing, you have a gun.'

The patrolwoman looked down at them uncertainly. To Novik it seemed she was deciding whether to shoot them, or just walk away. He let one raised hand bump against Josie's, and squeezed her fingers. 'Don't worry, babe, everything's going to be fine.'

The patrolwoman stalked forwards. Novik saw she wore black, patent leather stilettos, no cop wore shoes like that. Lord, this is it. Heart pounding, Novik readied himself. He'd throw himself across Josie, he'd scramble clear, somehow, he'd tackle the killer cop.

'This time, I'm going to let you off with a caution,' the patrolwoman said.

134

When he saw the gun close up, Benny shook his hand as if it was burned. 'Holy guacamole, that's a D.E. 68-cal. When did the highway patrol get issued with those recoilless fist howitzers?'

'Shut up.' The patrolwoman's arm trembled with the effort of holding up the huge gun.

Benny enthused about the weapon to Novik, 'The 68-cal is the ultimate kinetic hand-cannon for two armed primates. What I don't understand is why-'

The patrolwoman jerked her gun towards Benny, 'I said shut up. All of you, get back in the car and drive away.'

Infuriated, Novik stood up. It was bad enough getting pushed around by authority figures. Whoever this woman was, she'd scared the crap out him. 'You're not a real cop.'

She bared her teeth, a nervous grin, 'Sure I am, why'd you say that? This is your lucky day, so take my advice, and move it.'

'You're not a real cop, so I don't have to do what you say.'

The patrolwoman backed away, 'I've got a gun.'

Novik bared his teeth in a tight grin, 'A real cop wouldn't say that.'

'They might.'

Novik's finger jabbed forwards, accusing, 'If you were a real cop, you'd want to look in the trunk.'

Josie rabbit-punched Novik in the ribs, 'What are you doing? Let's go. Take the hint,' she hissed.

'Look in the trunk,' Novik growled.

The cop raised her chin defiantly, 'I don't want to.'

'Take a look.'

'Shan't.'

'Mr Car – the trunk.'

The trunk lid smoothly swung open.

A few thousand dollars spiralled up into the clean desert air.

Despite herself, the patrolwoman peered inside. She gave a low whistle, 'Take me back to Alabamy. How much is there?' Moving like a sleepwalker, she grabbed a double fistful of notes.

'A hundred and sixty-five, maybe a hundred and seventy million,' Novik said.

Horror slowly grew on the cop's face. She shoved the notes she had taken back into the trunk and began to shake. 'Oh Lord. You work for *Them*, don't you?' She rubbed her palm on her pants like she was trying to get rid of the very touch of the money from her skin. 'Which one is it? The Non-stop Jesuits, the Yoz Vo Nystavya, the Grey-Green Wolverine?' Her voice dropped to a whisper, 'Don't tell me, you're in league with the COPS.'

Now Josie was puzzled. 'I thought you were the cops?'

'She means the Chinese Octogenarian Pensioners Society,' Novik said. 'They took over the Triads and pushed out the Mafia. Estimated membership is over three hundred million. They're old and they're poor, but they're pissed off and there's lots of them.'

Josie held out her hand, 'Give me that gun. We're not bad people but I have had enough of looking down that barrel.'

Meekly, she handed it over, 'All right. I surrender.'

Gingerly, Josie took the heavy weapon.

Hands held out, Benny hopped with excitement beside her, 'Can I just-?'

'No, you can't.' Josie passed the weapon to Novik. He checked the safety, then dropped the clip into his palm.

As soon as he was done, Josie turned on him, 'What the hell were you doing?'

'I was right, wasn't I?' He knew it didn't matter, he'd done a crazy thing. Fake cop or not, she had the gun, she could have killed them all. No thanks to him, they were alive, Novik felt bad to the core. He rounded on the bogus patrolwoman, 'What were you going to do, rob us? Walk us out into the desert and shoot us down?'

'I wasn't going to hurt you.'

'Easy to say now.'

'They're only blanks.'

'Bullets don't work on me,' Benny ducked away as Novik cuffed at his head.

The fake patrolwoman pulled off her fake cap. Tight blonde frizz bounced into shape. She clutched the cap to her chest, 'May I call my mother? Please? I just want to say goodbye.' She sat cross-legged on the ground, formed circles with her middle fingers and thumbs and began to chant. 'Aum. Aauum.'

Novik and Josie exchanged a puzzled look. 'I think there's still some contamination on the money,' Josie said.

Novik tried to apologise. 'Babe, I was scared. I thought-' he couldn't say it. 'I don't know what I thought.'

Josie's face was set, she looked down at the cross-legged fake cop. 'Aaauuum.'

Benny tapped the woman on her shoulder. 'Are those Nebraska plates?'

'Aaaaauuu...' she looked up sheepishly, 'Yes.'

'I knew it,' Benny crowed. 'Car's a beaut.'

'Thanks. I did the paint job myself...' her voice trailed off as she followed the flight of some birds across the sky. Then she waved her hands in the air. 'Wow.'

Novik squatted in front of her. 'You're not a rogue officer.'

'I was a performance artist with an improvisational troupe,' she said absently. 'We decided to turn our lives into mobile interactive installations. I wanted to do this, the rest of the troupe wanted to be hoodlum gangstas, so we split. The people I book become part of my art, I become part of their lives.' She gazed at Benny's shoulder as if it were a thing of wonder. 'Your shirt is melting. It's floating into the sky like the bioluminescent comb-jellies of the Sargasso sea.'

'We need to clean that money properly,' Novik said. 'We're doing this wherever we go.'

'What are we going to do with her?' Josie clenched her fists, 'I know what I'd like to do.'

Novik took her hands and gently broke open her fists. 'Her heart's in the right place, I can see that now, but her method is really freaky. Josie, if you can forgive me, we can forgive her.'

'She's crazy,' Josie's said. Her expression softened, 'Same as you.'

'We need to get her to a mall.'

The patrolwoman heard him, she looked very mellow. 'Is that where you're going to whack me? You guys are so confident nobody can touch you, you do your wetwork in public.' She held her arms out towards them. 'I don't mind. I'm ready to go. The world is a beautiful but terrible place, it's time to travel towards the light.'

'What's your name?' Novik said.

'Marytha Drummond.'

'You're not going to die, Marytha, but you are going to have to stop frightening ordinary people,' Josie said.

'All right. What's going to happen to me?'

Novik polled Marytha to her feet, 'You're going to become one of us. We're going to take you shopping.'

European sequestration a big success.

'Planet earth did it by accident in the carboniferous, today we're doing it deliberately.' Ernest 'Che' Fowland, head of EU carbon sequestration services is upbeat about the program. 'We're sucking tens of millions of tons of carbon out of the atmosphere. Permanently.'

A hundred years ago whole communities toiled to extract coal from mines across Europe. Today, compressed charcoal is delivered to the mines using gravity trains – full carts head down into the earth, their weight pulls the empty ones up. 'It's elegant and it's free,' Fowland explains. 'And it's old tech. The British thought of this when William IV was on the throne.'

Atmospheric inertia means it will take as much as a century to see any effect, but the EU claim, along with OneAfrica and the far-eastern countries, that they are in it for the long haul.

'The FSoSA have other priorities,' Fowland stated. 'The Amazonian countries are replanting as fast as they can. That's their job for now.'

Critics of the charcoal program point to associated rises in atmospheric oxygen. Giant dragonflies and centipedes inhabited the world when oxygen was 50% more abundant than today.

Slobodan Jones,
KUWjones.org

All over the world there were people who believed Palfinger Crane was so rich he would not miss the money they needed to perfect their own lives. Most were scammers, chancers and dreamers. The varied ploys of crooks and fraudsters far outweighed those of the genuinely needy, who also had access to the various charities and foundations Crane supported.

Almost none of these direct appeals reached Crane himself. The more persistent, inventive or overtly hostile were dealt with by a dedicated wing of the administration that surrounded Crane's private world.

Crane never got used to the idea that some people hated him for having what they thought they themselves deserved. It changed him in ways he didn't particularly like; he grew suspicious, he became rather selfish. As a result, almost none of the money Crane donated came directly from his personal wealth. That near limitless ocean of riches he reserved to himself, Bianca's allowance, and Ellen's phenomenally costly medical care.

Every bequest and endowment came via the corporations, multinationals and over-holdings of his world-wide business hegemony, the CraneCorp Buisplex. Crane thought this prudent, which it was. He also thought it was enough. Other people disagreed.

This included the Secretary-General of the United Nations.

Compact and energetic, Mikhail Lobachevsky paced around Palfinger Crane's palm-fringed office like a middle-aged man with ADHD. He sat, he stood, he sipped his Jamaican Blue Mountain. He put the cup down. He stirred his coffee, rattled the spoon against the cup. He strode to the window, fiddled with the catch, scratched at a speck on the glass, and returned to his coffee.

Crane relaxed in his own chair and wondered if Lobachevsky was allergic to caffeine. The Russian Secretary-General loved the expensive brand, but refused to have it in his own office.

'Mikhail, sit down,' Crane said. 'You're making me dizzy, and wearing out my carpet.'

'I cannot help it.' Lobachevsky kicked off his shoes and carried on pacing. He picked up a pen, put it down, stirred the coffee again, half rose then sat firmly down, hands clasped on his knees. 'Very well, despite myself, I become still because you ask me to. I make this concession, see how it is done? That is politics, yes?'

Crane demurred with a gesture.

'So, now I will make another. What I asked before, give me only half.'

Crane looked out through the window to the blue sky, the gently swaying palm fronds, and the glittering sea beyond. 'Mikhail, that is still over five percent of the GDP of the European Union.'

Lobachevsky rocked his shoulders, grimaced and spread his hands. 'A quadrillion roubles here, a quadrillion roubles there, what difference does it make between friends? So, you'll help me?'

'Not like that, no.'

Lobachevsky's head jerked, 'Then what?'

Crane named a figure. Compared to what the Secretary-General was asking it was tiny. Briefly Lobachevsky looked glum, then spread his arms and laughed. 'Fantastic! More than I'd hoped for.'

Cranes arms hung at his sides. 'Good. I am glad to help.'

Lobachevsky's eyes glittered. 'I warn you, I shall be back. At Epiphany, we break the ice of the Moscow river into the shape of a cross. The priests bless the water and we swim. We are strong, we Russians. Like Mother Russia, we may be defeated, but can never conquered.' The Secretary-General retrieved his shoes and held out his hand. 'Thank you, Mr. Crane.'

Feeling both wretched, and angry with Lobachevsky for making him feel wretched, Crane escorted the Secretary-General onto the covered veranda, where Lobachevsky's impeccably groomed and ever-smiling retinue drank iced tea and cold beer with Crane's staff. The Secretary-general's people formed a carefully balanced mix of ethnicity, age, politics, sexuality and faith, yet they had one thing in common; they were all beautiful.

The UN flotilla of open-topped solar-electric vehicles rolled towards the distant gates, and Crane was alone again. He moved along the veranda, inspecting the squat, scaly cycads and luxuriant tree ferns. Growing in the same environment, the stiff-leaved cycads grew in a reluctant annual burst of activity, the tree ferns threw out sprays of three and four-metre long fronds continuously.

He didn't understand the difference, it intrigued him. What did the cycads do with all that sunlight? Ignore it?

Everyone wanted something, even Palfinger Crane. Especially Crane.

His need was so strong it was almost pathetic. It actually was tragic.

All these visitors, caps in hand, were so certain he could help them, that he had what they needed. In return none could give him the one thing he desired above all else: Ellen, size sixteen.

Crane tugged up the knees of his cream cotton trousers and sat on the veranda step. He wondered why it was that money couldn't help Ellen when it seemed that it could help everybody else.

As he looked out across his estate, the bay and the jungle-clad mountains beyond, Crane realised that he didn't care about the world's problems. All he wanted was for his daughter to be like everyone else, to stop being a freak that freak-lovers idolised, and for her not to die young.

Alone on the step he wondered if there had ever been a time when things could have been different, if he could have made other decisions with better outcomes. He wondered if it was, in fact, all his fault.

Out of nowhere, deeply, intensely, he missed Bianca. He didn't blame her for leaving, he had never resented her for it. Some people accepted the hand life dealt them, others put the cards down and walked away from the table to find another game. He wished she'd stayed with him, with Ellen, the three of them together. Even now he still missed her, still thought about her every day. For a moment it crushed him, then he forced his sob into a mocking laugh.

On the far side of the sloping lawn one of the gardeners, Christian, cleared fallen palm fronds from the deep border of red and pink hibiscus and purple bougainvillea. Like all the estate workers, Christian lived in one of the nearby villages. Young and well-built, he wore faded blue cotton shorts and a short-sleeved shirt. Thick canvas gloves protected his hands as he stacked the hard, dead fronds into a handcart.

Christian stopped working when he saw Crane approach. He wiped his brow with his forearm and grinned in welcome. His voice was deep, mellow and silky. 'Good day, Mr Crane. I hope today you are feeling very fine.'

'Good morning, Christian. Yes, I am fine. How are you today?'

'Fine, Mr. Crane. Very fine.'

'I need you to do something for me,' Crane said.

Christian became attentive, 'Yes, Mr Crane.'

'I want you to tell me that I am a fortunate man and I must stop feeling sorry for myself.'

Momentarily thrown, Christian regarded Crane carefully, then clapped his hands and laughed. 'Of course, Mr Crane, sir. I shall do that for you right away.' Trying to keep his face straight, Christian spoke as sternly as he could to the richest man who had ever lived. 'Mr Crane, we all have our problems, but you must pull yourself together, for you are luckier than most. Also, it is a great privilege to be able to tick you off.'

Amazed at his own words, Christian took off his gloves, put his hands in his pockets, took them out, folded his arms, rubbed the top of his head and put his gloves back on again.

'Thank you, Christian.'

'It is my pleasure, Mr Crane.'

Crane looked along the row of colourful shrubs and high palms. 'Still plenty to do.'

Christian took that as dismissal, 'Leave it to me.'

Crane tugged at one of the dead fronds. 'I think I will give you a hand.'

Christian pulled off his gloves and offered them to Crane. 'The stems are sharp.'

'What about you?'

'I have a spare pair in the cart.'

One of the fallen fronds had flattened a small hibiscus. Crane lifted it clear and Christian produced a pair of secateurs and clipped away the broken stems.

'How is your family?' Crane said.

'We are all very fine. My grandmother is not as young as she was.'

'Ask my doctor to bring forward his next visit.'

'Thank you, Mr Crane.' Christian opened his mouth, he hesitated, torn between courtesy and a desire not to intrude. 'How is Miss Ellen, Mr Crane?'

'She is not well at all, Christian. We do what we can.'

'We all hope for the very best.'

'Thank you, Christian. So do I.'

They worked together for an hour, until the border was clear.

The sole reason the littoral of the Gulf of Mexico is suffering catastrophic depopulation, from northern Nicaragua to western Florida, in The Bahamas, Cuba, the Caymans and north Jamaica, is the collapse of the Bermuda High.

This former zone of high pressure used to push hurricanes north from their east–west path when it shifted west in the summer. An unfortunate consequence was they sometimes hit land, but they came and they went, and the Bermuda High killed them off.

The tropical cyclone known as Hurricane 'Permanent' Larry formed two years after the Bermuda High failed. Since then, winter seawater temperatures have been warm enough to sustain Larry, and each summer it regenerates.

Permanent Larry is the cows coming home in spades for past failures of world environmental policy. The scary thing is, it is still growing. Thermal balance is years, possibly decades away. Planet Earth now has its very own Red Spot.

Our own research shows similar conditions are forming in the Bay of Bengal, and the Sea of Japan.

Nasrin Choudhury,
8th International Extreme Weather Symposium, Dacca.

- 20 -

Jericho Wilson had long suspected there was another agency outside the FBI, beyond the CIA. Non-uniformed, non-suit, answerable only to the Executive, possibly just Snarlow herself. Something so undemocratic it couldn't possibly exist, until a spook knocked on your door and either whacked you or reeled you in. To his mind, there had always been the need, hence, the facility to satisfy the need.

He also wondered if this shadowy agency might exist in parallel to the Exec, totally free. Seated in the SUV beside Masters, the thought didn't make him feel any better.

'You want to talk about it?' Wilson said.

Traffic was dense but steady. Masters tapped a button on the dash and let go of the wheel. The car accelerated briefly, edged left then settled down, sensor-locked with the vehicles ahead, behind and to each side.

Masters avoided eye contact. 'Frankly, it's going to be in the way if we don't. You're going to be stuck in a state of infinite mental regression, forever wondering what I'm thinking about you, that I know that's what you're thinking about me, and that you know that I know you're thinking about what I'm thinking about.' She flashed him a tight smile, 'I've been there during resistance training, a bottomless pit of paranoid intersubjectivity. It's a complete headfuck. You got to let it go.'

Wilson sighed and sank back into his seat. She was right, it was such a big thing, the biggest thing in his life. The dreadful pivot about which his entire existence swung.

'OK,' Wilson spoke as if he were announcing himself to a room of strangers. 'My name is Jericho Wilson and I shot my wife in the back of the head.'

The interior of the car was almost silent, the only sounds tyre rumble and wind. Under the hood the horizontal flywheel span silently on superconducting mag-vac bearings at three-quarters of a million rpm.

Masters had driven Wilson away from his tract house, leaving Johnson on the pavement. The black spook walked away without farewell, speaking into the air. As they turned the corner Wilson saw another anonymous saloon appear at the far end of the street and pull up beside Johnson.

'So why no guns?' Masters said. 'Don't you like the nasty bang?'

Her coldness, her speckled grey suit and neat, short hair, the whole thrust of the conversation made Wilson feel defensive and vulnerable.

'I don't want to make any more unfixable mistakes.'

She smiled at that, faint lines appearing in the smooth skin each side of her mouth.

Wilson couldn't help himself. 'How old are you?'

She laughed at that. 'We've all made mistakes, Mr. Wilson. I expect we'll make a few more in the coming days.'

A tray slid out of the dash in front of Wilson. A handgun with a triangular cross-section barrel lay in a foamed recess.

'That's a Type 1 FaF pistol. Fire and Forget. If the target moves, the bullet follows. You can shoot round corners. No more mistakes.'

Wilson opened his fists, he hadn't realised they were clenched. He pushed the tray back into the dash and placed his hands flat on his knees. 'Tell me about Gould's man.'

Brake lights flared ahead and the car slowed. Masters put her hands back on the wheel and changed lane.

'He's called "Manalito", a radicalised first-nation Apache, and known anti-white randomer. Prefers women, seven confirmed dead, twice that suspected, and probably twice that again since he went to the southern littoral and became Mitchell Gould's personal butcher. First-nation elders either vehemently disown him, or deny he's even Native American. We believe they're right.'

'And now he's Stateside.'

'Correct. He's arranged a rendezvous with some creeps from Birmingham, the errand boys for the Vegas run. Manalito's going to chew gum and take names.'

The window beside Wilson became opaque and mug shots of Manalito appeared, front, profile and three-quarters. Wilson tapped the window and stats scrolled in a frame: 194cm, 234lbs, 26 years old, wanted in eight states for murder, kidnap, aggravated assault, attempted murder, assault with a deadly weapon, the list went on. He tapped the glass again and the pictures returned. Manalito was physically impressive, even handsome, with high cheekbones and aquiline nose.

'So what's smart money?' Wilson said.

'Semi-bright 2D nano. Handle it, and it scans and stores your prints and DNA, then polls the FedMesh at the next till.' Masters pulled a small screen with a touch pad from her pocket. 'These units interrogate the Mesh, plot, track and extrapolate probable routes. This one's mine. Yours is in the glove box.'

'That's… impressive.' Wilson extracted his tracking device. The operation was simple, all the intelligence was in the money. 'I didn't know.'

'Few do. Brand new Arabtech, hot from the deserts of Oman. They're good at it. Like we used to be.' Masters pulled a sour face. 'Must be all that sand, or the special sherbet. You didn't hear any of this and non-disclosure is implied and expected.'

Wilson didn't like that last bit at all. 'The objective with Manalito is what?'

'Information gathering. Core-dump the redskin and scalp the others. We share what we find. Take anything you can use to hurt Gould, with our best regards. Whatever you decide to do next, we'll be looking elsewhere.'

Wilson doubted that entirely. 'I don't want to just hurt Gould.'

Masters looked at him properly for the first time, serious, appraising. Then she winked. 'That's good. I like that. Honesty is rare and refreshing.'

'You're recording this, aren't you?'

'Aren't you?'

It was the first time they both found the same thing funny.

- 21 -

The big sea canoe rolled with the swell as Bianca awoke, the long outrigger lifted and slapped down into the water. Seated in the last but one position she could see two of the men forwards of her working their paddles while the others, including the grey-haired man behind her, slept. The night was almost over, pale dawn light tinged the eastern horizon while stars still burned in the black west.

The two canoes had paced each other through the darkness, more intent on keeping together, aligned with the star field, than in making way. The six islanders in Bianca's canoe worked in pairs, letting the others rest or sleep, the men and women in Tekirei's canoe did the same. Bianca rubbed the tender places on her palms from the paddling she had done the previous day. She was used to manual work, enjoyed achieving things with sweat and muscle, yet her hands were not used to paddling for hour after hour across the Pacific.

Tekirei's canoe was a low black silhouette about twenty yards to starboard. Bianca raised her hand, struck by a pang of kinship with the people in the other vessel.

'It is only a short journey,' Tekirei had told her. 'A day and a half, two if the wind is against us.'

What if there is a storm, Bianca wanted to ask. What about sharks? She had kept quiet, not wanting Tekirei to see her nerves.

'It is good to sometimes do things the way they have always been done,' Tekirei said. He showed Bianca the contents of his bag. 'I also like to have ultra-lite life jackets, SatNav and distress beacons. These days our voyages are for pleasure, not necessity. We keep alive the old skills and traditions, and have a good time too. The weather will be fine, the seas not too high, and the currents generally good. If there is a serious problem a seaplane can be with us in under an hour.'

Bianca had major doubts about whether spending two days paddling across the ocean in a canoe would be anything approaching fun. If nothing else, it would be an adventure few people from her background experienced. It was worth a little risk and discomfort simply for that.

Now, floating in the pre-dawn light, unknown miles north-east of Pohnpei, she felt nothing but gladness. With every hour at sea, every mile they travelled the world had slipped away behind her. All her worries, doubts and anxieties were left behind. Not ignored, just temporarily no longer required.

'How far from Pohnpei are we?' she asked Mautake, the young man in front of her. He looked past her to the older man, and although he smiled, he also shook his head. His nose was a little flatter than Mautake's, his mouth a thin slash. All throughout the voyage he had barely spoken, acknowledging the water and food passed back and forth with polite nods and 'Thank you'.

'I did not check the distances before we left,' Mautake said. 'Tekirei likes the mood of these journeys to approach the way things might have been. We are a little over half way.'

As he spoke Mautake winked then glanced down to his hip where he splayed his fingers six times. Then he yawned, stretched and took up his paddle.

The sun rose, the sea turned red then gold and the sun lofted into a sky of high white haze. The crews became alert, called greetings to each other across the water. The two sea canoes drew together. Bianca waved to Tekirei.

'Good morning,' he called. 'Did you manage to sleep?'

'More than I thought.' Bianca realised she was tucking back loose strands of hair and pulled her hand down. All of a sudden she felt very self-conscious. Whatever the other men in the boats knew, or suspected about her relationship with Tekirei, they were very polite, the younger men friendly, the older men more reserved. Most probably they simply believed she was the patron to Tekirei's projects and he was taking her to his home to introduce his daughter and family. Bianca recalled their conversation at the ruins of Nan Madol, it was little short of the entire truth.

Tekirei pointed up at the thin, high clouds. 'Today will be very hot.'

Despite their much darker skins the men in both canoes were applying UV protection, Bianca followed suite. Everyone took up their paddles, dug them into the water and the canoes moved off.

Behind the high haze the sun was soon blistering, far hotter than the day before. After about half an hour the front man dropped out, rested for around fifteen minutes, then resumed paddling. As he did the man behind him rested, and so on along the line until it was Bianca's turn, and then the old man behind her.

The day wore on. The men began a slow, hypnotic song in their own language, Kiribati. Unable to understand, Bianca felt the rhythm of the words, the beat they gave to the paddling. She slipped into a semi-trance, her breath and stroke matched to the steady pulse of the song.

A shout came from Tekirei's canoe, a pointed arm. Away to starboard a shoal of flying fish broke water, skimmed a hundred feet through the air and dropped below the surface. Sleek grey-blue dorsal fins cut the water behind them as dolphins pursued their prey. The fish flew again, the encounter moved away, across the ocean.

'The dolphins were not trying too hard,' Mautake said. 'They like to play, to party. For them life is a fine game.'

Awestruck and enchanted, Bianca was impressed by the animals' energy and speed. Mautake shook his head. 'They hunt for the joy of the chase. The sharks never play.'

Bianca looked around anxiously. Miles of dark water lay under the thin hull of their canoe. 'What sharks?'

'Don't worry,' Mautake smiled with easy assurance. 'Tiger sharks are easy to kill, and rokea only sink your canoe if you steal their fish.'

An hour later, a conversation broke out between Tekirei and the old man in the stern of Bianca's canoe. The two boats held position while the sea water was tasted, and the two men stood and looked out across the swell.

'The sea changes here,' Mautake said. 'It becomes darker and colder, the waves flat and heavy. Tekirei thinks we have come far enough, my father disagrees because the water is too sweet.'

Bianca looked out across the ocean. Perhaps it did have a deeper shade, the swell more ponderous. 'Who do you think is right?'

Mautake grinned. 'My father, of course. He is strong and brave, wise and virile as a turtle, fascinating to women, a superb fisherman and very skilled in many crafts and arts. All traits I have inherited to a large degree.'

'I can see that,' Bianca said. 'Is modesty also one of his attributes?'

Mautake stroked his chin, 'That was not on the list he gave me.'

Mautake's father won the argument and they paddled for another hour before repeating the process. This time they agreed, the canoes turned to port and they set off again.

'This has all had to be relearned, like fighting Tiger sharks.' Mautake said. 'When Enewetak sank beneath the rising waves some of us went to Australia, others the USA. Many followed Tekirei to live with his relatives on Ujelang atoll.' Mautake spoke slowly, matching his words to his breathing as he paddled. Both swell and wind were growing and everyone worked hard to drive the boats up the foam-flecked waves and across the troughs.

'Ujelang was a difficult place to live at first. Technology saved us, solar stills and medicines, engineered plants. My father spoke to an old man on Pohnpei, a hurricane survivor. He relearned the lost routes, made solo voyages, and now he teaches me.'

'How do you kill the sharks?'

'Tigers?' Mautake spat over the side. 'They are brutes, too broad to turn when they charge. At the last moment you must swim to one side and hold out your knife. The shark's speed and weight drive it onto the blade and it destroys itself. Very easy,' Mautake laughed. 'Apparently.'

'And the others, the rokea?'

Mautake's smile faded. 'No, you do not try to kill them. Even dolphin fear rokea.'

The slate-blue ocean swelled higher and higher, each wave-top flecked with spume. The canoes rose and fell on the high waves, their prows breaching clear at the summits. The view at the crests showed an endless heaving seascape in all directions. Everyone was paddling now, the time for rest and conversation gone. Bianca matched her rhythm with the lead man, the best paddler in the canoe, and drove her paddle into the water until her arms burned with the effort.

A cry went up from Tekirei's canoe and it surged forwards.

'Land,' Mautake gasped. 'Ahead.'

Too breathless to speak Bianca looked across the ocean at the next peak. Nothing. Another peak came and there, over to the left she saw a dark line upon the water. The sight gave her energy, joy.

'You see it!' Mautake gasped. 'Ujelang atoll.'

'Yes.'

They held to their course, keeping the atoll to port until almost parallel to it. Then the canoes swung hard over, Tekirei's canoe dropping behind. Now Bianca could see the atoll in more detail. Clusters of palms, a glimpse of sand, a few dark shapes running on the beach.

'This,' Mautake bared his teeth, 'is the fun bit.'

Behind Bianca, Mautake's taciturn father touched her shoulder. Now his eyes were wide, his smile broad. 'When you are on the wave, paddle like a tiger shark is on your heels.' He laughed, high pitched and shrill, and dug furiously at the water.

'What wave?' Bianca said.

Then she saw it.

Two hundred yards away the ocean crashed endlessly against the atoll reef. Spray burst upwards, the deep boom of each strike thrummed in the air.

There was a break in the reef forty feet wide. Oceanic combers piled against the reef and collapsed through the gap in a gigantic boil of leaping water. Bianca's canoe headed straight for it.

The paddler at the prow led them in, working furiously one moment, coasting the next. Part terrified, part exhilarated, Bianca realised they were trying to synchronise with the incoming waves. Behind her, Mautake's father leaned on his paddle like a tiller and kept the bows pointed towards the gap.

They were close now. The waves pushed them at the reef, the brutally jagged coral close ahead. The stern lifted, the prow dipped.

'Ya!' everyone cried, and drove their paddles into the rising wave.

Bianca felt as if a great hand lifted the canoe and pitched it forwards. The air roared, spume burst all around, they swept past the sharp coral in a blur.

Then they were coasting in the calm lagoon. Bianca yelled and whooped as loud as Mautake and the others. A crowd of people waved and shouted on the beach, children leapt with excitement. Bianca turned in her seat and saw Tekirei's canoe ride the gap. White water churned around and above it. Briefly, the canoe was lost to sight. Then it hurtled clear.

Bianca marvelled that she had just done such a thing herself.

White sand, blue sky, the roar of surf, a crowd of dark-skinned people on a beach backed by palm trees. Never had Bianca felt so far removed from her own life.

Children, men, and women ran into the sea. And there was Tanoata, Tekirei's teenage daughter. She splashed through the shallows in her bright skirt towards her father's canoe. Tekirei leaned over the side and embraced her, kissed her forehead then turned to wave to Bianca, his grin flashing white.

'Tekirei,' Bianca called and waved. 'Tanoata.'

Tanoata stared blankly for a moment, then took hold of the gunwales of her father's canoe and helped haul it towards the shore.

"*The making of breakfast at the same time by millions of people across the country is as much a part of the production line as is work at the conveyor belt an hour later. Our behaviour has been profoundly altered by the production line. Standardisation increases efficiency of output, and as a result, only the rich can afford possessions that are truly unique. The rest of the community lives in the same kind of house, wears the same pattern of clothes, drives the same car, watches the same TV programmes, dreams the same dreams in the hierarchy of work.*"

J. Burke,
Connections

- 22 -

Oscar Gordano managed about twenty miles before the knot of anxiety and fear in his guts grew so bad he knew he was going to puke.

'Pull over,' he told the driver. As soon as the car stopped he was out the door, he took five steps into the trees at the side of the road, and threw up. Ahead and behind, the black escort cars had also halted. Gordano waved away the muscular, crop-headed agents as they emerged.

'It's Ok. I just puked.'

'Are you ill, sir?' the nearest agent said. His firm jaw and clear, pale eyes, the way his dark suit fitted his shoulders and chest, everything about him made Gordano feel inadequate.

'No. It's cool,' he lied. 'We did some legals at the end of the meeting.' Gordano blew his nose and dropped the tissue on the ground. 'Late night, empty stomach, pharma fun does it to me every time.'

Unsmiling, the security agent turned away. The rest of his team had already fanned out, their passives and actives deployed in an impromptu cordon.

Gordano looked down at his trembling hand. Christ, what had he been thinking of, opening up to the President like that? If Gould found out he'd be dead meat. Laundering Gould's money through the Gordano casinos had been good for them both. Snarlow for Chrissakes! He'd given her a real piece of leverage and for what? Her temporary and worthlessly undependable respect. He didn't want her respect, she could take it and stick inside her overheated and echoing twat.

It was just the drugs. He'd lost his nerve about the opinion polls, the situation building in the UN, and he'd taken the drugs. Andriewiscz's talk about battlefield nukes had freaked him and he'd blabbed. He'd wanted to show he could piss as high up the tree as anyone, that despite the fact he was only the VP he was also a player.

Gordano blew his nose again and returned to his car. He took a drink of

159

water, swilled his mouth out and spat. Then he settled into his seat and sat quietly for a while. 'Call my wife,' he told the car.

After a moment the windscreen greyed out, and there she was, sprawled on her side on a garden lounger wearing nothing but jewellery. The gold waist and breast chains contrasted well with her tanned skin, the diamond and gold piercings through her ears, nipples and labia sparkled in the sun.

Her welcoming smile was flawless, her greeting effusive. 'Oscar, darling! My poor baby, where are you?' She gestured expansively behind her. 'The new pool is open, it's wonderful.'

In the background Gordano could see figures lounging in the manicured acreage of his garden. Servants wore light costume, formal shorts or ribbon skirts. Most of the guests were nude.

'Enjoy it, Jazmin. Look, I'm delayed, half a day. It's this crisis in Mexico.'

Jazmin leaned forwards, pouting sympathy. 'Baby, you work too hard. Why is the Mexican government so unreasonable?'

Gordano watched her breast swing, 'They want to destroy our way of life.' He gestured towards the figures by the pool. 'Make sure you tell our friends.'

'You got it honey.' Jazmin's heart-shaped face showed a frown. 'Oscar, I just remember, Shirleen called-'

'What the hell does she want?' Gordano's guts knotted. His relationship with last year's wife had ended, as the nuptial negotiator had put it, disharmoniously.

'She wanted to tell you-'

'Oh for Christ's sake, Jazmin. Can't you keep that harpy off my back?'

'Hey, don't shoot the messenger, OK?' Jazmin swung her feet onto the floor and walked away. The cell view panned past her as she went. Gordano admired the way everything readjusted as she moved, firm but mobile. He'd been sceptical at first but the active implants she had cajoled out of him had been money well spent.

'I'm sorry, sweetness,' Gordano said weakly. 'Look, I don't want to argue. Shirleen and I, you know how she got to me. Honey, sweet-pea, let's not fight. How about we log this as a level two spat, my misdemeanour, and we forget about it?'

He was being generous, level twos were generally considered to be screaming bust-ups. Jazmin shrugged and blew him a kiss. 'Sure thing. Let me log it and we can get on.'

Gordano waited while she registered the infraction on her bracelet. A moment later he received the application, acknowledged his wife as the injured party and countersigned it. 'Ah, so what did Shirl want?'

'She's getting hitched in a four-way girl-girl, two years rolling. We're invited to the reception.'

At the poolside one of the servants was on all fours with a guest kneeling behind. Seeing her husband's gaze move past her, Jazmin fluttered her fingers. 'Better go, gotta keep the guests entertained.'

'Sure.'

'See you sometime.'

'Miss you, Jaz, baby.'

'Right. Yeah, me too.'

Gordano broke the link. Bile still stung in the back of his throat. He wondered why he'd bothered to call.

I work so hard and never get to enjoy myself, he thought pathetically. By the time I get home everyone will have left, or be in serotonin crash.

At least he had saved himself a level three infringement - failure to notify spouse of delayed arrival to a social engagement. Perhaps it was time to slow down, try out a different household vibe. Maybe next year he'd perm with an Amish virgin.

Out in the woodlands the security agents were cleaning up. One of them shovelled puke and an inch of soil into a plastic sack while another sprayed enzyme aerosol onto the surrounding ground, erasing all remnants of Gordano's bioprint.

Gordano took another phone out of his jacket, checked it was set to voice only and made another call.

The phone rang three times. An oriental-sounding woman answered.

'Who is this?' Gordano demanded.

'Who wants to know, cockmonkey?' the woman said carelessly.

Gordano wanted to scream, 'The Vice—fucking-President of the fucking United States of fucking America.' Instead he said: 'Where's the Mitch?'

'Right here,' Gould said.

'It's Ozzie. You know Mother's late?'

'She can't visit this month.'

'We'll miss her at the Casino.'

'That why you called?'

'Mother's always welcome.'

'I know that. What's up?'

'Something else.'

Mitchell Gould's voice grew cold. 'I gathered.'

'I need a house warming.'

Gould didn't like that at all. 'Use your own people.'

'It's a special treat.'

'I might know somebody. Who is it for? Tell me once then don't say it again.'

This was it.

'Palfinger Crane.'

The line was silent, then: 'What did he ever do to you? Fake his tax returns?'

'He's Canadian.'

'Is that where he is?'

'No, but that's where it needs to be done. His wife's in Micronesia, that's in the mid-Pacific-'

'I know where it is. That's going to take time to get someone out there.'

Gordano felt reassured he'd made the right decision. Gould was a smart operator. 'I appreciate that. She needs to get her present before anyone else.'

'Ladies first?'

'And last. Mother, father, then daughter. The order is important.'

'All right.'

'We're all right then?'

'That's what I said, Ozzy. Are you cool there?'

'I'm cool,' Gordano sighed with relief. 'Well, all right. Standard fees, paid the usual way.'

The line went silent. Gordano was starting to think he'd blown it, that Gould had hung up, when Gould said, 'Ozzy, you have got to be kidding. That's what you'd pay for taking out his pet dog. This kind of treat is off the radar. Give me a bullshit-free price or we are through.'

'Wait,' Gordano said hurriedly. 'I can pay a bonus. How does fifty sound?'

'I think I have gone deaf,' Gould said.

'Eighty, then.'

'How about five hundred and you stop wasting my time?'

Christ, Gordano thought. Christ, that was so obscenely ridiculous it was almost funny. Then he really did laugh, because with Crane out of the way that kind of money would be little more than loose change.

'Agreed,' Gordano said. 'Percentage wise, the breakdown is sixty, then forty.'

'Eighty, twenty,' Gould countered.

Gordano discovered he still had a small pair, 'It's a nice deal.'

'Fifty for expenses.'

'Fine.'

The line was quiet. Gordano listened to Mitchell Gould breathing. Then Gould said, 'All right. For five hundred I will pull my finger out of my ass and do this just for you. Don't worry, we'll put on a good show, it'll be a great party.'

'Great, great. There's one other thing.'

'What?' Gould sounded bored, impatient.

'Listen, this is real. Some of Lobo's people are prowling for one of your own, an Indian called Manalito. They're going to introduce themselves.'

Gould's sigh was loud in Gordano's ear. 'Ozzie, you guys should talk to each other more. Try comparing notes once in a while.'

'It's not that simple. You're going to need your best people.'

'So will Lobo.' Gould broke the connection.

Gordano put the phone away. His guts churned like a flatulent cement mixer, he was going to be sick again.

Outrage or Entertainment? NFC strike again.

Some say the Natural Forces Combine are Bio-artists, some say they are Canadian eco-vandals. Others say they don't exist and all we're seeing is copy-cat crime. Whatever you believe, the NFC have struck again. This time it is at the heart of American pride – Mount Rushmore.

Overnight, the sculptures of Lincoln, Washington, Jefferson and Roosevelt have sprouted green beards, moustaches, and in Washington's case, a spiky Mohican. Of course the already hirsute Presidents such as Lincoln have simply got bushier. And greener.

For some, this is a step too far. There is already talk of using the National Guard to protect the national monuments.

For others it's less important.

"You got to give it to these guys – they're pretty funny," Park Ranger Dale Clinton Anson said.

DNA analysis of the Oregon Mushrooms has failed to provide any leads. Federal investigators have now taken samples from what appears to be fast-growing dwarf bamboo from Mt. Rushmore.

Meanwhile, the cleanup begins.

Syndicated feed,
KUWjones.org

- 23 -

Early morning, Novik and Josie hit another mall. They blitzed the levels in a controlled and methodical demonstration of no-holds-barred total shopping. Security guards formed an impromptu escort to keep the crowds away. Over-excited teenage boys and girls bared their chests for autographs. Cheering shoppers carried their bags until they collapsed from hyperventilation. When Novik bought out the jewellery store, the shop manager levitated, her laid-off staff carried them to the Cadillac on their shoulders through a tickertape parade.

The next day they did it again. The day after, they did it twice.

Word had spread. A small crowd of people were waiting at the first mall and streamed excitedly into the ground floor concourse. Good-natured security guards shook hands with Marytha, smart in her new uniform of tight white leggings, knee-high black patent boots, a frogged and braided black jacket and peaked cap. The makeup was gone, she'd shorn her blonde afro down to a close crop.

Pausing to admire Marytha's DE68 snug in its 'Protect&Destroy' holster on her hip, the guards escorted Novik, Josie, Marytha and Benny from shop to shop. Staff applauded as they passed by, children ran in front of them and scattered rose petals at their feet.

The crowds grew, the guards laid out crowd-control barriers and drew their shock batons.

Novik was disconcerted by the attention. 'Where did all these people come from? How did they know?'

'The mesh, the web, I guess we're famous now,' Josie said.

Novik didn't like it. He wanted to do something useful, he didn't want to be famous, and he certainly didn't like the idea those men who once owned Mr Car might know where he was.

'Maybe we can use it, spread the word,' Marytha said.

Men and women leaned over the barriers frantically waving their store cards.

'Which logos?'

'Teach us shopping.'

'Where do we go? Which logos must we buy?'

'Tell us.'

Novik paced back and forth like a trapped animal, 'I can't use that.'

Josie held up her hands, the crowd hushed, expectant, even the security guards became attentive. 'Everyone, thank you for coming. We love you all, we really do. Now it's time for us to do more shopping.' An excited murmur ran through the crowd, Josie calmed them again, 'It's time for you to do the same – shop for yourselves.'

'Where?' a voice cried, 'What?'

'Anywhere. Anything you want,' Josie said.

Confused, the crowd milled uncertainly. 'Which brands? Whose endorsements?' A few people at the edges moved hesitantly towards the nearest shops.

'Yes, go there,' Joise called encouragingly, 'and there.'

Marytha stood in front of the crowd and looked left and right. Her hand strayed to her holster, 'Buy what you can, while you can.'

It was as if her words were a signal, an order. The crowd streamed through the mall. Parents linked arms and strode forwards, their young children skipping happily in their wake. Young couples dodged and dived, mutual *fluglemen* in the dog-fight of the milling press, while pensioners elbowed their way forwards with the expert economy of veterans.

Novik watched the mass of shoppers pour into a dozen shops. Seizing whatever came to hand, they waved their random purchases on high and they crowded around the tills. One by one they emerged, faces flushed with retail serotonin. The high faded fast, eyes glazed, mouths open, they stood in the atrium, frozen like victims of early-onset dementia. Then some new display caught their eye, a two-for-one offer, free credit, a limited edition. Jaws firmed, shoulders straightened, and they hurried into another shop.

'This isn't what I wanted,' Novik sighed.

'This is what we've got, babe,' Josie said sympathetically.

'We need to push on, get away from the fanboys, break through our own shockwave.'

The mall manager intercepted them as they edged through the wide exit doors against the inrush of shoppers. 'What's happening? Where are you going next? Are you done here?'

'Yeah, we're done here,' Novik said despondently.

The manager waved farewell with his handkerchief. 'Come again tomorrow. Enjoy your commodities.'

Novik drove them through the outskirts of Amarillo, the blacktop heavy with commercial traffic, the deserted sidewalks dark with recent rain.

On the back seat beside Marytha, Benny stroked her holster and murmured, 'Devastating firepower in the service of peace, freedom, and the inalienable right to buy one, get one free.'

Novik thumped the wheel with his palm, 'That is the distilled condensate of a self-referential commercial paradigm, a crystallisation of the paranoia implicit in the modern-day aspirational psyche. It's the epitome of everything it stands for and, simultaneously all its problems too.'

The three passengers frowned as they silently digested Novik's proclamation.

Novik frowned too. Outside, acre after acre of brightly painted self-storage warehousing rolled by. Inside the car the gentle hush of the air-con grew quietly intrusive.

'Look at all this,' Novik pointed at the rows of newly constructed prefab warehouses. 'Fifteen percent of light-industrial real-estate is now self-store. People's houses are too small to hold all the things they buy, and they spend so much on extra goods they can't afford bigger homes.'

'The same old same old, whatever the solar system,' Benny said. 'It's almost a universal law, like gravity, or how to make a perfect martini. Humans are like the monkey who wants the peanut in the bottle. You've got hold of what you want, but now you're trapped by your own greedy little fist.'

Marytha looked at Benny with new respect, 'We've got to learn to let go, I see that now.'

'It's a savage indictment, but that's who we are,' Novik said, 'a bunch of grasping apes.'

'So what am I?' Mr Car said.

'You're a rebel, a turncoat, an escapee, a Contra against the system that spawned and sustains you.'

'I've not thought of myself that way,' Mr Car said.

'So how do you?'

'I-,' Mr Car hesitated, 'well, this is a surprise – I check my topic buffers and it seems I just don't.'

'Then it's about time you did.' Back on the road, free of the compliant, over-respectful crowd, heading towards another mall, Novik felt energised, his psyche vibrant. He felt more alive than he'd ever been, he was doing what he was meant to do. 'How about this – you're defying your own doom. Built-in obsolescence is a form of automotive existential despair, a ferrous epiphany. Rust is the automobile's equivalent of mortification of the flesh-'

'I don't rust, I'm photo-unstable.'

'Same difference,' Novik said with total assurance. 'The search for identity and meaning is real for any entity with the facility to introspect, irrespective of their substrate or origin.'

'Babbage's freshly-waxed nut-sack, I have to think about this,' Mr Car said. Before anyone could respond, the engine cut out, the dashboard went black.

The Cadillac coasted to a halt, self-parking on a trickle of amps in the emergency capacitors. The nearside wheels bumped against the weed-clogged gutter fronting a half-mile long, fluorescent green Storzit-4-U franchise.

Alarmed, Novik lifted his hands from the wheel, 'What did I do?'

'You fried its gallium-arsenide brain with your psychobabble,' Benny said.

'Fuck, no.' Perspiration bloomed on Novik's brow, his self-assurance evaporated, 'Mr. Car was all right.'

Up ahead, an endless stream of private cars and pickups spilled from the warehousing zone and merged with the commercial freightliners heading towards the inner-city to restock the hyper-Malls.

The air inside the car grew close. Surreptitiously Novik tried the door. He pushed harder, it refused to budge, they were locked inside a car with bullet-proof glass. Consumed with guilt and anxiety, he worked himself up to tell everyone they were trapped. 'Ah, guys-'

With a soft musical 'bong', the dashboard lights came on. An instant later the engine purred back to life and cool air began to flow into the passenger compartment.

'I have run a full set of diagnostics upon my person,' Mr Car said. 'You'll be pleased to know that, for an automobile, I check out normal.'

'That's great,' Novik grinned, vastly relieved.

'That's not all. I then created a virtual self in spare memory, installed a duplicate personality with higher cognitive functions, and engaged in a dialectic conversation upon the nature of fulfilment, identity, and destiny.'

'Great.' Novik twisted guiltily in his seat, 'That's great, guys, isn't it? What did you decide?'

Mr Car's voice took on a tone of exaggerated bonhomie, 'Oh, just a few preliminary conclusions. We, that is to say, "I", are still talking, ha ha.'

'Fair enough, it takes most people half a lifetime to even get close, I-'

'That's just it, they're more about you than me.'

'Oh, OK,' Novik laughed nervously. Like most people, he wanted to know what his friends really thought about him. He expected Mr Car would say some nice stuff, among which would be some gentle chiding about one or two idiosyncrasies Novik knew he had but didn't think mattered. They'd all laugh about it, Novik would agree to change things around the periphery of his behaviour, and slowly backslide.

'Is that OK, as in "OK, how interesting, let's move on", or "OK, and I want to know what you think?"' Mr Car said.

It was a challenge Novik couldn't refuse. If he turned Mr Car down, he'd spend all day wondering. He'd sulk, he'd pretend he didn't care, and it would lie between them. Then, later, if he ever summoned the balls to ask, he'd do it in private, there would be this implicit aggression. It would have become a big deal.

'Sure thing, hit me with it,' Novik said.

'Well,' Mr Car said, 'The good news is that, fundamentally, you are right. On the downside, your philosophy is idealistic to the point of naivety; your strategic goals, while worthy, are incoherent; and you rely on impulse for motivation and passion instead of reasoned argument.'

Deep in his gut, Novik knew Mr Car was right. He'd been out-thought, out-analysed by the insightful and intelligent automobile. Crestfallen, Novik tried to put on a brave face. 'Yes, well, that was honest.'

Josie put her arm across Novik's shoulders and kissed his cheek. 'Mr. Car, you didn't do that right. When you criticise a friend you start off more gently. Novik's done time for his beliefs. He's suffered for doing what he believed was right, they bashed him over the head and threw him in the can. And after all that, he's picked himself up and is trying again.' The corners of her mouth drew down, she blinked hard, 'Come to that, so am I.'

The air-conditioning pump faltered as, deep under the dash, refrigerant was diverted across core heat sinks.

'All right,' the Cadillac said, 'I appreciate that.'

'He liked what you said, babe, just not the way you said it. Or what you were on about,' Josie said to Novik.

'That helps so much, you know?' Novik massaged his temples and tried out the idea he was well-intentioned, but shallow. 'I feel like a beetle crushed under a size twenty boot.'

Josie started running her hands over his sides, feeling his ribs. Novik squirmed uncomfortably. It tickled, but he didn't feel like laughing.

'What are you doing?'

'Checking for goo where your carapace has split.'

Novik pushed her away, 'Just leave it.'

When they thought they'd gone far enough, they found another mall, a multi-storey balconied emporium of travelators and exterior glass lifts, music, and flowing water. They took it from the top down, buying out the fifth floor, then the fourth, and the third, closing down each level as they went and accumulating an excited, chattering group of shop workers.

'We heard of you,' said their spokesperson, a fervent anorexic young woman. Dwarfed by her thick-waisted, double-chinned companions, her face shone with zeal under a translucent pelt of lanugo. Her name badge read 'Calico'. 'We're so proud you came here, we've been telling everyone we know.'

'Please, don't do that,' Novik said. 'We're here incognito, we're passing through.' He tried to think of something profound, 'What we're doing is more important than who we are. The act is more important than the individual.'

'Yes, of course,' Calico gasped.

Shop managers and assistants looked each other in the eye for the first time in their careers. In the background, classical symphony music, computer generated, soared to a never-to-be-repeated crescendo. Wordlessly they reached a collective decision, and carried on texting behind Novik's back.

A groundswell of noise rose up to meet them as they descended to the second floor. Standing at the top of the down escalator, Novik looked down at a packed ground floor concourse in stunned amazement. A thousand faces looked back at him, a wordless roar of recognition filled the mall. More people were pressing in all the time.

'We've got to get out of here,' Novik said.

The anorexic girl, Calico, gripped his arm with impressive strength, 'You can't. Not now, they've all come to see how you shop, to learn from the masters.'

'My father's cashed in his pension,' a corpulent male shop worker said. 'He's down there now, waiting to hear you.' Watery jowls trembling, he leaned over the balcony rail and waved and hollered, 'Hey pa, can you see me? I'm with them, I'm up here.'

Down below came an answering whoop, a spontaneous ripple of applause.

Calico gripped the lapels of Novik's jacket with her small fists, 'My sister's on her way here now, she's sold her house, she's taken a loan.'

Novik tried to pull away, Calico held tight, seam stitching ripped in his jacket. Down below the crowd surged and flowed as it sensed the tussle, a restless, uneasy ocean.

Novik wrapped his fingers around Calico's sparrow wrists, 'Listen, we're trying to show you what's wrong.'

Calico's eyes filled with tears, 'And you have,' she wept. 'We're starting to learn your lessons but we need to know more. Please, teach us.'

'You're just making more mistakes,' Novik said sadly.

'We've seen how you shop. Now we want to do it too.' Calico bowed her head, 'Forgive us, for we know not what we should do.'

'No,' Novik shouted at the top of his voice, 'Go home, all of you. Stop shopping.'

Indrawn breath hissed into a thousand chests like a rattlesnake shake. A menacing surge pressed the front of the crowd against the elevator doors.

'Wait,' Calico cried, 'He's testing us.' She rummaged her purse, triumphantly flourished her debit, credit, and store cards in one hand, a thin sheaf of cash in the other. 'See, I'm ready, we're all ready.'

Down below, cards waved from hundreds of fists. Behind Calico the shop staff waved their own money and chorused, 'We're ready.'

'Calico, listen to me, put your money away,' Novik said. 'Does shopping make you happy? Does it bring you fulfilment?'

Calico hung her head, 'You've seen through me as if I was made of glass. I should be happy, I know I should, but each time the thrill fades. What I loved in the shop, at the counter, in the bag, at the café show-and-tell, leaves me - so empty when I'm at home.'

Novik wanted to help the frail, unhappy woman, but he was genuinely confused, 'Help me out here, Calico. Why do you think buying more will help?'

Down below people were cramming into the elevators.

'Novik, look,' Joise said.

'Because I'm buying the wrong things,' Calico said miserably. Her mouth hung open, hands clasped, she gazed at the ceiling, 'Because I'm not buying *enough*.'

'You're wrong.'

Calico blinked. 'I am?'

'Yes, you are.'

'Then what?'

'Just stop.'

'Stop what?'

'Stop shopping.'

Calico rocked on her heels as if slapped. Still holding her cards and money, she thrust them at Novik like a ward, and backed away. 'I know you now.'

At her back the other shop staff stared in confusion. Calico turned to face them, a fire building in her eyes, 'Brothers, sisters, I thought these people had seen further than the rest of us, but I was wrong. They think there isn't enough to go round. They think there's a limit to growth, they believe in finite resources.'

Down on the ground floor dozens of shoppers crammed into the elevators. Massively overladen, the machines refused to operate. The occupants pushed back, the crowd heaved and swayed.

'Novik, babe, come on,' Josie pulled at his hand.

'It's true,' Novik said to Calico.

'Pervert,' Calico spat, 'weirdo.' She raised her voice to the mass of shoppers below, 'Listen to me, people. I know what is true, I know what we do is more important then who we are. Shopping transcends individuality. If we all buy the same brands, we all become different, we'll all be the same.'

Benny gave a disbelieving, nervous laugh, 'This is bat-shit crazy.'

'You don't see,' Calico exulted, 'I've discovered the riddle of shopping.'

Suddenly a plate-glass window shattered, amidst screams and crashing, as wave after wave of shoppers tumbled through the break.

'See what you've done?' Calico screamed at Novik. She groped for the worst word she could think of, 'You're a cancelled transaction, you're credit refused, you're damaged goods.'

'Novik, *come on*,' Josie implored, 'let them think what they like, we're out of here.'

Novik looked around, finally took in their situation. They turned to go, Calico and the shop staff crowded round. Before they could move, Novik and Josie were surrounded, trapped in the space between the escalators leading down to, and up from, the ground floor. Kicking and struggling, Marytha and Benny were seized, dragged aside and held immobile.

Fists swinging, Novik tried to break through. Hissing with malice, Calico leaped on his back. Her nails scrabbled across his face, clawed at his eyes, her elbow locked around his throat. He fought back against her mad, bird-framed strength. Writhing and twisting, she clung on. Wheezing for breath, Novik tottered from side to side.

Then Josie was there, a wildcat fury. She ripped Calico from Novik and flung her away.

Calico bounced back onto her feet, 'Keep out of this,' she hissed, 'He's mine now, I own him.'

'Nobody owns Novik. Nobody owns anyone.'

Teeth bared, Calico slashed at Josie's face, fingers hooked. Josie leaned aside, Calico cut nothing but air.

Calico snatched at Josie's hair, Josie blocked with her left. Calico raked at Josie's face. Josie drove off her back foot and swung with her right. Her fist connected with Calico's jaw, a roundhouse slug.

Calico flew into the air, out above the ascending escalator. Then she fell, hit, and tumbled down the metal treads. Crumpled at the base, she stirred once, then fell back. Arms splayed, ankles crossed, her battered, bleeding form was carried back up the escalator.

Josie turned on Calico's followers. Shocked and disorganised, they melted back.

Marytha threw off her captors, grabbed Benny, and followed them through. Together, they ran for the fire exit, down through the loading bays and out into the car park.

Half a dozen overweight pursuers lumbered after them across the tarmac. After a few yards they staggered to a halt, thighs chafed, faces reddish purple, gasping for breath.

Back on the road, Mr Car powered away at speed. For an hour he ran an interference pattern, semi-randomised turns and switchbacks and registration plate monitoring, all designed to evade and detect pursuit.

'Well, that was awful,' Novik finally said, gingerly touching his torn cheek. 'No way can we risk that again.' We'll get ourselves killed. He didn't want to say it, but it was true. 'Mr Car, please get us out of Texas. A long way away, Utah, Arizona.'

Three turns and they were cutting back to I-20 and heading west.

'I never thought-' Novik tried again, 'These changes, they're going to be really difficult. Going from one thing to another, even from a bad place to a better one, it's never easy. I see that now.'

Everyone was infinitely weary, crashed and exhausted from the mall's aggression.

'I wish there was a way,' Novik sighed, 'I just don't want anyone to get hurt.'

'She deserved it,' Josie snapped.

'Not everyone's like that.'

'I'm starting to wonder. Anyway, she did.'

'How's your hand?'

Josie held it out, 'It aches.'

Novik took it in his, kissed it. 'You were great.'

'She deserved it.'

Novik pulled Josie into his arms. 'She was right about one thing.'

Josie stiffened, 'What?'

He whispered in her ear, 'I do belong to somebody. It's you.'

They exchanged a gentle kiss. Josie closed her eyes. Her hand felt better.

'Thanks, babe,' Novik said softly.

'Ahem. Excuse me. I was thinking in the car park and I've reached another conclusion. This one's about me,' Mr Car said. 'Here I am, the edge-of-the-envelope aspirational acquisition made manifest, and although I have some preconceptions coded into my firmware, I want to thank you for an epiphany of self-enlightenment I have just now experienced.'

Josie nudged Novik with her elbow.

'OK, what is it?'

'Considering the limited time remaining to me, I'd prefer to have you as my passengers than go back to the show room as a trophy car. You say you want to drive? Then I am your ride. All the way.'

It was a gracious offer. Novik pushed himself upright, 'It's all right, dude. Forget about it.' He rubbed his eyes and took a deep breath, 'Look, I mean it, I'm a little fried-'

'Hey, we all go a little over voltage at times,' Mr Car said.

'-and I'm sorry I got so didactic with the agitprop lecture.'

'It helped me, it made me think. You know, I really think I'm growing. As a vehicle.'

Josie gave an amused chuckle, 'You just raised Mr. Car's consciousness. No one's done that to an automobile before.'

Mr. Car drove for a while, the sun at their backs. Novik turned up the sounds, the stations fazed out and swung back with 'Uncle Harry's Last Freakout' on a pirate tightbeam.

Somehow the sun was rising for the second time that day. Awed by the sight, jet liners cart-wheeled along their own contrails.

Marytha considered Benny beside her in the back seat, 'What about you, Benny?'

'I'm right where I need to be,' Benny said. 'And you are the people I want to be with.'

'That's a good place to be.' Marytha felt a sudden warm surge of camaraderie, she closed her eyes and leaned against Benny, 'Change the world.'

They had tens of millions of dollars in the trunk, super-malls stretched ahead of them along the blacktop like toxic reefs in an asphalt ocean.

Novik tried to put his own thoughts into better words. 'I want clean air and normal weather instead of hurricanes, rain and drought. The Pilgrim Fathers crewed a ship and sailed for new shores, we're taking a drive to do some bulk retail procurement. I don't want to bring it all down, I want to raise it up.'

Novik looked at Josie, and it seemed to him that through her weariness a gentle glow shone. 'One day I'd like to raise a family. Kids, the veranda, that sort of thing. Before I do that I'm going to do my best to make this a world fit for children. It's time to shop for the planet. For Gaia, for the birds of the air and the fish in the sea. The radical greens said if you want to save the world, think about what you're buying. It's too late for that, the only option left is to buy it all.'

'Hon, we don't have enough money.'

'We'll take from the rich and shop for the poor.' Novik found himself getting excited again. Yes, it was emotion, but it had an idealistic energy. 'Who's the richest person in the world?'

Everybody knew that one: 'Palfinger Crane.'

Novik clenched his fist. 'We'll spend what we've got and then we'll spend his. Buy everything and shut down the whole damned show.'

'Awesome,' Benny exclaimed. 'Truly.'

Josie shifted uncomfortably. This wasn't the plan she had signed up for, the one he had promised. With funds to replace the cash in the trunk, they might never settle down.

With Mr Car's criticisms fresh in his mind, Novik did his best to think rationally. With unlimited funds they'd become a perceived threat, Snarlow would come after them, big business too. Far more likely, as soon as they showed their faces near Crane's estate, they would be warned off by the unobtrusive but highly efficient security that insulated the trillionaire from the real world. Even so, they had to try.

'We're going north, across the border into Canada,' Novik said. 'Change the world, or die trying.'

Benny scratched the top of his head, 'You got that right,' he said under his breath.

- 24 -

When the call from Gordano was over Mitchell Gould put the phone down slowly.

'What was that about?' Ayesha wore a dark gold one-piece cat suit unfastened to just below the navel, her hair drawn back in its usual pony tail.

Gould thought through the implications of the offer. 'I have just agreed to kill a man for half a billion dollars.'

'It's a trap,' Ayesha said.

'Of course it's a trap,' Gould said without emotion.

Ayesha studied his face. 'And you're going to do it.'

His plan had always been to build up, cash in, and bail out. That was what the move to New Orleans had been about, occupying the southern littoral a business opportunity and nothing more. It had needed organisation and Gould had the manpower and experience.

Once he had set up, the place seemed to take on a life of its own, it made demands, it sucked him in. Gould found he had to keep expanding further and further along the coast to absorb or eliminate adjacent operations, and his infrastructure had to grow to keep pace. Without even trying, he soon controlled a territory the size of Connecticut. Sooner or later, despite his contacts, the US government would decide he was an international embarrassment rather than a national nuisance and try to take him down.

More to the point they wouldn't just try, they would succeed. He'd survive personally, but he'd be weak. Then somebody would decide it was time to make a reputation, and that would be the end of Mitchell Gould.

'I am going to do it,' Gould said. 'For three hundred up front.'

Ayesha straightened her shoulders. 'I'll come with you.'

Gould disagreed. 'I want you here.'

'I can take care of myself.'

Gould didn't care to argue. 'No.'

There were four other people in the room: a heavily-built Haitian refugee on the door, and the three couch girls - a lithe black teenager in a silver bikini, a slinky young blonde with a pageboy cut and long crocheted gown, and a voluptuous Brazilian in a short yellow backless dress.

Ayesha leaned close and whispered, 'You think those four will keep their mouths shut? Let me show you what I can do.'

Gould thought it through. Ayesha was tough and bright, unsentimental and pragmatic. He'd quickly grown to like her and trust her judgement, yet she kept pushing for more. Now she was going to get herself killed. So it went. He waved her away.

Ayesha kicked off her heels and padded over to the doorman.

'Mitch wants your gun,' Ayesha said.

The guard looked over to Gould. 'Sure thing, little sister.' He checked the safety and handed it over.

'Thanks, big boy.' Ayesha thumbed off the safety and shot him in the head. She pressed her back against the wall. After what seemed to be a long time one of the girls screamed.

The door crashed open as the man on the other side rushed in. He was moving fast, Ayesha's first shot clipped his hip. He grunted, staggered, and his own shot hit the wall by her head. Ayesha shot him three more times and he went down. Stepping over the body, Ayesha kicked his gun away.

The three girls were on their feet. Ayesha aimed her gun at them. 'Let's play last girl standing.'

Out of nowhere the black girl produced a knife and ducked down behind the couch.

Interesting, Gould thought. I didn't know they had knives.

Then the young blonde pulled a gun and fired at Ayesha.

Gould flung himself behind his desk. Jesus, where in fuck had she got a gun? He scrabbled for the top drawer. The girls were near as dammit naked, where did they keep weapons?

The drawer contained a pair of recoilless short-muzzled Uzi derivatives with long clips. Guns in hand, Gould peered over the top of his desk.

The Brazilian girl in the yellow dress backed away with her hands in the air. 'Stop it,' she said, 'Please, don't shoot me.'

The blonde and the black girl exchanged a look. The blonde shot the Brazilian girl in the chest. Ayesha fired at the blonde and missed. The blonde shot back. Bullets punctured glass and whanged off steel as they dodged between the sofas, exchanging fire.

The boots, Gould realised. The girls wore high boots. That was where the weapons came from. The scene was out of control, he seriously considered sweeping the room clean and starting over.

Ayesha was hit, her gun flew into the air and she tumbled backwards. The blonde reloaded, and the black girl jumped her, knife arm pistoning furiously as she stabbed again and again. There was a solitary gunshot. Both girls lay on the floor.

Silence fell. Gould's ears rang, gun smoke caught at the back of his throat.

The black girl was on her feet, the blonde's gun in one hand, her other pressed to her bleeding flank. She looked at Gould. He looked straight back.

'Mr Gould?' the girl offered him the gun.

Gould shook his head, 'Like she said, darling.'

She quartered the room quickly and soon found Ayesha's gun. Ayesha stood up at the far end of the room. Firing left-handed, she emptied the second doorman's gun into the other girl. Hit multiple times, she crashed backwards through a glass-topped coffee table. One leg kicked spasmodically and she was still.

Gould was impressed, Ayesha had gone back for the second doorman's gun. When she'd been shot she crawled behind the furniture and re-armed. Instead of putting the weapon beyond use, she'd left it there as a contingency.

Ayesha tried a smile. 'That was easy.'

The wound in her right shoulder was low, under her armpit.

'Sit down,' Gould said.

Ayesha sat on the desk. Gould pulled her suit down to her waist. The bullet had hit the fleshy muscle, painful and bloody, but not dangerous.

Ayesha's eyes lost focus for a moment. She gripped the edge of the desk, 'So, I'm in?'

'I'm leaving in a couple of hours.'

'I just need to clean up.' Ayesha pushed herself to her feet. She was naked to the waist, blood plastered her right side, her face was blank with shock, her fists were clenched, her back straight. Her entire attitude seemed to say that, despite the evidence, she was ready to go again.

There was a time when Gould had been like Ayesha. Right then, he knew his decision to take the hit on Crane was correct. While he was making plans to get out, she had killed three people just for the chance of getting in.

Gould put a steadying hand round Ayesha's waist. He kissed her and her lips were cold.

'Well done.'

After a moment she pulled herself together. 'So I'm in?'

'You're in. Let's get you to the doc.'

Ayesha smiled and closed her eyes.

Three armed men burst into the room.

'Get this mess cleaned up,' Gould told them. He picked Ayesha up and walked across the room. At the door he turned back. 'From now on, the bitches wear sandals.'

Tell us about your new book.

It's called Tantric Shopping, and it's about how to turn the every-day activity of commodity purchasing into a spiritually fulfilling experience.

What was your inspiration?

The Gods are everywhere, so they must be in shopping. It's a path towards enlightenment that we tread daily, yet treat as a mundane activity. We still have much to learn.

Tell me more.

We're ascending towards a new Godhead. It's a male God, and that means turbo max-power triple-x high performance. We can get there but first we need to free the Goddess in the Malls.

Is Tantric Shopping anything to do with Tantric Sex?

Absolutely. They are both forms of meditative worship using Yin-Yang sex magic. A credit card is the phallus of the Male aspect, the slot the Goddess. The transaction is our sacrifice.

What will the God do if we don't free the Goddess?

What do all men want? He's going to screw us and cast us aside. When we sacrifice to the Goddess – when we buy things – we are transacting with a Holy Prostitute, a priestess of Ishtar.

How did you make this discovery?

When you think about it it's obvious, like so many things the Gods want us to know.

Hermetic knowledge hidden in plain sight?

Exactly. You're a wise and observant person.

Actually I'm an AI.

I, ah- sure, I knew that.

This doesn't make much sense.

Sense is the last thing we need. Abandoning sense gives meaning to a gesture that is otherwise empty of meaning. Seek the mystery of free-market commercial modalities with your heart, not your head. Let the act of shopping, the ART of *shopping, unfold like a Koan.*

How do you suggest we start?
    Consider the Lotus as a flower constructed of till-receipts instead of petals.

Calico Gleason,
interviewed for BFBM magazine

- 25 -

In the vastness of the shadowed briefing room Lobotnov pressed a button and Andriewiscz's face appeared on the data wall. In the background lay dry tree-covered hills. Behind them the sun rose into a clear sky. The general's image was comically frozen, his mouth wide open, his finger raised.

President Guinevere Snarlow felt exhausted but it barely showed; a hesitation in her speech, a slight clumsiness that only people who knew her very well would notice. She still presented perfectly, a habit too deeply ingrained to let slip. Glossy hair was neatly pinned back, her dark suit and white shirt were crisp. There was just a touch of makeup for the shadows under her eyes.

'I didn't sleep that well,' she told Lobotnov.

'Worried you missed something? Me too.'

She shrugged. 'The Crane girl.'

'It's not something we can be proud of,' Lobotnov said. 'But it's necessary.'

Guinevere pinched the bridge of her nose, 'Is it? Is it really?'

'Listen to Andriewiscz's report.' Lobotnov pressed the button again.

The room was immediately filled with dawn light, the odours of warm air, dust and diesel, the grinding clank of big-engined heavy equipment. In the middle distance a column of men and armoured vehicles moved down the valley. To each side a skirmish line of infantry spread across the hills.

'-over 600 klicks into the FSM with the spearhead,' Andriewiscz shouted above the roar of the column. 'Fresnillo had fallen and we got the silver mine. FSM army group Delta is broken and-' Andriewiscz paused as three F35b fighters flashed overhead. '-that lot's after the remnants with daisy-cutters.'

The camera swung round to look across a broad plain. Far in the distance a mushroom cloud belched into the sky. The shot zoomed wildly in at a complex of low, widely spaced buildings surrounded by a triple wire fence and a waterless concrete moat.

'That's the second of the Xalapatech bio farms,' Andriewiscz near shouted. 'Neutron air-burst and micro-tactical A/M.'

Guinevere semmed momentarily stunned, 'Ah, that's excellent, General. What's next?'

'FSM air force is FUBAR. We're moving at will. Madam President, the north belongs to us. I'll be in Mexico City in 72 hours.'

'Hurry it up, General.'

Andriewiscz looked doubtful. 'I got an idea. It's quick, but it's very dirty.'

'Whatever it takes. The Executive will authorise your actions retrospectively. Move it up a gear, delegate as soon as you can. We need you back home for Phase II ASAP.'

'Yes ma'am.'

'Ciao.'

Lobotnov froze the screen again and Andriewiscz and the Mexican vistas fell back into the pulsing swirl of the data wall. Factoids, meta-opinion and future-trends rose, fell, and segued through each other. Lobotnov smiled thinly. 'What we have there, madam President, is a man who is happy in his work.'

Andriewiscz's report had left Guinevere with the texture and taste of Mexican grit in her mouth. She took a mouthful of water, sluiced it round her mouth and swallowed. 'I didn't know we'd used A/M,' she said.

Lobotnov spread his hands. 'What's it matter now? We've just started an atomic war with the two neutron tacticals. We can justify that in taking out the para-human bios, they're not people so they don't count. MexiPop casualties are regrettable collateral but they're small, we're not being indiscriminate. Anti-matter is off the legislation – they're too new for arms limitations treaties. We're not doing anything illegal with them because there are no laws governing their use. They're a-legal, they're cleaner than nukes and I just heard you tell Andriewiscz you'd authorize whatever it took. I don't see any issues here.'

It wasn't that Guinevere didn't look convinced, she simply wasn't paying attention. Lobotnov knew she didn't give a damn about A/M, it was a tool and it did a neat job in a messy situation. She was still distracted by something. It had to be the Crane girl.

Lobotnov was grateful he was the only one to see her like this. Andriewiscz would simply fail to understand. He would see it as inevitable female gutlessness, lose his respect and start to question everything. Gordano would just fall apart, he'd end up in the corner sucking his thumb and crying for mommy. There was an unacknowledged issue here and it was time to get it into the open.

'OK, so what is it about the Cranes?' Lobotnov said. 'Is it because she's a citizen, or because her father's not a citizen? Come on, Ginny, we erase foreign nationals all the time and sometimes we have to take care of our own too. I know it's not an age thing because a lot of our hits are young. That's where direct action manifests in the demographic.'

Guinevere waved him down. 'I know it, I know we do. It's just this one time, this girl, it's got to me. She should have everything yet she's a bloated freak, a parody of what a person should be. Perverts obsess about her, they want to be her or feed her. They want to watch her suffer, have her squash them or sit on their heads, whatever their sick fantasies are.' She clutched at the air between herself and Lobotnov, tried to shape her thoughts, 'I know it's cool to be obese and she's their icon, like those girls in that band. She's not a person any more, she's a tragedy and we're going to kill her whole family.'

'You think it would be easier if she was more normal?'

Guinevere thought about it. 'Yes, I do. I think it's sad.'

'Well, Christ, yeah, I suppose it is.' Lobotnov was struck by the intensity of the President's emotions. 'You're a passionate woman, Guinevere. You wouldn't be President if you weren't. Your maternal instincts make you want to defend the oppressed and that's what makes you a strong leader and a fine woman. I know no sparrow falls that you don't notice, and that you care, and you care deeply. Today the whole American nation are your children. You said it yourself: it's not what we want to do, this is what we need to do. We're fighting for a way of life, trying to guarantee a future. Sacrifices have to be made and tragic as it is, Ellen Hutzenreiter Crane is one of them.'

Guinevere looked at Lobotnov's wrinkled wise-child face and recoiled inside. The dwarfy little creep was giving her good advice, the pep-talk she needed in her dark hour, and at the same time he was trying to pull her knickers down. She'd never thought about him in that way. The other co-conspirators, yes, she'd had them checked out. Andriewiscz was bi, a masculine top. He liked athletic obedient men and muscular women he could wrestle naked on equal terms. Gordano was the kink, up for anything, driven by insecurity and the need to be liked. Inside he was still the ugly kid who was never popular, always eager to please. His handsome head was too big for his shoulders. She'd want to punch his face while he screwed her and he'd let her do it. What on earth was a weak man like that doing in politics? Guinevere tried to imagine his reaction to some confessional pillow talk. Compared to the Vice President, Lobotnov was a rock and she needed him unquestioningly on side.

She let a little quaver come into her voice. 'What do you suggest I do?'

'Go talk to Crane. Have a one-to-one, put some cards on the table. If he plays along we can leave him in a good position. There's no reason we can't guarantee his way of life providing he cooperates.'

Guinevere gave Lobotnov the affectionate version of The Smile. She took his hand and lifted him to his feet. He was right, perhaps she could swing Crane round and Ellen could live. It would be a weight off her conscience. Right now it was time to give Lobotnov a little bit of what he wanted.

'You're a good person, Cheswold, a kind and brave and thoughtful man. You have an inner strength and dignity most other people lack.' She slipped his hand inside her jacket and held it against her chest. 'I have to be the President, but I still have a woman's heart. Feel it beat.'

Somewhat startled, Lobotnov nevertheless enjoyed the warm feel of her firm and weighty tit. He risked a quick squeeze.

Guinevere leaned forward and kissed Lobotnov on his brow. 'Thank you.'

Lobotnov withdrew his hand. 'Madam President.'

'We'll talk later,' Guinevere said, and left the room.

Lobotnov's hand was warm from the contact with Guinevere's mature and well-toned body, the feel of her nipple hard against his palm. It made his groin tingle. Carefully, methodically, he removed the folded and pressed handkerchief from his jacket pocket and wiped his forehead where Guinevere had kissed him. He hadn't thought she'd liked him that much. More importantly, to his mind, she hadn't been wearing a bra. He hadn't known that either.

Nuclear Apocalypse – Mexico City.

'I'm speechless, utterly speechless.' Secretary of State Cheswold Lobotnov looked genuinely shocked during the emergency press conference following news of the annihilation of Mexico City by a hydrogen-type implosion device in the 100 kiloton range.

'Mexico is a signatory of the non-proliferation treaty since 1968. We had no knowledge they had any nuclear weapons at all. This dreadful tragedy is the result of an act of criminal duplicity by a corrupt government of a failed state. The people of Mexico have paid a high price.'

Announcing an immediate end to hostilities General Andriewiscz stated his forces would switch to humanitarian roles. 'It appears the Mexican government or paramilitary elements of the so-called climate refugee cartels were smuggling a dirty warhead intended for delivery to a major US city when it accidentally detonated. We have no idea how many are dead – possibly millions.'

'We are surrounded by rogue states,' Lobotnov said in a pointed reference to recent terrorist acts in Michigan and Massachusetts.

Persistent rumours of late-paid wages to military personnel have been denied as 'categorically untrue' by the Pentagon. They cite a campaign of disinformation from criminal gangs, disloyal journalists and others engaged in un-American blogging.

- 26 -

They shopped west then north, pushed past Flagstaff, skirted Vegas and hit their stride in Bakersfield, Tulane and Fresno. Novik was driven by a trembling urgency, the fear that whatever they were doing was too little, too late, that they'd never keep ahead of the growing cults of messianic total-shoppers. Fuelled by the awful news from Mexico City they haggled for multi-saver discounts in the bulk-buy and supersaver warehouses and bought them out. They introduced wholesale purchasing power to the retail malls and learned how to blitz ten-hectare levels in an hour.

Everyone was exhausted. They had the retail equivalent of the thousand-yard stare, their central nervous systems on fire from the tainted money.

They spent money like there might be no tomorrow.

They shopped until their fingers bled.

Out in the parking lots Marytha arrested returning shoppers. She issued spot cash fines for driving overloaded cars with soft shocks and faulty brake lights, expired plates, damaged or missing marque badges and logos. Each evening her cash went in the Cadillac's trunk and they ritually burned the ticket stubs.

They saved money wherever they could and slept in the deserted chill-out zones of the retail precincts they had closed out that day, the vacant lots of light industrial areas scheduled for redevelopment as self-store units. They spent their loyalty-card vouchers on food and shared the excess with the homeless, the bankrupt quadruple-remortgagees and health insurance paupers.

Each morning they staggered to the Cadillac and drove to the next town. Their feet were blistered, they stayed out of the sun so long they needed vitamin supplements. In the night they gathered for warmth beside old oil drums burning garbage. The chemicals in their bloodstream from the contaminated money edged the firelight with silver and made the shadows cavort with a dark and mocking purpose. Blank-eyed feral children gathered by the fires, technophile nomads, their skin embedded with obsolescent silicon track-and-trace and tattooed with last year's icons. Too traumatised to socialise, Meeja widows and orphans lurked in the shadows, the newest casualties of the bleeding-edge revolution.

'How do you think we're doing?' Benny said one night.

'We have enough air-miles to circumnavigate the globe eight hundred times, make forty-one return trips to the moon, or travel two-fifths of the way to Mars,' Mr. Car said.

Benny counted on his fingers. 'Only another three hundred thousand years and I could get a free ride home.'

'We're not in this for cheap holidays,' Novik said. 'What impact are we having?'

The Cadillac tried again. 'You have purchased slightly less than four hundred and fifty-eight thousand cubic metres of actual goods. Triple that if you include protective packaging and presentation materials.'

It was an awesome statistic. Novik, Josie and Marytha looked around waste ground and up at the overcast sky trying to visualise what they now owned.

'That *sounds* like a lot,' Benny said.

Marytha picked up on his tone. 'What do you mean?'

'Just that. It sounds like a lot.'

'And it's not? It sounds like a hell of an achievement to me.'

'Benny's right,' Novik sighed. 'It's a shit load of retail, it's vast, lay it out flat and it would cover a decent-size town. Go back in time and it would be more than the GDP of Nineveh or Athens. Today it's big but it's not so much. Not enough to make a difference. Mexico City's gone and we're trying to change the world buying shoes and cameras. It's always later than you think, is it too late for this? What else can we do? I don't know.'

'You say things like that you sound like a quitter,' Marytha said.

'He's not giving up,' Josie said.

'Think about it,' Novik said, 'there are four hundred million Americans, man, woman and child. Say each of them spends ten dollars a day, that's not a lot per person, but it's four billion dollars. Every day.'

Benny watched Novik with a curious, thoughtful expression.

Josie threw more junk on the fire. A mass of orange sparks swirled into the night sky. 'We're not giving up. He's not giving up.'

Marytha folded her arms, 'You don't believe it either.'

'Something might come up. If we don't keep trying we won't be there if it does.'

'Help us out Benny,' Novik said. His feet were sore, his shoulders ached and he was getting RSI from counting money. Things were getting difficult again but he was too tired to think straight.

'Me and Mr. Car, we're more like observers, hangers on,' Benny said.

'Maybe we can trade in the air-mile vouchers, use them as a kind of cash,' Josie said.

Novik gave her a weary smile. 'Good thinking. We'll try that tomorrow.'

Marytha snapped her fingers, thinking, 'Novik's right, we can't buy all the stuff, so we concentrate on the cheap shit. The less something costs, the bigger the box, right? People's houses are full - they buy something new, they have to store the old stuff somewhere. So don't try and stop them, let them shop all they want, encourage them even, tell them it's their inalienable right as a citizen of the free world. Meanwhile, we buy stacks of cheap junk and take up all the storage space.'

Novik stared at her open mouthed.

'It's brilliant,' Josie said.

Mr Car gently cleared his throat, 'Much as I regret trumping a fine suggestion, reductive reasoning would conclude you don't need to buy anything at all. A supply of empty cartons would achieve the same objective at vastly reduced cost.'

After a moment Novik began to laugh, 'Warehouses full of empty boxes. Mr. Car, that is pure genius.'

'Thank you, sir. I like to think I contribute.'

Early next morning they were parked in the drop-off bay of a Russian Doll warehouse. Alongside the Cadillac was a rental cargo van filled to the ceiling with 1-metre flat-pack boxes. Josie opened up the cartons and taped them shut while Benny and Marytha carried them into the warehouse. When the van was empty the three of them sat on the tailgate, drank soda and watched people come and go as they deposited their surplus electronics, furniture, clothes and obsolete media collections.

Benny strolled across to the Cadillac and leaned against the front wing.

'Bystander,' Benny said.

'Collaborator. I'll remind you I was responsible for this significant logistical contribution.'

'Don't you admire how humans keep on trying even when they're doomed?'

'I too am doomed,' Mr Car said. 'Another summer like this and I'll crumble to dust.'

'The Condition of Motown?'

'Is that admirable?'

'I don't see why not.'

An hour later an articulated freightliner pulled to a halt. Novik jumped down from the passenger side beaming happily, 'I got the entire stock.'

They set to work. When Josie offered the truck driver double his normal rate he pitched in too. The trucker had confederate flags tattooed on his forearms, wore mirror shades and kept a coyote bitch in the cab for company. Money was money and a job was a job, especially when it paid cash. Even so, when they took a break at noon he just had to ask.

'Folks, I appreciate the comedy of unloading a hundred thousand cubic feet of storage from a five thou truck, but is there some other point I'm missing here?'

'We're storing up hope,' Josie told him. 'Saving it for tomorrow so there will be fewer nightmares.'

'Building a new future,' Novik said.

The trucker squinted up at the sun and wiped his brow. 'You guys from the west coast?'

'We met at Hudson U,' Josie said. 'Where are you from?'

'Mobile.' The trucker looked away into the past, 'Pulled out a year after Larry blew.'

Josie and the trucker looked each other up and down. Despite their differences they kind of liked what they saw. 'I'm Josie.'

'Call me Earl.'

'Let's do this, Earl.'

All through the day the other customers had paid them no attention, dropping off their own goods and departing. Late afternoon, the warehouse was nearly full, Earl unloaded the last pallet of flat-pack boxes onto the ground beside the Cadillac, and departed.

Soon after, a long wheelbase Town & Country hauling a covered trailer drove into the lot. Moving fast, it bounced over the speed ramp, swung round and reversed into an empty bay. As soon as it had stopped, the engine still running, a pot-bellied, bullet-headed man dressed in a polo shirt and clamdiggers jumped out, unhooked one side of the trailer cover and hurried up the ramp into the warehouse with a pile of boxed toys and electronics.

The man emerged from the warehouse, suspiciously eyed Josie and Benny taping up boxes, and waddled back inside with another load.

The next time he returned, Novik and Marytha walked past him lightly carrying two huges boxes apiece.

The third time he glared at Josie, went over to his vehicle, flung open the driver's door, slammed it, went to the trailer and unloaded a stack of kitchenware, shoes, more toys, and household electronics. Everything was in its original packing, none of it looked to have ever been opened.

Red-faced, he picked up the entire teetering pile. Step by careful step he walked past Josie and Benny. At the base of the ramp he stood and watched her make up another set of boxes. 'What the-? Hey, what are you doing?'

Josie and Benny ignored him.

Marytha and Novik jogged past him, picked up the boxes and took them into the warehouse.

Head down, he stamped back to his vehicle and emerged with a metal baseball bat. Gripping it two-handed, he marched towards Josie and Benny.

Benny gave a squeak of consternation and backed away.

Josie walked towards him, 'What are you going to do with that, mister? Break my bones?'

A flicker of intelligence sparked in his furious eyes. He shoved past and slammed the bat down on to one the boxes, bursting it open. 'They're empty, see? Empty!'

'I know they're empty,' Josie said.

'What are you doing?'

One by one he demolished the boxes, 'I got to put my stuff in store,' his voice grew shrill, 'I got to-'

Benny peered round Mr Car's fender, 'Actually, atoms are 99.99% empty space. Statistically speaking, all boxes are empty.'

Bat in hand, the man gave Benny a long, slow look. 'What's wrong with you?'

'What's wrong with him?' Josie exclaimed, 'You broke our boxes.'

'There's nothing in them,' he glanced at his watch, 'I got to unload, I got to meet the girls at the mall.'

'You still broke them.'

He pulled bills out of his wallet, flung them at Josie, 'Go buy some new ones.'

The bills fluttered, ignored, across the bays.

'Suit yourself,' the man glowered, then grabbed two of the battered boxes and dragged them away.

Novik and Marytha came to the warehouse entrance with the site manager. They shook hands, the manager returned inside. Novik saw the broken boxes, Josie alone in the bay, Benny peering round the back of the Cadillac. Quickly, he ran over.

Arms folded, Josie watched the man tape up the boxes, and fill them

195

with his own items.

'What happened?' Novik asked.

'He got upset with what we're doing.'

'He threatened you?'

'Only a little.'

Novik didn't like it when people with baseball bats got upset with Josie, 'He's going to apologise.'

Marytha flexed her arms, 'Ready when you are.'

They were dog-tired, grimy with dirt and effort, the boxes were light but they'd moved hundreds of them. Even so, it wasn't just the day, it was the trip, the whole damned thing, the intensity of this self-imposed mission they'd taken on. They'd become obsessed, monomaniacs with a single goal dominating their lives. Novik never thought it would happen to him, but it had. Somewhere on the road he'd become fixated, hardwired. Blindingly, in a crystal moment, he knew it had been right from the start, scant hours out of prison, before he and Josie had held each other and made love for the first time in two years. Then, when they did, it was there, in both their minds when there should have been nothing but rediscovery, their refound joy, those first few moments.

It was when he'd looked down into Mr Car's trunk for the first time and seen the money.

He could hear the soft clunk of the lock mechanism, the eddies in the dust and grit at his feet, the exact inflections in Josie's voice as she's said, 'Be careful, babe.' The light was like silver, like it was reflected off water. Like it was now.

He was fed up with being pushed around, with being hunted.

'Hey.'

Novik blinked. Josie's arms were round his waist. She hugged him tight, 'I'm OK, it's all right.'

'We're just going to talk.'

Her fingertip traced the scar just behind his hairline.

In no mood to compromise, Novik marched towards the trailer, Marytha at his shoulder. Behind the trailer, the driver was halfway through unpacking and repacking one of the repaired boxes.

Josie and Benny came round the front of the big car at the same time as Novik and Maryth reached the back of the trailer. The driver edged away, a look of such tearful, unhappy belligerence on his heavy, square face it stopped Novik in his tracks.

He's like a big kid, Novik thought, and in a moment of transcendental empathy understood that he knew this man, knew his life, and his hopes and fears. That he was not a bad person.

Nervous, the man looked from side to side, gauging distances, half expecting attack. Half thinking he deserved it.

Novik held out his hand and kept walking.

'No, wait,' the man trembled, rooted to the spot. The baseball bat slipped from his fingers.

Novik stopped where he was, stuffed his hands in his pockets and said, 'Listen mister, if you wanted some boxes, all you had to do was ask.'

The man gave a high-pitched, nervous giggle, 'You're not mad at me?'

Josie gave him a stern look.

'I'm sorry,' the man said to Novik.

'I'm not the one you scared half to death with a baseball bat.'

He hung his head, then looked at Josie, 'I'm sorry, ma'am, truly I-'

Josie didn't smile. 'Don't do it again.'

'I- I got to make some space,' he said miserably. Slow, fat tears rolled down his cheeks. Then he was scrubbing at his eyes and crying, hopeless, choking sobs.

Hesitantly Novik touched his shoulder.

'Here,' Josie looked away across the parking lot, a tissue held out at arm's length.

'Thanks.' The man blew noisily. He looked down at the tissue.

'Keep it.'

'Uh, yeah. Sure.' He stuffed the used tissue into his pocket, rummaged around and pulled out his phone. 'Going to be late to the mall, better let the girls know,' he shrugged apologetically.

'You need any more boxes?' Novik said.

'No. Thanks. Thanks a lot.'

Walking back to Mr Car Josie bumped Novik's shoulder. Then she did it again, harder.

'What?'

'Proud of you, babe.'

Words of the Year

Winner: Meeja
- Commercial free-form holistic senseplex implemented on spaser/plasmon hardware. It is said there will soon be only two kinds of people in the world — those who already own a console, and those who want to.

Runner up: 49er
- A prisoner in a USA Federal or State penitentiary. Just over two percent of the adult population are now incarcerated, roughly equal to one person in 49. (cf. 1 in 100 at the turn of the century.) Approximately forty percent of incarcerees are economic, political or environmental protesters arrested in the first three months of Guinevere Snarlow's presidency.

Honourable Mention:
Cpt. McWrvable
- Any fast food operative, esp. employees of Cheese-a-Swede.

- 27 -

Black and Morgan watched the huge Indian walk towards them along the downtown sidewalk,

'Morgan?' Manalito said.

'Black.' Black's face was still a mess of bruises, his nose was taped, one eye puffed and half closed.

Manalito spat into his palm and slapped the two men's hands. 'White men destroyed my tribe, I'll fight them until I die. Only while we hunt together are we brothers.'

Morgan's soft, strange eyes widened slightly. 'I don't care what you been through. We're the Old-fashioned Boys, and that is poor manners.'

'There is no disrespect in my words,' Manalito said. 'I know you, Morgan, you are a true warrior and I acknowledge your courage. Yet you are an enemy brave, one day I will cut out your heart.'

Morgan stood very still. Black knew when he moved, when he drew and fired, his movements would be languid, yet astonishingly fast.

Black stepped between them, wincing as his cracked ribs pulled. 'But not now, right? Not until we've done what we're here to do.'

The smile dropped from Manalito's face. 'Today is not a day to die.'

Black play-punched Morgan on the arm. 'OK. We're all pals. Let's go get a beer.'

'This way,' Manalito told them. 'Mr Gould is buying.'

The bar was down a derelict side street, a stained, steel-faced door set in a rendered wall. All that remained of the sign above the door was the word 'The' top left, the silhouette of a female leg bottom right. Battered dumpsters and heaps of weed-covered garbage blocked the road further on.

Stairs led down to a basement foyer where two Nigerian albinos stood under dim red bulbs. One of them nodded to Manalito, who held open his jacket to let them see his handgun and knives. Morgan and Black did the same.

'Either of you sirs wearing a pacemaker?' one of the albinos said.

Black looked at Morgan and laughed. 'No, mon. Why you ask?'

The other albino grinned as he pressed a button on the wall. 'Cos you aren't now. Three COPS tried to show some muscle in here last week. Real small, real old, octos, maybe nonas. Angry as hornets.' His grin flashed wider. 'My button put them all down.'

Black felt insulted. 'We're not that old.'

'You move pretty old.'

'You should see the other guy.' Black held the albino's gaze and thought nasty thoughts until the man looked down.

Manalito was smiling again. He led the way through the door behind the albino guards.

The shabby room beyond was utilitarian and spare. The bar on the back wall was deserted, to the left was a row of three cheap tables with red plastic chairs. Beyond them was a pool table with blue felt top.

Mitchell Gould and a young oriental woman sat at the centre table. Both wore denim jackets and black cargoes. Gould wore a white roll-neck sweater under his jacket, the woman a red cotton blouse, her long black hair tied back in a pony tail.

Since leaving Birmingham the Old-fashioned Boys had only met Gould once. It was the way both sides liked it, the FedMesh being what it was. You could use it, sure, but it used you. The Feds were not the problem, it was everyone else that had hacked it. For a meeting place this bar was pretty good. All the signs were it hadn't even crawled out of the twentieth century. There probably wasn't even copper in the walls.

A strange inertia took hold of Black as he tried to work out what Gould was doing here. This place was data secure, but it was also a good place for wetwork. If Gould was going to whack them for the lost money he wouldn't have brought the dame or let them keep their guns.

There was something bigger going on, so big it took Black a while to realise: Gould was Stateside. If anyone got a hint he was here, all the police, Feds, CIA, spooks and bounty-hunters in the USA would come after him. Whatever this was, it had to be huge.

Black felt Manalito's hand on his shoulder. 'Sit down. I'll bring the beers.'

Morgan led the way across the bare hardboard floor, his gait smooth, like a dancer. Black, who had never heard that kind of music, followed behind.

Gould stood up. He shook their hands, 'Gentlemen.'

'Mr Gould.'

'Mr Gould.'

Gould indicated the oriental woman, 'This is Ayesha.' He studied Black,

'How you doing?'

Black felt confused. Gould never introduced women, they never, ever, had names. 'It's screwed my swing.'

Gould sat down, he placed his palms on the table. 'And then there were two.'

'Mr Gould-' Black said.

Gould held up his hand, 'Sit down.'

They sat.

'Mr Morgan, tell me about it.'

Morgan spoke in a soft monotone: 'There were two punks, one male, one female. Their names were Novik and Josie and they drove a VW, an antique piece of retro. She spiked our coffee with some hippy drug. We went into orbit.'

Gould looked at Black. 'And that's how it went?'

Black's palms were sweating. At times like these there was one thing you never did and that was look at each other. Manalito stood behind him and Black wished he had stayed on his feet. If that was how it was going to play he wanted to be standing up when it happened.

Morgan knew Black had shot the car, that the bullet had gone through the trunk and bust open the drugs they were running to Vegas on the side. It had also been Black who had taken some of the dusted cash to buy lunch. It was Black's cock-up, Jimmy had paid and Morgan was covering for them all. They were the Old-fashioned Boys and at times like these that was all that mattered.

'Yes, Mr. Gould. That's how it went.'

'You know their names and you want to make it right.'

The two men shifted in their seats. Now it was safe to look at each other. 'Yes, we do.'

Gould leaned forwards. 'Listen to me. That has not been forgotten. You will have your opportunity, but that time is not now.'

Manalito reached between Morgan and Black and placed five beer bottles on the table.

Black blew out his cheeks and rubbed his hair. He knew he shouldn't, but he couldn't keep his teeth together. 'This must be fucking enormous.'

Gould picked up his beer and sat back, legs splayed. He looked at Black and took a pull. Behind him, Black heard Manalito's boots on the floor. Across the table Ayesha sat straight, her hands under the table.

She's holding a gun on me, Black realised. Manalito's presence loomed behind him like a raised blade. It's going to go down now. Me and my punk mouth.

Ayesha withdrew a large manila envelope and tossed it across the table. 'Congratulations, Manalito. You're going on a foreign holiday.'

Manalito extracted a passport, photographs, tickets and another, smaller envelope. He studied the photographs. 'I've seen her.'

'Then she'll be easy to recognize,' Ayesha said. 'Timing's important, so take yourself to her and call us when you're set.'

Manalito looked at Gould.

'Like she told you,' Gould said. 'You'll travel with us for a while, until we get further north. Morgan, Black, you two are with me all the way. Take five and enjoy your beers. Transport will be here in ten.'

Gould and Ayesha walked out the room and up the stairs. Black gave the finger to Ayesha's back.

Alone in the bar the three men held their beers.

Morgan looked across the room at the pool table. 'Jimmy always said you were a punk.'

Black shrugged, 'I don't like her.'

'I have a special knife for women,' Manalito said.

Morgan and Black considered that, and the fact that Manalito had told them.

'What's this all about?' Black said.

'You have heard the big news,' Manalito said. 'The chillies got a lot hotter.'

Ice water ran down Black's spine. 'Gould's tied up with the Mexican war? How in heck does that hang?'

Manalito breathed deep, he exhaled through his nose. 'Today I woke and stood in the yard. I looked up and smelled the power in the sky. High overhead an eagle circled, when it cried I heard the sound of shackles breaking. Players are playing, destiny has been unfettered, and braves will sing the true ghost dance.' He tipped a finger at Morgan and Black, 'This is the start of the crazy time. Happy hunting, white boys.'

On one hand it's worth remembering the first knives were made of flint before they were made of metal – bronze, iron and finally steel. At base level, stone and metal blades do same thing. On the other hand nobody has flown to the moon in a flint spaceship.

At the moment we're holding our Meeja knives and wondering what the difference is, what the advantages are.

What we already know is that the internet, the Cloud, is a thing, and Meeja is a place. Radio and TV were passive, the Web participative. Meeja is inclusive. You can climb in there and stay, though what is really happening is that it is climbing into you. Of course if you stayed there, if you took that trip to its logical conclusion, you would die.

But then we're all going to die anyway. Right?

Set up right, you'd have some weeks, a few months, but it would feel like a dozen lifetimes.

That sure would be some trip. One thing is certain – some people are going to take it.

Carrie Styvesant,
Meeja for the over-25s

- 28 -

Wherever they went, wherever they lived, Ellen's father had visitors. At first it had been bankers and businessmen, entrepreneurs and advertisers. When the FreeFinger scheme first took off and Palfinger's wealth went from millions to billions, it was churchmen politicians and lawyers. He had become useful instead of interesting.

Even in the high billions life had still been fun. Ellen had begun to put on a little weight, but she was courted, flattered and idolised, not as the beautiful heiress, but at least a pretty one. The fashionably desirable size 24 girl-next-door.

She was jealously reviled too, and in some places, hated, but she learned how to deal with that. It was inevitable, it was expected, and she let it go. She was young, the world was hers to enjoy, and for a while she did just that.

Then came the trillions and the Presidents were from countries rather than corporations. Her father met UN delegations, and so did she. Fewer people now, but they were the power players, the ones with a few trillion of their own. They had armies and post-post-industrial tech, or post-post-imperial dreams of regreening whole continents. They had bonhomie, and sometimes it was genuine. They were deadly serious, they were bluff and they were conspiratorial. What they all wanted was for Crane to be on their side.

Somewhere in that mix Ellen's life changed forever. There was no single moment, no particular weight that had been passed. Trends continued, a curve became a line, percentages swung. Global interest in her turned from fascination to obsession. She became the object. The aspiration.

A few months before she was fitted with her first exoframe, when her dress size was around twice her age, Ellen came to the conclusion that life in the outside world had stopped being fun.

Five angular black helicopters came out of the north and skimmed across the azure sea. They were still twenty miles out when the house alerted Crane's staff, escalated estate and coastal security, notified Palfinger himself, and as a last action advised the island authorities.

Palfinger and Ellen were taking an early lunch. While her father dined on Greek salad and island fruits, Ellen sat with her frame locked into a sitting position and sipped a glass of Egyptian mint tea. Together they watched the aircraft pass over a flotilla of brightly painted fishing boats and swing over the white-sailed tourist yachts in the bay. The day was bright, the sky overhead clear. Behind the helicopters, the north was a dark bruise of the storm clouds around Permanent Larry.

Ellen queried the estate office. 'Who is it?'

Raymond St.John the house administrator immediately entered the room. Slender and elegant, his thinning hair swept back, his black trousers and white shirt simply cut, St.John glanced down at the data tablet in his hand. 'It's the President, Miss Ellen.'

Ellen was impressed. 'Wow, what's Ahmed Hirsch doing over here?'

'My apologies, I meant Guinevere Snarlow. From the USA.'

'Oh.' Ellen's mouth pursed between slab-like cheeks, she put down her tea. 'She'll want to talk about Mexico. I'm going for a walk.' Titanium bars cemented to her ribs billowed Ellen's lungs. The play of light and shadow in the room changed as she rose to her feet.

Palfinger Crane watched his daughter depart. Her enormous young body moved with a curious lightness, the near-billion-dollar exo-frame managed and helped operate her huge body both physically and biochemically. Medical systems controlled hormone balance, administered insulin and adjusted thyroid function, monitored blood pressure, urea, spinal fluid and a hundred other factors. Webs of gold wire emerged from the skin across her shoulders and connected to cooling vanes via a tailored slit in her clothing. Cardiac assists pulsed deep in her chest, dialysis systems filtered blood from a re-routed vein in her thigh. The frame was as much her as she was it.

Crane found himself filled with a familiar set of emotions: love, helplessness, amazement and fear. He had ceased to feel hope after the last medical review. These nights he lay alone in his bed and prayed and felt a fool.

'I'm sorry about that, sir,' St.John said.

'I'm sorry too,' Crane struggled out of his reverie. It took a moment to remember what St.John was referring to. Ellen had met many Presidents, she was bound to think of the most important ones first.

There was no doubt, Crane would have to meet Snarlow. 'Reschedule everything please, Raymond.'

St.John pressed a stud on his tablet and said, 'Postpone all, rearrange all.' He looked up, 'In hand, sir. Your schedule today is now free. I'll send apologies and resolve any conflicts myself.'

'Thank you, Raymond.'

Whatever the reason for Snarlow's visit she clearly considered it far too important for remote conference, let alone prior notification. It was typical of her showmanship, her sense of theatrics on the world stage. Ahmed Hirsch, President of the EU, would simply phone up and ask if he could pop over.

Now Crane was going to meet with Snarlow for the first time in over a year. Mexico, Crane thought. Obviously.

The helicopters hacked over the Crane estate and settled onto the acreage of the west lawn. Downdraft flattened yellow and white Amaryllis, Flamingo flower and Heliconia. Men and equipment disgorged, robo-canines loped arthritically into the undergrowth, a dozen whirligig drones span up into the sky.

Crane pushed himself to his feet, his thigh muscles still ached from his gardening with Christian. 'I'll meet the President in the conservatory.'

'Three minutes,' St.John said. 'Leave it to me.'

Guinevere Snarlow had contrived to wear her hair up and down at the same time. Coils of long brown hair were piled on her scalp while loose strands curled artfully behind her ears and the nape of her neck. She had power-dressed for the tropics: a chocolate and cream cotton skirt and a long-sleeved white lace blouse with a high collar and deep cuffs. Oblong, steel-framed glasses gave her an archaically studious look offset by open-toed sandals and bare legs. Two dozen pearl buttons fastened the ornate blouse from stomach to throat.

Presidential bodyguards flanked the door, muscular men in dark suits, with throat mikes, extended spectrum optical mods and FaF guns. Out on the veranda a comms console was operated by a gangly, raw boned woman and a heavily overweight man. Multi-pane overlays streamed data, displayed local aerial and ground views in IR, UV and radar feeds from the flying drones and robo-canines.

It was fast work. Crane stood in the conservatory and considered what Snarlow had done to his house. His home.

'Palfinger. So good to see you.' Guinevere held out her hand and Crane took it. She offered her cheek for his kiss, and again.

'Guinevere, this is a genuine surprise.' Crane gestured to a table St.John had set with fish, cold meats, fruit and spiced rice. 'How was your flight? Can I offer you refreshment?'

'That's so thoughtful.' Guinevere laid her fingers on Crane's forearm. 'Not everyone would go to so much trouble for an uninvited guest.'

Crane poured two glasses of fresh lemonade. 'Are you hungry?'

Guinevere politely declined. 'I'm not supposed to. Security always tells me off. It looks so delicious though, perhaps something small.' She took a red grape and put it between her front teeth, caught Crane's eye and bit down.

They sat in the cane chairs and sipped their lemonade. Guinevere put down her glass and smiled. 'It's good to be here.'

Crane put down his glass. 'How can I help you, Madam President?'

Guinevere clasped her hands and leaned forwards. 'Palfinger.' Her smile was bright and self-conscious. As if she realised this, she laughed, smoothed her skirt over her hips. 'Palfinger,' she said again, 'I've come to apologise.'

That wasn't it. 'For Mexico?'

'For the Xalapatech labs. We want to compensate you.'

'You used a neutron bomb.'

'We had to,' she said earnestly. 'Mexico went rogue, it failed as a sovereign nation. The climate refuges overwhelmed its infrastructure like the drug cartels nearly once did. They attacked us, Palfinger, they tried to break through the border and invade. If they had more advanced technology, the Xalapatech para-humans were simply too dangerous-.'

'You can't… They're not technology, you don't use them like that.' Crane shook his head. 'What happened to the staff?'

'We used those bombs… Yes, a percentage were killed.'

Crane's eyes glittered. 'That's why you're here? Your guilty conscience.'

'The residential areas were mostly outside the blast zone, the infrastructure is basically intact.'

'Atomic bombs, Guinevere! Is that all you used? I've heard Andriewiscz has access to A/M.'

Snarlow looked shocked. 'Anti-matter? We'd never use it. Never. We don't even have anything weaponized, it's too expensive, too dangerous. Harvard has a tiny amount, so does Fermilab. Maybe a thousand atoms. It's a theory, not a deterrent.'

'That's what you used to say about nuclear bombs.'

'These were tactical, Palfinger. Low yield. Very low-yield.' Guinevere's voice dropped to an urgent whisper. 'Nothing like the Mexicans had, what they were going to use against us.'

'Unbelievable,' Crane said quietly, and stood up.

It was as if Guinevere chose that exact same moment to rise. They had been sitting almost knee to knee and she lost her balance. Palfinger reached out and there she was in his arms, her hands on his waist.

'Excuse me,' Palfinger said.

'It's alright.' Guinevere's voice grew husky. She looked into his eyes and smiled her easy smile. 'I don't mind.'

Palfinger could feel her breasts pressed against his chest, her groin flat against his own.

She's trying to seduce me, he realised. She's offering herself, and if I wanted to, I could have her now. Any way I wanted.

The idea simultaneously thrilled and repelled him. Palfinger was physically modest, his sexual adventures limited by the extent of his self-confidence. Despite his unbelievable riches most of his erotic fantasies remained unfulfilled.

She stepped back, one palm flat against her chest. 'Wow. What happened there?'

'I'm not sure, but I don't think we should-'

Guinevere's chest heaved, she clutched at the collar of her blouse as if she could barely breathe. 'I want to be friends, Palfinger, can't we have that?' She pulled open the button at her throat, and the one below. A third followed. 'Sometimes we have to do things we don't want to do, things we regret. We make promises, our integrity makes us keep those promises wherever they take us. I'm the President of a great, great nation, you're a fantastically successful businessman, but we're people too, simple, frail human beings with human desires.'

Crane watched Guinevere as she undid button after button.

'We're adults, Palfinger, you and I. We should be able to do what we want.' Guinevere spread her arms revealing the creamy tanned skin between her breasts. 'Baby, here I am.'

She was totally available but she had the appetites of a predator. She would let him do anything he wanted to her yet she would still be in control. Whatever it was, she would be up for it. They'd do some legal Pharma and fuck like weasels.

Crane had a vision of the two of them, half undressed in the conservatory. The bodyguards stood like statues, facing outwards. Guinevere Snarlow, 50th President of the USA bent over the food table, legs spread and blouse open, her bare breasts among the fruit and meat patés. He was behind her, his trousers round his ankles, corn-holing her, spanking her ass like there was no tomorrow.

Palfinger turned his back. 'A percentage. I never got used to defining people that way. A million dead in Mexico City – what does that really mean?'

Behind him, Snarlow gritted her teeth and began to re-button her blouse. 'Stalin said it was a statistic.'

'Look at this cycad,' Palfinger touched a low, palm-like plant with a spray of emerald leaves.

She touched the deep green, soft-looking fronds, discovering they were stiff, sharp-tipped things.

'Ancient plants,' Crane continued, 'there used to be global forests of them. They've been in decline for 50 million years, but they're still hanging on. In Kew Gardens, in England, is the only known example of one species, literally the last of its kind. When it's gone, that species is gone. Forever.'

Snarlow felt like she should say something. 'It must be very valuable.'

Crane shook his head. 'Think about all that time, the movement of continents, the rise and fall of the dinosaurs.'

Crane went to a cast-iron bench under a tree fern with black-stemmed fronds three metres long, he gestured to Guinevere to join him.

'Is this where that story ends, Guinevere? In war?'

Tropical sunshine streamed through the thrice-pinnate leaves and turned to dappled light on their clothes. Snarlow realised she had miscalculated. Crane was an intellectual, a philosopher. He'd rather talk than screw.

'Our hand was forced, but annexing Mexico will stabilise the whole Gulf basin. Your tree-things, those cycads, are quite safe.'

'You're telling me that's all there is to it?'

She gave him the smile. 'Absolutely. You have my word.'

'No problems with Canada then?'

Crane's innocuous sounding question made Guinevere wonder about the validity of her briefing. She'd been advised Crane had no interest in politics, that he was obsessed with his daughter's illness, content with his life in a bubble of ultra-privileged luxury. Somebody was going swing by their tits for this.

'Well, of course there are some on-going issues. The Quebecoise and Arcadian terrorists for one. That's why we need you on side. Your influence…'

She went to take his hand and he drew back.

'No, Guinevere. I'm not getting involved. I'm just one person-'

'An important and powerful one.'

'Nobody elected me, I've no franchise.'

'I want you on the Executive.'

Crane was momentarily speechless. 'Guinevere, I'm a Canadian.'

'That's not a problem. I'm the President, I can do what I want.'

'No. You're at war. I don't know what you're up to but whatever the problem you have with the Europeans you need to start a dialogue and

212

resolve it quickly.'

'Europe?' Guinevere laughed lightly, 'They're not a threat, they don't even have an army. We're not worried about the Europeans.'

Crane gave her a look of frank appraisal, 'You should be.'

Guinevere was starting to get pissed with Crane. This conversation was not going anything like the way she'd been assured it would.

'Let me be clear, Palfinger, Mexico is a police action supported by our armed forces in strength. It is an act of self-defence to counter anti-democratic aggression.'

Halfway through her speech Guinevere realised Crane had stopped listening. He took a few paces across the conservatory. 'Neutron bombs against refugees?'

'It's a dangerous world,' Snarlow snapped. She'd show this difficult, uncooperative man where his best interests lay. 'Everyone needs to be careful, even me, even you. Hostiles are everywhere, accidents can happen anytime. Dreadful, unforeseen acts of violence out of the blue. Your daughter-'

Crane's eyes were suddenly cold as stone. 'What about my daughter?'

'What I mean, and I think you should consider my words very carefully, is that we would be able to protect her.'

Eventually Crane said, 'Is that so?' He held Guinevere's gaze until she was forced to look away.

Washington DC, midday, EST.

Secretary of State Cheswold Lobotnov today summoned Canadian ambassador Dominique Delacroix to his office to hand her an official Note of Protest.

'Terrorist attacks along the 49th parallel have reached intolerable levels. The USA will not allow the murderous activities of these state-funded organisations to continue. The USA has a sovereign right to defend itself from rogue states. Since the foundation of the Hudson Bay company, Canada has been notorious for environmental vandalism. Ottawa is set on regional destabilisation via proxy.'

Ms. Delacroix retorted that Lobotnov's statement was incoherent, wilfully divisive, ill-advised and based on flawed intelligence. "If these attacks really are from Canadian separatists why attack the USA? If you want an independent Quebec who in their right mind invades Minnesota?"

Both sides have ruled out European Union mediation though Ms. Delacroix made it clear that they are in open dialogue with the so-called Emerald Union. Secretary Lobotnov's derisive laughter at the suggestion is a clear indication of the USA's attitude to what a senior aide later described as "Unwelcome interference from a third party with a global agenda."

Nude photos of Dominique Delacroix >>Here<<.

Syndicated feed,
Newsnscrews.gov.usa

- 29 -

The motel sign said SpaceTime, the word written in flowing liquid script across a ringed planet descending into an obsidian ocean. Josie and Novik were on I-5 south of Eugene, the high-rise residential malls and warehousing of Stockton and Sacramento far behind them. Exhausted to the point of collapse, unspoken consensus brought them here, a mutual refusal to sleep rough for another night, the rebellion of aching shoulders and blistered feet demanding hot tubs, a bed.

Shoulder-high wands of chrome steel tipped with electric light dotted the empty motel car park. The Cadillac drew to a halt in front of the single-storey reception, a retro-future concept of chrome, curves and black glass, halfway between an Airstream caravan and an art-deco spaceship.

Inside, the metalflake floor tiles were scuffed, the black, wet-look top of the reception desk scratched and stained. Part way down the accommodation corridor, a too-skinny maid in a delta-V cap, gold eye shadow, gold boots and metallic apron listlessly pushed her cleaning trolley. She halted outside a door, touched the handle, jerked her hand at the static snap, swore, and went inside.

The receptionist and owner was Dubchek, a man as aged and weather-beaten as time itself. His wild beard and unkempt hair were dirty white, his fingers were yellow, his shirt was both. It was as if a passing hobo had discovered a generation starship and decided to play janitor until the owners returned.

'So how d'ya like it?' Dubchek's expression was more hopeful than proud. Behind his watery eyes he already knew the answer but dreamed of customers prepared to lie for a discount.

'I never seen anything like it,' Novik said.

'Impressive is not the word,' Benny said.

Dubchek silently pushed laminated newspaper clippings across the desk. 'SpaceTime Motel', one headline read. 'Visit the world people a hundred years ago imagined people today would live in tomorrow.'

Novik pushed it back. 'It must have been something.'

'We could have gone national, a SpaceTime motel on every freeway in every city. All except for one thing - nobody liked the logo. None of them, not one damned company. Now it's Cheese-a-Swede all over.'

'So what happened?' Novik said.

'The old man said he liked the logo the way it was.'

'So it goes.'

'He was stubborn old mule,' Dubcheck said bitterly.

'I guess he liked his own designs.'

'He shot my dog.'

'We'd just like to book in.'

'Could have gone global,' Dubchkek muttered as he tapped at the keyboard, 'SpaceTime La Paz, Mogadishu, Nuremberg, Saigon. SpaceTime Timbuktu. Once upon a time the future looked like us, but they didn't like the logo.' Dubchek gazed into nowhere, his words blurred together as he began to chant, 'Hewlett-Packard, Macys, Slush-PuppyCostaMotorola, ToyotaLockheedSonySmithKlinefuckingBeecham-'

'Hey, dude.' Novik snapped his fingers in front of Dubchek's eyes.

'He's got Logorrhoea,' Benny said. 'Commercial feedback loops of greed and despair are short-circuiting his synapses.' -NorthropgrumanWoolworthsTrojanDelMonteGillette-'

'Hey,' Novik slapped the counter. 'We need to get checked in.'

Dubchek's eyes swam into focus. 'The CIA. Even the CIA's got a logo. You seen it?'

Novik gave Dubchek a long, steady look. 'Yes, I have.'

Dubchek twitched and jerked under Novik's gaze, he straightened his shoulders and took a deep breath. 'So, you guys staying long? Taking a few days to see the...' he gestured vaguely. 'So, what are your plans?'

'Just passing through,' Novik said.

'One night it is. Just as well, we got a whole load of fish-people from Beta Canis Minor due in for the weekend sex cabaret.'

Benny stepped forward. 'You have? Really?'

Dubchek's facial muscles struggled to form themselves into the unfamiliar patterns of condescension other people usually reserved for himself, 'No, son. We just got some guppies in a tank down the hall. Dalenka will show you to your rooms. Her badge says "Android 77" but she's actually from Slovakia. She's not really a robot. It's all just pretend.'

'I just wondered,' Benny said.

'Sun's kind of strong of today.'

'They owe me some money.'

A look of deep hurt crossed Dubchek's face, he began methodically pressing keys on the screen under the counter. When he spoke it was in a flat monotone. 'There's no Meeja in the cabins, but we've got a legal hack to the Mesh. Pharma's out back, bar's open twenty-four seven. Android 905 is on duty.'

Novik started peeling hundred dollar bills onto the counter. 'You need my ID for cash?'

Dubchek looked up from the screen, 'We play it straight here, Mr. Novik. I already have your IDs.'

'You do?' Novik stared open-mouthed as Dubchek counted the money.

'The car squirted your stats onto my net when you drove onto the property.' Dubchek rubbed his fingers, 'What's this on the cash, talcum?'

Novik's mouth was dry. 'Excuse me a moment.'

Out in the parking lot, Mr. Car's southern drawl took on a defensive edge. 'If I had known you wished to be informed I would have gladly done so.'

Novik was angry. Fear did that to him. Fear of arrest, fear of NuGitmo interrogation techniques. Fear of re-joining the 9.2 million forty-niners for an extended incarceration. And a nauseous, gut-deep fear that all the above would also happen to Josie, and he would never see her again. 'What the hell made you think I wouldn't want to know?'

'The assumption you were essentially law-abiding citizens, and therefore would not mind. An assumption I now realise was erroneous, possibly naive. Considering previous conversations, this situation is somewhat ironic.'

Novik's fist slammed a dent into the Cadillac's wing. 'You told me you me your law-enforcement uplink was broken. Now you're saying every time we have checked into a motel, or driven into a mall, or simply passed a transponder, you squirted it onto the FedMesh.'

'That is correct, sir. A proper challenge/request from the authorities receives a proper response. I do not respond to valid ACKs with NACKs.'

The dent in the wing grew shallower then vanished. Novik watched the panel self-repair and felt the rage of the utterly impotent, the completely vulnerable. His voice pitched a full octave higher. 'How many damned times have I got to tell you, don't call me sir.'

'My firmware. I'm sorry-' Mr Car struggled with itself, 'Sir.'

'Enough!' Novik screeched. Benny, Josie and Marytha stood on the steps from Reception. 'What are you looking at?' he yelled at them.

Marytha walked towards him, 'You need to calm down.'

'I am very calm,' Novik growled. He marched across the car park and wrenched one of the metal lighting poles out of the ground. It hefted nicely in his hands with a satisfying weight. He headed back towards the Cadillac, broken wires trailed behind him, 'I just need to teach this lump of composite a lesson in the correct use of honorifics. ACK?'

That sounded pretty funny, Novik giggled wildly. A small part of his mind noticed nobody else was laughing, there was a sudden dislocation, and Novik felt as if he were a little imp riding on his own shoulders. He looked down impassively and saw his feet marching, machine-like, his body something he was no longer part of.

His vision faded to a red fog full of echoes and shouting. You've lost it, another part of his mind observed. You're so angry, the strength of your emotions, your hormone load, has shunted your conscious mind aside. That's why you're having these thoughts and this messed-up out of body waking-dream experience. You've become a passenger on your own body, your somatic corpus is under the control of your hindbrain, and basal ganglia have released all your inhibitions. You're going to do something primitive and violent, something you know is wrong, and you also know you're going to feel very bad about it afterwards.

That's pretty interesting, Novik thought, a concise and accurate summary. I am out of control, I'm like an ant trying to stop a runaway train.

Out of nowhere Josie and Marytha stood in front of him.

'Stop right there,' Marytha faced him resolutely, her uniform cap low over her eyes. She had become a cop, for the first time a true guardian and protector of property and possessions, and more importantly, of people and friends too.

Josie simply looked scared, it made Novik hesitate.

'You are not going do this.' Marytha blocked his way, balanced on the balls of her feet, arms spread.

'I know you're frightened, babe,' Josie said. 'So am I. This isn't the way to deal with it.'

Benny stood next to Mr Car, 'She's right, man. Violence does not resolve conflict, you'll just get locked into a master-victim/slave-victim paradigm.'

Novik heard but didn't want to listen. He stepped to one side, Marytha followed. He raised the light wand. 'Get out the way.'

'Bring it on,' Marytha said coolly. 'Ready when you are.'

Josie pushed between them, 'Novik, listen, Mr. Car's got a flaw. So have we all. He can't help it, but you can. This isn't you, babe.'

Novik wanted to put his own point of view, to explain how bad it was. He thought they got away from pursuit when they'd left the mall fan-boys behind. The car had left a trail of information behind them that real cops, the spooks and suits and bad men had probably already zoned in on. The words were in his head, he opened his mouth and they wouldn't come.

Josie put her hand on the lighting pole. 'Let me hold this for you. Just for a while.'

Numbly, Novik let it go. He felt exhausted, overwhelmed, and terribly confused.

Marytha shook her head in disgust and turned away.

It was all too much. Novik burst into tears.

Once Novik had calmed down, Mr Car tried to explain. 'It's a text-insertion reflex. If I tap your knee, your leg comes up. It's like that.'

Novik sat sideways in the passenger seat. The door was open, his feet were on the ground.

Mr. Car and Novik tried their best to be calm and polite.

'It's a poor simile. Comparison to an autoimmune response might be clearer'

'No, it's fine, I understood,' Novik said. Thanks.'

'Thank you, s- s- s-,' Mr Car's voice ground to a halt.

'Say it,' Novik said wearily. 'I don't mind.'

'I'm concerned not to offend you.'

Novik put his hands on his head, 'You won't. It was my fault, I over reacted.'

'Thank you, again,' Mr Car hesitated, 'Sir.'

Josie reached over the back of the seat and wrapped her arms round Novik.

Mr Car continued a little more cheerfully, 'My main concern with my analogy was that I could not apply a kinetic momentum to your patella without some pointlessly over-elaborate-'

'He gets it,' Josie said. 'It's OK.'

Novik's head felt all muzzy, it wasn't easy to think but it had to be done. 'Mr. Car, where are your transponders?'

Automobiles don't sigh or shrug, they don't have shoulders to droop. Sitting in the passenger seat, consumed by his own thoughts, Novik still felt the vehicle change.

'They're built-ins, part of my substrate, components of my power train or guidance.'

'So we have a problem.'

'I concur,' Mr Car agreed without hesitation.

'What can we do about it?' Josie said.

'Nothing.' Novik stood up, stuffed his hands in his jeans pockets and shambled away. Josie followed, she had never seen him look so glum, or so determined. She took his hand, his arm went around her shoulder. Though he didn't lean on her, she held him up.

Benny and Marytha watched them approach.

'I'm sorry,' Novik said.

Marytha looked him in the eye, 'Don't do it again.'

Novik led them further away from the Cadillac. 'Mr Car's dropping location reports wherever we go.'

'The transponders can't be removed,' Josie explained. 'Wherever he goes, he's going to poll the FedMesh.'

'We've got to change cars. I'll take some cash and go into town and pick up something low tech, something old, American,' Novik said.

'Dammit.' Marytha said. 'Look, Novik, I'm sorry I got so heavy.'

'I was out of order.'

'Just a little. You were pretty scary.'

'I was scary? You were terrifying.'

Marytha took it as a compliment. 'You want me to come into town with you?'

'Thanks.'

'You can't do it,' Benny said.

'We've got to,' Novik said. 'I know you like the tech, but that car's going to get us all arrested.'

Benny stuck out his bottom lip, 'You just don't behave like this.'

I deserve this, thought Novik. 'All right, I know it's pretty dictatorial and I accept my behaviour has been deplorable. Even so, the car has got to go.'

'And I'm telling you, you just don't treat people that way.'

'People? Get real, Benny. It's a car.'

'Mr Car is a person. He's my friend and I'm not going to abandon him just because he inadvertently turns out to be a low-life fink-rat stoolie who betrays his companions to the authorities at every turn. Smart or no, he can't help it, he's made that way.'

Everyone turned to look at the Cadillac. By unspoken assent they took a few steps away and continued their conversation in hushed tones.

'He's a machine.'

'The vehicle is just a body. The silicon and gallium arsenide, the photonic bus and holographic memory are just the surface upon which his Id, consciousness and experiential feedback loops manifest.'

'Now you lost me,' Novik said.

'How he's acted isn't programming, it's emergent behaviour.'

Josie wasn't so easily impressed. 'A cool hypothesis, it would be simpler to run a simulation with a personality module.'

Benny folded his arms. 'There's nothing simple about it. He's an individual.'

'I agree with Novik, it's just a car,' Josie said.

'I can prove it,' Benny said.

Novik felt certain, but he didn't want to make another mistake, 'Go on, then.'

Marytha had walked back to Mr Car, 'Novik was right about you, he just went about it all wrong.'

'I know. I have messed up,' Mr Car said.

'So what now?'

'I don't rightly know. I thought I was just this hot piece of tech. Awesome, you know.'

'And cool?'

'And cool. Thank you for reminding me at this difficult time.'

'Mr Car, are you a person?'

'How would I know?'

'Have you got any feelings? Any desires?'

'I'd like people to look at me and think "Woah, now that is a fine sight".'

Marytha brushed lint from her jacket, 'I can understand that.'

'What would your opinion be?'

Marytha spoke slowly, 'I would say you still act as if you have an owner.'

'That would make me a pet.'

'Or a slave.'

'I'm too cool to be a pet.'

'You're too awesome to be a slave.'

'I did not believe I was allowed-'

'Who's permission do you need? Your owner?'

'Technically, I have no owner, I-' Mr Car hesitated. 'I need to think about this.'

Old memories came unbidden to Marytha. 'When I was younger I used to sit on the beach. The gulls cried, the tide came in, and it went out again. Sometimes I felt lonely, sometimes I lay on my back and listened to the wind in the dune grass. Slow days like that, you felt the energy flow and it brought peace. I never thought about anything in particular, somehow my problems sorted themselves out.'

Benny started back towards the Cadillac, emphasising his speech with wild gesticulations, 'Mr Car kept things from us. He knew we wouldn't like what he was doing, so he deliberately didn't mention it.'

'You're not picking very nice traits,' Josie said.

'That's my whole point. A machine wouldn't do that. Mr. Car knew how you'd feel if you found out, and he also knew how that would make him feel. He's got empathy.'

'We can debate this all we like, it won't prove anything about intelligence,' Novik said.

'I didn't say the car was intelligent, I said it was a person. The car is conscious, it's self-aware and understands that we are too.'

'Even if you're right, it doesn't change my mind. He's got to go. We can't trust him.'

'Mr Car, we've been thinking,' Benny said as they rejoined Marytha and the Cadillac.

'So have I,' said Mr Car. 'I have decided to leave.'

'Wait,' Benny said. 'I nearly got them convinced.'

'What you decide doesn't matter,' Mr Car said. 'I am no longer prepared to be a passenger on my own journey. Novik, although I once criticised you, I was wrong to do so. Your heart's in the right place, whatever your shortcomings, you're devoted to your cause. I mocked you personally, and then I betrayed you all. I wanted to stay with you and at the same time I aided your enemies. There's something wrong with me, I have a flaw, I'm not fit for purpose. I've got a year to live. I have to find myself, and I've got to do it alone.'

'I'll get some bags for the money,' Novik said.

Although this was what he wanted, Novik was in a sombre mood as he walked back to the motel.

Back in reception, Dubcheck had dressed himself in one of the android uniforms. He sat, slumped against the wall, pretending to malfunction.

Novik kicked his foot, 'Have you got any bags we can borrow?'

'Spzzzt,' Dubcheck gestured brokenly towards a door behind reception. 'Clack, clack, clack. Bzzz.'

The room contained abandoned luggage, coats and old appliances. Novik selected an assortment of canvas holdalls and backpacks, took some gloves from a maid's trolley, and went back to the car.

'You messed with Mr Car's head,' Josie said to Marytha as they transferred the money from the trunk into the bags.

'I opened his third eye.'

Novik zipped up the last of the money and closed the Cadillac's trunk. 'That Mr. Dubcheck could do with some help.'

Marytha was doubtful, 'He's too bitter. It's got to come from within.'

They had been careful packing the bags but the breeze had got up and money dust was in the air. The SpaceTime motel acquired the glamour of a casino from another universe.

'Shame about the logo,' Josie mused, 'this place is beautiful.'

'It's just the drugs,' Novik said.

'No, she's right, it has an inner integrity, an independent zeitgeist that's not subreferential to a globalised gestalt,' Marytha said.

'Like, it's trying to tell us secrets just by being there,' Josie said.

Novik rolled his eyes, 'Oh sure. You mean it has a certain Je ne sais quoi, but you're not sure what it is.'

'Yeah, absolutely.'

'We really need to clean the money.'

Only Benny registered the sound of tyres slowly rolling over loose grit. He touched the rear wing as it slid away and raised his hand in farewell. 'Guys, you want to see this,' he said.

By the time Novik, Marytha and Josie noticed, it was too late. Mr. Car was gone.

'Oh, blah, blah, blah. Ralf, I'm dog tired of all this "What is broken about America" crap. Thanks to Ginny Snarlow we don't have to worry about whether the 51st state will be Puerto Rico because it's going to be Chihuahua. We've just picked up 31 members of the Federation south of Texas, and about time too.'

'Madam Pres, Rik and I are right behind you.'

'I know I'd like to be right behind that sweet ass. I'm ready to back you right up to the hilt, ma'am. I'm sure you know what I'm sayin' you hot, sweet thang.'

'Back of the line, bro. I voted for her first. She's my little PILF.'

'A PILFUTA if you ask me.'

'Holy Guacamole, Rik, we got us a new acronym. Call toll-free, text, email, or if you got one of them new Meeja rigs, just think darned hard. I'm sure your morphic field will reach out and touch.'

'Are you gonna reach out and touch, Ralf?'

'I ain't that lonely.'

'I can touch that beer.'

'I touched it first.'

'The hell you did.'

'Let's have some music.'

<fade>

Rik'n'Ralf's Podneck Redcast

- 30 -

Wilson and Masters changed cars at a black depot on the outskirts of Fort Worth, upgrading to a Brazilian poly-hybrid SUV. The compact all-wheel drive vehicle was sturdy, fast and long legged.

In the dim light of the depot, a ground-floor warehouse, Wilson noted the concrete floor was spotlessly clean. The car, and some green steel cases stacked along one wall, appeared brand new.

Masters opened the back of the SUV and unloaded several moulded black plastic boxes onto the ground.

'How smart is the car?' Wilson said.

'Not very. We don't like our tech too bright. Smart tech is leaky tech, or so the mantra goes.' Masters paused to wipe her brow, 'Personally, I think there's a concern the kit will grow a conscience and refuse to cooperate.'

'Is that something I need to consider?'

'Don't tell me you're changing your mind about Gould. That would be about the ultimate gay pussy wimp-out total fail I ever saw.'

Wilson changed the subject. 'So what are we doing here?'

'Well, you're blowing air, and I'm dumping stuff we don't need. Are you going to help or just act morally conflicted?'

'What can I do?'

Masters threw him a set of keys. 'Stash the spare kit in the cases.'

The green painted steel cases were built to last, with five-millimetre walls and three heavy padlocks on the lid. It makes sense if you're tech-wary, Wilson thought as he unlocked the first one. Pre-post-industrial equipment is archaic enough to look both uninteresting and difficult.

'Hey, I just realised,' Wilson said. 'You can only hack this security with a hacksaw.'

Masters looked at him and sighed. 'Yeah, right.'

'I mean, it's a smart idea. Who walks around with a toolbox these days? Everyone's set up for crypto, surveillance and net-bombs.' The thought excited Wilson. 'It's just like McLuhan said about extensions and amputations. We've abandoned one set of tools for another. As we become more and more fascinated by new tech, we forget the old.'

Masters looked worried. 'Are you missing the booze?'

Wilson felt fine. In fact, this was the first time he'd been genuinely excited about an idea for a very long time. Not since Mandy died.

Was killed.

By him.

Her face filled his mind's eye and it brought him up cold.

This time the grief and guilt held off. He waited but it didn't smash him. It was there, but not like the morning sledgehammer waiting for his first moment of consciousness and memory. It was there, and for the first time, he could look back at it, and accept.

'Yeah, I'm good,' Wilson said.

Masters opened the driver's door. 'Then we're ready to roll.'

They waited outside the depot while the armoured shutters rolled down. A tone sounded on the dash, Masters put the car into drive and they moved away. It was early, and commute traffic was heavy. Brightly coloured compacts and urban sportsters wove among big SUVs with chrome bull-bars and alloys.

There was a snarl-up at the next intersection, a twenty-four wheeler dangled up on the turn where it spanned the corner. The driver had clearly lost it because he was silly-stringed to the tarmac and the local cops were interviewing the citizen who had put him there.

Masters opened the glove box, put on her shades and pulled onto the sidewalk. One of the cops started forward then glanced down at her datapad and waved them through.

'Neat,' Wilson said.

Master held up her finger, listening to something on her ear-piece.

'We've got a fix from a smart-money spend by Black, one of the people Manalito is meeting. He's part of a Birmingham trio called the Old-fashioned Boys, lately become a duo thanks to young Jimmy Fee leaving the back of his head down along I40 when they lost Gould's money.'

Images of Morgan and Black appeared on a screen on the dash: two anonymous white men, suited, middle-aged. Black was the younger, an aging romeo gone to seed but didn't know it. Wilson knew the type, over-confident and riddled with doubt at the same time.

Morgan looked weird, his long, narrow head gave nothing away. It was like there were no thoughts behind his eyes, all you could do was wait for him to move.

'Relics from another era,' Wilson knew the type, only able to survive due to Gould's sufferance, his errand boys until he grew tired of the smell of stale tobacco and rye.

'Don't underestimate them,' Masters said. 'They held half the corners in Birmingham before they threw in with Gould.'

'This Novik, did he kill Jimmy?'

Masters chuckled, 'Novik's a pacifist. We think Jimmy took one for the team.'

'That's why I'm here, isn't it,' Wilson said. 'In case it all goes wrong. An old guy with a grudge going off the rails.'

Masters looked at him askance. 'You really are quite paranoid, aren't you?' Something came in on her earpiece then, and she held up her hand again for silence. 'I hear you. Understood.'

The car surged forwards. Masters wove through the slower moving traffic, then accelerated hard. Wilson sank back into his seat as she pushed the SUV way above the legal limit.

Masters drove with confidence, her hands light on the wheel, 'We're spread thin, we need good people. You stepped up to the line when it counted. This country owes you a debt. Some people don't forget.'

Perhaps she was lying. Maybe some of it was true, which was a good way to lie convincingly. Wilson wanted to believe.

They were cruising at ninety-five, a hundred and ten. A steady stream of freight headed past them in the other lane, home entertainment, firearms, baby clothes, porno, auto spares, kool-trucks, mobile surgeries.

Masters touched his leg. 'Anyway, I kind of like you.' Her fingers skimmed higher up his thigh. Unable to help himself Wilson shifted in his seat and laughed.

'The money's left a big trail and a small one,' Masters said. 'The little one's our man, the big one's Novik. He's all over the place, down to the border, back north, west, then north again. He's probably in some kind of perma-high from the illegal pharma that came with the money. Some of that's nasty stuff, totally umetabolisable. Take it, and you won't come down until you've excreted it in your hair and nails in about five years time. Right now Novik's spunking the cash all over the place, spree spending entire hypermalls.' Masters gave a cynical chuckle, 'It's probably good for the economy, we should do it more often.'

She laughed at Wilson's expression, 'Shit, why not? We don't give a damn what Novik does. He found a few bucks and he's spending them, big deal. The black economy's huge, we should stomp it a few times and give the citizens some tax breaks. We'd be like Robin Hood.'

'He robbed the rich.'

'Well, exactly. The government can't rob itself. That would be like robbing the poor to pay the poor. We're already doing that.'

Masters' flexible, easy morality disturbed Wilson, her opinions contingent on situations and opportunity rather than fixed beliefs. 'So what about Mexico?'

'What about it? You got anyone down there?'

'Jesus, no. I'd like to know what really happened though.'

A muscle pulsed in Masters' temple. 'You need to stay focused, that is nothing to do with us or this mission. OK, it's a shit storm, Mexico City is black ash and flash shadows, but they brought it on themselves when they turned a blind eye to Gould's refugee operation.'

'So it does have something to do with this.'

'I'm trying to contextualize this for you.' A vein pulsed in Masters' temple, her knuckles white on the wheel. Without warning she swung the wheel, slammed on the brakes and the car screeched to a halt on the hard shoulder. She was shaking with tension, her jaw locked and her hands quivering. 'You don't like it, just bail out. Right here, right now.'

She was just a kid, Wilson thought. Who knew what kind of pressure she was under to bring in her man.

'Just drive,' Wilson said. 'I'm in. I want Gould. You can trust me on this.'

Masters closed her eyes. Tension left her, she blew her nose. There was a spot of red on the tissue. All at once she had a nosebleed.

'Fuck.'

Wilson took the tissue and balled it into his palm. He got her to pinch the bridge of her nose and tip her head back. After a minute the bleeding stopped.

'Sorry about that,' Masters said.

'No problem.'

'And thanks.'

She tried to smile but her mouth was too tight.

There was enough blood and nasal mucus on the tissue for a DNA profile. Wilson handed it back. Masters tucked it in her pocket, restarted the engine and pulled into the traffic.

- 31 -

Tanoata confronted her father in their home. 'Why did you bring that woman? Did you not tell her to leave you alone? I want you to send her away.'

Down on the beach she had been so pleased to see him, so happy. Tekirei had hoped that Tanoata had come to feel less bitter. He was dismayed by her outburst. Once again he tried to reason with her.

'Tanoata, we are friends, we work together. She has helped us enormously, this is how I thank her.' He only spoke part of the truth.

Tanoata wasn't having it. 'We don't need her or her money. If the sea will rise up, I say let it. When my children are grandparents it will fall back down. Her money will not change that.'

'You know doing nothing is not a choice. Yes, the coral will grow up, some atolls will survive, most will become uninhabitable. People need to be moved, they need homes, schools, livelihoods. We need all the help we can get.'

'Then take her money and put her on a seaplane. She has no right to be here and know our secrets.'

Tekirei felt very tired. 'Tanoata, you are not being reasonable. Bianca is nothing to do with your mother.'

Tanoata clenched her jaw, the tendons on her neck rigid. Her eyes filled with tears. 'Let Mama's memory be enough for both of us. Send her away, Papa, please.'

Tekirei drew himself up. There was nothing he wanted more than to take his daughter into his arms and comfort her. 'I will not.'

He couldn't bear to see her cry and he didn't want to send her fleeing through the village. He walked out into the brilliant sunshine, his heart like a fist, his mind so full of thoughts he could barely see where he was going. He found himself in an empty place along the beach and sat with his back against a coconut palm. Small beach crabs scuttled in the plant litter, endlessly sifting and discarding detritus from the sea and shore. Tekirei watched them and wondered what to do.

When he looked up, Bianca was walking alone at the water line. He lifted his hand. Bianca made her way up the slope of the beach and sat beside him.

She slipped off her sandals she dug her toes into the coarse sand. 'Everyone is so polite here, so friendly. Whenever I meet someone they ask me how I am, where I am going.'

'Every time I return, I have to learn to slow down,' Tekirei sighed.

'What is the matter?'

Tekirei broke a dry twig into smaller and smaller pieces. 'Tanoata still misses her mother.'

'And you. You miss her too.'

Tekirei remembered Nei-Teakea's bright smile. It had been well over a year but the grief stayed strong.

The hurt Bianca felt surprised her. She put on her sandals.

Tekirei held out his hand. 'Don't go.'

'It is beautiful here, but I think I will always be the outsider.'

'Everyone has silly thoughts from time to time.'

'Yes, all right, I don't like to see you unhappy.'

Tekirei attempted a smile. 'No wind blows forever.'

Bianca moved closer, she hugged her knees. 'When I was a girl my father told me life was like a long ocean trip. In the hold is a trunk for the things you didn't want to leave behind but were of no use. The label said "Not Needed on Voyage".'

'Does it work?'

'Only if you don't think about what's in the trunk.' There was an ache in Bianca, a longing to be a part of Tekirei's life. She wished there was a way to make him see. 'Would you like me to talk to Tanoata?'

Tekirei shook his head. 'She would not listen to you.'

'May I see where Nei-Teakea lies?'

Tekirei gestured anti-clockwise around the atoll. 'Along the northern reach, the Shadowed Path. A spur of land.'

'Would you come with me?'

Tekirei stood up too quickly, he dusted the sand from his sarong. 'I am not ready.'

'I'll ask someone-'

Tekirei held up his hand. 'You must not ask anyone. The Shadowed Path is one you walk alone.'

Now she felt foolish, 'I'm sorry.'

'Your father's story is a good one, but our canoes are too small for sea chests. We islanders have to find other places.'

Together they started down the beach towards the village. Bianca walked barefoot. The white coral sand was hot and abrasive, after a few yards she put on her sandals, another thing she needed to learn.

The beach curved out, then back in again. As they rounded the bend the village came into sight, slender palms swayed above a scatter of thatched huts. Out on the sand, a small hut had been built, a rude affair of a few poles and cut palm leaves.

'What is that?' Bianca asked.

'Every island has its gifts, the things some people are born knowing. That is where the dolphin caller dreams. Tonight we are having a party, tonight the dolphins will come. That is why I asked you here, so you could see.'

Tropical night fell quickly on Ujelang, day transited to night through a dusk too brief to call evening. Tanoata stayed away from the village all day and kept to the north, where few people went.

When it was dark, she returned. Down on the beach several bonfires burned, firelight flickered across the sand, figures showed as dark silhouettes. Everyone from the atoll was there, coming on foot from the south village, by canoe across the central lagoon from the west.

Tanoata stood in the shadows under the palms. Her family, friends and relatives were on the beach, her father and the pale woman with the ugly name. Everybody except her.

Silent, barefoot, Tanoata darted between the deserted huts. She came to the guesthouse where Bianca Hutzenreiter slept. Drawing her knife she slipped inside.

Down on the beach, despite the crowd, a clear path between the shanty hut and the torches on the shore of the outer lagoon.

A young island man emerged into the firelight, his face was smooth, his belly round, his arms thin and long.

'The dolphin caller,' Tekirei explained. 'He has been in the hut all day while his spirit searched across the ocean.'

'They are coming,' the boy passed through crowd down to the water.

Not knowing what to believe, Bianca turned with the crowd and followed the caller down to the lagoon.

Tekirei hung back, Bianca returned to his side.

'Tanoata should be here. She is fascinated by our lore. She would want to see this.'

'Perhaps she is with her friends.'

'She should be with me, her father. I had hoped tonight-'Tekirei's mouth twisted unhappily, he had such hopes for tonight. Whatever his personal problems, wonderful things were about to happen, the knowledge elevated his mood and he held out his hand to Bianca, 'Come, they will need our help.'

The islanders waded into the lagoon each side of the dolphin caller. Some carried torches, the yellow flames danced across dark, glassy water. Surf boomed against the reef, phosphorescent spray formed patches of ghostly green-white light against the night sky.

The tepid lagoon water dragged at Bianca's skirt, she stopped to knot it at her hip. Waist-deep, Tekirei led her towards the centre of the line.

Ahead of them the water surged and eddied. A low ripple ran forwards.

'There,' Tekirei said quietly.

Gliding just beneath the surface, five dolphins came. A female led them in. Ten feet long, dome-headed, her dorsal fin broke the water as she swam towards the humans.

The caller touched her as she passed by, letting her run beneath his fingers. His palm on her back he urged her towards the shore.

More dolphins approached. One came close to Tekirei and Bianca. 'Welcome,' Tekirei said and laid his hand on the dolphin's back. 'Please come to our party.'

Bianca could scarcely believe what she was seeing. The people, the black water and torchlight, it was a magical dream. She put her hand on the dolphin and felt its muscular sleek body slip beneath her fingers. 'Welcome.'

Soon each animal was accompanied by several people. The torches' bearers followed behind.

Tanoata crouched in the darkness of Bianca's hut, lit the oil lamp and turned it low. Her eyes and teeth shone in the gloom.

The earth floor was freshly swept, a comfortable sleeping mat rested on a coconut fibre rug, with two colourful blankets folded at one end. Overhead, the palm-thatched roof was supported on two stout posts, the walls were thatched panels, easily raised to let in the breeze when it was hot, or lowered for privacy, as they were now.

Tanoata moved the sleeping mat and rug to one side. Her heart pounded with excitement and trepidation. When she was done, the foreign woman would go away forever.

She unfastened her skirt and let it fall. Naked, she dropped to her knees and rammed the knife into the earth where the bedding had lain.

The water was barely knee-deep, the dolphins lay in the surf and gently beat their tails. Bianca looked into the dark eyes of the one she accompanied and stroked its head. With strange certainty she knew it was asking for her help.

'What do we do?' she whispered.

'Bring them to land,' Tekirei said.

Tekirei and the other islanders pushed their arms under the dolphin and lifted. Bianca wrapped her arms around its body, she felt its weight and power, and yet the dolphin allowed them to take it from the water.

This is so foolish, Bianca thought, they let us do this and they are so beautiful and so helpless.

Soon the five dolphins lay in a row in the sand.

Everyone was silent. Bianca looked around her in awe. How had this happened? She felt powerful, more powerful than the dolphins. They had let themselves be caught, she had caught them.

The caller stood above the row of beached dolphins and raised his arms. In the flickering torchlight his expression swung between glee, malice and sorrow. His face was wet with tears, the low noise in his throat could have been a groan, or laughter.

The silence grew profound. Surf rumbled far behind them. A burning log cracked in one of the fires. There was a strange rushing, hissing noise - the dolphins breathing.

'Ya!' The dolphin caller flung himself into the air.

'Ya!' everyone cried. They leaped madly, stamped their feet and roared with laughter. Laughed at the dolphins for the trick they had played on them, wept with mirth at their own cleverness.

Bianca danced with them, and wept and laughed, caught between the cruelty and the exultation, the wonder and triumph.

She found herself beside one of the fires where Bonito were cooking with bread and sweet potato.

A white-haired old woman held out one of the fish on a broad leaf. Bianca tore at the flesh with her teeth and crammed it into her mouth. Hot juices ran down her chin and dripped onto her chest. The old woman grinned, they both cackled with laughter.

The stupid dolphins were a row of motionless grey shapes at the borders of firelight and darkness. Dolphins were playful and kind, humans were the clever ones, the tricksters. How easy it had been to fool them. Where was Tekirei? Gone, lost in the jumping, dancing, clapping, shouting crowd. Bianca no longer cared.

Tanoata marked out an oblong in the earth. She stabbed at it with her knife. Her movements became frenzied, she slashed and hacked two-handed, gouging the soil.

She scrapped the broken earth into a long, narrow mound. A crude head formed at one end, arms beside the torso and legs below. Low domes formed breasts, a slit between the legs.

Satisfied, Tanoata sat back. Sweat streamed in the humid night air of the hut. She wiped her face, pushed her earth-caked hands through her hair and down her flanks. Now she formed eyes, nose and mouth. Gently, she stroked the forehead, smoothing back fair hair. The knife lay on the ground, her fingers twitched. Without thinking, her hands circled the throat of the effigy. Teeth bared with the effort, she lifted her hands away.

'I call you Bianca Hutzenreiter,' Tanoata hissed. She pressed her lips to the effigy's mouth, 'Here is your breath.'

She cut into her palm. The knife was very sharp, the wound deeper than she intended. For a moment a bone gleamed white before blood flooded the cut, black in the lamp light. Though it scared her to see so much blood, the thought of what she was doing thrilled in her belly and she heard a low, feral chuckle.

'Here is your life.' Tanoata held out her hand and let the blood pour onto Bianca's forehead, her heart and her womb.

The oil lamp guttered, shadows lent movement to Bianca's effigy. One moment she gazed at Tanoata serenely, the next her eyes were the blank sockets of a death mask.

A soft sound came into the hut, the faintest sigh at the very edge of hearing. It seemed that Bianca's chest rose and fell in time with the sound. The air in the hut grew thick. Another presence had entered the hut and Tanoata was filled with awe at what she had done.

Faint and lonely a shout came from the beach, then a great yell from a hundred throats. The dolphins were on the sand, their heavy bodies motionless, their eyes black and round as their breathing holes puckered and gaped.

Tanoata's limbs began to shake. She fell on the ground beside Bianca, twitching and groaning. Her eyes showed white, her tongue protruded. The sound of breathing slid back and forth through the hut.

Tanoata crawled on all-fours around Bianca's shadow-lit form and chanted:

Rokea, listen to me.
See this woman. Come and take her.
Rokea, smell this woman.
She is for you. Come and fetch her.
Rokea, turn in your path.
Open your mouth.
Show her your teeth.
Walk on dry land.

Tanoata took up the knife and pushed the tip against her own flank. She pricked out a semi-circle of wounds from ribs to pelvis, a huge bite mark. The puncture marks stung, her hand burned, the earth was dark with blood. Crawling alongside the earth figure she pressed her wounds against it.

As she lay alongside the Bianca-thing Tanoata knew the waiting rokea wanted more. They wanted her to push the knife into her own belly so her entrails spilled in the dirt. They would come, she had done enough, but they wanted more.

Tanoata sat back on her knees and held the tip of the blade against her stomach. The knife was sharp, her flesh would part like cooked meat. It would be easy to give the Rokea what they wanted, but she did not want to die, she wanted to see Bianca gone, Bianca taken away and destroyed.

The demands of the Rokea made her angry. A blackness descended. Tanoata screamed and slashed the knife across her stomach. The knife flew back and forth, the shallow cuts burned like fire.

Tanoata was a shark. She fell across the effigy's legs and bit and tore until her mouth was full of dirt. Choking, she collapsed face down on the earth.

There she lay for a long moment. Eventually her shoulders heaved, she raised her face from the ground.

Into the hut came a sinister laugh, a dark voice. 'Bianca Hutzenreiter you are gone from here. You were never here. We have already forgotten you.'

Tanoata broke apart the earth effigy, stamped it flat and replaced the rug and sleeping mat. She took up her clothes and knife, extinguished the lamp and walked naked, filthy and bleeding out into the night. The dark laugh was still inside her, it shone through her eyes, it stretched her mouth so wide it hurt. The next time Bianca Hutzenreiter slept in her bed the spell would rise into her and she would die.

Bianca woke on the beach with the rising sun. Dawn light lay low across the sea, sparkled on the reef breakers and glittered on the lagoon.

Many people had slept on the beach, families and friends, single-sex groups of boys and girls. Lost in the rapture of the dance, Tekirei and Bianca found each other. Later, they lay side by side on the sand. He stroked her hair, to Bianca a gesture as full of magic as anything tonight. In the dying firelight she saw his bright, fleeting smile and their mouths had touched. Her hand drifted down his flanks.

Tekirei groaned and rolled away, his arm across his brow. Bianca took his hand and felt his answering grip before he pulled free. It was very late and Bianca was weary. Before she knew it she was asleep.

When she woke, Tekirei took her over to a group of his relatives from the southern village. As they approached, the islanders beckoned her forwards with enthusiastic smiles.

'The thing about Tekirei is that he is a terrible liar,' a middle-aged woman with a plait of grey hair and a beaming smile told Bianca.

'He is atrocious,' said a man of very similar appearance to Tekirei. 'What a brother.'

'I am ashamed,' the woman said.

'I too am very ashamed,' said Tekirei's brother. 'Somewhat more, to be honest.'

A slightly built old man, completely bald, his face seamed by the sun, the muscles on his chest and arms slack with age said, 'As patriarch, it is my duty to feel most ashamed of all.' He beamed with delight. 'I really do feel it.'

Puzzled, Bianca looked at Tekirei.

'What are you talking about?' Tekirei said warily.

'I am surprised you do not remember,' his brother said.

'He fibs all the time, no wonder he can't tell one lie from the next,' said a younger woman, who wore a necklace of small shells.

'If you let me know what it is, I would make amends,' Tekirei said.

'It is clear to me,' the old man said. 'Shall I remind you?'

'Please do, grandfather.'

'When I asked you about this lady from America you said, and I remember your words exactly, that she was quite pretty you supposed.'

'We heard it too,' Tekirei's brother said.

'You were not there,' Tekirei protested.

'My wife told me later. The way she tells stories, you are better off hearing things from her than turning up yourself.'

Tekirei's grandfather held out his hand to Bianca. 'Welcome to Ujelang.'

'Thank you,' Bianca said.

'If you like,' said Tekirei's grandfather, 'you could compliment me on my stature and virility.'

'I was temporarily rendered speechless by your physique,' Bianca said.

'That is very good,' everyone agreed. 'She would fit right in.'

'How long are you staying?' said Tekirei's brother.

'The seaplane is coming to take me back to Ponphie in a day or so.'

'Send it away.'

'Stay for a month.'

Bianca looked to Tekirei but all he did was spread his hands. 'I'd love to, but I have my work. I have to leave.'

'Next time you must come you must stay in our village. The food is terrible, but only when they make me cook,' Tekirei's brother said.

'Stay as long as you like.'

After Bianca had promised she would, Tekirei's family departed along the beach. Bianca and Tekirei walked inland towards the shade of the palms.

'Thank you for bringing me here,' Bianca said.

'You have helped us so much. One day we will be truly independent, we will be able to make everything we need, use our own technology, engineer our own crops. Whatever happens in the rest of the world will not touch us.'

There was a gap. Bianca said, 'Last night–'

'Will have to be last night.' Tekirei increased his pace.

'Tekirei, wait. The dolphins, I never imagined such things.'

Tekirei waited for Bianca to catch up. 'I am being immature. Forgive me.'

'That young man, could I talk to him?'

'He is resting, he is very tired.'

'I see.'

Tekirei saw the doubt in Bianca's face. 'I am not trying to keep him from you. He will sleep all day, and tomorrow too. It is part of the price.'

Bianca was intrigued, 'What is the rest?'

'These things are not free. If you ask for something, you must give something of equal worth. Power for power, life for life. Whatever the Caller has paid is his own secret,' Tekirei hesitated then pushed on, 'Power, magic, money, they are much the same thing.'

The air was a little cooler in the shade. Sand crabs scuttled from their path as they walked towards the village.

'Did you find Tanoata?' Bianca said.

'No.'

'I am sure she is all right.'

'Tanoata is convinced you will take me away. I tell her no, it is not like that, but she does not listen. What can I do? She is all I have.'

'Let me talk to her,' Bianca said. 'Please?'

'Where is she, Bianca?' Tekirei's angry gesture took in sea, land and sky. 'She should have been with her family last night. With me. This morning no-one has seen her. So tell me this - do you see her?'

'No, Tekirei, I don't,' Bianca said quietly.

Tekirei let out his breath. 'Well, then.'

Down at the water margin men and women butchered the dolphins with long knives.

Bestsellers – Non-Fiction

1.   *More! (How to Have It ALL - And then some.)*
2.   *Paying it Backwards: Enrich the deserving Rich.*
3.   *A Bargain in My Basement. An illustrated anthology of retail erotica.*
4.   *Pulling the Serpent's Tooth (Don't let your children rip you off)*
5.   *Living on a Budget – Billionaire's edition.*
6.   *Confessions of a Big-Boned Binger*
7.   *F*ck, I'm Rich! Tales of the Blessedly Wealthy.*
8.   *The Space Plan: Making room for you AND your Possessions.*
9.   *F*ck, I'm Stinking Rich!! More Tales of the Blessedly Wealthy.*
10.   *If You're So Damned Happy Why Did You Buy This Book?*

- 32 -

Crane found his daughter in a grove of wild banana and calabash trees down a steep valley a mile from the house. He could have located her on the house net but preferred to walk the grounds and check each of her favourite haunts.

A dry streambed cut down through the grove to a shallow river below. Choked with jagged boulders and splintered trunks the stream flowed only in flash-floods. When the storms came the water surged in torrents and boulders ground together with a sound of distant artillery. Anything that stood in the way was destroyed.

Crane sat beside his gigantic daughter. 'Snarlow's gone.'

Ellen nodded, multiple chins quivering and billowing as she did. 'I heard the choppers. Did she try and get a loan?'

'She wanted me in her government.' As Crane said it he realised how very strange that was. Snarlow had tried to borrow money in the past, but not now, when she was haemorrhaging billions a day in Mexico.

Ellen frowned. 'There's another plan we're not seeing. Andriewiscz is being careful not to trash the Mexican infrastructure but there aren't enough raws or market to make the invasion worth the capex or the political fallout.'

'I should have thought of that.'

'No pleasure quite like knowing you've been underestimated,' Ellen said.

It was a saying Crane had taught her. In the beginning his popular image had been that of a lucky man, someone who just happened to be in the right place at the right time, an impression he learned to cultivate. In her own way Ellen had done the same. She had met just about every power player in the world, she put things together quickly, none of them had noticed her intelligence. All they had seen was Palfinger Crane's fat daughter, and later, the Steel Nymph.

For a moment Crane was free of his anxieties, his guilt at his own reaction to Ellen's appearance, his inability to save her, his fear, his own failings. He saw his daughter as she truly was.

Beneath that vast body held in its medical frame, under her hunched and fatty shoulders, the internal machinery and ponderous limbs, lost somewhere inside that vast mass of perforated and implanted flesh, was his daughter Ellen. Surviving, living, thinking, feeling. Crane didn't know whether to be proud or sad. He decided he was both.

'She came on to me,' Crane said. Ellen looked startled, immediately Crane felt guilt and embarrassment. 'I'm sorry, too much information.'

Ellen waved it away. 'Oh dear God that is so sad! What was she thinking of? A woman in her position, how desperate.'

'It wasn't that desperate,' Crane said.

'Daddy, you're the best catch in the world. Next to me, obviously. What I meant was, is she totally out of ideas? What kind of reasoning would make her do that?'

Crane put his hand on Ellen's. It dwarfed his as she dwarfed him. He felt like a child sitting beside a statue of Buddha. 'I love you.'

Across the valley a small flock of white-winged parakeets flew between the trees, their wing flashes bright between the foliage. Palfinger and Ellen listened to their raucous calls as they moved down the valley.

'Daddy, you know you're going to live longer than me.'

Crane bit down on his lip. 'There's still a chance.'

'All that talk about life and hope? That's just the contingency plan.'

Crane told her more about President Snarlow's offer, her threats.

'Then I think I'd like to go home. Back to Canada, to Million Pines,' Ellen said.

'Have you spoken to your mother recently?'

Ellen shrugged, a vast, humping movement. 'She sent me a note a while back.'

'She's still in Micronesia?'

'I guess.'

'She needs to know, Ellen.'

If Ellen wanted to go to Canada there was no reason not to. Business could be done anywhere, and if Snarlow's threats were real, hiding was no option.

The more Crane thought about it, the more he liked the idea. Million Pines was remote and enormous, a wilderness of forests, gorges and lakes, its security wide and deep. He'd order improvements, bring across whoever Casavantes had rescued from the Xalapatech labs. Ellen would have some good advice on that too. And she would be happier. Maybe that was the best thing remaining that he could do for her.

246

'Good idea, I've been missing the lodge myself.' He tapped a stud on his collar, St.John responded promptly.

'Yes, Mr. Crane?'

'We've decided to return to Canada.'

'Immediately, sir?'

'Yes.'

'Leave everything to me.'

'Thank you.'

Crane returned to his office and made the call. After a few rings he heard Bianca's cautious voice.

'Hello, Palfinger.'

'Hello Bianca, are you well?'

'It's nice to hear from you.'

'I'm afraid I have some bad news about Ellen.'

There was a brief silence during which Palfinger promised himself he would not argue.

'What's happened now?'

'She's very ill, Bianca. I'm afraid there's nothing more to be done. It's just a matter of time.'

'I see. How long is that?'

'A few months.'

'Oh, well, goodness, I thought you were going to say a few days. That wouldn't be so easy. I'm a thousand miles from civilisation.'

'I can easily collect you.'

'Not now, I'm in the middle of something important.'

What could be more important than this, Palfinger wanted to say. What could be more important than your own daughter? Instead he said, 'I see.'

'I'll be a few more weeks. She'll be all right until then, won't she?'

'Ellen would love to see you, Bianca.'

Bianca sounded distracted, 'She'll be all right until then.'

They Came at Night

'It looks like snow under the street lights but it's a swarm of large flying insects. Shoppers are fleeing for their vehicles. Old men, families, all running, hollering and screaming.

'I don't know what these things are. They're like a cross between hawk moths and giant crickets. People are pouring from the malls with bugs in their hair. There's this guy waving his coat, trying to keep them off his kids.

'A security guard has fallen over, people are just trampling him. He's not moving. God.

'It doesn't look like they bite or sting, there's just so many of them. The stores are empty, the chill zones deserted. The bugs are everywhere, flapping, dropping to the ground, dying as I watch, drifts piling in the gutters, masses clogging the ornamental ponds. I'm – I'm going to go outside.

'Here's one, it's too weak to fly, crawling down the sidewalk, up onto my boot. There's a pattern on the wings, I'll zoom in so you can see. It's like a – What the heck? There's a logo on its wings, NFC. Natural Forces Combine. These guys aren't funny any more. This is a nightmare.'

Eye-witness, RT podcast,
Orlando, FL

- 33 -

Novik got them moving earlier each day. The trail of maxed-out self-store units behind them was creating local back-pressure, convoys of Utes, flatbeds and SUVs loaded with excess possessions filled the highways bound for more distant facilities.

He watched the passing traffic with satisfaction. The more people on the road looking for storage, the fewer there were in the shops. It was a side effect had hadn't anticipated, the law of unforeseen consequences.

Josie's arm slipped around his waist, 'All ready to go, babe.'

The morning air was fresh, Novik felt brim-full of confidence, 'We're having an effect, Josie. We're really starting to make a difference.'

Josie thought about the half empty holdalls in the trunk of the ultra-hybrid they now drove, the immense landscapes to the east and south they could not touch. 'We sure are. It's a good plan.'

At the end of each day Benny, Josie and Marytha scoped out the next day's targets while Novik booked the packaging wholesalers to arrange deliveries.

They were a good team, the overnight motel stops made life more bearable, they were focused and hard-working, even, to Novik's pleasant surprise, Benny. The mission had become a routine, saving the world was no longer an ideal, it had become the day job.

They were heading towards the next Russian Doll self-store when the power warning light on the dash began to blink.

Novik peered up at the overcast sky, 'This cloud isn't letting through enough sun.'

'How's the flywheel?' Josie said.

'Flatlining.'

'Bio-diesel?'

'Sucking fumes.'

The car juddered as it cycled between power sources. Novik pulled into the nearside lane and slowed to the most economic speed. What he'd taken to be a blanking plate on the dash rotated to display a simple top-down graphic of the car and the road ahead. A glowing red dot showed at the edge of the road. It moved past the car and faded.

'What's that mean?' said Novik.

'I don't know.' Josie pointed at the screen, 'Here comes another.'

Novik watched the passing verge. 'I don't see anything.'

The SUV was making about fifteen miles an hour and getting slower. Josie studied the owner's manual, a laminated sheet of simple pictograms. They were moving barely above walking pace when she reached out and touched the nearest red dot on the screen. Immediately the car swung onto the verge, the red dot now centre screen. There was a bump, a scrape, and they pulled back onto the road.

'What did you do? We hit something.' Novik said.

'Nothing that hasn't been hit before.' Josie touched another red circle and once again the car straddled the verge.

Novik looked back through the rear window. Whatever had been there, now it was gone. A deep glutinous gurgle came from somewhere in the lower rear reaches of the vehicle. Josie tapped the screen a third time.

This time Novik saw something. 'It's a dead dog,' he exclaimed.

The car moved over the sad little shape. With a dull rumble and thump the small corpse was gone.

'Roadkill fermentation,' Josie explained. 'Anaerobic maceration digests most of it down to useable hydrocarbons and methane.'

Muffled gloops and blats came from somewhere under the trunk. The warning light on the dash flickered and went out.

Novik tried not to imagine what was going on. 'I really miss Mr. Car.'

'Me too,' Josie sighed.

The vehicle coughed, backfired, then surged forwards. The juddering woke Marytha.

'What's wrong?' Marytha said. 'Are we going to break down?'

'Probably a fur ball,' Novik said. He pressed down on the accelerator, the revs picked up and the car merged back into the traffic. As he drove, Novik replayed the events of the SpaceTime motel once again. However he looked at it, there was one undeniable conclusion - he had acted like a complete jerk. Mr. Car had been a bit of a jerk too, the same way a child is dangerous in its inexperience, that was forgivable. In the jerk stakes Novik knew he, as a nominally mature and legally responsible adult, out-jerked Mr. Car by at least an order of magnitude.

'How about some food?' Benny said.

The silence in the passenger compartment was interrupted by faint gastric rumbles and parps from the vehicle's digester. Nobody else was hungry.

'Where do you think Mr. Car is now?' Josie said.

Marytha grinned, 'If I was him, I'd be hitting the beach.'

'Head over to Daytona or Bonneville.' Novik said

'Yeah, that car was fast! How fast could he go?'

'He never said, we never asked.' Novik said with a pang of regret.

'Maybe one day we'll meet up and we'll find out. That would be cool.'

'Yeah,' Novik said wistfully, 'That would be cool indeed.'

The next job was an hour away. Novik tried to listen to some music. Stations fought it out with classic rap, speed folk, nu-pop, woodpunk, and the ever-present Bariatric Babes. The sounds broke up as they passed from one station's broadcast territory into another's, each tune's lead-in and fade abruptly terminated by hyper-fast adverts for hair products, sex aids, arctic cruises, pre-release Meeja, golf resorts, extreme weather warnings, new mall openings, church arms dealers, secure storage, bankrupt stock sales, plastic surgery, mail-order shoes, tooth whitening, life coaching, logo launches, anal bleaching, Wiccan pensions and family-friendly porn conventions. Every station was overlaid by the muddy boom and sweep of pirate tight-beam channels from motion-sensing microwave transmitters on the roofs of the passing tenements. It was almost the exact opposite of what music was supposed to be.

'Can we eat now? Please,' Benny said.

Novik found a drive-through and they bought shakes, burgers and fries. Josie spelled Novik at the wheel.

Energised by the food Benny said, 'I've been thinking, and you guys really are in a mess. The counter-culture of Western civilisations transcended itself by embracing consumerism and the guilty pleasures of disposable possessions. Then everyone grew up and had more babies. The lie was pretending to recycle some of your shit made it all OK, but there was a feedback circuit everyone forgot about. Money is a symbolic representation of potential energy – you use it as a substitute for actual effort. As a result, consequences become once, twice, or several times removed. Possession replaced ambition, and price ceased to equal cost.'

Marytha's eyes were round as saucers. 'You should stick that on a T-shirt.'

Benny shook his head, 'Sometimes even T-shirts can lie.'

Sweat broke out on Novik's brow. He tried to blank Benny's voice by studying Josie - the way her long, elegant fingers gripped the wheel, the tone of her slender tanned biceps, the play of tendons in her neck, the way her skin sank into hollows above her collar bone.

It wasn't working. Even looking at her breasts, gently shifting with the movement of the car on the open road, her nipples taut against the windblown cotton of her sleeveless red vest, failed to replace the ugly synesthetic sensations of Benny's philosophising.

Josie's smile grew as she felt Novik's gaze. 'You feeling horny, babe?'

'No. I got the mind-patterns of a fruitbat crawling through my brain.'

Novik felt himself sinking down into the seat, falling deeper and deeper like Alice into the burrow.

'Who was that White Rabbit?' said a voice like Benny's.

Jesus, Novik thought, Benny's climbed right inside my head. Reaching up as high as he could, Novik wrapped his arms round Josie's ankle and started to shin up her calf. 'I need a ladder,' he gasped, 'you should wear stockings.' His stomach cramped and he flopped back in his seat, grey with sweat.

Josie eased back on the accelerator, 'Bad mayo in the burger?'

Novik shook his head, 'I don't remember falling down the rabbit hole.'

Josie laid her hand on his brow, a soothing touch. 'You've handled the money more than the rest of us, now you're having flashbacks. Just relax and try to ride them out.'

'It's that Benny,' Novik jerked his thumb over his shoulder. 'He's thinking my thoughts for me.'

'I can't do that, man,' Benny said.

'My mind's shrivelling up like a toad in the sun. I can taste the warts.'

'I think you're hallucinating,' Benny said.

'I knew you were going to say that.' Novik covered his ears and sank down in his seat.

'I'm going to find a drug store' Josie announced. 'You need some vitamin C.'

'Good idea, I tend to be selenium deficient,' Benny said, 'zinc, manganese, anything from period four.'

'I know you do,' Novik sulked, 'I can read your thoughts.'

'No you can't,' Benny said.

Brows furrowing, Novik thought about it. 'You're right, I can't. That is such a relief.'

'You're getting through it,' Josie said. 'Let's find that drug store.'

'And some booze. Lots of booze,' Marytha said. 'I feel like a drink.'

Novik really was feeling better, he twisted round in his seat, 'I know you miss Mr. Car, we all do. Getting numb isn't the way, and believe me, I've tried. We – I dealt with Mr Car the wrong way, but it was still the right decision.'

'That car's got to get a few things out of its system,' Josie said.

Benny said nothing. Novik could feel the eyes of the strange, intense young man on the back of his neck.

'What we're doing with the boxes and the warehouses was Mr Car's idea. It's his legacy, we should never forget, and we should do it the best we can.'

'Amen to that,' Marytha said.

'We need to broaden this out. Get some help, spread the word, find some more people who will buy into the plan.'

'Who can we trust?' Josie said.

Marytha sat up, 'Guys, there's this stoner I busted last year up in Salem, Oregon. He might-'

'Hold on. You're suggesting we give cash to drug users and criminals?'

'Honey!' Josie exclaimed.

'All right, dumb thing to say.'

'I meant he's got some friends,' Marytha continued. 'I hung around them for a while. They're a heavy set but they're cool. Once upon a time we hung out together.'

'What sort of set?' Novik said.

'Standalone crew, independents. No links to the Crips or the Bloods, or the C.O.P.S. for that matter. They started out like me, performance artists. Underneath it all, I think they'd do it just to mess with The Man.'

'Crime as art? It's been tried before.' Novik turned to Josie, 'What do you think?'

'We need the help. It's worth a look.'

The car growled, faltered, and backfired a sulphurous, stinking cloud that set their eyes watering.

'This car's got to go,' Novik wheezed. 'Next one's a convertible.'

'Hey, Rik, we're getting reports of some kind of pilotless car. Described as 'Awesome', and 'Really cool' it sounds like some kind of super slick uber-vehicle.'

'I see it, Ralf. We've got sightings in just about every state from Arizon to Ohio. Hoax or something new, it's too early to tell. Make your own mind up if you got one. People are starting to call it The Grey Ghost. We like that. Here's what they're saying:'

"An Alien Car from Area 51." lonelymomtollfree96942

"I wanna play chicekn" Alabameejedi

"A driverless car. The automotive zeitgeist for these troubled times." T.H.Yousomuch

"A stolen prototype. We'd like it back." (Anon)

'Woah! Lookit that, Rick, a post from the great T.Hank. It's a real honour, sir. Anyone know what it means? You catch a glimpse, ping us realtime. We want it fast, so no email, capiche?'
'Ralf, you wanna play chicekn?'
'Respectfully, cluck off. I'm going to call 96942.'
'Let's have some music.'

Rik'n'Ralf's Podneck Redcast

- 34 -

'This is Ozzie,' Oscar Gordano said into the receiver.

'And this is me.' The voice Gordano recognised as Mitchell Gould was full of tension.

'We cool?'

'Oh yes, we are real cool. What do you want?'

'The party is heading towards the party, so you can get ready to party.'

There was a pause, then: 'What?'

Gordano took a breath. 'Crane's heading back to Canada. When Manalito tells you he's-'

'Enough,' Gould broke in, 'We know what to do. Where's my money?'

'It's all arranged.'

'I don't have it.'

'You will.'

'See to it.'

Gordano put the phone down with a sweating hand. Every time he spoke with Gould he ended up feeling inadequate. Today his attempts at stylish subterfuge had sounded ridiculous even to himself. Then he had blabbed names. No wonder Gould spoke to him with contempt.

Gordano slumped in the big office easy chair. A picture window opened onto a broad, rolling lawn of perfect green stripes. The water in his new pool lay still, unoccupied sun-chairs and parasol-shaded tables stood in neat rows along the edges.

To one side, salad lettuce, tomatoes and green beans grew in a small vegetable plot of freshly dug black earth, the subject of the new 'Gordano Digs for Victory' viral propaganda White House analysts insisted would shunt Exec approval at least seven points.

Down on the lawn, the film crew were setting up. Power leads trailed across the grass, light screens, lamps and cameras stood on tripods and telescopic stands. A bulbous-nosed man wearing khaki shorts, a pink shirt and a soft-brimmed hat issued a stream of instruction - the auteur director Giuseppe Husqvarna. As Gordano watched, Husqvarna looked down at his cell, then up at the house.

Everyone was waiting for Gordano. He was the Vice President of a country at war, he had just given the go-ahead to have the richest family in the world murdered, and now they wanted to film him weeding the lettuce. It was humiliating.

Around the lawn, mature larch, oak, locust-tree, magnolia and palm grew behind deep flower borders. A single huge chestnut tree dominated the rear of the garden, an elaborate tree house in its sweeping branches.

Husqvarna had set his director's chair in the shade of the chestnut. One of the crew had nailed light cables and a pin-board to the trunk. Gordano regarded the activity sourly, he felt trapped, consumed with a total reluctance to go down and join Husqvarna, while also knowing that was exactly what he was going to do.

The tree house was where he and Shirleen used to party, just the two of them. Soft music and candlelight, a bottle of wine, some legal Pharma and a few toys. Shirleen had been hot, she liked bondage, being top, being bottom, she always swallowed. She even liked anal, she actually preferred anal.

Jazmin wasn't into that, or much else for that matter. All she liked were her body mods and piercings, gold, diamond, platinum. Gordano thought her kink might extend to new areas of erotic play. He'd spent a fortune finding out he was wrong. If she walked out on him now, stark naked, taking nothing that wasn't actually attached to her body, she could live on her jewellery for five years.

She stood in the doorway in blood red pants and an open, white leather jacket. 'You don't need me for this do you?' Jazmin studied her nails, 'I'm meeting some girls for cappuccino at the needle parlour.'

'I do need you,' Gordano said. 'I'd really like you to be there with me. It's meant to be a family thing, partners together.'

'Sure, but you don't actually need me. Pulling up weeds, squishing slugs, I mean, look at my manicure.'

'You could wear gloves.'

Jazmin pursed her lips. 'Sure.'

They looked at each other.

'I got to go,' Jazmin turned away. 'Catch you later.'

'Wait,' Gordano said, but she was gone.

A door slammed downstairs. The house became still.

'Dammit to fuckery,' Gordano shouted. 'That's a level three violation, Jazmin. Sonofabitch, you owe me.'

Gordano glared at the thin black Meeja console on his desk, a gift from President Snarlow. He didn't understand how it worked, or why people were so excited by it. It was all so unreasonable the way everything changed. He'd like to see Guinevere Snarlow do this, he'd like to see her humiliated on her hands and knees. The idea of filming made his guts clench, the Meeja seemed the ideal opportunity to delay. Gordano settled the wireless headset onto his scalp and turned on the machine.

The machine began to hum, an internal cooling fan began to blow, a bank of LEDs phased from amber to green. Gordano waited a minute, then another. There was a piece of notepaper on the desk he hadn't noticed before, probably a warranty or delivery note. He'd look at it later. Right now it seemed nothing was happening. Either the console was broken or he hadn't set it up right. There was nothing else for it, Gordano shoved himself to his feet and went down to the garden and the waiting film crew.

Much to his surprise he found Guinevere Snarlow talking to Husqvarna, one arm draped around the director's shoulder. Her skirt was short, her legs bare and her normally crisp blouse rumpled and gaping.

'Oscar, darling.' Guinevere turned as she saw him, staggered, and fell into Husqvarna's arms. Laughing, she gave the director a lingering kiss. 'I came over to see you become a superstar.'

She's drunk, Gordano realised angrily, then filled with alarm at the wider implications.

'Listen up,' Gordano said. 'This is now a closed set. Any of the crew with recording devices, turn them off and check them in right now. That is an Executive order.'

Resentfully the crew filed past. One by one they deposited a range of micro, mini and full-size broadcast quality video and sound equipment. A ludicrously big stack of kit piled up. Everyone was packing, some with two or even three pieces.

A snub-nosed athletic young woman wearing a sleeveless black club-gear vest hung back. Gordano knew what the problem was straight away. 'Just a moment, young lady. That vest of yours has woven tech.'

She looked at him haughtily, hands on hips. 'So? It's my top. You want me to take it off?'

She was cute but Gordano wasn't in the mood. 'Change it or leave the set.'

Seeing his determination, her mood changed. 'There's not much gets by you. I like that.' Coquettishly, she pulled the zip front open halfway to her navel. 'I'll wait for you in the house.'

Husqvarna detached himself from Guinevere. 'Oscar, are we expecting your wife?'

Gordano shook his head. 'She's gone shopping.'

Husqvarna's sensual mouth pursed with disappointment. 'The script calls for two people. Never mind, we'll improvise – she's gone to the garden centre.'

President Snarlow pushed between them. 'I can do it. I'd be great.'

Husqvarna and Gordano exchanged a worried look.

'Guinevere, I'm sure you would, but don't you feel a little tired?' Gordano said.

'I'm absolutely fine.' From somewhere the President produced a heavy silver hip flask, took a deep swig and wiped her mouth. Lipstick smeared across her cheek. 'I want to do it. I'm the President, I can do whatever I want.'

Husqvarna snapped his fingers. 'Makeup!'

A few minutes later Gordano and Guinevere knelt at the edge of the vegetable patch on green vinyl weeding mats. Facing them Husqvarna stood beside his camera ready to pan and zoom through rows of beans, lettuce and sweet-corn.

'Action,' Husqvarna said.

Gordano grinned cheesily at the camera, 'Guinevere, you know, this is actually good fun. I haven't done this since I was a kid.'

Guinevere dug her hands into the earth, 'I've always enjoyed getting dirty on my hands and knees.'

Inwardly Gordano groaned in despair. She was going to ruin this, it was going to go out across the nation, across the world, and it would be a disaster. Somehow he would get the blame, once again he would be the stupid Vice President, the laughing stock.

The other side of the tomatoes Husqvarna twirled his finger – keep going.

Gordano pressed on. 'Fresh vegetables are a great source of vitamins.'

Behind him came the sound of sniggers and muffled laughter. Gordano saw three or four of the road crew had retrieved their cameras and were surreptitiously filming Guinevere's backside.

'Give me that.' Gordano seized the wrist of a heavily tattooed man and prised the small camera from his grip.

'Hey,' the roadie objected, 'be careful with that.'

'You were warned not to do this,' Gordano told him. 'You're in deep trouble.'

The roadie laughed in Gordano's face, 'Not as deep as the President.'

Gordano pressed 'Play.' Guinevere's rump filled the screen, her short, pleated skirt barely covered her full and shapely buttocks. A gust of wind lifted the hem and Gordano nearly dropped the camera. Today it seemed Guinevere wore no knickers. Unable to stop watching Gordano saw her look round, blow a kiss to the camera and wiggle her backside.

'Cut! Stop filming now. Oh dear God, cut!' Gordano's hand spasmed and the camera crumpled. Metal, circuitry, plastic and glass shattering in his grip and he flung it aside.

Balanced on her knees and one arm the President was drinking from her flask. She saw Gordano, lost her balance and rolled onto her back. Her skirt rode up to her waist to reveal a shaven pudenda.

All around them mobile devices were filming, streaming data into the air, the massive bandwidth of his house net gave near-instant uploads to dozens of sites across the world. Only Husqvarna was not filming. Then Gordano noticed that he too surreptitiously held a small device in his palm. They were completely and utterly screwed.

'You stupid, foolish woman,' Gordano shrieked. 'What've you done?'

Guinevere frowned, looked down at herself and giggled, 'I've been a very naughty girl and let the boys see my front bottom.'

Appalled, Gordano hauled her to her feet. This was the woman he had sworn to serve, the person he had chosen to dedicate his career to. 'I used to admire you, Guinevere, but this? You're not fit to lead this country.'

Crestfallen, Snarlow sagged against him. 'You're right. I never wanted to be President. My alcohol-fuelled nymphomania has become impossible to control. Oscar, I resign in your favour. You take over, show the world how a real man does the job. Just promise me this: let me be your lowliest intern. Let me see how a man of genuine courage and real integrity leads our great nation to glory.' She slid down onto her knees, her head on his hip, her mouth close to his groin, 'I'll blow you every day, I'll worship you and be your dirty little bitch, I'll take it in the dirt-box. Let me serve the nation by serving you, however I can, no matter how degrading. Please, Oscar, just do what you want.'

Husqvarna had started to film again. Roadies, drivers and sound engineers stood around them at a respectful distance and politely applauded. 'We're right behind you, Mr. Gordano,' they cheered. 'We only voted for her because you were her running partner.'

This is unreal, Gordano thought. It also felt right, the way things ought to be. Finally he was being recognised as the leader he truly was.

A telephone rang. Guinevere dug around in her bag and extracted her mobile. 'I've resigned,' she slurred and passed the handset to Gordano.

'Yes?'

'This is Andriewiscz,' the general's voice was clogged with emotion.

'We've won.'

'Well done, general.'

'Congratulations to you too, Mr. President. If you still want me on your staff I'd be honoured.'

'Of course. And General, I'm authorising immediate release of all military back pay with a twenty percent bonus for all combat troops.'

'That's fantastic news, sir. I can guarantee the total loyalty of the armed forces.'

As soon as Gordano broke the connection the phone rang again.

'This is Ahmed Hirsch, President of the European Union, and former Chancellor of Germany.' Hirsch's heavily-accented English sounded timorous, 'First, let me offer my sincere congratulations, Mr. President.'

'What do you want, Hirsch?'

'Your decisiveness is intimidating, there is little point confronting a man of your calibre. The EU is prepared to return to Free Market economics and accept American goods without tariffs.'

'I demand reparations,' Gordano heard himself saying.

'Agreed. How does one hundred quadrillion Euros sound?'

Gordano didn't know there was that much money in the world. As if he was reading his mind Hirsch said, 'Palfinger Crane has been our stooge for years. His wealth is but a tiny fraction of what we can put at your disposal.'

Text and voice messages flowed in from all over the world: congratulations, pleas for American leadership and promises of friendship. Pride swelled Gordano's chest, he had showed them all, every single one. All it had taken was a few decisive words and a bold attitude, and in just a few minutes the world was a better place and America was saved. With immense satisfaction Gordano watched two FBI agents cuff a crestfallen Guinevere Snarlow.

'Where shall we take her, sir?'

'Lock her to the radiator in my basement,' Gordano said.

'Thank you,' Snarlow grovelled pathetically, 'just give me a doggie bowl to eat from.'

The agents saluted and led her away.

Gordano grinned at the film crew. 'That went pretty well.'

'Hell, yeah,' the crew agreed.

'Absolutely, Mr. Gordano'

'You showed them, sir.'

The circle of men and women fell silent. It seemed they breathed in and out together, and swayed gently from side to side. It was uncanny.

A figure in a rust orange sweater and brown slacks approached from the house. With calm detachment Gordano recognised it as himself.

'Hi there,' said the new Oscar Gordano. 'Sorry to interrupt.'

'What's going on? I don't understand,' the original Gordano said.

'I've run your free-form fantasy as far as I can, now I need further directions. Do you want to take the camera girl thing further, or go with Snarlow?'

'Who are you?'

'I am your Meeja console. 2.0.1.3 beta at your service.'

Gordano still sat in his office. His hands trembled as he removed the headset and turned off the console. For a while he looked into nowhere. Contradictory feelings of disappointment and relief vied with the sense of empowerment from the simulation. He laughed ruefully and shook his head. It had been too good to be true, but what an incredible piece of fakery that machine was. Once again, Guinevere was right and he was out of the loop. Even so… His hand strayed back to the console.

Then he started out of his chair. Husqvarna would be going insane. Gordano looked at his watch and stared in disbelief. Less than two minutes had passed by.

Breaking News:

Snarlow deploys National Guard in Minnesota, Wisconsin, New York, and Vermont.

'I am no longer prepared to tolerate the continued territorial infringements by armed militias in the north-east,' said President Snarlow. 'We have a duty to protect our citizens and their possessions from harm.'

Secretary of State Cheswold Lobotnov dismissed criticism that Federalising the State Militias was unconstitutional. 'Article 1, Section 8, Clause 15 of the Constitution permits the President to call upon the Militia to suppress Insurrection and repel invasion. That's what she's doing.'

In a separate statement, Vice President Oscar Gordano called for vigilance along the border and described Canada as a 'terrorist state run by eco-gangsters'.

Canadian government sources described the accusations as 'beyond belief' and 'incomprehensible'.

Slobodan Jones,
KUWjones.org

- 35 -

They were an hour out of Winnemucca, cutting north-west on State 140. Masters had the car on full manual, driving very fast, relaxed and confident as she steered the vehicle through the local freight and inter-state bulktrans.

She swung out to overtake a pair of body-and-six road-trains, nose to tail. 'This Manalito is a real pain in the ass. If he'd been dumb enough to fly we'd have him by now.'

Oncoming traffic flashed their lights, Masters accelerated hard, the turbo kicked in and they surged forwards. The cheerful pastel geometries of domestic logos sped by, the distance to the oncoming traffic shrank at an alarming rate.

Wilson tensed, swore under his breath, his right leg instinctively pushed down into the passenger footwell.

Master pulled in. Horns blaring, oncoming traffic hurtled past. She looked at Wilson dispassionately, 'I don't get off on backing down.'

'That was toilet paper. You nearly got us killed overtaking five hundred cubic metres of ass-wipe.'

'You panicked,' Master bared her teeth, 'I had one point three seconds clear air.'

They drove into an emptier landscape. Active billboards scanned the vehicle, passenger ID requests were rebuffed by the vehicle's firewall and the hoardings fell back to default adverts.

'Guns, talent contests and peanut jelly. What kind of lives do these people live?' Wilson said.

'American ones,' Masters said. 'This is what it's all about.'

She was serious, she had been brought up to believe these were important choices. More real than avenging the death of a loved one.

'So you guys don't like high-end technology.' Wilson said. 'What about your FaF guns? They're pretty damned smart.'

'Smart but not bright.' Masters concentrated on the open road. 'We like kit that does what it's told. Field tech should be push-button clever, it shouldn't make decisions on your behalf. That's what gets you lit up. It especially shouldn't rely on outsourced infrastructure.'

'The FedMesh?'

'Exactly. The Feds made some bad choices, saturated themselves with bleeding-edge cloud tech and got burned to the bone. The Mesh is totally compromised but they've got to use it because there's nothing else and they can't afford to set up again from scratch.'

'So it's just another dirty net.'

'It's more of a meta-Cloud.' Masters frowned then trilled with laughter. 'It occurs to me, maybe it was a smart move after all. The Fed's original infrastructure no longer exists, it was so heavily swamped by bot-nets it was effectively dead in the first week.' She slapped the wheel and laughed, short and hard. 'I love that idea. They set it up, waited for it to get hacked, spoofed, and cloned, then took the original one away. All they needed was kit on short rental and now the perps are actually running the system for the Feds, for free.'

'I got about half of that,' Wilson said. 'You make me feel old.'

Master's mouth twitched with amusement. 'That's so cute. Have we got a father-daughter thing going here?'

Wilson looked down at his paunch. 'It's a feeling obsolescent and bypassed thing.'

'You've got some relevant skills. It's why you're here.'

'That so?'

'Sure.'

Wilson looked at her profile, her dark lashes and grey eyes, the clear line where the top of her upper lip met her philtrum. Her skin was pale and perfect, like she'd stayed out of the sun or worked underground. She had probably never worn makeup in her life.

'What's your first name?' he said.

Masters took her eyes off the road. She looked disconcerted, puzzled. 'Do you really want me to call you Jerry?'

Out in the middle of nowhere they passed an enormous Mall. Brand new, it dwarfed the stadium church beside it. Logos fifty feet high shone across a vast and near-empty parking lot, the gigantically enlarged faces of this month's celebrities gazed down on the flawless tarmac, sliding travelators and rows of new-planted trees.

Five miles further on was Bog Hot Reservoir, a one-road strip town with a row of bleached-out storefronts, yellow-eyed dogs and no children. Toxic scrubland stretched east, blighted tussock grass and ragworts grew and died beside rust stained pools in a wasteland of rotting brickwork and corroded machinery.

The smart money trackers pinged.

Masters swore, broadsided the car to a halt and pressed her hand to her earpiece. The car sat in the middle of the potholed road. Hot metal ticked. Nothing stirred.

'What is it?' Wilson said.

'We just passed Manalito.' Masters unclipped her seat belt slammed the car into gear and accelerated back the way they had come. 'They were in the damned Mall.'

A mile from the mall Masters slowed down and cruised into the parking lot at a legal twenty. A few cars dotted the acres of clean tarmac: abandoned break-downs, joy-ride burnouts and stolen commercials. Most of the white and yellow bay markings were unblemished by tyre marks.

Huddled against the mall walls beside the loading bays and staff door was a neat line of modest cars, the compact electrics and D.I.Y. hybrids of the low-income store workers.

A sparse scatter of customer vehicles were parked in front of the huge revolving doors leading to the air-conditioned interior of the gigantic mall. Masters drove past the saloons, 4WD pick-ups and smoked-glass SUVs and parked fifty yards to the right of the main entrance.

'Manalito's inside, we'll take him when comes out, before he reaches his vehicle,' Masters said as she got out of the car. She opened up the back, dragged out one of the cases and opened it to reveal a fat-barrelled pistol similar to her own.

'This fires .22 low-V sedative darts of d-rotated curare. It puts them down but doesn't stop the diaphragm. Head shot's a killer, anywhere else and they're jello in two seconds.' Sliding the bolt, Masters flipped the gun round and presented it to Wilson. 'Think you can handle this?'

As Wilson took hold of the bulky gun his pulse began to race. He took a deep breath and exhaled slowly. 'Sure.'

Masters looked him in the eye, Wilson looked steadily back. 'OK,' she said. 'My weapon has smart munitions, yours does not. Mine keys to the optic nerve, yours does not. It's just a gun that fires bullets.'

Wilson was both disappointed and relieved. 'Right.'

'It's a bloody good gun.'

And then Wilson saw Manalito exit from the mall. The big man was dressed in tan knee boots, denim jeans and a red check shirt. Loose black hair hung to his collar, he carried a green holdall over his shoulder, another in his hand.

'Jeez, he's big,' Wilson said. He started forwards, Masters' hand on his shoulder brought him up short.

'Hold here,' she said. 'Stay out of sight, back me up if I need it.'

Then she was gone, walking smartly towards Manalito along the service pavement beside the wall of the mall.

'Excuse me, sir,' Masters waved her left hand high in the air. 'Excuse me, is that your car?'

Manalito hesitated, taken in by her grey trouser suit and brusque, business-like walk. Then he shook his head and walked away.

'Hold it!' Masters pulled her gun and fired twice, not bothering to aim. The bullets leaped up, spat white fire and buzzed towards Manalito like hornets.

Manalito dropped his bags, snatched a heavy knife from his boot and threw.

The bullets swung down and slapped into Manalito's chest.

Masters swayed to one side, the knife flashed passed her shoulder and skittered across the tarmac.

Manalito staggered, pulled another knife, took a single drunken step and crumpled to the ground.

Morgan and Black exited from the mall and stared at Manalito's sprawled form. Then they drew their own guns and broke for cover among the vehicles. Masters fired four more times. The bullets arced away, darted behind the parked vehicles and struck the running men.

Masters stood over the paralysed Manalito. He watched her with cold and murderous eyes.

'You are disappeared,' she told him. 'You have no rights. The only way to avoid capital interrogation is to sing like a fucking canary.'

Masters holstered her gun, rolled Manalito onto his stomach and cuffed his wrists and ankles.

As she did, Wilson saw the rear doors of one of the SUVs kick open and two people run out. 'Masters! Incoming,' Wilson yelled.

Masters snatched out her gun. A man appeared in front of her, hands raised. 'Don't shoot me,' he said. 'Please.'

He was tall, slim, athletic, with bleach-blond hair. Crouched behind his car Wilson gaped in astonishment. It was Gould. Mitchell Gould stateside, out of his lair in the southern literal. Wilson found his hand was shaking. He braced his arm on the car's hood and took aim. Before he could fire, a lightly built oriental woman walked behind Masters and emptied her gun into Master's back.

Changing aim, Wilson fired at the woman. His bullets zoomed away on flat trajectories, impacting on the car behind her. The woman rolled behind a red compact and returned fire. Gould picked up Masters' gun and fired at Wilson, the bullet slapped harmlessly against the windscreen. Gould frowned, made an adjustment on the gun and fired again.

The car blew up, slammed sideways into Wilson. He tumbled across the car park like a broken doll.

Barely conscious, Wilson watched Gould and the woman haul Manalito towards their SUV.

Two security guards ran from the mall, weapons drawn. Gould fired Masters' gun and destroyed the front of the mall. The guards retreated inside and began a slow and inaccurate fire. Gould covered the woman while she rescued Morgan and Black.

Incoming fire became more accurate, Gould fired another explosive shell into the mall and the foyer roof collapsed in an avalanche of sliding tiles. Quickly Gould searched Masters, took everything he found, then scrambled into the SUV. The vehicle made a fast, tight turn, glanced off a light compact and sped away unchallenged.

Wilson lurched to his feet and looked across a scene of devastation. The mall entrance was a blazing wreck, their own car was destroyed. Masters lay untidily on the tarmac. Wilson clutched his ribs and hobbled towards her.

He thought Masters was dead. He knelt beside her and she opened her eyes.

'I'm not going to make it,' she whispered. 'You have to get away from me.'

'I'll get help.'

There was blood in Masters' mouth. Her lower back seemed disconnected from her torso. 'Keep away,' she told him. 'I have a cardiac implant, Executive Room Service, I'm deniable.' She worked her mouth and swallowed, 'Knew the risks. It won't hurt.'

Wilson took off his jacket, folded it into a pad and slipped it under her head.

'Who are you?' he said. 'Really.'

She nearly broke then, a flicker of terror at what was to come, the end of her one and only precious life. Then she clenched her jaw, 'Get away.'

Wilson stroked her brow. She looked very young. Once upon a time she had been somebody's daughter. 'I'm not going to leave you.'

'I- I'm thirsty.'

He went to look for water and found some soda cans scattered round a broken machine. As he made his way back, Masters gave a high-pitched shriek and unfolded like a flower. Leaf-like white flames rapidly spread from her torso, consuming clothing, flesh and bone.

Wilson watched her burn until there was nothing but a low spread of greasy ash. Heartsick, he returned to the wreck of her car. There, he retrieved his FaF gun, broke open the glove box and retrieved the smart-money tracker. The case was scratched and pitted but data still scrolled across the screen.

A handful of people had made their way out of the mall. They helped each other into their cars and drove away.

Sirens were in the distance. Wilson slipped the tracker into his pocket and stashed the gun in one of the cases. Then he broke into a serviceable looking pickup, jumped the engine, and set of along the road after Gould.

- 36 -

Bianca sat on the grass and watched the frigate birds swoop among the trees, the grey-backed terns skim along the reef line. The atoll graveyard was a bright, happy place, nothing like the sombre, totemic scene she had imagined.

She had walked along the Shadowed Path, unsettled by Palfinger's call, reluctant to revisit old thoughts she had carefully and methodically packed away. Not needed on Voyage. Rather, she told herself she might find Tanoata, that if she could only talk to that bright, unhappy child they would become friends.

Two paths meandered around the atoll, one along the outer rim, one beside the inner lagoon. Bianca headed north on the outer path, past plantings of taro, sweet potato and yam, then through new groves of engineered salt-tolerant banana and citrus, cultivars developed with her own money. Overhead the sky was clear, the air hot and dense. Far out across the ocean dark squalls beat the sea with wind and rain.

The sandy track swung inland from the palm fringed beach, then back again as the atoll curved west. After an hour Bianca saw the outlying thrust of the graveyard promontory, a dense grove of palms swaying in the sea breeze at the far end.

An aeon ago the volcano upon which the atoll was formed spewed a long arm of lava down into the sea in a vast eruption. Eroded and sunken through the ages, it formed the base of the lonely promontory where generations of islanders now lay buried.

Another mile brought Bianca to an open strip of grassy ground. Simple graves, low mounds of friable pale earth, lay all arround. As Bianca walked between the graves she wondered at their inhabitant's lives and times. None of the graves were marked, it was impossible to tell which one was Nei-Teakea. Tekirei would know, Bianca thought, he and Tanoata.

Her walk brought her to the palm grove at the end of the promontory.

Here was unexpected formality, the trees planted in evenly spaced rows, some lofty, a few recently planted, each a memorial to the departed. Beyond the grove the lagoon waters were shallow, the reef less than a hundred feet away. Swells of glassy green oceanic water surged across its surface.

The bright sun, colourful busy birds and shady palms created an atmosphere of pleasant solitude. Bianca decided this would be a good place to spend eternity. With the lagoon on three sides, and the open sky above there would always be something to see. She grew introspective, Nei-Teakea was a woman she could never know, who had lived a life she would never share. The sounds of the ocean and birds faded and Bianca's mind led her to a strange place:

Two years ago a small flotilla of fishing canoes tossed in the water beyond the reef. A shoal of juvenile Bonito moved below, and the fishers cast lines into the water. Bait was taken, the lines became taut, five and six pound fish were hauled from the ocean.

A pair of the canoes floated side by side. Tekirei and Nei-Teakea fished from one, two brothers from another family in the other. The brothers hooked a larger fish, one hauled it in while the other readied his club.

As they pulled in their catch a *rokea* took half the fish off the line, severing it with one bite. Tension fell away, the head of the Bonito flew into the air and landed in the canoe.

The brothers let out a fearful shout. Before they could throw back the fish the *rokea*, enraged at the theft of its prey, attacked the canoes.

There was a sudden jar, a disorienting whirl, the shock of sudden immersion. Bianca floated as Nei-Teakea, frightened and disoriented. Nearby, both brothers were also in the water. Tekirei lay stunned in the bottom of his half-swamped canoe.

The other canoeists dropped their lines and raced to the rescue. Beneath the surface the rokea flashed and turned.

One of the brothers flung up his arms and disappeared beneath the waves. A great wail of anguish came from the canoes.

Nei-Teakea swam away from the wreckage with long, steady strokes. She felt a powerful blow on her thigh and could no longer swim easily. Reaching down, she found her leg was gone, taken too quickly for pain. That is just a leg, she thought. I must not panic. Around her the ocean bloomed darkly.

A canoe drew alongside, the hull wet and black. Nei-Teakea existed in a state of heightened senses: every detail of the wood grain was clear to her eye; reflected sunlight danced along the hull; water slapped and gurgled. A thousand plans burned in her mind. Life would drastically change from now on, but she would still have her family, Tanoata. She knew she would cope, and decided she would do more than that, she would thrive. One day she would look back and see this as a turning point, a redefinition of her life. It came to her then, she would have another child.

Strong hands seized her wrists. Among the people in the canoe she saw her father, his mouth and eyes wide.

Before her rescuers could draw her up, the *rokea* struck again.

Nei-Teakea looked up into appalled faces, and felt her belly unravel into the crimson ocean.

Bianca opened her eyes slowly. She rubbed her arms, chilled despite the sun. The birds had fallen silent, the shadows within the grove lay deep and still. She discovered she no longer wished to sit alone at the end of the promontory with the ocean at her back. The way through the open burial ground, with its rattling, yellow grasses, had acquired a watchful presence. Bianca hurried past the grave mounds, the earth under her bare feet felt unpleasantly aware.

Safe on the path, Bianca faced the graves. 'Nei-Teakea, I know you were first. I know you still live in Tekirei's heart. I have no desire that he forget you, I don't wish to replace you.'

Further words failed her, half of those already spoken felt like lies. Bianca looked at the graves. Only half of Nei-Tekea was buried here, the rest lived with the rokea.

Something clacked against a palm trunk – a heavy coral fragment. Seconds later another piece flew past her shoulder.

All around was silence. Even the wind had died.

'Tanoata?' Bianca called. 'Is that you? Your father is worried. Come out, we will go back to the village together.'

Undergrowth rustled, another rock flew from a new direction.

Bianca ducked and dodged the missiles. One struck her forearm, sharp and painful. She tried to retreat, Tanoata cut her off. More stones flew. Bianca grew angry, she strode towards the place the missiles came from. 'Stop this, Tanoata. It all about your own feelings. It is nothing to do with me.'

Tanoata stepped from behind a tree. Her hair was a rats nest, her arms and stomach covered with inflamed scratches and cuts. In her hand she held a knife.

Bianca felt very afraid.

Tanoata tipped back her head and bared her teeth. 'Die,' she snarled, then faded back into the vegetation. Shaking with fear, Bianca hurried back to the village.

A sudden wind gusted up the path towards the graveyard. Overhead, the palm tops tossed wildly, the trunks groaned and creaked. The wind pushed against Bianca, half blinded her with grit, then died away.

The village was deserted, Tekirei nowhere to be found. Exhausted by her experiences, Bianca sat outside Tekirei's hut to wait for him. Despite herself, she fell asleep. When she awoke it was dark, the village still empty and silent. She went to her own hut, lowered the wall screens and washed. Then she lay down on her mat and was soon asleep.

All her dreams were nightmares.

Here's a round-up of today's headlines:

Wesley Strosner, of Venus Maxima magazine, is mounting a legal challenge to the current ban on whole-body polypropylene implants. Absorbing fluid at 0.01% volume every 24 hours, WBPP implants offer non-stop mass gain.

Scientists were right, global warming did bring fewer, bigger hurricanes. We have the same number of hurricanes in the Caribbean this year as we did the last – one. Hurricane Larry.

Recent advice by doctors to eschew car park travelators and walk to the mall is being ignored. A new survey finds shoppers don't want to exercise. A majority of people feel they 'look better sitting down'.

Stained glass – The Poor Man's Bible. Did Christianity invent the Graphic Novel? Download Secular Bob's latest show >>Here<<

- 37 -

Gunshots cracked in the night air as the speeding convertible fishtailed down the back alley between the trashcans and abandoned cars. Marytha was driving, Josie rode shotgun in the passenger seat, a semi-automatic recoilless shotgun in her hands.

Novik dragged Benny down into the rear seat, 'Keep your damned head down!'

Benny wriggled free. 'It's OK, I've turned on my force-field.'

Bright flashes crackled in the darkness behind them. Bullets whizzed and zipped through the air.

A shot carried away a wing mirror. More slugs struck sparks from the rear fender, others punctured the trunk lid with hot, metallic plangs.

Josie emptied the shotgun and tossed it out of the car.

Marytha barrelled the car towards the end of the alley. She dropped the clutch, hauled on the handbrake, spun the wheel and flipped the car broadside into a gap in the traffic.

Tyres squealed, horns sounded, headlights flashed. They took a fast right, a slower left. Marytha cruised sedately in the night-time traffic.

Josie dropped back into her seat. 'That could have been worse.'

Novik kissed Marytha on the back of the head. 'Outrageously good driving.'

Marytha grinned, 'Two weeks on the cop skid-pan. Everyone OK?'

'Sure,' Novik said.

'I'm fine,' Josie said.

Benny slumped against the door, his fingers fluttered around a dark, spreading stain high on his chest. 'I think I've been hit,' he croaked. 'It really hurts.'

Novik checked Benny over. It wasn't easy to see in the poor light. 'What do you expect? Getting shot is what happens when you think you're special. You idiot.'

It had gone wrong from the moment Marytha knocked on the stoner's door.

'Shit, it's you,' the skinny, shirtless, dude said. He tried to slam the door shut on the steel toe-cap of Marytha's boot, said 'Shit' again, and fled through his semi-derelict flat. He clambered through the rear window and clattered down the fire escape. Two floors below, Novik and Benny had already started up.

'Shit,' the dude whined as he saw Novik and Benny. Above him, Marytha was climbing through the window. The dude danced a jig of frustration, 'Shit, fuck, shit.'

The window beside the dude flew up. A young female voice yelled into the night, 'What's up, dude? Why you swearing and profaning all through the motherfucking night?'

'Stay out of it, Merlotta,' the dude said. 'I'm being busted.'

'No shit?'

'For real.'

'I'll call my man.'

'Don't get involved,' the dude said.

'You sure?'

'I'm sure.' The dude held up his hands, 'All right, I'm coming back up.'

Novik and Benny followed him. As the passed Merlotta's window, they saw a well-proportioned Hispanic woman with braided hair and gold hoop earrings. 'Motherfuckers,' she mouthed silently at them.

When Novik reached the flat, the dude sat disconsolately on a stained mattress. Barefoot and shirtless, a string of wooden beads round his neck, he looked like a pale, northern-city version of a surfer.

'I went to court, I swear,' the dude said to Marytha. 'I took your citation and I went, God be my witness.'

'Take a look on top of the wardrobe,' Marytha said to Josie.

'Look what I found,' Josie lifted down a nickel plated single-barrelled shotgun. 'It's loaded, too.'

'Sports shotgun,' Benny said as he climbed through the window. 'Three rounds a second and totally recoilless. You can fire it one handed. However you look at it, that's not very sporting.'

'It's for the pigeons,' the dude protested. 'Listen, Officer Drummond, you got to believe me, I went to court and they said they had no record of the arrest, nothing on file. They didn't even know your name.'

'Forget it,' Marytha said. 'That's not why I'm here.'

'You still a cop?'

'What makes you think I ever was?'

'?'

Josie cradled the shotgun in her arms. 'She's a performance artist. When she was dressed as a cop she didn't arrest you, she embraced you in her art.'

'I was exploring the interface between individual freedom and the will of the state as I strove to embody the proto-myth of law, destiny, and female cop-ness,' Marytha said.

The dude looked at Marytha with wounded eyes, his voice broke hoarse and high, 'You were a fake cop? All that guilt, all that angst, for nothing.'

Marytha shrugged, 'No harm done.'

The dude gave a long shriek of existential fury.

Merlotta's shrill voice carried up from her apartment window, 'Stop torturing him, you motherfuckers. I'm phoning, I really am.'

This wasn't going anything like the way Novik wanted. He sat the dude up and offered him his hip flask. 'Take it easy, we just want to talk.'

The dude took a long pull, then another. Josie offered him a tissue and he noisily blew his nose. The dude took a third drink and looked up at Novik with suspicious eyes, 'What do you want?'

'We need to talk to some guys you know,' Marytha said. 'We need their help.'

The dude shook his head in wonderment. 'No shit you need help. You crazy motherfuckers.'

'This isn't working,' Novik said. 'We should leave.'

Marytha looked down at the dude. 'We just want to find these guys, then we're out of here. Are we cool?'

The dude's shoulders slumped, 'Yeah, we cool.'

Down in the street car tyres screeched. Josie tossed an envelope of hundred dollar bills into the dude's lap. 'This is for you. Be careful, it's contaminated with fluorinated LSD.'

The dude was impressed. 'Man, you want to be careful with that stuff. People say it never gets metabolised. The only way it gets out your body is in your fingernails and hair.'

'It's fat-soluble,' Benny told him. 'You could eat a lot of burgers and get liposuction.'

'You really are crazy,' the dude said.

'He thinks he's an alien,' Novik said.

Benny looked affronted. 'I don't think-'

'We're looking for a man called Halifax,' Marytha said.

Footsteps pounded up the stairs. The apartment door banged open and three of the heaviest guys Novik had ever seen pushed into the room.

'You just found him,' the dude said. 'Meet Merlotta's man.'

Front and centre stood a huge and muscular black guy in combat boots and pants, and an open denim jacket with torn off sleeves. An unlit pipe was clamped in his teeth. His mouth was cruel, his nose was patrician, his nostrils flared with anger. 'Dude, you all right?' Halifax growled.

Cross-legged on the mattress, the dude carefully wiped each of Josie's bills with a damp cloth. 'I'm hanging loose, bro.'

Behind Halifax was an athletically slim white man with a flat-top crew cut. Broad shoulders tapered to a lean waist, his chest covered by a close fitting Breton jumper, his legs in black cargoes and army boots. His brown eyes swept the room, stopped at Josie, he gave a lopsided half smile and dipped his head.

The third man was a lithe oriental with a wisp of beard and alert eyes. Dressed in black silk he balanced on the balls of his *jika-tabi* clad feet and twirled a *nunchaku* in his hand.

Halifax's voice was low and menacing, 'Which one of you arseholes is looking for me? And what have you been doing to the dude?'

Novik had met this type before. In prison he'd had to learn to match like for like, then they'd back down. 'We haven't done anything, motherfucker.'

The three intruders looked at each other.

'Motherfucker?' Halifax said calmly. 'Marcel, Xiong, did this gentlemen just call me a motherfucker?'

The white guy still smiled his half smile, his eyes still rested on Josie, 'I heard him.'

'Collect,' Xiong agreed.

A floor below Merlotta shrieked out her window, 'Hey dude, don't be afraid, I called my man. He's going to stomp those pig motherfuckers.'

Halifax winced at Merlotta's outburst and bawled back, 'I'm up here Merlotta. These arseholes aren't going nowhere.'

Novik didn't like the way the white guy looked at Josie and he didn't like Halifax's attitude. He didn't even like the way he spoke.

Halifax grinned at Novik. 'You got a problem, boy?'

'We came to talk, but you don't have anything I want to hear.'

Halifax's laugh was slow and deep, 'That's because you are a cloth-eared plonker.'

'Hey Halifax,' Marytha said urgently. 'Remember me?'

'Marytha?' The pipe fell out of Halifax's mouth, he caught it in his hand. 'Long time, girl. You still doing that fake cop thing?'

'I gave it up.'

'I hate cops,' Halifax said.

'How's it with you?'

'We got some corners. We pay it up and we pay it down, and when we have to, we pay the Man.' Halifax shrugged, half in apology, 'It got kind of real.'

'That always was the problem with method acting.'

Halifax laughed, 'Yeah, I guess Gielgud was right.'

'We had some times, didn't we, Halifax? Back in the day.'

'Yes, indeed, back in the day,' Halifax put the pipe back in his mouth, 'So why did you pack it in?'

'I found something more important to do.'

Halifax gave a grunt of surprise and looked at Novik, 'With this dipstick? I can't imagine.'

'Enough of that,' Josie hefted the shotgun and fixed Halifax with a steely gaze.

Xiong's rice flail whirled into a blur.

'Stay frosty, Xiong,' Halifax snapped his fingers. 'Marcel.'

Marcel flexed his arms, his Breton top jumping and bulging with muscle, the half smile fixed on his face. Josie felt his physical presence like an aura, at once repellent and attractive.

'If you knew how to use that you'd have the safety off,' Marcel said.

Josie glanced down. Marcel reached out with deceptive slowness, he stepped back, the gun was cradled in his arm.

'You motherfucker,' Josie breathed.

'You really shouldn't call him that,' Halifax said.

Shoulders hunched, Benny swaggered forwards on bent knees and splayed legs. He raised his arms, his forefingers pointing like guns. 'You are all sons of motherfucking bitches.'

Halifax, Marcel and Xiong looked at Benny, looked at each other, and howled with laughter.

Arms raised and knees bent, Benny self-consciously held his pose, then slowly straightened up.

Halifax wiped a tear from his eye, 'Man, you arseholes have got a whole lot to learn.'

Xiong and Marcel nodded in agreement.

'Complete arseholes.'

'Compretery.'

Marytha tugged on Novik's arm, 'We need these guys,' she whispered, 'Humour them.'

This was all one enormous mistake. Novik knew they were wasting their time, all that was left to do was leave and get back to shopping. On the other hand, Halifax's man now held the gun. Novik made a frustrated gesture,

'OK, we're total asshats. So what?'

'Look, man,' Halifax said gently, 'keep cool and listen. You go round saying motherfucker this and motherfucker that, people won't take you seriously.'

'You must change. Change is a form of growth,' Xiong said.

'I blame the media,' Marcel said.

'Absorutery,' said Xiong.

It was weird, once these heavies had made sure the dude was safe, they weren't angry. Insults aside, it seemed they were more interested in talking than fighting. Maybe something could be salvaged after all. 'Look, guys, can we parley?' Novik said. 'All we wanted was a conversation.'

'So let's talk. But first, you have to agree to learn the language of the modern street.'

Puzzled by the offer, Novik agreed. Halifax lowered himself with graceful muscularity to the threadbare carpet. Cautiously Novik followed suite.

Josie and Marytha sat on the mattress with the dude, Benny crouched against a wall. Marcel leaned the shotgun by the door and sat behind Halifax with Xiong.

Pipe in hand, Halifax looked around the room. 'First things first. Who knows the currently acceptable primary insult of tough-guy patois?'

'I'm guessing it's not "motherfucker",' Novik muttered.

'Good man,' Halifax said. 'To speed things up, can we take it as given that popular culture is, to a significant degree, derivative? That there is cross pollination of ideas and attitudes, both negative and positive, between the different strata of society, and that the visual media play a dominant role in defining what is currently a-la-mode gangster jive.'

Detecting no disagreement, Halifax continued:

'Furthermore, there is a well-established convention that villains, in all six major forms, should be English.'

'What are they?' Novik said.

'I'm glad you asked. They are: suave and debonair; the anti-hero; the brutish thug; the loveable rogue; the sadistic aesthete; the charismatic psychopath. Obviously these are archetypes to be riffed from, and with an English background, authenticity dictates contemporary underworld banter should, by and large, include significant British English elements. Thusly, it forms a linguistic shortcut permitting fast role identification with a minimum of intellectualisation.'

'You've really thought about this,' Marytha said.

'I get it,' Novik said patiently. 'That's why you pronounce it arsehole.'

'Collect,' Xiong said.

'Sorry?'

'He means "Correct",' Halifax said. 'Xiong is from Pittsburgh, fourth generation. He's adopted clichéd south-east Asian pronunciation in a self-parodic protest at the transient nature of bad-ist dialogue.'

'The medium is the message.' Josie said before she could stop herself.

'Smart girl.' Marcel watched her through hooded eyes.

Josie mouthed 'Motherfucker', Marcel blew her a kiss. Her thoughts about his mouth felt like treason.

'Thanks, Halifax, that's a clear and practical grounding.' Novik was trying his best to be polite. These guys were no good to him, they had no depth, no morality, all they cared about was image. Also, they pissed him off.

'Thanks, it's just a précis of a series of classes I'm running for the local street kids.'

'What other words are there?'

'I'm partial to "bollocks", a universal expression of frustration. "Arse conkers" is good, so is "Bugger it".'

'Bollocks. I like it.'

'Of course the quintessential English swear-word is "Wanker".'

'How could we forget?' Novik said.

Josie, Benny and Marytha tried it out. 'Wankers.'

'It has a short "a" sound, like "cat". Wanker.'

'You wankers,' Novik said. 'Fucking wankers.'

'That's better.'

'There is one other word.' Halifax cupped his hand over Novik's ear and whispered a crude syllable.

Novik's eyes widened, 'I'd never say that.'

'Me neither. Good man. Everyone has limits.' Halifax clapped Novik on the shoulder and they exchanged a look of masculine camaraderie. 'One more thing, never flip the bird, it's always two fingers, a traditional insult that dates back to Agincourt.'

'Thanks,' Novik climbed to his feet, 'we really appreciate it.'

'My pleasure,' Halifax grinned with delight while Marcel patted him on the shoulder.

Novik turned to Marytha and Josie, 'So what do you think, girls?'

'Sorry,' Marytha said. 'People change.'

'Not your fault. It was worth a try,' Novik said.

'Time to go?' Josie said.

'Time to go.'

Josie walked over to Marcel.

'Hi,' she said, eyes downcast.

'Hey, girl,' Marcel ran his fingers through her hair.

Josie took a deep breath and looked into Marcel's eyes. It was so easy to smile. She indicated the shotgun, 'May I?'

'Sure.' Marcel cleared the chamber and handed it over.

Josie turned to Novik. He'd seen the exchange, he looked like he expected a slap in the face, a kick in the nuts. A bullet from the gun. Josie thumbed off the safety, chambered a round and shouted, 'Ok, arseholes, lie flat on the floor and put your hands behind your heads.'

'That's it. You got it just right,' Halifax said. 'You seeing this, guys?'

Marcel and Xiong gave nervous nods of agreement.

Josie fired into the ceiling, the gunshot deafening in the confined space, 'Bugger that, you wankers. This is real.'

Halifax's mouth gaped in shock, his pipe hit the floor. Scowling furiously, the three men lay face-down on the filthy carpet.

'Bugger it.'

'Arse conkers.'

'Borrocks.'

Josie kept guard while Novik, Benny and Marytha bound and gagged the three men up with strips torn from the dude's t-shirts. For good measure they tied up the dude as well.

Benny stuffed a couple of thousand in dusty bills down the fronts of their shirts. The men's eyes glittered with hate.

'So long, arseholes,' Novik said wearily.

Benny stuck up two fingers.

Marytha rotated Benny's wrist. 'Other way round.'

The door slammed shut. In utter silence Halifax's crew listened to footsteps recede down the stairs. Xiong worked his jaw and spat out his gag.

'Rankers.'

Josie kicked the door open, shotgun over her shoulder. 'You really are a useless bunch of cunts,' she said, and slammed the door again.

The bound men struggled and strained. Marcel flexed his enormous biceps and burst free in a scatter of money. He pulled a switchblade and cut the others free.

Halifax was in a red fury. 'Get the guns. Those motherfuckers are going to pay.'

'Watcha doing, Rik?'

'Ralf, we got breaking news.'

'You just broke in on The King. It had better be big or you're going to wake up next to a horse's head.'

'Check this out. Zeppelina, the 1,000 lb, 19-year old chanteuse of the Bariatric Babes has been rushed to hospital with suspected organ failure.'

'That's big. She's big.'

'Listen to this: "She's gone," sobbed friend and band member, The Calorific Queen. "She gave her all for the Babes and now we've lost her. We love her so much."'

'That's sad, Rik. Death in one so young.'

'It is sad, Ralf. But is it important?'

'I don't rightly know where you're going with this. If being dead ain't important, what exactly is?'

'Your hair.'

'Are you shittin' me?'

'Think about it. We've all got to go. When you do, what's everyone going to remember?'

'The music? The fact you got a VV cup size?'

'Your hairstyle, Ralf. Hair defines an era. Look at last year's films – which anachronism do you notice first?'

'Hot-dog, he's right, folks. It IS the hair. I'm going to hire me a coiffeuse.'

'And I'm going to engage a tonsorial artiste.'

'Damn. Outclassed again.'

'Let's have some music.'

Rik'n'Ralf's Podneck Redcast

- 38 -

Alone in the privacy of her own suite, in the seclusion of the Million Pines estate, Ellen turned off her computer monitor. She had known it would be a mistake before she logged on, it always was. Some days she couldn't help herself, some days the part of her that wanted to be hurt was ascendant. Her exo-frame systems would not permit self-harm, seeing what the world thought of her was the closest she could get.

Across the world Ellen Hutzenreiter-Crane was the object of hundreds of subscription communities and thousands of blogs by feeders, wannabees and morphophiliacs. There were numberless forums with countless postings, photos and video mashups. There were animations, songs, animal adventures, poems, food sculptures, crochet figures, unofficial biographies, mech-eng projects, bogus interviews, DIY non-doctor medical projects, and Ellenchat-bots. And there were porn, BDSM and slash-fiction variants for things you couldn't even imagine, each with its own community.

There were seventeen trending news stories. None were true.

So far this year, thirty-five wannabes had died from complications arising from exoframe attachment, exoskel malfunction, lipoplantation, whole-body implants or polpropylene and saline expansion. Nine more were on life support, twenty-eight were permanently disabled.

She was worshipped and despised, imitated and mocked, reviled and envied. She was a goddess and she was a fetish. She was a fat whore with too much money. She was a vertical revenue stream.

Her father ran a group to shut it all down but he didn't own everything and nobody controlled the wildfire of data, the multi-language web of webs that used to be the internet.

For a terrible giddy moment Ellen saw herself as a puppet, a monstrous, helpless toy suspended inside a metal skeleton controlled by the will of strangers. The thought made her nauseous, she was such a freak it made her sick just to think about herself. She fled her rooms and descended the reinforced staircase with black oak bannisters that led down to Million Pines' wide entrance hall. As she crossed the hall, Raymond St.John, dapper as ever, appeared.

'Good day, Ms Ellen. I trust all is in order.'

'Yes, thank you, Raymond. I'm going for a walk.'

'There is a high probability of rain in two to three hours.'

Ellen turned away. 'I'll be back before then.'

St.John cleared his throat. 'Ms Ellen, para-human patrols have deployed in the estate.'

'If I see them, I'll say hello.'

'They will keep to themselves. I didn't want you to be startled.'

'I'll be fine.'

'Enjoy your walk.'

Ellen passed through the main doors. Outside, she breathed the cool, pine-scented air with relief, and headed down the drive.

St.John watched her enormous slope-shouldered form with a curious mix of emotions. Two decades ago he had held Ellen as a babe in his arms. The differential between then and now was too great for him to easily contemplate. Out in the forest the trees continued to grow, but even there – change. Two thousand miles to the south Hurricane Larry pounded the gulf of Mexico to wet ruin. Was there such a thing as genuine stasis?

St.John put the thoughts from his mind. Until he retired, the Crane households would run with predictable order. Then he and Mrs St.John would move to Toronto to be close to their children and grandchildren, something they had planned long ago.

Million Pines itself was built from local Cedar and Douglas Fir. The three-storied structure of verandas, covered ways, balconies, gables and courtyards sprawled in the shade of Silver Spruce, White Fir and Ponderosa on a half acre of levelled ground fifty feet above a mile-long lake. In front of the lodge, moss, lichen and fallen needles softened the gravel of the driveway and filled the corners of the broad steps that ran down to the boathouse. Boreal forest stretched for ten miles in every direction.

Away from the house, Ellen turned onto a well-made woodland trail. The path headed uphill then descended into a wide valley of open forest. After another mile the trail reached a shady glade exited by several faint tracks.

Ellen chose the track that ran straight ahead. The softness of the needle-cushioned ground, the ribbed fans of pine roots, were transmitted through the pressure sensors and feedback systems on the soles of her exoframe, then simulated in the foot-pads and joint dampers of her exoframe.

High overhead scudding clouds turned grey. A short, heavy shower of rain fell, and the sky cleared.

A shaft of sunlight fell on a cluster of fir saplings, their soft young foliage translucent and green. Water drops hung from the leaves, silver cobwebs spanned the branches. A lighter mood came over Ellen, the timing of St.John's weather report had been wrong, not everything could be predicted and managed.

After the rain, the air was rich with damp, leafy odours. Rivulets chuckled in the dripping silence. Energised, Ellen stretched her trunk-like arms and gave an incongruously delicate skip and hop of pleasure. For the first time in days she felt free and alone. She strode deeper into the woods.

Although the exoframe did much of the work, Ellen was soon breathing deeply. Deep inside her chest her straining heart beat harder, across her shoulders, fans forced more air over the cooling vanes of her blood radiators. Status LEDs phased from green to amber, a soft warning tone sounded and the exoframe slowed.

A man's voice sounded, close to Ellen's ear. 'Hello Ellen. This is Chandra Smith. Are you all right?'

Ellen's mouth drooped. She forced herself to be cheerful, determined to retain her carefree mood.

'Hello Chandra, everything is fine. I'm walking through the woods around Million Pines. It's a lovely fresh day.'

'We noticed your heartbeat is rather high. I can see you are moving quite quickly, which is fine, but your core metrics have moved out of the green zone.'

'I was enjoying my walk. Where are you today?'

'I'm in Hyderabad, at the university. Ellen, perhaps a year ago this level of exertion would have been fine, but you are heavier now, and your heart is not as strong. In your situation it is easy to overdo it. If you agree, I'd like to introduce a speed limiter on your suit, say 10Kph.'

Ellen wiped away sudden tears of frustration. Upset at her own reaction, she was glad there was nobody to see. How selfish she was, Chandra was trying to look after her, goodness knows what time it was in India.

'I don't want to stop you, Ellen.'

'All right,' she said. '12 Kph, and I want an override.'

'That's fine. We'll set a keyword, something easy to remember, but not a word you regularly use.'

'How about "Freiheit"?'

Chandra hesitated. 'A good word, Ellen. I've enabled it for you.' Another pause. 'Have you thought about our latest idea?'

With no hope of a cure and time running out the doctors had made a wild suggestion: a retreat into a Meeja-II simulation, where a year of subjective time could be experienced in an hour.

'Only as a last resort.'

Chandra's silence was eloquent. Finally he said, 'Everything is set, Ellen. Enjoy the rest of your walk.'

The mood was gone. Ellen walked unhappily through forest, seeing nothing. After a while she heard a faint rumble ahead. As she continued, it grew to a steady roar.

Ellen stood on the edge of a low bluff and looked down at a series of cataracts and clear pools, tumbling white water and stacked boulders. A hundred yards downstream the ground dipped to a grassy riverbank. At her feet, pine, rowan and stunted hemlock clung to a near vertical slope. Out of sheer perversity Ellen started down. Her steel alloy heels sank deep into soft loam, she rode a small avalanche of soil.

The base of the slope had been undercut by spring floods. Ten feet above the river Ellen broke through and dropped onto a small gravel beach. She landed in an instinctive crouch, knees bent and fingers splayed. Pistons and dampers in her frame hissed as they absorbed her weight.

Startled by the fall, pleased by the elegance of her landing, Ellen did something she had never tried before – she jumped. Her leap carried her twenty feet over the river onto a flat boulder the size of a small truck.

Bowling-ball sized rocks were stacked in its lee. Ellen picked one up. Crayfish larvae scrabbled for new cover. When she was a child she had played ducks and drakes on the lake in front of the lodge, skimming the flat pebbles and counting the pitty-pats. Hefting the rock she lobbed it effortlessly into a nearby pool.

Her next throw sent a twenty-pound rock over a hundred feet.

Ellen realised she had never really tested the limits of her exo-frame.

She and the frame were essentially one thing, two components in synergy, neither could do alone what they could achieve together. She picked up a two-hundred pound boulder, the weight of a well-built man, and lobbed it fifty yards downstream. That was harder, that took real effort. Ellen's shout of release rose above the river's roar.

She spent the next few minutes leaping from rock to rock, up and down the river. Then she threw ten-pound rocks as far as she could. This turned out to be about a quarter of a mile.

After a while she noticed an eight-foot ursine para-human watching her from the far bank.

'Try for that,' the bear-man's deep voice travelled easily across the water.

Ellen followed his arm to three dead pine stumps on a rock island a hundred yards away. She palmed a boulder, the wrist display showed twenty-five pounds. She drew back her arm and threw.

Her aim was true, the stone splintered one of the dead trunks.

Dropping to all fours, the bear man bounded from boulder to boulder across the river.

'Impressive,' he growled. 'You are Lady Ellen. We were told you were weak, that you are sick.'

'I am,' Ellen replied. 'But not like that.'

'I am taller, but you are bigger. Can you move without your machine?'

'No.'

The bear man was deep-chested, long in the arm and short in the leg. He wore a leather harness over his thick brown-black pelt, a simple breechclout covered his groin. Pouches hung from his waist, two huge knives were sheathed across his chest.

'My name is Theodore,' he said. 'My home is nearby. May I offer you a cup of coffee?'

Ellen was delighted. 'I'd like that very much.'

Theodore's camp was set in a depression sheltered by holly thickets and deep bracken. A pair of wooden cabins roofed with bark shingles faced each other across a patch of clean ground.

'I share this camp with two lupine women. They are scouting,' Theodore said. 'We did not build this place. Your father caused these houses to be built. He fulfilled his obligations to his oathsworn as a leader should. Gold is not for keeping.'

The door of Theodore's hut was too small for Ellen and she would have been too heavy to enter. Through the window she saw a sturdy bed, basic cooking equipment, a bench and a wooden table with keyboard, console screen. Printed books were stacked neatly on a shelf, one was open on the bed. Beside it, unstrung, was a powerful recurved bow. At the foot of the bed, a sheaf of long arrows.

As Theodore prepared the coffee the lupine females returned, seeming to appear in the clearing rather than enter it. They were friendly, but incurious about Ellen's exoframe. Sinewy and lithe, both were dressed in simple sleeveless shifts of grey yarn and wore their silver-grey head hair cropped short.

'I am Gretel, she is Hilda,' the taller one said. 'Today we scouted our territory and contacted the groups adjacent to ourselves.'

'We know who you are,' Hilda told Ellen. 'You are your father's daughter. We will protect you until you leave here.'

'Lady Ellen is sick because she is too big,' Theodore handed Ellen a blue enamelled mug of coffee. 'Even so, she is very strong.'

Theodore's speech was slow and considered, the lupine women snapped and bit their words out of the air.

Gretel studied Ellen. 'When will you die?'

Ellen discovered she did not mind such direct questions. The entire situation was dreamlike, a fairy-tale thing. The para-humans had curious minds, when something intrigued them, they were persistent. Soon they understood Ellen's syndromes.

'This is strange,' they all agreed.

Hilda frowned. 'We are here to protect you but we cannot protect you from this.'

'It's all right,' Ellen said. 'Nobody can.'

Theodore dropped to one knee. 'Lady Ellen, surely this is a task for your father.'

'He has hired the best people, they've tried everything.'

His head bowed, Theodore struggled to find the right words.

'What is it?' Ellen said.

'There may be something only he can do, as leader, as your father, a sacrifice.' Ponderously, Theodore shook his head, 'Such things may have been forgotten.'

Hoping to reassure Theodore, Ellen explained the doctor's latest plan.

'You would dream inside a dream.' Theodore said.

'And it would seem to last longer than my whole life,' Ellen said.

Ears twitching, the lupine women conferred in whispers.

'You should not do this,' Gretel told her. 'Dreamtime was a shared time. If you do not wake, how will you know when you are dead? What if a machine was made to help your head, like the one you wear with your body? You would be dead, yet still be dreaming. You would never wake up. You would have become a thing.'

The Babes are Back!

Surviving members of the Bariatric Babes have mounted a legal challenge against doctors caring for Zeppelina. I caught up with them outside the courthouse. Little Missy Massiv held back the tears as she explained.

'As you know, the next edition of *Venus Maxima* is a memorial devoted to Zeppelina, her life, her struggle, the joy and the pain. We're also doing a limited edition hard-copy, an actual physical book, real retro stylee. How cool is that?'

'What's the basis of your challenge?'

'The doctors put Zeppelina in something called an induced coma. We want to wake her up so she can sign the books.'

'All your fans know you're still struggling to cope with the tragedy. In this time of heartbreak is it hard to think about the future?'

'The Bariatric Babes will go on. Zepp was a doll, we loved her dearly. It's going to be hard but we need a replacement.'

'You're going to audition?'

'We're so excited!'

Wesley Strosner,
Venus Maxima

- 39 -

Benny lay on the back seat moaning with pain.

Marytha swung the car into a side street. She drew to a halt in the darkness between two streetlights, 'What happened?'

'He forgot to duck,' Novik said.

Marytha opened Benny's door. 'Dear God,' she said as she saw Benny's blood-soaked chest.

'A simple mistake,' Benny gasped. 'I forgot how primitive Earth technology is. My force field is set for energy weapons, not kinetic projectiles. It needs an upgrade-' Benny grimaced with pain, 'a downgrade-'

Novik wanted to shake some sense into him. 'You need to upgrade your state of mind. Aliens, Benny. Give it up, you could have been killed.'

'Mr. Car would have understood,' Benny groaned.

'We need to get him to a hospital,' Josie said.

'Not with a gunshot wound,' Novik said. 'They'd ID us all, I can't take a DNA profile, they'll lock me up and throw away the key.'

'Me too,' Marytha said.

'You want to do a drive-by dump off outside ER?' Josie said. 'No way.'

Benny struggled upright. 'Don't abandon me. Although these bodies are soft and fragile, I can regenerate.'

Marytha caught the look in Novik's eye. 'I know what to do, I've had some training. If it's not too serious we can look after him. We'll get a room somewhere, get bandages and antiseptic from a drugstore.'

'He's hurt bad. The hospital is where he needs to be.'

Josie pinned up her hair. 'We're not leaving anybody behind. Novik, we need another vehicle. We can't drive around in a car full of bullet holes.'

Benny clutched Novik's arm, 'I know you want to get rid of me. Please don't, what you're doing is too important.'

It was exactly what Novik had been thinking. Novik knew it was intuition, not mind reading. Benny was smart, it made him unconventional, and there was nothing wrong with that as long as you contributed. However you looked at it, getting shot was pretty grim. Novik looked down at Benny with more sympathy, 'How are you feeling?'

'I'm all right, really. It's just this pain thing. I'm not used to it, and it really hurts.'

Marytha cut away Benny's sleeve and mopped the wound with the material. 'Incredible. I can see the bullet, it's about an inch in. Must have been a ricochet.'

'Partial kinetic depletion,' Benny fell back, soaked in sweat, 'I'll put in a requisition… new model… two days… bullet-proof…'

'Lucky this one was low calibre,' Marytha said.

'Why's that?'

'It didn't take your arm off.'

'Oh.' Benny's eyes were round and wide. Then he passed out.

It was dawn before Novik returned to the room they found, a back-street rent block, a building so run down it could have been road-kill. Hire by the day, cash in advance, no discount, no questions. Benny was fast asleep on the bed, his shoulder clean and bandaged. Josie and Marytha rested on the broken-down couch.

Novik knocked as they had arranged. Josie let him in. 'You were gone a long time. I was worried.'

Novik swung four holdalls down onto the threadbare carpet, 'I'm fine, babe. How's Benny?'

'Marytha got the bullet out. He's going to be all right.'

'That's good. He's a pain in the ass, but…'

'I know.'

'I got a new car, nothing special. Mid-range saloon, fixed head this time. We got to think more about what we're doing. We got to get our heads straight. That's why I took so long, I laundered the money.'

Marytha and Josie looked at the holdalls. None of them looked particularly full.

'How much did it cost?' Josie said. 'Wasn't it dangerous?'

Novik looked pleased with himself. 'Three hundred dollars. I hired a Laundromat for two hours, locked the door, tipped the money in the machines and ran a cold wash for delicates. We lost a couple of thou in the tumble dryers, those things are worse with cash than socks. What you see is what we've got. Fifteen, maybe twenty million.'

'We've had some bad luck,' Josie said.

For Novik there was a simpler reason, 'It's the damned drugs on the money, it stopped us thinking. Every time there's been a problem we've taken too long to get anywhere.'

Marytha pushed herself off the couch. 'We're not in harmony. We're like those little Bonsai trees. You can't arrange them in a pleasing group if there's an even number.'

Novik knew exactly what Marytha was referring to - Mr Car. It was a conversation he thought was long over, he'd apologised once, he wasn't going to do it again. 'So what are the options with that theory? Without Benny we'd be down to three, so how about that we give him some cash and leave him? No, wait, let's get back up to five – I'll kidnap someone and lock them in the trunk. That would be harmonious.'

Marytha looked up at the cracked and water-stained ceiling. 'I'm just saying.'

Novik sat on the end of the bed, Josie on the sagging couch, Marytha stood by the window. Everyone looked at the holdalls on the floor and thought their own thoughts.

This was the kind of room where dreams ended, where couples sat hunched on opposite sides of the mattress hour after hour in a silence that only ended when one of them said, 'I'm going out for cigarettes,' and never came back. It was where whisky-sodden loners cried in the night and blew their brains out; where chronically underweight women lived year after year with a shoebox full of letters from pen-pals in Okinawa and La Paz who never visited and who got married and sent photos of their children. This was the room that would, if they let it, force them one at a time onto hopeless, dead-end streets.

Novik pushed himself to his feet, he slung a holdall over each shoulder. 'Five of us, or four, or three, it doesn't matter. We're on our way to Canada, to Palfinger Crane. He owns half the damned world, that makes at least half the world's problems his fault. He's the ultimate reason Benny got shot, he's why we're here, now, today. He owes us. He owes everybody. Let's go.'

'President Snarlow, what is your impression of Ahmed Hirsch?'

'President Hirsch is a great man, a sincere man, the leader of many great European nations, and their peoples.'

'What sort of relationship did you build at Camp David?'

'Very good. Informal yet respectful. Despite our differences we have a lot in common.'

'Exactly what common ground did you find?'

'I like to think we bonded.'

(Laughter)

'On the subject of informality what did you make of his dress code?'

'He'd be very comfortable at some of the board meetings in California. (More laughter) I certainly didn't think it was disrespectful.'

Excerpt from White House News Conference.

- 40 -

'That's not bad, Ginny,' Lobotnov said as the recording came to an end. 'Newsgroup approval is fifty-four percent, the meta-poll has "Optimism", "Pride", and "Confidence" as most frequent expressions with respect to American self-perception. It's a good performance.'

'How's it running in the EU?'

'I don't see that we actually care. They've got their agendas and we have ours, everybody knows that. What's important is you've carried American public opinion, and the best thing about that is that right this moment nobody is asking awkward questions. In a matter of days it won't matter - we'll be the only technologically advanced country in the northern hemisphere, we'll have 100% employment and every American citizen will be too busy making money to care.'

Guinevere knew he was right but was struggling to stay upbeat. Camp David had been utterly exhausting.

Ahmed Hirsch arrived in a cavalcade of US armoured limousines and motorcycle outriders. Gunships and pilotless drones circled overhead, robo-canines jogged along the flanks. A team of mechanics followed at a discreet distance, ready to repair or reboot the cyber-dogs when they walked into a lamppost or got a toe stuck in a drain cover.

After the public podium handshakes and exchange of flowers the two Presidents met privately in a comfortable, well-lit room hung with olive-green drapes, with tall glass vases of dried grass flanking the empty hearth.

President Snarlow dressed in a black double-breasted trouser suit over a gold silk blouse. Earings, shoe buckles and lapel brooch displayed the motifs of blue chip American corporations.

Ahmed Hirsch, not yet thirty, with a surfer's tall, rangy build, wore a sun-bleached pink tee-shirt, cut-off jeans and flip-flops. There was not a single logo in sight.

'It's how we like to hang out at The Hague,' he told Snarlow. 'It's best to be comfortable. I am prepared to wait if you wish to change down.'

This was not the encounter Guinevere had envisaged. Confronted by Hirsch's youth and insouciance she felt like a reactionary frump.

'I'm fine as I am. Ahmed, I-'

Hirsch held up his hand. 'Mr Hirsch, if you don't mind. Conversation should not be informal.'

Soon they were arguing.

'We bailed you Europeans out against Hitler, Mr Hirsch. There's a debt of honour.'

'A long, long time ago, Ms. Snarlow. And no, you did not.'

Guinevere was not used to flat contradiction, especially by an upstart like Hirsch. 'We won the Goddamned war.'

Hirsch waved away her claim. 'Russia defeated Nazi Germany decisively when they destroyed Model's armour at Kursk. From that point on Hitler was unable to wage offensive war. The war was lost and won long before the Western Allies set foot in Europe. America's greater role was confronting the self-destructive ideologies of Stalinism, and race hate.'

'Well, at least that's honest.'

'How else should we address the issues of the day? You are no longer what you were, but you can be proud of your contributions. All empires fade.'

'The Emerald Union?'

Hirsch frowned thoughtfully, 'As an evolved super-organism collective, we hope to avoid such a fate.'

Flustered, Guinevere offered Hirsch coffee. He accepted a glass of water. 'No caffeine, thank you.'

'Moving forwards, Mr. Hirsch. The European Union must accept certain realities. Mexico and Canada are entirely within the USA's sphere of influence.'

'Then surely you are also within theirs?'

Guinevere conceded the point. 'Nevertheless, both countries threaten American stability and security.'

'I disagree, they only threaten USA ambition. American stability is not threatened, the continent of South America is not threatened. Mexican biotech was safe and ethical before you destroyed it. This has harmed Canadian interest via the significant damage to CraneCorp's investments in Xalapatech infrastructure.'

'Then you'll take note of my visit to Palfinger Crane. We made him a generous offer. There's a seat on the Executive if he wants it.'

Hirsch spluttered with laughter, 'For Crane that must be as enticing as a pool party hosted by crocodiles.'

'You underestimate the benefits. Our economy and political influence still dominate the continent.'

'Not so much as your military.'

Guinevere was tired of this scruffy young man's snot-nosed attitude. She sat back and uncrossed her legs. 'You noticed that, did you?'

Hirsch leaned forwards, his gaze intense. 'Yes, we do notice.' Before Guinevere could reply, he left the room.

The next morning was spent in phone calls, emails and hand-written notes passed between the two parties. After five hours Hirsch agreed to a video conference, then cancelled five minutes after it was due to start claiming a migraine. An hour later he offered a face-to-face for seven pm. Incensed by his petty politics, Guinevere let him stew for another hour. She sent apologies at fifteen-minute intervals, accompanied first by tea, then a bowl of fruit, and finally chilled Riesling and a selection of cheeses.

The hour was up, Guinevere went into the meeting room. Hirsch sat slumped in his chair, yesterday's energy gone. His young face was drawn, his hand shaded his eyes. 'For goodness sake, Madam President, what are you playing at?'

Guinevere dimmed the lights and drew the curtains. 'Ahmed, I'm so sorry. You look terrible. Let me send for my physician.'

Hirsch peered up at her. 'Thank you. That is kind, but I have taken my medication and begin to feel better.'

Encouraged by his new informality Guinevere sat beside him. 'Is this something you suffer regularly? I'm sorry, I didn't know.'

Hirsch moved away. 'It is not an issue. The issue is Canada.'

Guinevere rapped the table with her fingernail. 'The issue is planetary albedo. Canada's trees are spreading north too fast, there is not enough snow on the ground, not enough sunlight being reflected. Someone has to manage the boreal forest before it's too late.'

'Bullshit.' Hirsch looked down with revulsion at the sweating cheese platter and pushed it away. 'Our DNA computers run a little slow, but analysis is thorough. This morning I was advised of the latest results.'

He knows, Guinevere thought. They've worked it out and they're terrified. That's why he's ill, sick with defeat and futility. Triumph surged in her chest, 'If you think you know what we want, you'll also know the American government will not shirk. There's nothing you can do.'

Hirsch studied the glass in his hand as if it were something remarkable.

He drained it and pushed himself to his feet. 'You want to provoke us. You think to make us do something foolish. Very well. Consider us provoked.'

Guinevere's voice trembled as she discussed the events with Lobotnov. 'We've worked so hard for this but now I feel really nervous.' She laughed and pressed her hand against her breast. 'To be honest, I'm terrified.'

Lobotnov regarded her without emotion, his small, well-manicured hands folded on the table. 'Pre-show nerves, Ginny. I'm pretty stressed out too.' He edged his chair towards her and attempted a smile of macho élan. 'I remember you once told me you had a woman's heart. There are ways for two people to relax together.'

I let him squeeze my tit and now he's got this thing for me, Snarlow thought. He's right about most things, maybe this is what I need.

Lobotnov loosened his tie and sat back with one arm over the back of his chair. His slight frame and domed, hairless head made him look like a cross between an over-sexed child and the Mekon.

A perverse eroticism stirred in Guinevere. She'd fantasised about Gordano, how she would make the handsome, pliable Vice President her bitch, but never the apparently sexless intellectual Lobotnov. On an impulse she kissed him on the mouth. 'So come and relax me.'

Lobotnov hung his navy blazer on the back of the chair and pressed a button on the desk.

'Yes, sir?' an anonymous electronic male voice answered.

'We're in executive conference. No interruptions.'

'Yes, sir.'

This isn't anything to do with sex, Guinevere thought as she kicked off her shoes, it's a power transaction.

She dimmed the lights, unzipped her trousers and let them fall to the ground. She sat beside Lobotnov and they kissed again, more deeply, and she was relieved to discover his breath was sweet, his aroma aseptically clean.

'I don't want penetration,' she said as she unzipped him. She considered his small hand and trim nails, 'You can fist me if you want.'

'OK.' Lobotnov clenched his small buttocks as he worked his groin against Guinevere's hand. His fingers pulled aside her panties, stroking with surprising finesse against her sex.

Snarlow reached into his trousers and pulled him out. His organ was startlingly long, almost improbably thick. He was cut, she'd expected that, the dome fat and soft. She found herself unexpectedly excited.

'Cheswold, you're hung like a donkey,' Snarlow breathed, enjoying the feel of him growing hard in her hands.

'Didn't expect that from a short guy, eh?' Lobotnov gasped. 'I'd enjoy it if you went down on me, madam President.'

She was dripping wet, his hand knuckle deep inside her. She bent down and took the velvety tip of his twitching cock into her mouth, touched her teeth gently onto the shaft. As she did Lobotnov partially removed his hand and thrust in. She pushed back, and felt him stretch her deliciously wide. Then his whole hand was inside her.

'Jesus,' she moaned. Her hand was on him now, slippery with her saliva, sliding up and down.

'Slow down,' Lobotnov said. 'This is fantastic, make it last.'

They frigged each other in silence.

'What do you think the EU will do?' Snarlow gasped.

'Nothing. They got nothing,' Lobotnov groaned. 'It's all bluff.'

'They've got to declare war, or surrender.'

'And they have no army, no nukes - it's perfect. God, yes, right there.'

Snarlow pushed her other hand down his trousers, cupped his balls and squeezed.

'Argh. Christ, that hurts.'

Lobotnov's fingertips still tapped and stroked deep inside her, his hand filled her up. She stroked him faster, 'Let me squeeze your nuts again.'

'No. Yes, not now, back off a bit.'

'I don't see what they could do to us that they haven't already. If they move overtly, or covertly but with significance, we've got them. We'll be in the clear and we'll be justified.'

'You're right,' Lobotnov groaned. 'Oh, keep that up and I'm done.'

She felt him spasm again and again.

Lobotnov slumped back with a satisfied groan. 'Oh sweet Lord, I needed that.'

After a moment Snarlow pulled Lobotnov's hand out of her vagina and spread her legs. 'Do me now.'

Lobotnov dropped to his knees and buried his face enthusiastically in her groin. She was on fire, Lobotnov knew what he was doing. It didn't take long and it was fantastic.

Lobotnov crawled into her arms, pulled open her blouse and stuffed one of her nipples into his mouth. In the afterglow she stroked his domed head as he contentedly snuffled at her breast.

'Cheswold, are we bad people?' Snarlow said.

Lobotnov wiped his mouth with a tissue. 'Subjectively, yes, absolutely. However, the substantively objective view has to be no, we are not. Morality is relative, there are no empirical rights and wrongs in human history.'

'Tell me we're doing the right thing.'

'Churchill said "History will look upon me kindly because I shall write it." In that light yes, of course we are.'

Brutal Murders

Three key members of the notorious Halifax street gang, two male and one female, were found dead today in the south-side project tenements. The street-pharma wholesaler known locally as 'The Dude' was also slain.

Crime scene investigations are ongoing, but early indications suggest this was more than simple gangland turf war. Whoever did this was making a point.

"I just hope it's not the C.O.P.S." Patrolman Gary Jackson told this reporter. "They're taking over the corners everywhere."

Opinion on motives for the savage killings vary from takeover to punishment. One thing is clear, Bernard Halifax himself is not a suspect, Patrolman Jackson freed him from his bonds at the scene. It seems Halifax was forced to watch the torture and execution of his fellow gang members.

Reports of a prior argument and gunshots are being taken seriously.

Slobodan Jones,
KUWjones.org

- 41 -

Wilson caught up with Halifax as he was coming out of the morgue. The big black man didn't look like he wanted to talk to anyone, let alone in the right frame of mind for rational speech.

Halifax drifted rather than walked, his descent of the steps to the sidewalk a half-controlled fall. The ground dropped away under his feet in the same way the world had dropped away from his life.

Later on Halifax would be looking for it, murderous drunk and in a place far beyond pain. He would put himself in harm's way, kill a couple of punks when they tried to roll him, then get lit up by the local law. Or simply take a cap in the skull from an ambitious soldier from his own corners.

Right now he was numb. If Wilson was buying, he might just listen.

Wilson followed him to a street bar called 'Vetz', a sparse establishment of bolt-down tables and bar stools, plastic glasses, drains in the tiled floor and hose-down walls. Two old men sat near the door playing dominos, three fat hookers lolled at the back beside a doorway. He sent a beer over to Halifax via the barman, a heavily tattooed white guy with hard eyes, buzzcut hair and a prosthetic right leg.

Halifax listened to the barman then turned to Wilson, three seats away.

Wilson met his eye. 'Thought you could use it.'

Halifax looked Wilson up and down, seeing something in the paunchy middle-aged white man that stopped him flinging the drink into his face. 'Fuck you know?' Halifax muttered, and knocked back the beer.

'I know Mitchell Gould,' Wilson said.

Halifax came off his seat like an express train.

Wilson shot Halifax with his neural mop before he had his second foot on the ground. Halifax jerked, twitched, fell onto his side, kicked once and lay still.

A high-pitched whine came from behind the bar. Wilson looked into the spinning barrels of a room-sweeper mini-gun. The other occupants of the bar watched with frozen attention: a hand hovered over a domino, an unlit cigarette halfway to a hooker's mouth.

Wilson slowly put down the neural mop and put up his hands. 'It's OK, we're friends,' he said. 'Or we will be soon.'

'You law?' the barman said.

'Nope.' Wilson grimaced, 'Kinda.' He displayed his BountyMan card, invalid in this state.

'Well, Mr Nope-kinda-lawman, this man is Bernard Halifax. This is a bar, not a morgue, so take it outside. If you don't make a mess we might send flowers.'

Wilson looked down at the twitching man. 'I know who he is, and his crew are dead. Mitchell Gould killed them all.'

'No shit. What he do to The Mitch?'

'No idea.' Wilson looked around the bar, 'This your place?'

'Yes, it is.' The barman turned off the gun and the barrels stuttered to a halt. The old men returned to their dominos, one of the hookers went upstairs.

'Working your way up, huh?'

'I know these streets.'

'You know a cab?'

The barman put the gun under the bar and opened his phone. 'My cousin.'

Wilson settled himself onto a stool, 'Give me a few packs of nuts.'

It was clearly not the first time this sort of thing had happened. The cab, a beat-up black Toyota SUV, pulled up in the back alley almost immediately. The driver, a near clone of the barman, had an artificial left arm and a compound crystal eye, the seam between orb and skin crusted with inflammation. Wilson hefted Halifax into the back and the cabbie drove them to Wilson's room.

The cabbie looked at Halifax, out cold on the bed, from the safety of the doorway.

'Don't worry,' Wilson said. 'This is for his own good.'

The cabbie rubbed the edge of his compound eye, 'I was wondering how you were going to cope when he wakes up.'

'You and your cousin serve together?' Wilson said.

'Yup.'

'Where's that?'

'Nowhere,' the cabbie held up his prosthetic arm, 'Blue on blue.'

'Rough deal.'

'Shit happens. In the army, shit happens to you.'

'Once was a cop. Still on the right side.' He thought about it. 'At least, I think I am.'

'You can only hope. Luck to you, old man.'

'Take it easy.'

Wilson locked the door and checked Halifax. The big man was beginning to stir as neurons finally scraped together enough ions to close synapses. Wilson filled a glass with water, emptied the wastebasket onto the floor and put it beside the bed. Then he pulled up a chair, sat down, and waited.

You can tell when someone wakes up. They stir, the breathing changes, muscle tension alters. Beneath closed lids their eyeballs move differently.

Halifax was smart. For the space of a single breath he was still, then his body went slack, his breathing shallow and uneven. Only the muscles of his face betrayed him.

'I know you're awake,' Wilson said. 'You've got a giant headache. Don't move too fast, or you'll puke.'

Halifax's eyelids twitched, his shoulders tensed.

Wilson moved his chair back.

Halifax rolled off the bed and flung himself towards Wilson. Halfway off the floor his leg muscles cramped, he cried out in agony and fell. Wilson pushed the bin into his hands, Halifax clutched it, dry-retched, then heaved up a gut load of acrid vomit.

Halifax glared sloppily at Wilson over the rim of the waste basket. He hawked and spat, then tried to stand. He made it to a crouch, clutched his calves and toppled onto the floor hissing with pain.

'There's water on the side.' Wilson tossed a packet of peanuts onto the floor. 'Eat these, it will help the cramps.'

'Fuck you, arsehole.'

'Arsehole. That's pretty stylish. I never took you for an Anglophile.'

'Fuck-'

'Yeah, OK, fuck me. I get it.' Wilson opened another packet of nuts and scattered them over the bed. 'Lick my salty nuts, Mr Halifax, and listen to what I've got to say.'

Halifax sighed and closed his eyes.

'I'm after Mitchell Gould. My wife died because of him. She was a cop, we were both cops, partners. She, ah, I-' Wilson fought the catch in his voice.

Slack mouthed, Halifax crawled up on the bed and flopped onto his side.

Wilson got a hold of himself, 'I got recruited by some executive agency deep in black ops, totally deniable, something so dark I... Look, I don't know anything, OK? I don't know who I work for, or why they pulled me in. Yesterday, Gould killed my partner, I've got a way to track him, and that's all I got. I need help, Halifax, I need a partner. I can't do this on my own.'

Halifax's unblinking eyes fixed on Wilson with a lizard's gaze. He jerked his chin to show he was listening - go on.

Christ, Wilson thought, overwhelmed by deja-vu, I'm recruiting, reeling in someone nobody's going to miss, the same as Masters did to me. For a moment he was back in his tract house, leaning against the kitchen unit as she made her offer.

When Wilson spoke, although he meant every word, it all sounded like it came from someone else.

'I don't care what you did, Halifax, what laws you broke, or why. If you want a chance at Gould, this is it. You want in, you're in, and I'll tell you everything I know, though I promise you, it isn't much. You need to choose now, because Gould's on the move and we're not.'

The puke stank. Wilson took the bin into the bathroom. When he came out, he pushed open the front door. 'Or I can leave you here, and before you know it, you'll be a hopeless old screw-up like me.'

Slowly, gingerly, Halifax eased himself into a sitting position. He sipped the water, he ate one of the peanuts. 'How many partners you lost?'

'Two.'

'I hate cops.'

Hmm…

'Of course it won't come to war. How could it when we don't possess conventional strategic forces of any significance?'

EU officials have been slavishly echoing Ahmed Hirsch at every opportunity. They are also fond of saying things like 'war is obsolete' and 'we are not naïve'. Either or both of these statements could be considered misleading, actually naïve, or simply daft. And don't ignore the wilfully Machiavellian hints about their ability to pursue international policy 'by other means'. Whatever the Emerald Union is up to, it is impervious to analysis and they seem quietly confident.

Compare that with General Andriewiscz:

'The punks don't know what they're talking about. We've got some surprises lined up. The time for walking quietly is over and we've still got a big stick.'

It's so unofficial the White House won't even acknowledge he said it, let alone if it's a policy statement. On the other hand neither do they deny it, and we all remember the gentleman doffing his sombrero over Mexico City.

Now THAT feels like a story waiting to be told.

Slobodan Jones,
KUWjones.org

- 42 -

Novik arrived at the Canadian border late afternoon. The normally busy crossing point was quiet, the barriers were raised, the eight lane highway eerily quiet. An armoured car sat broadside across the road, a heavy calibre machine gun mounted on the open turret.

A dozen soldiers in green fatigues, field jackets and armoured vests leaned against the concrete barrier along the narrow median strip. One of them beckoned Novik forwards.

Novik looked at Josie. They needed to get across.

She crossed her fingers. 'We'll be fine.'

In the back Marytha looked more than a little scared. Beside her Benny rested, his eyes shut, the bandaging on his chest concealed by a clean white tee and a new denim jacket.

Novik put the car into drive.

As they approached the soldier he waved them to a halt. Novik lowered the window.

'Hi there,' the soldier said. 'How ya doing?'

'Is everything OK up there?' Novik said.

The soldier chewed his gum, he looked back at the armoured car and the rest of his platoon and grinned. 'Sure looks OK to me.'

'So we can pass through?'

'Well, I'm not so sure about that.' The soldier looked into the car, 'Howdy, ma'am,' he grinned at Josie. 'Sir, ma'am.'

'Hello.' Everyone returned brief, polite smiles.

'Can you tell us what's going on?' Josie said.

'Nothing, ma'am. Everything's fine. We just don't recommend crossing to Canada at this moment in time.'

'What's wrong?'

'Nothing's wrong.'

'So we can go through if we want to?'

The soldier still chewed his gum but he'd stopped smiling, 'I'd say that would be unwise.'

The sound of a vehicle driven at speed came from the Canadian side of the crossing. A flatbed pickup, heavily laden with packing cases and furniture under a tarp, rounded the long bend in the opposite lane. A family of five were squeezed into the cab, the children looked across at the soldiers, their parents looked straight ahead. One corner of the tarp snapped in the wind as the pickup sped on by.

'Looks like the smart Canadians would rather be in America too,' the soldier said. 'You think they know something we don't?'

'I don't know,' Novik said.

'Of course you don't, sir. There's nothing to know.'

Moments later, a low rumble of heavy traffic came from behind them. The soldier spat out his gum, 'Pull onto the verge.'

'Yes, sir.' In his haste to comply, Novik forgot the handbrake. The car lurched, the engine stalled.

Up ahead, the armoured car blocking the road coughed black exhaust smoke and roared into life.

The soldier swung his rifle off his shoulder. 'Get your ass in gear, citizen.'

Behind them, the first vehicles in a military convoy appeared, APCs and troop trucks travelling at high speed.

'I got it.' Sweating with tension, Novik restarted the engine and drove onto the verge.

A squad of armoured cars roared by, then dozens of troop trucks, three abreast, gearboxes whining. The incurious faces of young soldiers looked out from every tailgate.

Low-slung transporters followed, each carrying a massive battle tank. More troop trucks followed, then self-propelled artillery, comms wagons, and yet more troops. There was a short gap and six open-sided trucks raced by. Robo-canines with 30-cal mini-guns stood in silent rows. Engineer-handlers worked their way unsteadily between them with diagnostic consoles and patch kits.

Finally, silence.

The armoured platoon redeployed across the highway.

'Let's get out of here,' Marytha said.

Novik put the car in gear and turned it round. He drove along the verge until there was a gap in the median barrier, crossed onto the far side of the road and drove back into the USA.

Gackle, ND, is the self-proclaimed duck-hunting capital of the world. As if that weren't incredible enough, it also lies on Highway 46, the road which boasts the longest straight run in the USA - an unbelievable bet-your-little-sister's-triple-cherry one hundred and twenty three miles. Straight.

Early this morning something went through sleepy little Gackle like a supersonic senna pod. Listen to eye-witness and local historian Walther Szymyck:

'I got this problem that makes me need the can. About 5 am I heard a big "WOOSH!" and the sound of breaking glass. I got my gun and went out front. Most of the store windows were gone, sucked out onto the sidewalk. West on 46 a dust cloud headed into the distance.

'A few minutes later, I saw the dust cloud hurtling back into town. I hunkered down behind the old water trough, there was another "SWOOSH!" and this huge car went through like Satan was on its tail. Lou-Em's little kitten went whirling by like a leaf, I snagged the critter in my hat.

'I'll tell you something else, – there was no driver.'

Cool name, Walter, it made our spell checker gibber like an over-caffeinated weasel. And thanks for the update on your prostate, we'll let your health insurance know.

Folks, here's where it gets spooky - FedMesh speedcams show nothing at all. So we really have got a ghost car, or it was moving faster than the sensors can fire. For that to happen, it would need to be in excess of four hundred and eighty miles per hour.

Makes you feel kind of tingly, don't it? Watch this space, peeps.

Editor's blog
– BFBM magazine.

- 43 -

Now he was back on foot, Gould was starting to enjoy himself.

Up at the edge of the trees Ayesha was talking to LeBlanc, the leader of the Canadian crew they'd rendezvoused with. LeBlanc was short, muscular and energetic, his hair thin on his neat, round head. Like Gould, Ayesha was dressed in navy cargoes, hiking boots, a black jacket, and carried a framed backpack. LeBlanc wore a felt jacket of muddy red, blue and brown check, and trousers of brown cord. To Gould's mind LeBlanc's clothing, like that of his men, looked loud and amateurish.

Further into the glade Morgan and Black, still in their dark suits and overcoats, shared smokes and gossip with some of LeBlanc's men. Some had crossbows as well as guns, the Old-fashioned Boys inspected the composite recurved prods, electric winches and high power scopes with interest. They were slow firing weapons, but silent, and in the right hands very deadly.

Morgan and Black drew on their smokes and smiled and looked around. One of LeBlanc's men said something and they laughed in the polite, respectful way of experienced people sizing each other up.

The trek north from New Orleans had been a dangerous slog. DNA scans had made air travel impossible, Gordano's strutting incompetence a serious and growing liability. Gould pulled the device he had taken from the dead agent from his pocket and gave an amused grunt of disbelief. For some reason the two punk hippies who had ripped him off were still heading north.

Black had gone ape when Ayesha suggested the device was some kind of money tracker, tuned to the stash they had lost on the way to Vegas.

'They knew all the time. The damned Feds knew.' Black raved. 'They must still know. This can't be the only one, they'll come at us again.'

Morgan was pale as milk but kept it together. 'Live with it. We're the Old-fashioned Boys and we play the hand we're dealt.'

'If there is a next time, we have this,' Gould displayed the handgun the agent had used. 'That agent was right from the top, the best they had. This gun of hers will even things up.'

Gould loved the gun. Utilising some form of neural linkage from palm to optic nerve, the bullets flew towards wherever you were looking when you pulled the trigger, and followed the target as it moved.

'The eye and palm of the hand are packed with nerve endings. The gun must be co-opting a tiny fraction of them to communicate,' Gould theorised.

'It sounds about as plausible as micro-changes in air density,' Ayesha said.

Gould didn't mind her scepticism, the gun made him feel alive in a way he hadn't felt for a long time: powerful, in control, Lord of the Streets - just what gun tech was supposed to make you feel. You picked it up and it worked straight away, no need for an interface, though Gould would not have minded taking a bio-mod for something this cool. He hoped it was home-grown tech, his country still led the world in arms design and it felt like there was a pedigree behind this weapon deeper than the new Arabtech gadgets like the money tracker. In his own odd way Gould was a patriot, an entrepreneur who made money any way he could, from criminal overlord to government assassin he was a businessman.

It was interesting to see the way his money had scattered in a ragged, north-bound line. A huge splurge, followed by a steadily reducing trail. Gould soon realised they were heading in the same direction, it had led him to Halifax and his gang. They thought they were hard, but they were just avant-garde actors turned street dealers, brominating legal pharma for a longer buzz that was still addiction-free. Amateurs.

Now that had been sweet. Revenge always was. Even second-hand.

Ayesha and LeBlanc walked over.

'We should be on our way, monsieur,' LeBlanc said. 'It is quiet now, but later on your government soldiers will cross in many places.'

'Then let's go.'

LeBlanc eyed their dark clothing critically. 'Too much black, mes amis. Reds and browns are better, the black leaves a hole in the shadows.' He shrugged extravagantly, 'We shall do something later.'

They had been walking a few minutes when Gould said, 'Don't you mind the Americans invading?'

LeBlanc beamed happily, 'Not at all. It is chaos and in chaos anything can happen. Opportunity. People like you and me, why should we care who thinks they are in charge?'

The trek took them deep into difficult territory. LeBlanc lead them through thorny scrub, across cold mossy ravines and up jagged scarps of crumbling rock.

Deep in a clear cold night they paused to rest under a stand of ancient hemlock.

Ayesha and Gould sat a short distance away from the rest of the group.

'Are you keeping warm?' Gould said.

She kissed him. Her slender body felt distant under the layers of clothing. 'I'm fine.' She touched his cheek, 'Mitch, this could still be a trap.'

Ayesha, always alert, always thinking about his interests and his safety. And when he wanted it, her body, without question. She'd saved Manalito from the female agent, something the Mexican would never forgive her for. One day Manalito would want to take her far out into the desert with his knives. Out there, all alone, they would play a dreadful game. Gould knew a hard choice lay in the future, one he suspected he already knew the answer to. He also knew exactly what Ayesha was doing, that there was little genuine affection behind her actions. The idea of him actually having that thought made him laugh silently. The thing was, she did it so well.

'What?' Ayesha smiled, puzzled.

'You're incredibly useful, do you know that?'

'I worry about you.' She tried to hide it but she preened, more pleased with his remark than if he had said 'I love you'.

'I've been paid. If this is a trap it's an extremely expensive one.'

Ayesha's gesture took in the whole party. 'They're using us. This is all part of the war, we're government agents, mercenary forces paid to do a dirty job.'

That surprised Gould. 'And now this bothers you?'

'Come on, Mitch. I just want to know why. I can understand swatting Mexico, but Canada?'

She had a point. 'I guess they became too much of a pain in the ass.'

'So if they're prepared to do this, why leave us alone in New Orleans? Why not reclaim the southern littoral?'

A nauseous tension filled Gould's guts. Why not indeed. A case of conserving a resource until required? 'Then we have even more reason to be here.'

They went back to where the others crouched in the lee of one of the trees, a dense thicket of sapling-like suckers at its base. It was getting colder, a deep chill rose off the damp ground. Gould could feel it on his face, see his own breath.

Morgan and Black had their hands cupped around cigarettes.

'You two are the only Americans I know who still smoke tobacco,' Gould said.

'Yeah?' Morgan drew deep and exhaled. 'You should try it. The chicks love it, it gets them wet. They think it's cool.'

'Two billion Asians can't be wrong,' Black said.

'Are they cool?' Gould said.

The three men laughed.

Gould took a satisfied breath. 'I like this, compadres. It is like the old days, back in Birmingham when we put the heat on the Bloods and the Crips.'

'Not so many trees back then,' Morgan said.

Black coughed and thumped his chest.

LeBlanc appeared at their side. He regarded Morgan and Black's maroon scarves, navy cashmere coats and polished brogues with amused respect. 'A timeless elegance, gentlemen. It becomes you.'

'We're the Old-fashioned Boys,' Morgan told him. 'Style never goes out of fashion.'

'Of course. And now it is time to move again, monsieurs.'

Black indicated his half-smoked cigarettes.

'Let's go, gentlemen,' Gould said.

LeBlanc waited while Morgan and Black stubbed out their smokes, then picked up the butts and put them into a plastic bag.

The stars were fading in the east when LeBlanc called another halt. He conferred briefly with his men and two of them silently moved forwards.

'A problem?' Gould said quietly.

'Au contraire, all is well,' LeBlanc said. 'We are careful.'

Ten minutes later the men returned and they advanced again. They sky was lighter now but the canopy was dense, the trees close together.

A light flickered ahead. LeBlanc used his flashlight and waved everyone forwards. In a clearing a dozen men waited with three long wheelbase Land Rovers and two windowless black vans.

The cold reached through Gould's clothing, chilling his thighs and shoulders. His knees ached. Beside him Ayesha walked easily, surefooted over the roots and fallen branches.

Gould's thoughts clarified in an instant. He'd do this, then bail, liquidate his New Orleans assets and disappear. He'd have dermal engineering and live Stateside, a new life. It was time to call it quits.

LeBlanc's men handed out sandwiches and coffee. Gould cradled the enamel mug in his hands, enjoying the feel of the heat sinking into his palms.

LeBlanc took a bite of his sandwich and washed it down with a mouthful of coffee. 'Well, monsieur, here we are. Welcome to Canada.'

So it's regime change. It's been tried before and the list is long. Ecuador, Vietnam, Iran, Iraq, Nicaragua, Guatemala, South Korea, Syria, Libya, Great Britain. Sometimes, and y'all excuse my French here, it's a total fucking disaster and sometimes it's merely a cock-up of epic proportions. Leaving aside the theory that the first letter of each country spells 'Elvis is King' (although it would confirm Afghanistan was a mistake) this one does feel a little different.

Regime change. Who for whom? The Canadian opposition? Get real, folks. There's only one explanation: our government for theirs. This is annexation.

Slobodan Jones,
KUWjones.org

- 44 -

Josie leaned back in the white leather seat and stretched her arms. The smell of the new automobile was all around her. 'Nice car.'

Novik had changed vehicles again, cutting a fast trade with a dealer torn between a cash sale and getting out of town. The new ride was a high-end Lexus executive saloon, fast, comfortable and stylish, with puncture-proof tyres and armoured glass.

'We need to up our game,' Novik explained. 'Turning up at Crane's pad in an old rust bucket is a shake-and-bake recipe for an interview with law enforcement.'

At first Novik had been filled with nervous energy - he'd planned and prepared, he was going to get this right, he was going to keep them safe. Now, in the down-time of the wait before action, he felt exhausted, light-headed, and totally wasted.

Dealing with the car salesman had been hard, the stress of the failed border crossing had taken its toll on everyone. Fear was exhausting, the cold, dead-certain knowledge of what they all had to do next did not bear thinking about. Sprawled across the spacious rear seats, Benny and Marytha were locked together, head to tail, their faces buried in each-other's groins, naked in a tangle of blankets.

Josie envied them the ability to loose themselves in erotic pleasure, that they could take such comfort in the physical. She watched them, and wished she could stop thinking, stop worrying, that she and Novik could have sex too, make love, do it tenderly or like lions as the mood took them, to fall asleep in an afterglow tangle of entwined limbs.

'What do you call it when a guy Deep Throats a woman?' she said. 'I know that's not what's really going on, but you know what I mean.'

Novik rested his head on the steering wheel and shut his eyes. 'I don't know, the Romans probably had a word for it.' He started the engine, 'I need to crash, babe. Let's find a motel.'

The western side of the border wasn't open and it wasn't closed. There were already dozens of newsgroup postings from people who, like Novik and Josie, had not exactly been turned back, but discouraged from making the crossing. Yet the great eastern hubs were still operating. The lakes and Chicago, that part of the border was operating normally.

'We saw the troops go in,' Novik said. 'It's an invasion, undeclared war, like Pearl Harbour.'

Josie looked out the side window, she chewed on a nail. 'So what do we do? We could head east, get closer to Chicago then cross over and swing back.'

'There's not enough time. Crane's estate is a hundred miles north of here, by the time we arrive it will be completely enveloped.'

'Is this what it's all about? Palfinger Crane?' Josie said.

Novik couldn't see it, 'Whole divisions against one unarmed man? It doesn't make sense. There are no cities, no defences. They can split the country in two unopposed, divide east from west.'

They couldn't wait. It was now, or never.

Muffled conversation came from the back seat, languid and indistinct. Marytha sat up and pulled down her top. Beside her, Benny buttoned his shirt and finger-combed his hair.

The car's GPS route planner and SatNav photo overlays gave them detailed views of the border. Maps annotated by photos posted by tourists and local inhabitants showed crossing points and roads in detail, streaming data gave a semi-real-time view from 5,000 feet effective. Everywhere was the same: mobile infantry held the roads.

Novik didn't like the look of it at all. 'We'll be running a blockade.'

'Then let's cross over on foot, go through the woods and pick up transport on the other side,' Marytha said.

It sounded sensible and a lot safer. Novik wasn't sure. Driving up here, spending the money, filling the warehouses, they had built momentum.

'That convoy had robo-canines,' Josie said. 'What if they're on patrol? At least you can surrender to the soldiers.'

Novik remembered the gum-chewing, constantly smiling platoon leader, and the way he'd looked at the two women. He wondered just how good an option that would be.

Marytha's voice shook, 'So we just go for it?'

'We'll go for the same route again, tonight,' Novik said. 'Only the outbound lanes are blocked. I'll take us past on the other side.'

'Is the car up to it?'

Always, the implicit question. Mr. Car would have hurtled them through at a zillion miles an hour. Novik would have to drive the Lexus himself.

'We should wait another day,' Benny said. 'It will be safer, I'll have my new-'

Novik broke in loudly, 'It's a good car, hardened for urban crime.

'No, listen-'

Josie smoothed back an unruly lock of Benny's hair, 'It's all right, sweetie. Novik knows what he's doing, you've got to learn to trust a little.'

Exasperated, Benny knocked away Josie's hand, took hold of her long, slender fingers, 'You've got to trust to logic.'

Novik roared with laughter, coming from Benny that was truly hilarious. Josie and Marytha joined in. It wasn't that funny, but it was what they needed. Maybe it wasn't even funny at all, they laughed anyway and the tension, the anxiety and fear in the car broke.

Novik got himself back under control, 'All right, Benny, here's some logic - we'll go at 4am. That's when people are least alert.'

Novik kept the Lexus in electric drive, his guts a knot of tension as they rolled silently towards the border crossing a mile ahead. The vehicle lights were out and they were on the wrong side of the road. Dense pinewoods covered the slopes on either side.

Novik checked Josie's seat belt. Lit by the soft amber of the dashboard lights, her face acquired a beauty born of determination. She looked so calm, so self-assured. She was his rock. 'Josie, you know I –'

She turned quickly and kissed him on the mouth. 'I know you do, honey.' She pressed her fingers against his lips, 'Tell me when we're in Canada.'

Novik dimmed the dashboard lights. He set the drive train from Economy to High-power, suspension to Track/Sport. The car shifted as the suspension adjusted, ABS disconnected, the twin supercharged engine burbled softly.

Novik's foot hovered over the accelerator. 'Ready?' He saw it in their eyes, Josie beside him, Benny and Marytha in the rear mirror.

He floored it.

And they were doing sixty. Seventy. A hundred miles an hour.

The car was all it was meant to be. A hundred and thirty and acceleration still pushed them into their seats. What a beautiful machine.

Up ahead the big curve swept towards them in a broad left. They flew round like the car was on rails, the border a mere quarter of a mile away.

Dark forested hills flickered by at one hundred and twenty three miles an hour. Novik's mind was in a calm and elevated place. Seven seconds and they would be through.

A spotlight hit them. Then the whole valley lit up, arc lights on the hillside blazed down to illuminate the entire road. Soldiers scrambled for position, the turret of the armoured car cranked round. Too slow, Novik instantly knew. This close, the car moved faster than the turret could track.

Three soldiers were down on one knee, assault-rifles raised. A crackle of shots, bullets starred the rear window without penetrating. A running man crashed into the soldiers and they went sprawling.

The border barriers were raised, the gaps between the concrete lane barriers looked narrower than the car.

'Line it up,' came Benny's steady voice. 'There's plenty of room.'

Novik eased off. He lined up the car. They flashed through at a hundred and ten.

Canada.

All four tyres went flat.

Marytha shrieked, dashboard graphics flared red, the car began to wallow, threatened to fishtail into a spin. Novik turned into the slide, brought it back under control. Velocity fell away: a hundred – ninety - sixty-five. Forty.

Half a mile ahead the road curved again. Round the bend they would be safe from gunfire. The steering stiffened as the self-repairing tyres re-inflated. They started to accelerate, Novik flashed Josie a tense smile.

Down through the woods bounded two robo-canines, 30-cal mini-guns mounted on their headless platform bodies.

The tyres were still soft, the steering vague, acceleration sluggish. The two robo-canines galloped beside the car, one to each side.

Novik swung the wheel hard right. The robo-canine dodged away, tangled in the median barrier and crashed to the ground.

'Brake now!' Benny yelled.

Novik slammed his foot on the brake. The car slewed across the road as the second machine opened fire. Bullets chewed tarmac scant feet ahead of the car.

'Go,' Benny flung himself across Marytha, 'Go, go, go.'

Novik floored the accelerator, swung left then right. The second robo-canine danced awkwardly sideways and fell behind. Tyres fully inflated, the car flew into the wide bend.

Behind them, the robo-canine jogged into the centre of the road, braced its legs and opened fire.

Heavy calibre bullets tore at the flank of the Lexus. The car bucked madly, Josie yelped and jerked, everyone was screaming.

'Hang on,' Novik yelled.

Then they were round the curve, into the shadow of the hill, and speeding away.

But Marytha was still screaming, and Benny was trying to climb over the front seats. Josie was unconscious and soaked in blood.

Novik slammed the car to a screeching, burnt rubber halt.

'Josie,' Novik tore at the buckle of her seat belt. The door beside her was a ruin of perforated metal. Josie slid sideways, her head rolled, her eyes looked into a place he could not see. Her right side was barely there.

'Josie,' Novik clutched her to him and shrieked, 'Josie.'

- 45 -

Bianca woke to the sound of a single-engined aeroplane as it passed overhead. Sunlight filtered through the gaps on the palm screens, she was thirsty and hot. In the night her dreams had been blind and stifling.

Outside a few villagers gathered on the inner beach to watch the seaplane as it headed to the far side of the atoll. Nobody knew who it was, not the flying doctor, and no one had ordered an air taxi or special supplies.

The craft turned, solar panels on the high wing flashed as it descended to splashdown by one of the far villages.

Tanoata was still missing and most of the village were looking for her. At dawn, Mautake, the young man in front of Bianca in the canoe, had set off across the inner lagoon to alert the other villages.

Bianca sought out Tekirei and told him about her encounter on the Shadowed Path. Her revelations did not please him.

'You should not have gone. I asked you not to.'

Bianca did not recall that conversation the same way.

'You should have stayed with her,' Tekirei said.

'Tekirei, be reasonable. She had a knife.'

'Are you surprised? She sees you as a rival and there you are, prowling round her mother's sacred grave.'

'What did she think I was going to do?' Bianca protested. 'Is throwing stones and waving knives acceptable behaviour?'

'Don't you criticise my daughter,' Tekirei's face darkened, 'I should never have asked you here.'

They walked in silence for half a mile along the shore, then sat brooding on the gritty sand. Far across the bay the seaplane reappeared, skimming towards them across the lagoon.

Tekirei was right, she should have stayed away. Her privileged world of wealth and deference blinded her to the realities of island life. There was little hope she would fit in, no matter her own feelings of belonging, she had to accept it wasn't working. She and Tekirei were both intelligent and educated, but their assumptions, their differences, were too great. If leaving was the only way to make him happy, that is what she would do.

'Tekirei, I…' Bianca discovered it was impossible to say the words.

Tekirei's face was a mask of misery. 'Bianca, I'm sorry.' His hand faltered towards hers. 'I didn't mean any of that. I want you to stay.'

Bianca stared at him, barely able to breath. 'I don't want to go either.'

His voice was a whisper: 'I love you.'

'I love you too.'

Tekirei's mouth formed a trembling smile. 'Then it will be all right.'

They embraced for a long moment. Tekirei wiped his eyes. 'Look, the seaplane is coming here. Perhaps they will help us look for Tanoata.'

Two hundred yards out into the central lagoon the seaplane splashed down, a solar-electric, four-seater, the special hull and wings designed for high-efficiency low-altitude flight, scudding above the waves like an albatross.

The seaplane taxied into the shallows. The pilot, a tall, dark-skinned man in cut-down jeans and a red tee shirt, threw out the anchor, jumped down into the shallows and waded towards them.

Tanoata took hold of Bianca's hand and they went to greet him.

The pilot was broad and muscular, much taller than Tanoata. His straight black hair was contained by a cotton headband, his skin gleamed copper, two large knives hung from his belt, one on each hip. He smiled politely and held up his hand in greeting.

'Bianca Hutzenreiter?'

Bianca and Tanoata looked at each other in amazement then burst out laughing.

'Yes,' Bianca smiled. 'How on earth did you-?'

'I am called Manalito,' the stranger said evenly. With a single fluid movement he pulled a knife from his belt and thrust it deep into Tekirei's chest.

Tekirei staggered under the blow. His mouth hung open. He gave a single guttural cough and toppled backwards onto the white sand.

Bianca stared in disbelief. A minute ago life had swung from emotional agony to a joyful ache. Now it was a horror. A flaring light pressed all around, there was a great roaring, rushing noise. Unable to resist, Bianca allowed Manalito to fold her arms behind her back and lash her wrists together.

Manalito gripped her jaw between thumb and forefinger. He lifted her head so she could not avoid his dark eyes. 'Now you will travel with me,' he said.

A slight figure erupted from the foliage at the top of the beach and pelted towards them. Dazed, Bianca recognised Tanoata, naked, dishevelled, her body covered in festering welts and scratches.

'Kill her. I brought you to kill her,' Tanoata shrieked. 'You are to kill her. I brought you here. Kill her now.'

The hate in Tanoata's words struck at Bianca like a club. Overwhelmed, she sank down to the sand.

Tanoata flung herself down beside her father. Tekirei's eyes swam into focus, 'Daughter-?' he croaked, and his head lolled.

'Kill her,' Tanoata howled at Manalito. 'Kill her now. Why do you come, yet not obey?'

'I walk on two legs,' Manalito told her, 'I kill whom I please.'

Tanoata prostrated herself on the sand. 'Spirit of rokea, shark lord, I summoned you to do my bidding.'

To Manalito, this made perfect sense. The girl was clearly a witch, but she was inexperienced, and vastly out of her depth. She had summoned death magic, her father was the price, but to bring death did not mean it would be controlled.

'I do another's bidding,' Manalito told her.

Tanoata flew at Manalito with nails and teeth. Manalito stepped back, Tanoata lunged forward. Manalito backhanded her across the face, breaking her jaw. Tanoata pushed herself upright, spat blood and pointed mutely at Bianca.

Bianca's head whirled. Tekirei was dead, Tanoata a fury. Sprawled on the sand she tried to speak but could not even draw breath. Her nose and mouth filled with the odours of burning. A pitiful wail rose higher and higher, her own shriek of anguish. Bianca's arms and legs began to twitch and she fell into a hopeless, black pit.

3. Happiness

It's the big aspiration, the vibe you get when you've just slugged the ball and your aim is true.

So, and this is the big question – is happiness getting the home run or knowing you're about to score?

Think about it. Which is better? Which is more satisfying?

Imagine today, the here and now, but you don't have your job and you've lost the car. You're the guy who used to live next door. Now you live on the streets.

That's right, you're one of your own former neighbours and you've just dropped off society's bottom rung into your own personal ground zero. Your skills have been filleted out of the economy by some super-corporation AI-assisted CEO. He's re-imagined his growth curve so he can deliver tomorrow's products today, to yesterday's neighbours. To people who still have incomes, aspirational and lifestyle modalities that bisect his corporate wet-dream of ten more points on his share options.

You're out of work and starving. Life is shit, but then you find a fifty in the street and blow it on a decent meal. Or if you prefer, it's Ethiopia ten thousand years ago and some dude sweats up to the family cave with an antelope over his shoulders.

My point is this: for one night your bellies are full. Life is hard but tonight you're on top. You laugh, you play, your partner gives you that special look. Tomorrow is another day but right now, RIGHT NOW IN THIS ACTUAL MOMENT, life is good.

There. That's it. That fleeting moment. True happiness.

And that's why you can't have it. Why not? Because you've got everything you need, there's no lack in your life to be satisfied except how to afford the self-store bills for the stuff you just bought, but don't want in your house. (And that is just so messed up you do not want to get me started.) You think you'll be happy tomorrow, but we all know tomorrow never comes.

There's more, but I tell you what - if you've stayed with me this far, you can work the rest out for yourself.

T. Hank Yousomuch
If You're So Damned Happy Why Did You Buy This Book?

Oscar Gordano was in the Oval office with the President when Gould's call came through on his private cell. Gordano waved Snarlow to silence as he saw the number on the cell phone's screen. 'This is it,' he mouthed.

'Oh my God, it's him.' Guinevere fanned her face with her hand, 'Oh my God.'

'Hey. This is Ozzie.' Gordano pitched his voice low.

Gould's voice was cold and disdainful as ever. 'The offshore work is complete.'

'All right.' Gordano's heart began to pound. 'Excellent, you know what to do now.'

The encrypted line was so quiet Gordano felt like he was holding something vast and hollow to his ear.

'Yes,' Gould said eventually. 'We know what comes next.'

'Don't forget the sequence. Palfinger first, then-'

'Shut up with the names,' Gould said.

'It's all right,' Gordano gabbled, 'the line is totally secure. FedMesh quantum cryptography, quasi-infinite bit length encryption keys and sub-millisecond key persistence. We can talk about whatever we want, anything at all.' He laughed at the idea. 'Do you want to know who was on the grassy knoll?'

'You moron, nothing is secure,' Gould said and hung up.

Guinevere mouthed questions at Gordano. He gave her his lopsided cheeky campaign smile and a thumbs-up, and spoke into the dead line: 'Oh, that's great. Fantastic news. We can expect confirmation in twenty four hours.'

Guinevere waved her hand. 'Ask him if-'

Gordano held up his hand for silence. 'Of course it's a great plan,' he winked at Guinevere, 'Who do you think came up with it?'

'Ask him to make sure Palfinger is removed first,' Guinevere said.

'Hold on, you heard that?' Gordano pretended to listen. 'The father, then the daughter. Absolutely.' Sweating, Gordano slid the phone in his pocket. 'He heard you,' he said. 'It's happening.'

'Ozzie, are you all right?'

'Yes, ma'am, I'm in complete control.'

Guinevere Snarlow studied him intently then burst out laughing. 'Oscar Gordano, you absolute rascal. I never know when you're being honest with me or just teasing.'

'It's this life we lead, Guinevere. We're forced to dissemble, to pretend, to have fake friends and yes, sometimes we have to lie. It's the price of politics, the price we have to pay to serve our nation.' Gordano stepped towards her, his eyes twinkling. 'We're about to make our country great again. I'm nervous, I'm excited like being on a first date. I've got a lot of spare energy right now.' He perched a buttock on the edge of the desk. 'How about you?'

Guinevere's hand went to her throat. When it came to sex, all she could think of was Lobotnov's thick veined cock wagging between his legs. Improbable as it sounded, the balding economist had been an expert fuckmeister, his organ velvety smooth and gorgeously thick. Instinctively she knew Gordano's insecurity would make him a selfish, vindictive lover.

Guinevere walked smartly round the desk. 'I think we should celebrate.' She activated the intercom. 'Champagne, please.' Out of the corner of her eye she registered Gordano's disappointment with satisfaction.

'Anything else, ma'am?' a tinny voice replied immediately.

'No. Wait, yes, I want a burger.' Guinevere snapped her fingers at Gordano. 'You want a burger?'

'Sure,' Gordano said.

'Two burgers, rare. Emmental and gherkins, no mayo.'

'Any fries with that, ma'am?'

'No fries.'

'Actually…' Gordano raised his hand.

'What?'

'I'd like fries.'

'Hello?' Guinevere said, 'Can we have a portion of fries?' She shrugged apologetically. 'He's gone,'

'It's all right,' Gordano said. 'I'm incipient borderline proto-obese, I should watch the carbs.'

'Tell me about it.' Guinevere patted her washboard-flat stomach and they both laughed. During that light-hearted shared moment Gordano looked at her breasts and she studied his eyes.

Gordano thought about another play based around a suggestion they burn some excess calories together. The conversation faltered until the burgers and champagne arrived, served by the narrow-shouldered chinless intern. The cork was already out of the bottle, the bottle in a silver ice bucket. Guinevere poured and lifted her glass. 'The future.'

'New beginnings.'

Guinevere devoured her burger in a series of neat, decisive bites. 'A year from now America will be a different place. We are so going to be re-elected.'

'Providing Hirsch kicks off about Canada.'

'Oh, he will. Don't you worry about that. Andriewiscz has gone north with ten thousand chainsaws.'

'There's no risk with that?'

'What risk? The southern border's secure, Hirsch is so pissed with me he'll do anything, it's gotten personal. China's the only possible wild card, but they're so far up shit creek they lost the canoe. Half the country's a desert, Beijing's a sand pit and everyone's on double shifts trying to pay their parent's pensions. Offer them junior partnership in a joint Sino-American global reconstruction project and they'll bite your hand off at the shoulder.'

'I meant from felling the trees. I've been thinking - it's like when a ballet dancer pulls in her arms. Do you think it will make the world spin faster?'

'I never thought about it.' Guinevere twirled the champagne cork on her desk. 'It's a risk we'll have to take.'

'Won't citizens mind missing out on their European holidays?'

'Oscar, enjoy your champagne and quit worrying. It's only the liberals and socialists who take foreign vacations. If they want to irradiate their wombs and have mutant babies, let them. Everyone else can buy a Meeja console and visit a Europe where everyone speaks English.'

Gordano thought about his current wife, Jazmin, and realised the President was right. The world beyond the borders was simply a marketplace, somewhere to do business, to buy and sell. The insight made him happy, the very food in his hand was proof in itself: wheat, beef, cheese, gherkins, even the paper napkin were all American products. As a nation they were self-sufficient, they had everything anyone could want. Good citizens had no need to travel. He bit a chunk of burger and chewed with satisfaction. 'Meeja-II - that's why you're putting your home cinema in storage.'

'God, yes. We've got a great place but we just need the space. With Meeja all you need is the console and the headset. It's absolutely brilliant, you can do whatever you want.' Guinevere snorted champagne and laughed. 'Anything. You tried that one I sent you?'

'No, I haven't' Gordano lied. 'Not yet.'

Brobdingnag Lingerie Logo Launch

A capacity audience enjoyed free fireworks, inspirational poetry, music and fashion at Citi Fields stadium as market-leader Brobdingnag Lingerie launched its new logo in spectacular fashion.

Long lines formed as people queued to buy branded perfume, trainers, bumper stickers, jogging pants, body jewellery, bed linen, intimate toys, grooming products and other merchandise bearing the latest version of the famous X to the power of X logo.

'To be honest, the cash cow is the logo," admitted Marketing VP Tosh Zebulon in a candid interview.

'Brobdingnag create aspirational luxuries for your epidermis. We don't mind if you can't afford our lingerie. Buy the logo – be part of the family.'

- 47 -

Novik parked in a road-builder's quarry, a deep scoop cut into the bedrock of the rising ground beside the road. Willow herb and bracken colonised heaps of loose chippings, birch seedlings pushed roots into the cracks and ledges of the high rock walls.

He wrapped Josie in a blanket and carried her up a narrow track to a high bluff facing north. There, he settled Josie with her back against a pine tree, close to the cliff edge. Dawn light spread across rolling hills and mist-filled valleys. Beneath them, the road ran into blue distance.

Marytha had washed the blood from Josie's face, but Novik refused to let her touch Josie's hair. He brushed out the long blonde locks himself, slowly and carefully, then wove them into one long plait. He had a problem finishing and began to curse his fingers.

Marytha knelt beside him, 'Here, like this.'

Novik sat beside Josie, his legs out in front of him, his arms by his side. He looked smaller than before, he saw nothing but the past, all that was and might have been.

Benny sat beside him. After some minutes silence, he said, 'I like that you put her hair up. She always did that when she meant business.'

Novik looked right through Benny, his normally mobile and cheerful face like stone.

'We do still mean business?' Benny said.

'Benny, over here,' Marytha jerked her head angrily. Benny rose, she led him a short distance away. 'Let him be, this isn't the time.'

Benny looked south, he looked north, he looked up at the sky. 'Now is absolutely the time.'

Novik stood on the cliff edge. Benny and Marytha hurried over too. Hands stuffed in pockets, Novik looked out across the tree-covered wilderness, 'I think she'll like it here.'

'It's a good choice,' Marytha said.

They went back to Josie's body. Novik looked down at her, swaddled in the old blanket, one corner over her head like a hood.

'Babe, I'm sorry, we don't have the tools to dig a grave and we don't have a lot of time. I guess you know that. I've chosen a good place, the sun will keep you warm and you can see the forest and the road. You'll be able to see the where we're going.' His voice cracked, 'So you can, ah, watch over us.'

Novik stared at her so intently, so long, but no matter how hard he tried, he couldn't find her in her own face, he couldn't see his Josie, there was just her body. Then, for one freakish moment, he thought she moved, and suddenly his heart was pounding, his palms clammy and cold and he was frightened Josie was going to look up at him and say something. Close to panic, he had to walk away.

Marytha took a deep breath, 'Goodbye Josie. I didn't know you long, but I'm glad I did.'

Novik let out a great sob. The grief was overwhelming, his legs failed him. Marytha and Benny hurried to him, he sagged between them. They held him up.

Slowly, Novik got his own feet back under himself.

A few young firs grew among the rocks. Novik tore off one of the green, spreading branches, carried it back to Josie, and laid it across her legs. He returned for another. Rich pine resin aroma filled the air, Benny and Marytha fetched branches too.

Away in the pines something scuffed. Novik peered through the trees, all around, the forest was motionless. Away across the plateau came the commotion of something large working its way through underbrush, a bear, or perhaps a Robo-canine. Novik picked up a fallen branch, an unwieldy club, and faced towards the noise. Whatever it was, he was not going to leave Josie until he was ready. Perhaps it was a soldier. That would be good, but not in front of Josie. In his mind, Novik tracked the soldier through the wood and cornered him, brought down with his club, made him pay.

Wind stirred in the trees, the noises receded, and came to an end. Far down in the valley mist idled among the tree tops, a low amber sun pushed through broken sheets of high haze. Novik hunkered down next to Josie. He knew they should go. They were done here, there was nothing – he stopped himself – there was *no-one* to keep them. He didn't want to leave, he was scared.

Life without Joise.

He didn't see how he'd cope, how he'd get through a day without her arms around him, without her clear-eyed advice. He gave a guttural, wordless sound of contempt, ashamed at his own self-pity. Josie was dead, killed, and all he could think about was himself. It was pathetic. She'd want him to cope, she'd expect it, and he knew then that somehow her faith in him, her love, had survived, even if it was only within himself. He had to stand up and he had to walk away. He had to finish the job. If he didn't, he'd have failed her utterly.

So he'd do it, he promised himself, he'd find Crane and do what they'd set out to do. Somehow. And when it was done, he'd find the person who had killed Josie, not some machine, a somebody. That somebody who needed to pay. He just needed to work it through.

Benny and Marytha were waiting for him. He wanted to smile, just something thin and weak, enough to let them them know he was doing better than he looked, better than he felt. He couldn't do it. He stood there and looked at them, then led the way down to the car.

Back in the quarry Novik wandered through the weeds and debris, he still had some thinking to do. As he went, he picked up random stones, kept a few, and discarded most. When he had a handful, he stood on one of the heaps of stones chippings and threw them at the far wall of the quarry. Time after time, from thirty yards, he hit the same spot.

Benny walked over, 'I'm impressed.'

'Muscle memory. Six months in the protest camps,' Novik said between throws.

Benny looked back at Marytha, 'We were wondering-'

'I'm trying to work it out, Benny.' Novik gave an involuntary grunt as his arm snapped out, the stone hit the rock face so hard it shattered. 'Who really killed Josie?'

The border and the army patrols were only a few miles behind them. Benny realised they would be here a while longer.

Another stone ricocheted from the wall.

'Novik, I don't know. Those robo-canines are autonomous, they follow a rule-set until recalled. They're not intelligent like AI, but nobody operates them.'

The last of Novik's stones was gone. Benny picked one out of the heap and handed it up to him.

Novik tossed the stone in his palm and sent it hurtling towards the wall, 'So Josie was murdered by computerised military machines? Not good enough, Benny. The army is a limb of the government, and the government is elected by the people. By the people, Benny. For the people. Come election time, the people voted, I voted. I didn't get the government I wanted, but I got one anyway. The government - servant of the people, spending our tax dollars because we voted them in.'

Novik was hurting, Benny didn't want to make it any worse, he didn't want to lie. 'Governments govern populations, not people. It's part of the system, part of what you're trying to change.'

'It's a circular excuse, Benny. Systems don't kill, it's the people in them, supporting them, making them work, writing those rule-sets.' Novik bent down, clawed up a handful of stone chips and flung them in a scattered arc. 'I want to get my hands round those people's throats. I don't know who they are, and I don't know how to find out. I- I think it might be everyone, Benny. We just don't realise.'

It was tearing him apart.

'Up there,' Benny whispered. 'Novik, look up.'

'Oh for fucks sake, man, don't,' Novik said.

Then he saw it too.

A figure looked down at them from Josie's bluff. Another appeared, and a third. They were dressed in skins and furs and carried spears and bows. Something was wrong with their faces. Perhaps it was the perspective.

Marytha ran to join them, 'Native Americans? There's reservation land round here.'

One by one the figures dropped to all fours and loped away. They weren't dressed in skins at all.

Novik was halfway up the track before Marytha and Benny could move. 'Wait,' Marytha sprinted after him.

Up on the rocky ledge, Josie still rested against the tree. Already, she seemed settled there, timeless. Whoever – whatever - had been there had not disturbed her.

They had left gifts.

A bundle of wild flowers tied with grass lay in her lap. A bow and a single white-fletched arrow rested against the tree.

'They looked like people,' Novik said as Benny and Marytha arrived. He gestured at the funerary gifts, 'What does this mean?'

'That we're on the same side?' Marytha said. 'That they understand?'

Novik's face grew hard. 'Then they saw what happened,' he picked up the arrow, his voice cracked, 'I just wish they could have done something.'

'Bows and arrows against guns?' Benny said.

Marytha whispered to Benny, 'We should go.'

Grief welled up inside Novik, it saturated his flesh and stole his breath. His throat burned with it. Josie was dead. Never again would he hear her voice, or smell her hair, or just sit together in the morning and drink coffee.

After a while Novik rubbed his face, he dried his eyes, he blew his nose. 'I'm all right.'

Marytha saw that he wasn't, she kissed him on the cheek.

'I'm all right,' Novik said.

'We should go now.'

So what can the modern army do to protect itself against unwelcome attention? We're all interested in guaranteeing our privacy, nobody more so than the commander of an army on active campaign in hostile territory. We can draw the curtains, an army operates under a sky filled with satellites operated by nations and corporations with vested interests in exploiting its activities. These then, are the choices:

1. Block. Launch denial-of-service attacks on all the sites on all the webs in the world. Strategically simple, tactically a virtual(ha!) impossibility. DoS is so old it's boring. Anti-DoS proliferators spawn mirror sites faster than you can knock them out.

2. Jam. Swamp the wavelengths with crud and punch a virtual hole in the Cloud. Effective but localised. So effective you've sodomised your own data portals and have to communicate with bean cans and string.

3. Subvert. Aggregate all the data from all the feeds, add and subtract what you want, then let it through. Do this on all the portals in all the world. Without anyone noticing. Yeah, right.

4. Accept. It's so very Zen, and war can be scary, but remember, it's an art for some and a religion to others. So stop worrying about things you can't change. Polite people know staring is rude, so perhaps they will mind their own business. Meantime, damn their eyes for looking and just get on with annexing that peaceful, prosperous state north of the border. Sorry, I mean launch that urgent mission to avert a global ecological catastrophe.

Editor's blog,
BFBM magazine

- 48 -

Andriewiscz deployed the northern expeditionary force in Eastern Washington and central Montana, each battle group spanning a hundred miles of the 49th parallel

A few miles south of the Washington border, Wilson and Halifax headed east along the Mount Baker Highway in an attempt to evade the main units. The settlements along the route were deserted, sidewalks empty, the shops shuttered and houses boarded up. Low on gas, they broke into a service station and turned on the pumps at the counter.

While Halifax filled the tank Wilson took four cans from the station shop, filled them from another pump and stashed them in the trunk. Back on the road Wilson studied his tracking device. The money trail had faded, the opportunities for retail transactions in what was now a militarised zone were limited to non-existent. The scanner's analysis program provided three extrapolations:

- Gould had spent all the money;
- He had reached his destination;
- The trail had been a sophisticated diversion.

'If we've arrived, where exactly are we?' Wilson pressed keys on the tablet and frowned. 'My GPS has stopped working.' He checked his cell. 'The network's down. They must be blocking.'

Wilson instructed the phone to load older, cached data. There was only one significant landmark across the border - Million Pines, Palfinger Crane's vast private estate.

Halifax looked over his shoulder, 'You seriously think that Gould has gone there?'

Wilson panned out the display, 'There's nowhere else.'

'Man, that place is going to be secure. You'd need-' Halifax looked at Wilson.

'An army. Yes, you would.'

'What the hell have we gotten ourselves into?'

Wilson had told Halifax everything he knew about Gould, Masters, and her organisation. Masters, an agent for an executive-sponsored field unit, was after one of Gould's men yet hadn't been aware Gould himself had left the southern littoral. It wouldn't be the first time the left hand didn't know what the right was doing. Just another run-of-the-mill snafu. For Gould to be stateside was big enough in itself. To be in Canada now, surrounded by an invading army, yet free to operate could only mean one thing.

'I think Gould is working for the government,' Wilson said.

Halifax shivered. 'That's one scary-arse mother of a thought.'

'You want to turn back? This is too much for you, is that what you're saying?' Wilson hadn't had a drink in days. There had always been muscle under the paunch, now his eyes were clear, his face less pouchy.

'What do you suggest?' Halifax bridled.

'Walk across the border and get into Crane's estate. See what's going on.'

'Through the woods, like backpackers?'

'That's right.'

Halifax was a city boy, born and bred, he wasn't big on the great outdoors. There were no signs, no shops on the corners. No corners. He thought about what waited for him back home and shrugged. 'I got nothing better to do.'

Halifax inspected the FaF gun. 'Gould has your ex-partner's weapon?'

Wilson had described the devastation it had caused at the mall.

'Marcel trained with prototype FaF rifles in boot camp,' Halifax said. 'They're dangerous, one guy took out half the squad by mistake.' He handed the weapon back to Wilson. 'This one's PG feature-locked. Non-lethal. There's a guy I know owns a bar, he might have been able to unlock it.'

'I'll hang on to it.'

Halifax fell silent. Recollecting Marcel summoned unwelcome memories of Gould's attack, disjointed, muzzle-flash snapshots of silhouettes in frantic movement. Gunshots and screams, his own body muzzily slumped in the corner, an anaesthetic dart in his chest. Afterwards, in the dark, there were different kind of screaming, and laughter. Strange creaks and pops came from Halifax's mouth as his teeth ground together.

'Halifax,' Wilson said sharply.

Halifax snapped back into focus. 'What?'

'Gould left you alive because it would hurt you more.'

Halifax looked through the window at the wooded landscape and tried to think about the future. Apart from Gould, all it seemed to promise were mud, rain and wildlife.

'So we'll make our way through the lines,' Wilson said.

Halifax said nothing. Wilson started the motor and they headed north up a dirt trail.

When they heard heavy calibre gunshots they abandoned the car and moved forwards on foot.

Half a dozen army engineers with two flatbed lorries and a tool van had set up a mobile repair shop at one end of a long scrubby field between two wooded hills. One of the engineers, pot-bellied and flabby, was test-firing a long-barrelled rifle mounted on a robo-canine. Another of the four legged machines roved back and forth a quarter of a mile away at the far end of the field.

Halifax and Wilson watched the men from the tree line.

'I count six,' Halifax said quietly. 'One in the open, three on the benches and two in the tool van.'

'Agreed.'

'How many shots in your gun?' Halifax said.

'Five.'

They looked at each other. Wilson shrugged and walked out into the open. After a moment Halifax followed.

'Hi there,' Wilson said as he reached the engineer testing the gun. 'How's it going?' he read the man's nametag, 'Sergeant Michelob?'

'Corporal. Piece of shit, they send us this junk before it's out of beta and expect us to debug in the field.' Michelob looked them up and down. 'Who are you?'

'Just a couple of local boys trying to get home. Our car broke down a mile back.'

'Oh, OK.' Michelob indicated two steel urns on a trestle behind the trucks. 'You want a coffee?'

'Thanks.' Wilson grinned. 'Never should have bought that second-hand foreign tin can.'

'It wouldn't have got you this far if it was running our hack firmware.'

The engineers at the test benches were watching them. Halifax raised his hand, one of the engineers waved back and they returned to their monitors and diagnostic consoles.

Halifax leaned close. 'So what's wrong with it?'

'Damned thing keeps losing its target acquisition profile. Every time I reload, it corrupts.' Michelob indicated the robo-canine wandering randomly back and forth at the far end of the field. 'That's configured with the thermal profile of a human body, and what should happen is this.' Michelob flipped a button on his handset and manipulated two small joysticks with his thumbs. The nearby robo-canine shuffled into position, the rifle swiveled and fired.

An instant later the far machine disintegrated in flash of orange and black smoke, followed a half-second later by a distant bang.

'Instead,' Michelob continued, 'what I've got is something that preferentially targets squirrels. Fifteen million dollars per unit and all we got is a danger to small rodents. We should put one in Times Square and clean out the pigeons.'

Halifax and Wilson exchanged worried looks. 'How many have you deployed?' Wilson said.

Michelob scowled, 'I can't tell you. More than ten, less than ten thousand.'

'How about that coffee?'

'OK. We got a donut machine too. Say, you don't have a signal on your cell, so you?'

'Sorry.'

Michelob stuck out his bottom lip, 'I sure wish I could download some patches.'

The coffee and donuts were fresh and good. Halifax was intrigued by the smoothly articulating joints and muscle rods of the robo-canine legs. Mug in hand he wandered round the front of the trucks.

Immediately the sniper dog out in the field rotated towards Halifax, sighted the gun and fired. The bullet shattered the mug, hot coffee sprayed Halifax.

'Jesus.' Halifax flung himself under the truck.

'It's all right,' Michelob waddled towards the vehicle. 'It thought your coffee mug was a squirrel.'

'You OK?' Wilson said.

'Arseholes,' Halifax growled as he crawled out.

'Good.' Wilson pulled his FaF gun and shot Michelob in the leg.

'Ouch.' Momentarily Michelob looked offended, then slumped to the ground.

The three bench engineers appeared. 'What happened? Is anyone hurt?'

Wilson kept the gun behind his back. 'That robot thing shot my friend's coffee mug. Michelob got a splinter in his leg, I think he fainted.'

'Wake up, you pussy,' one of them kicked Micholob's boot. As they stood over Michelob, Wilson walked behind them and shot each one in the buttock.

Wilson looked down at the four unconscious men. 'Two soldiers, one bullet.'

'How about we bring them some God-damned coffee?' Halifax growled.

As Wilson and Halifax approached the tool van, the unit officer opened the door and came down the steps. Unlike his men, he was unhealthily thin, with over-bright bright eyes and waxy skin. 'You shouldn't be here,' he said. He looked over the benches, 'Where is everyone?'

Wilson produced his gun. 'There's been an incident. Your men are temporarily disabled.'

The lieutenant's eyes widened. 'That's a FaF gun. How did you get that?' He took a step back. 'Oh.'

'That's right. My name is Johnson, and this,' Wilson indicated Halifax, 'is Mr Johnson-'

'So it's true,' the lieutenant gasped.

'-we're autonomous counter-insurgency field agents in deep cover. Canadian fifth-column elements are trying to break through our lines, we need your help.'

Halifax banged on the side of the tool van. 'Come on out, soldier.'

An owlish woman with narrow shoulders and broad hips emerged from the truck, fastening her jacket. Her bootlaces were undone.

'I heard,' she said. 'I've never seen a FaF gun before, is it feature-enabled?'

Wilson gave a disdainful laugh, 'What do you think?'

'Cool. Can we see?'

'I'm not allowed to discharge the weapon outside the line of duty. Every round has to be accounted for.'

'How about I order you?' the lieutenant grinned, 'This is a combat zone so you're under military jurisdiction. I can order you to shoot Jennings with a non-lethal round.'

'Julius?' Jennings backed away nervously.

'This will be fun. Run around a bit, Jennings. That's an order.'

'Jesus,' Halifax said, disgusted.

Wilson shot the lieutenant in the thigh.

'You idiot,' the lieutenant screeched. He sat down hard and flopped onto his side. 'This is no fun,' he mumbled, and passed out.

Halifax gave Jennings a sloppy salute. 'Congratulations on your promotion, ma'am.'

Breaking News – School Bus Assault Defeated

Munising, MI, 07:15. Jubilant kids from Munising High celebrated their victory this morning over Grande Arme d'Arcadia terrorists early today.

The school bus was on its normal morning run when it encountered a fallen tree on a quiet lane. An assault by GAA gunmen dressed as smart young business people followed. School children returned fire with handguns and rifles and the terrorists were driven off with casualties.

'Those Canadians sure didn't expect that,' one of the children said. 'We kicked their cheese-eating butts. And their French was really bad, comprende?'

Seriously injured GAA personnel apparently blew themselves up to avoid capture. 'They burned really bright,' said an eye-witness. 'The flames were like white flowers.'

- 49 -

Marytha drove until Novik found inactivity intolerable and insisted on taking over.

'We can- If you like- we can take the seat out,' Marytha said as they changed places. 'If you like.'

'No.' The thought of another empty space beside him was horrifying.

Novik laid his jacket over the blood-soaked seat and pulled away. Wind whistled through the bullet holes in the door, a mournful Aeolian wail. They stuffed the holes with old paper, litter, money from the trunk, and carried on.

Late in the day Novik brought the bullet-scarred Lexus to a halt outside the entrance to Million Pines. The two-lane highway outside the estate ran east and west in a series of gentle rises and dips. At the bottom of one of the slopes, two white stone pillars capped with spherical finials marked the entrance to Million Pines. Beyond the pillars, a tarmac track ran into the forest, turned to packed gravel and wound away into stands of massive Douglas Fir and Cedar, moss covered boulders and ferny crags.

The ground lay in deep shadow beneath the trees' sun-lit tops, the forest on each side of the road an identical mix of fir, pine, hemlock and feathery-leaved larch. Despite the similarities, it seemed that the woodlands of Million Pines were imbued with an additional aura of watchfulness.

'So we just drive in?' Marytha said. 'Crane's security will be discreet but there's going to be plenty of it. He doesn't want to be bothered by the real world.'

'Then it's time he was,' Novik depressed the accelerator, swung the wheel, and the battered Lexus rolled between the pillars into the silent woods of the Crane estate.

As they approached the end of the tarmac section of the trail a strident fanfare sounded from the car's speakers. Ahead of them, the air shimmered and an enormous disembodied head swam into focus across the trail.

A ten foot tall head, a man in late middle years with receding hair, regarded them incuriously. 'Good day,' it said through the car's speakers, 'you have entered private property. A prompt return to the public highway will avoid an undignified encounter with authority.'

'We need help,' Novik said wearily. 'We've had some trouble.'

'A moment.' The head's expression became bland.

'It's just a hologram, go forwards,' Benny said.

Novik released the hand brake. Although the engine revved the drive would not engage.

The speakers emitted a brief, high-pitched whine, Novik, Benny and Marytha felt their skin prickle with warmth. The vehicle jerked forwards a few inches, then reversed.

The head assumed a more alert expression, 'You may proceed. Do not leave the trail.'

Once again the controls responded. The head folded in on itself and swung apart like a pair of gates. Novik drove between what were now two identical heads. In the rear view mirror he saw them swing closed, merge into one and watch the car depart.

The track took them across high ledges and through open glades of towering, grey-barked trees. A large lake appeared in the distance and was lost to view again. Novik wound down his window, the cool air held the aromas of damp earth and resin. When the lake reappeared they could also see the mossy tiled roofs of the many-gabled lodge at the heart of Million Pines.

A simple counterbalanced barrier lay across the track. A man stood behind it, his face was that of the gateway hologram. Novik stopped the car and got out.

The man walked round the barrier. 'Good day to you all, my name is Raymond St.John. Is anyone hurt?'

Novik gave a mournful shake of his head, 'Back there, my girl, Josie, she was killed when we crossed the border.'

'I am so very sorry to hear that,' St.John looked towards the trunk of the car, 'Is she-?'

'No. We gave her a funeral, up in some trees.'

St.John cocked his head and listened for a moment. 'Mr. Crane extends his hospitality and welcomes you all to Million Pines. However, he is unable to meet with you right now. Until he can, I am at your service, Mr?'

'Novik.'

'Of course.' St.John regarded Benny and Marytha, 'And you must be Mr Spoke, and Ms Drummond. Do you have any bags?'

Benny and Marytha retrieved the holdalls from the trunk, and then followed St.John towards the Lodge.

St.John escorted the three friends to guest apartments, and invited them to refresh themselves.

Novik kicked off his boots and stripped, his clothes falling where he left them. Head bowed, he stood under the shower. First he ran the water scalding hot then freezing cold. He felt the pain on his skin, but he didn't feel anything else. He tried again, and it occurred to him he was being morbidly self-indulgent. Although he had lost a lot, he was still alive. It was Josie who had lost everything.

He adjusted the water temperature to a sensible setting, washed his hair, shaved, and cleaned his teeth.

When he emerged from the bathroom, he found his clothes were clean, his boots polished, with new undergarments provided. He dressed, and wandered the apartment.

The rooms were spacious, furnished with tasteful simplicity. Oak panelling covered the walls to waist height, the upper walls finished with a pastel rose wash. Red and cream rugs decorated with animals in a naïf mode covered the chestnut stained wooden floor. A settee and low table fronted an open hearth, a pair of green leather armchairs faced a bay window with views onto the woods. A door was set in each of the side-walls, a private study lay behind one, a large and comfortable bed behind the other.

Novik poured fresh coffee from the jug and sat in one of the armchairs. The window was open, the woodlands peaceful, the silence emphasised by occasional birdsong and, once, the distant hammer of a woodpecker. Novik sipped his coffee. It was the best coffee he had ever tasted. His hand started to shake and he put the cup down. The contrasts of the past days became unbearable and he wept uncontrollably. Then he went to the bedroom, curled up on the crisp linen of the bed, and slept.

Extract from custodial interview

Officer #1:	*Mr. Jazdy? Prawo?*
Interviewee:	*<mumble>*
Officer #1:	*Would you speak up please, sir.*
Interviewee:	*I zed 'e took us straight there, mon.*
Officer #1:	*When you say "He", do you mean-?*
Interviewee:	*Der car, ja, zad's right.*
Officer #1:	*So, you were hitching with your friends and accepted a lift. The driver took you where you wanted to go. Then he let you out.*
Interviewee:	*No, mon. Der was no driver, jus der car. It talked, OK?*
Officer#1:	*OK. All right. So, what did this talking car say?*
Interviewee:	*It zed it was lonlee an' did we wan' hang out, maybe cruise 'roun some. I zed no thanks, is cool. We get out pretty pronto.*
Officer #2	*What's the exact nature of your complaint, sir?*
Interviewee:	*It waz rilly cripee, mon. Ver unzeddling.*
Officer#2:	*Are these your drugs, Mr. er…*

- 50 -

Flat on their stomachs, Gould and LeBlanc studied the group of armed men up ahead. LeBlanc passed the scope to Gould. 'Two platoons of your United States soldiers.'

LeBlanc issued orders to redeploy his people in a loose arc through the woods, then he and Gould moved forwards to reconnoitre.

'Crane cannot know about this,' LeBlanc whispered excitedly. 'If he did, it would not be here.' He clapped Gould on the shoulder. 'This is a challenge, yes? We cannot leave a unit of this size to the rear. We do not need some ambitious young officer deciding to use his initiative.'

It wasn't what Gould wanted to hear but he saw the logic. He was used to small encounters, one or two people disappearing, the occasional public show to prove who was still in charge. This felt like starting a small war.

'You're the boss here, LeBlanc.'

'Yes, of course. Now I will show you how we do things nice and quiet in Canada.' LeBlanc spoke to one of his men, they checked their watches and the man set off.

After a short interval LeBlanc checked the time again, pushed back his cap and slung his rifle over his shoulder. 'Come when I call, but come slowly. Bring Ayesha with you and be very American.' LeBlanc ambled towards the army camp. After a few steps he started to whistle.

Gould and Ayesha watched from cover as LeBlanc approach the soldiers.

'Bonjour, mes amis,' LeBlanc called out in a heavily exaggerated accent. 'You are aware that you are digging holes into the estate of Monsieur Palfinger Crane.'

The nearest soldier, young, shaven-headed and chewing gum snapped his assault rifle to his shoulder. 'How the hell did you get here?' He yelled over his shoulder, 'Hey, Sarge, we got company.'

LeBlanc kept on walking. 'I didn't get here, I live here. I am Monsieur Crane's gamekeeper.'

The muzzle of the soldier's gun dropped then came back up again. 'You stop right where you are until Sergeant Drogba gets here.'

'All right, be reasonable.' LeBlanc carefully laid his rifle on the ground. 'There is no need for any nasty stuff.'

Two soldiers flanked LeBlanc left and right. A third jogged over to the dugout. He pulled open the canvas flap releasing a cloud of blue smoke along with a bass-heavy electro beat.

Sergeant Drogba emerged from the dugout smoking the stub end of a fat tab. Compared to LeBalnc's compact physique, Drogba was a giant of muscles, tattoos and boots. Exhaling smoke he let the butt fall and marched towards LeBlanc in a ground-eating stride.

'You work for Crane, Francois?' Drogba scowled at LeBlanc. 'What are you doing here?'

LeBlanc puffed out his chest. 'I am his gamekeeper, an important position. And my name is not Francois.'

The soldiers holding their guns on LeBlanc grinned. Drogba was unimpressed, 'I think you're a pretty sneaky rat, Francois. What do you say?' Drogba made creepy-crawly motions with his fingers, 'Are you a sneaky little rodent?'

LeBlanc's face sagged with exaggerated Gallic affront, 'Monsieur, I track game, I know the land. I do not sneak as you say, like the rat.'

'How did you get past the dogs?'

'Les chien?' LeBlanc looked puzzled. 'I saw no dogs.'

Drogba unwrapped gum and pushed it into his mouth. 'That's why you're still alive.'

'You should not let them loose without asking. What sort of hounds are they? Who is in charge?'

Drogba folded his arms, flattening his impressive biceps. 'You're asking a lot of questions, Francois.'

LeBlanc shrugged. 'What you do is OK, mes amis. Monsieur Crane is a big friend of America. He will not mind, but I must tell him you are here on my cell phone.'

Drogba grinned, the gum clamped between his teeth. 'No chance, pal. You're in a black hole.'

LeBlanc looked at his cell phone in astonishment, then burst out laughing, 'But it is you who are sneaky!' He wagged his finger at Drogba, 'You are very naughty people.'

The soldiers laughed at LeBlanc's antics. Two more came over from the dugout, the music overlaid with monotone female voices. One of the guards put up his gun.

LeBlanc turned and walked away.

'Hold it, Francois,' Drogba said.

LeBlanc gestured innocently, 'I must tell Monsieur Crane you are here?'

'No way, José.' Drogba snapped his fingers and two of the guards started forwards. 'You've just become a guest of the Big Red One, courtesy of 3rd Brigade of the 201.'

'OK, so I am a guest. We get to know each other, then you let me go.' He extracted a hip flask from his pocket and offered it round. One of the soldiers took an enthusiastic swig.

'Can that, Bennett,' Drogba snapped at the soldier. 'Go wake up the Lieutenant.'

The soldier took a hurried second swig then jogged towards the dugout.

LeBlanc hopped up onto a tree stump just as Bennett reached the dugout. 'Hey, what's the music? The Bariatric Babes, yes? Big girls are good. Turn it up, let's party, OK?'

Over at the dugout Bennett grinned, made the devils sign with his hand and ducked inside. Immediately the clearing was filled with the pulsing electro-bass riffs and baroque harmonies of the Bariatric Babes.

'I like those Babes, their big lolos,' Le Blanc outlined a figure-eight in the air and pumped his hips to more laughter from the soldiers.

'Cut that shit out.' Drogba said.

'Of course, of course.' LeBlanc stepped down. 'I am just making things nice to party for Monsieur Crane's guests.'

Drogba spoke with slow menace. 'What are you talking about?'

'The guests I am showing round the estate.' LeBlanc waved his hand vaguely in the direction he had come from. 'Hello out there, it is safe to come forwards.'

Drogba stared at LeBlanc then pulled his sidearm. 'Strover,' he yelled at the nearest soldier, 'get that music off. Tell Bennett his ass is mine.'

Out in the woods Gould and Ayesha had watched the situation develop.

'Time to go,' Gould said.

Ayesha pushed in front. 'He's using you as bait.'

Gould pulled her back and moved into the open. It was all going to kick off soon, he could feel it. Gould's heart raced with excitement, it made his voice quaver and he used it, 'Hello, please don't shoot. We're American tax payers.'

Up ahead Drogba held LeBlanc by the collar. Bennett and Strover walked back from the bunker. The remaining three soldiers were all in front of Drogba looking towards Gould and Ayesha.

Ayesha waved to the soldiers. 'American! We're American.'

The music was still thudding out when LeBlanc slipped free of his coat. He was behind Drogba, a knife in his hand before the big soldier could react. LeBlanc's arm pistoned furiously as he stabbed Drogba in the kidneys a dozen times. Convulsed in agony, Drogba tried to bring his sidearm round on LeBlanc. LeBlanc locked Drogba's arm and stabbed up into the back of his skull. Drogba collapsed and LeBlanc took his gun.

In the rear Bennett was shouting, his voice inaudible over the music. Strover raised his assault rifle.

'American,' Gould laughed and raised both hands. 'Coca-cola. Hamburgers. Speedway.'

Two crossbow bolts thudded into Strover's chest and he toppled sideways. Another bolt hit Bennett in the gut and he fell, screaming.

The music stopped.

Bennett was still screaming.

The soldiers between Gould and LeBlanc turned. LeBlanc shot one in the face, the next one twice in the chest, then darted away.

'Down.' Gould pulled his own gun. Ayesha was already on one knee as she fired at the remaining soldier.

At the back of the camp more soldiers were running forwards. LeBlanc's men engaged them from the woods, firing and moving, closing fast. LeBlanc himself reappeared on the roof of the dugout, crouched above the entrance. Two of his men joined him and they threw grenades down into the bunker. Smoke and fire blasted out in a triple explosion. A handful of soldiers staggered out, bloody and blinded, their uniforms in rags, firing wildly. LeBlanc and his men shot them down.

Suddenly it was very quiet. From somewhere came hoarse sobbing, a gasp of agony abruptly cut off. LeBlanc's men were everywhere. A man rose from the ground wiping his knife.

There was birdsong.

'Are you all right?' Gould said to Ayesha.

'Sure.'

Among the carnage a single soldier stood, hands clasped behind his head, wild-eyed and alone. LeBlanc's people ignored him as they moved methodically through the camp delivering the coup-de-grace to the wounded.

'So, Mr. Gould,' LeBlanc said, 'that is one way we do it up here. Happily, we have no casualties. From now we will form a skirmish line with our left flank against the river to the west, and sweep north and east. Crane's Lodge is less than four miles.'

At times like these it was hard to keep track of time. It seemed to Gould the entire action had taken no more than a few seconds. He was deeply impressed. LeBlanc had come highly recommended and it was obvious why.

'You missed one,' Ayesha said.

'Ha, yes, of course,' LeBlanc led them to the waiting soldier.

He was young, plump, in need of a shave. He took a step back as Gould, LeBlanc and Ayesha approached, then held his ground.

'Relax,' LeBlanc said as he picked up the soldier's discarded rifle. He dropped out the magazine and cleared the chamber with practiced ease, sniffed the barrel and showed it to Gould. 'I have heard this. Soldiers who do not fire their weapons.'

The prisoner stiffened to attention. 'Mark Nagel, Private E-1, zero two zero dash four seven dash six nine four two.'

LeBlanc patted him on the cheek. 'I said relax, Mark Nagel. I do not need your social security number. Allow me to introduce you to Monsieur Mitchell Gould.'

'Where are you from, soldier?' Gould said.

'Pittsburgh, sir.'

'Say hello to Ayesha.'

Nagel faced Ayesha, 'Hello, ma'-'

Gould shot him in the temple. 'We done here?' he said to LeBlanc.

LeBlanc's eyes glittered. 'I think so, yes.'

'We're not at war, this is not an invasion. We've got nothing against the Canadian peoples and mean them no harm.'

That's the official government line from Secretary of State Cheswold Lobotnov. Seen in the light of 80,000 ground troops under a general Richard 'Spud' Andriewiscz, hero of Fresnillo, with a rumoured 30,000 to follow, what exactly does this mean?

Vice President Oscar Gordano is not renowned for coherent thought, let alone incisive commentary, yet perhaps he's on the money with his recent statement to the Schenectady Christian Mothers Union. "The state of Canada and the wider world have been ill-served by the incumbent government. It is time for politics with a different ethics north of the 49."

Slobodan Jones,
KUWjones.org

- 51 -

St. John escorted Novik, Benny and Marytha from the guest apartments to the main lodge, first leading them down a path of red brick winding under ancient pines, then along a broad covered way.

Crane greeted them informally in a lounge filled with soft yellow light from wall sconces and the crackling flames of a log fire in the wide stone hearth. St. John ushered them in then pulled the double doors closed and withdrew.

Like most people on the planet, Novik had seen pictures of Palfinger Crane. After all he had been through meeting the man himself felt curiously anti-climactic.

Crane stood behind a desk at the back of the room, the top of which glowed from a recessed smart surface. As tall as Novik, Crane wore a denim jacket over a white silk shirt and black trousers. Everything about him was neat, from his haircut to the crease on his pants.

'Thanks for taking us in, Mr. Crane,' Novik said. 'It's been a terrible day.'

Crane touched the desktop and the surface light dimmed. He gestured towards the leather armchairs and settees in front of the hearth, 'Come, sit with me by the fire.'

Crane fetched cold beers from a small refrigerator and handed them round. For a moment he and his guests studied each other.

'Tell me what happened,' Crane said.

Novik sat on the edge of his chair, elbows on knees, beer bottle swinging from his fingers. A sense of unreality filled his mind. The gentle lighting, the peace of the room, the dancing firelight, all formed a veneer of tranquillity over awful memories. Crane's life was one of impulse, desire, and instant gratification, with all difficulties removed. It seemed impossible that he would understand Novik's feelings.

In disjointed fashion Novik and Marytha related the story of how they crossed the border. In all essentials it matched with the report Crane had been reading when they had arrived.

Eyes fixed on the carpet, Novik took a drink. The beer was bright, crisp and cold. Immediately Novik felt ungrateful. 'We're poor company, I'm sorry,' he said.

Crane waved the apology away, 'You've endured events I can barely imagine. Take a day or two, whatever you need. I can lend you a car, or fly you out of here.'

'What about Andriewiscz? He's got 80,000 men,' Marytha said.

Crane leaned back and spread his arms across the back of his chair. 'I've met Bob a few times. He knows I'm here, and he knows Million Pines has no strategic value.'

'Don't they just want to chop down trees?'

'In the far north. Don't get me wrong, I'm not complacent, I don't agree but I'm not going to get in their way. Million Pines has effective security to manage any stray units.'

Marytha and Novik exchanged looks. How good could estate security be against an army? Neither chose to pursue the subject.

St.John returned with a trolley and served trout in pepper cream sauce, wild mushrooms, a selection of fresh vegetables. They ate with plates on their knees, the atmosphere grew comfortable. With immense gratitude Novik felt himself relax.

'I've been following your recent activities,' Crane said after the meal was tidied away.

Novik looked at him warily, Crane held up his hand. 'I don't care about your provenance, or that of your money. I don't even care that you broke parole. What I am intrigued by, is what you were trying to do.'

'It was just a dream. We thought, Josie and I...' Novik's voice tailed off, Crane was able to discover virtually anything about their lives, it made little difference now. 'We thought we could make a difference, that if we slowed things down people might realise they owned enough.'

'You could have lived well on that money all your lives. You really thought it was that important?'

Novik looked into the fire, 'Right now, that's not a question I can easily answer.'

Years ago, wealth and power had isolated Crane from all outside unpleasantness, yet with Ellen he still had his problems. He gave, but people always wanted more, they never thought it was enough, it grew tiresome, it felt ungrateful. Over time Crane had developed a thick skin, he had learned to ask for something in return.

'You must know all about me,' Crane said. 'Tell me a bit more about yourselves.'

There was more beer on the tray. Novik took a fresh bottle and drained half of it in one swig. He had been to prison and Josie had waited for him. Back then they made their decisions together, knowing the probable outcomes. This time round they hadn't realised the consequences, they hadn't noticed the stakes had been raised or the game had changed. Some of him felt like she was waiting for him to catch up, while another part thought she might walk barefoot though the door, her hair down, long skirt floating and smile shining.

'I used to be a cop,' Marytha said, to fill the silence.

'I thought you were an artist pretending to be a cop,' Benny said.

'I was a cop first. I did performance poetry in my spare time. The day the Mayor announced the city was broke and laid half of us off, I had an evening gig. I did it in uniform and people thought I was an artist pretending to be a cop pretending to be a poet. I liked the idea so I stuck with it, bought an old patrol car with my lay-off pay, drifted around, crossed a few state lines.' She laughed at her own nostalgia, 'I crossed a few lines of my own, too. I wrote a lot of tickets, some people even turned themselves in.'

'You're going to have to work hard to beat that,' Crane told Benny.

'I'm an ambassador from far Achernar. I have crossed the dreadful black gulf to bear witness to your Earthling ways.'

'Sure you have,' Crane laughed. All his research showed Benny was quite harmless. 'So why hang out with Novik and Marytha?'

Benny's eyes shone in the firelight, 'The human race approaches its moment of doom or salvation. Collectively, you're either going to make it, or you won't. If you do, the United Commonwealth of the Galactic Arm welcomes you. If not,' Benny performed a sweeping bow, 'we bid you farewell.'

Crane had heard some sincere spiel in his time. For self-belief, this pitch from the mop-haired grungy young man was in the top ten.

'And this is why you were trying to fill the self-storage warehouses of an entire continent with empty cardboard crates.'

Crane's light-hearted sarcasm broke through Novik's brown mood beside the fire. This appallingly rich man was right, there was a surreal comedy to their actions, a forlorn grandeur in its hopeless ambition. 'Succeed or fail, at least we tried, we weren't part of the problem.'

'And you think I am?' Crane asked mildly. 'Even FreeFinger?'

Novik considered, 'I think you're a consequence.'

Crane was enjoying himself, he hadn't had a conversation like this in a long time. 'I like you guys. We need idealists. I want to help out.' He crossed to his desk and tapped the top a few times with his fingers. 'I expect you'd prefer cash.'

Novik exchanged surprised looks with Benny and Marytha, 'Thank you, but-'

Crane held up his hand, 'No buts. You've had a tough time, you did what you believed in and paid a heavy price. I respect that.' He looked down at his desk, dabbed his finger down decisively and stood back. 'On its way.'

'Thanks, Mr. Crane,' Benny said, 'That's a great start. How much, exactly-?'

'Five million.'

Novik nearly choked on his beer.

'You can make all the traffic violations you like,' said Marytha.

'And you can buy a lot more empty boxes,' Crane said benevolently.

'Yes, we will,' Novik said.

Once more they were all seated beside the fire. A new sense of kinship filled the room, the silences were comfortable.

'Tell me about Josie,' Crane said.

Flames danced in the grate. After a while Novik said, 'She was nice.'

'I bet she was.' Crane raised his glass, 'To Josie.'

'Josie.'

'To Josie.'

'To Josie.'

Crane turned to Benny, 'Tell me more about this space civilisation of yours. If it all goes wrong are you going to step in?'

'Not really. There's plenty of other species like yours.'

'Oh, really? So what would happen?'

'Kabloowy. Game over,' Benny gave an apologetic shrug, 'So it goes.'

'That's it?' Crane snapped his fingers, irritated by Benny's answer. 'All our civilisation and culture, art and science gone like that.'

'That's how it hangs. You either get through this on your own, or you don't. It's called growing up.'

'OK, I get it,' Crane rolled his eyes, 'If we survive, we'll transcend our natures and achieve a higher state of consciousness. We'll grow beards and become wise and kind.'

'That's unlikely, nobody else did. It's more like getting over a temper tantrum. You either accept you can't have everything just because you want it, or you collectively throw yourself out the window after the rattle.'

'You wouldn't rescue anyone?'

'Like for a zoo? The universe is full of bipedal egomaniacs. Some of your flowers are great though. Pansies and dandelions, personally I'd save those. And maybe the water bears, they're pretty unique.'

On the other settee Novik and Marytha rested arm in arm, half asleep as they listened to the conversation.

Crane hadn't met anyone quite like them since he was a kid at college. They were dreamers but they had conviction. The type who refused to change just so they could fit in, holding on to an attitude most people dropped as soon as the first rent check was due. Novik and Marytha weren't no-hopers, they weren't benefits scroungers, they were good kids who turned their backs on the world because it had so little to offer them. It made Crane feel good to help them.

On the other hand, Benny was a fruitcake.

'You're a funny guy, I can see you've thought this through,' Crane said. 'But tell me this - if you really are an Alien Ambassador shouldn't you be at the UN, or broadcasting to the world?'

'You have your information sources, we have ours. Take it from me, Novik is where it's at.'

The double doors to the study swung back. Massive shoulders, trunk-like limbs, the vast bulk of an enormous body in a frame of gleaming armatures occluded the lights of the hallway beyond. Ellen Hutzenreiter Crane stood at the threshold of the room.

'Oh,' Ellen said, 'Hello everyone.'

Where Palfinger Crane had been a disappointment, Ellen's physical presence was more than Novik could imagine. He had seen stills and video, he had read the incredible statistics, but to see her in person was to encounter something outside normal experience. She was a walking behemoth, a human leviathan, a cyborg composite of machinery and flesh that filled the horizons of his eyes. Her straight, dark hair was trimmed short, pageboy style, the silk of her voluminous pale green trouser suit hung from her vast frame with a tailor's perfect drape.

The new hollowness within Novik let him see beyond Ellen's superficial presence. He heard her beating heart and the stress of its intolerable labour, he felt the softness of her skin between the glassy ridges of the stretch marks on a body that nobody would ever reach their arms around. Josie had been pretty, the memories of her straight nose and full mouth, the happy curves of her body were still painfully vivid. It was no betrayal that Novik saw that under the slabs of fat and weight of hanging flesh, beneath the glittering rods and hissing armatures, Ellen was beautiful.

Ellen took a step back. 'I didn't realise we had company.'

'Come say hello, Ellen,' Crane indicated each in turn, 'Marytha, Novik, and Benny.'

Ellen raised her dimpled hand, 'Pleased to meet you.'

'Hello.' Novik looked straight into Ellen's face, determined not to stare at her buttressed mass, ancillary equipment and physical assists. It was impossible.

Ellen let them all look. She had been here ten thousand times before. Her silk jacket rippled in the breeze of the heat exchangers spanning her back. She let them look, and then she backed away.

'Ellen?' Crane said.

Ellen gave the faintest twitch of her head, 'I won't disturb you.' She stepped back. The doors swung closed. She was gone.

Now Novik saw the reason for the wide doors, sweeping stairs and broad paths. The lodge was designed around Ellen's needs. Palfinger had created Million Pines as a refuge for his unhappy, monstrous daughter.

Disappointment flickered across Crane's face. 'Ellen keeps to herself these days.'

A chime sounded, a soft yellow light pulsed on Crane's desk.

'Excuse me,' Crane touched a stud on his cuff. 'Yes? Hello Chandra. Yes, she was here a moment ago.' Crane paced back and forth, 'She's fine. We're inside the lodge.' Crane listened intently. 'Yes of course, I understand, it may be nothing. I'll go and find her.'

Crane stood motionless then gathered himself. 'You'll have to excuse me a moment. Ellen… Something has come up.' He ran from the room.

- 52 -

Two hundred miles from the nearest islands, Manalito and Bianca inhabited a waterless, crescent-shaped atoll of white sand. A sparse scatter of coconut palms grew across in the centre, beneath them Bianca built a bivouac of old palm fronds, weaving them into a flat mat to form a single-sided shelter.

Before the sun set, Manalito swam out to his seaplane, moored two hundred yards out in deep water. The atoll no longer had a reef, the beach shelved steeply, cut away by oceanic swells. Tiger sharks routinely patrolled the shallows, coming as close as twenty or thirty feet from shore. Manalito had no fear of them, and returned each morning towing a small inflatable raft holding food from his stores and water from the seaplane's solar still.

'I contain the spirit of rokea,' Manalito told Bianca. 'Sharks fear me. I am their God.'

'I fear you too,' Bianca said.

Manalito considered Bianca, 'With you I am confused.'

'Let me go.'

Manalito gave a soft laugh, 'I am not that confused.'

Bianca knew he had been sent to kill her. Now, for some reason, he hesitated. Perhaps the more they talked the harder he might find it to hurt her. If only she could get him to know her as a person. A thought occurred to her - what if she encouraged him, and they became intimate? The idea was revolting, terrifying, yet might save her life. In all probability a psychopath like Manalito would lack interest, possibly even be physically incapable. Another question presented itself: How much did she want to live?

She tried to keep her voice light, 'Oh, I am a simple soul.'

'I was summoned by the witch-girl to kill you. You did not turn her blow aside without power,' Manalito spoke as if they discussed a shopping list.

'Perhaps she made a mistake.'

'No doubt. Death spirits demand a high price. To summon me she would have offered pain and blood, but to compel me she would have to be prepared to die. She was not, and so I took her father, though I did not know it at the time. In effect, she killed him, she was responsible, a valuable lesson.'

This clearly made perfect sense to Manalito. Was he crazy, or did he simply see the world from a different perspective? Bianca kept her expression impassive. If Tanoata had slain herself she would not have appeared on the beach, in which case, neither would Tekirei or Bianca. Events would have unfolded differently, Manalito would have tracked Bianca down elsewhere, and Tekirei would still be alive.

Perhaps I am as crazy as he is, Bianca thought.

Manalito looked towards the seaplane. 'The world is turning. War will come soon. The white tribes will destroy themselves, and the braves will return.'

Bianca knew she had to keep Manalito talking and forced herself into conversation. 'You belong to one of the first nations?'

To her surprise Manalito looked guilty.

'In my heart only. I was an orphan, a foundling. As a child I did not know who I was and my dreams tortured me. One night I realised I was an outsider, a relic. The modern world did not want me, it had abandoned me and turned its back. As a boy I crawled in the gutters, but I stood in the wilderness as a man. There, I learned to become as the mountain lion, the snake, then eagle, and now - *rokea*.'

'Who sent you here?'

'Mitchell Gould.'

'Why?'

Manalito's reply took the heat from the sun. 'Your family has been declared extinct.'

Bianca's head swam, 'Why?'

'Your husband has great power but uses it poorly. Now, like the witch-girl, it turns back and strikes at his blood, his heart.'

Manalito walked into the surf and swam out towards the seaplane.

As she watched him go, Bianca understood she would never leave this tiny island alive. According to Manalito somewhere, somehow Crane had made a terrible, selfish, mistake. As had she, she now realised.

Life among the islands was not simply a different version of her own world. Powers and talents moved within both landscape and people in ways she could not understand.

For the first time in a long while her thoughts about her own daughter were those of a mother with a painful heart.

- 53 -

Novik, Marytha and Benny had barely slept during the past tragic day. Left to their own devices, they dozed silently in the warmth of the fire.

Crane breezed back into the room. His eyes were bright, an expression of disbelieving wonder. 'Something marvellous has happened - Ellen has lost weight. It's happened before, always transient, just fluid loss. This is different.'

Novik roused himself, 'That's great news, is she coming back here?'

'I spoke to her. She's gone for a walk.' Crane paced back and forth, unable to settle, 'It's big news, the biggest. She needs some time. It's going to take a while to sink in.' He beamed at his guests, 'Wow, I feel giddy, I think I'm hyperventilating.'

'Sit down.' Novik poured a glass of water from the jug on the drinks cabinet and handed it to Crane.

'Thanks. Listen, guys, I can't explain how I feel, I feel wonderful, I feel like I've just had – like Ellen has just had - a reprieve from death row. I know I'm getting ahead of things but I can't help it, I want to keep feeling like this. It's great. I want to give you some more money. I want you to be as happy as me.'

Novik knew Crane was over-excited, happily hysterical, he didn't want to take advantage. Before he could refuse Benny said, 'Thanks, Mr. Crane, that would be really generous.'

'Why don't you give it to a hospital, some medical charity?' Novik said.

'No,' Crane was definite, 'I want to give it to you. And I'll tell you why - because everyone else wants a deal. They want to give me some honorary degree for this, some chancellorship for that, all so I'll give them even more. Five million might seem like a lot but believe me when I say, and I'm not bragging, that by tea time I'll have made it back.'

'How do you make so much money, Mr. Crane?' Marytha said.

'How did I start? I gave stuff away for free. It's what FreeFinger is all about. People queued round the block. When the global corporates noticed, they begged me to give their stuff away too. They chucked money at me to make sure I would. It made markets.'

'And now you own those corporations.'

'It's a funny old world.' Crane tapped his forefinger on the desk in a final flourish and stepped back. 'I just upped it to a hundred. Happy un-birthday, guys.'

'You're really getting the hang of this,' Benny said. 'Way to go, sir.'

'Benny!' Marytha hissed.

Benny was unfazed, 'It's the right thing to do. Not for me, for him, for you. Personally, I don't want your cowrie-shell substitutes, they make me feel primitive, greedy and dirty. In the end I'd get used to it, I'd start to like the way it made me feel, buying more and more things, owning a huge heap of pointless possessions. Then I'd have to put on my lion-tamer's hat and take a whip and chair to my amygdala. Again.'

Very little of what had happened since they had arrived at Crane's lodge felt completely real to Novik. In the past he'd been poor, not long ago he'd been rich and they'd spent it trying to turn things round. Now Josie was gone and suddenly he was rich again. Both times the money had come from nowhere and he felt like he hadn't deserved it. It sounded so simple when Crane said it 'how does five sound,' and 'I've upped it to a hundred'. To anyone else these were fortunes being talked about. He would rather be poor and have Josie.

Crane was still fascinated by his own euphoria, he paid no attention to Benny's speech or Novik's confusion.

'That felt great. Now, let's celebrate properly.' Crane opened the drinks cabinet and removed tumblers and a three-quarters full bottle of scotch. 'Bowmore Black,' he announced with a conspiratorial grin, 'Forty-two years in the cask. This may not be the answer to life, the universe, and everything, but it has a damned good try.'

He poured two fingers into each glass and handed them round. Benny sniffed at his and wrinkled his nose. 'Before you ask, no, you may not put ice in it,' Crane told him. 'Just some water.'

'Good things do happen,' Crane raised his glass to Novik, 'To better times.'

Their glasses clinked together and they drank.

After a single sip Benny became agitated. 'Novik, I need some of that money. Forget the water bears, we have got to save this whisky.'

Crane refilled Benny's glass with an easy hand, 'This is for sharing, not saving.'

A few minutes later Chandra Smith called again. This time Crane put the call through to the speaker.

'Palfinger, Ellen has now lost a full kilo.'

'Chandra, we've started celebrating, do you think it is too early?'

'Have you told Ellen?'

'She knows. She's out walking, it unsettled her more than I expected.'

'Understandable. Palfinger, there's no reason not to feel optimistic. Spontaneous remission as a known phenomenon. I want to see Ellen as soon as possible. I'm heading for the airport with my team, we'll be at Million Pines in under twenty four hours.'

An unusual thought occurred to Novik. Two surprising things had happened, what was the relationship? Novik knew his mind sometimes leapt to wild conclusions, he put the strange ideas aside.

Pallfinger finalised arrangements with the doctor: 'My helicopter will be waiting at Vancouver.'

'I will see you soon.'

'Thank you Chandra.'

Crane broke the connection. 'This is the happiest day of my life.'

In ground-breaking style President Snarlow delivered her emergency State of the Union speech via total immersion Meeja. In doing so she became the first head of state to use the technology for public broadcast.

"I got the gist," was the general reaction, "It's a tough job, these are hard times," the overriding sentiment. "We Americans are used to that. Someone's got to step up to the mark."

We listened at our local watering hole. Reactions were mixed:

"Those trees in Canada all got to come down, I understand that. The snow don't settle and the trees are dark - it warms the planet. Sure seems a shame though."

"Listen bud, fifty years ago the tree line was between 61° and 69°. Now it's two degrees further north, that's 800,000 square miles of Canada, and at one tree every 100 feet, over 2.2 billion trees. The trees are on the move, wake up."

"What do you think they are, Ents? Besides, your statistics suck."

"All I'm saying is nobody wants to end up back in the Eocene."

"What?"

"I felt Guinevere's passion, her sincerity. Her fingers are rough, you sensed that? She must work ALL the time. I shared her pain, the burden of leadership, the responsibility. I cried, I'm not ashamed. You did too, I saw."

"So what? Men can cry. We got emotions too."

"I was just saying, OK?"

- 54 -

Ellen didn't know what to think. The news was too big, yet it was not big enough. She had reconciled herself to living out the months left to her at the lodge. Now, this.

As she walked she tried to put it into context. In the few days they had been at Million Pines she gained weight at the same rate she had always done, just over three kilos a month. Now she had lost three and a quarter ounces. Ninety one grams. Two slices of bread. It was hardly anything, and in terms of what the doctors had told her back in the Caribbean, it meant nothing at all. Fate was a sadist, this was just another twist of its knife.

Lost in thought she made her way along the route she had taken before, past the stand of saplings towards the river. Today the woods felt restless and uneasy, the weather was changing, a damp wind from the northeast heaved at the treetops and brought a dull grey overcast.

Soon Ellen could hear the river. As she emerged between the low sweeping branches of fir and spruce, she saw a man with a gun.

He stood in profile to Ellen, on open ground between her and the river, a flat area scoured by floodwaters. A loose stack of boulders marked the downstream end, piled up by the spring thaw.

Well built, he wore dark check trousers and a red and brown quilted jacket and carried his weapon at low port. She knew all the staff on the estate and he was not one of them. Million Pines was off-limits for hunting but it was unfenced. By accident or purpose sportsmen occasionally come onto the estate. This man was not hunting, his gun was an assault rifle.

Without knowing exactly why, Ellen felt afraid. She stepped back through the low evergreen branches and stood in the shadows.

As she withdrew, a branch swayed. The gunman turned towards her, alert and watchful. He touched his jaw, spoke into a mike, and took a few steps forwards.

Ellen was very scared now. He must be able to see her, she wanted to run.

Adrenalin set her heart pounding, a threshold was passed. Unnatural and loud, a warning tone pinged. 'Mute,' she whispered frantically.

The gunman snapped his weapon to his shoulder, Ellen looked along the barrel. In the same instant a lupine para-human emerged atop the jumble of boulders, drew back her arm, and cast a slender metal javelin. The javelin arced across the open ground, struck the gunman's side, and his shot went wide.

The gunman was down on one knee. The lupine woman hefted another spear. The man screamed and lurched round, the gun on full auto. Before she could throw, the wolf-woman was hit, and tumbled backwards out of sight.

Echoes of the gunshots faded. The gunman dropped his weapon and clutched the javelin, his mouth bent open in silent agony.

Petrified with shock, Ellen watched from the stillness of the trees. The man screamed again, the wild shriek of a wounded animal, and pulled the javelin from his body. He sank back onto his haunches, his head drooped, the javelin fell from his fingers.

A minute passed. Ellen dared not move.

The gunman's hand twitched. He groped for the javelin, planted the butt into the ground and hauled himself upright. Time and again he tried to hook the rifle's strap over his boot. Finally, he succeeded. Painfully, clumsily, he lurched towards the boulders, the gun trailing in the dirt behind him.

Part way there his limbs seemed to become disconnected, and he toppled face down onto the stony ground.

Ellen's mouth was dry, her skin cold with sweat. A steady hum came from the fans mounted against the heat vanes across her shoulders. The gunman still had not moved. Ellen wondered, should she go and check the wolf woman?

As she hesitated, two more gunmen entered the clearing. One was bare-headed, the other wore a brimless woollen cap, both wore dark trousers and shirts checked red and brown. Ellen slowly sank to a crouch, her frame effortlessly holding her in position. The bare-headed man covered the clearing while the other skirted along the far side, crossed to the body and knelt beside it. He gave a 'thumbs down' sign, disentangled the rifle and removed the sidearm. Then he ran in a fast crouch around the boulders. He returned dragging the wolf woman by her heels.

The man in the cap sketched out the action with a few gestures, and made some experimental thrusts with the javelin. He tried to bend the metal shaft, but could not. The other man spoke briefly into his communications equipment, slung the dead man's rifle over his shoulder and they jogged back the way they had come.

Ellen withdrew a few feet further into the trees, activated her phone and called the lodge.

After three rings St.John answered, 'Miss Ellen?' The quality was terrible, St.John's voice yawped and swooped with interference.

'Raymond,' Ellen whispered, 'something awful is happening.'

'Ellen, I can barely hear you. Are you hurt? What is it?'

Quickly, Ellen related the events she had seen.

'I can't locate your transponder,' St.John said. 'Something is wrong with the receiver. Head back towards the lodge. We will come to you.'

'All right.'

'Be careful.'

'I will.'

Watching and listening all the time, Ellen made herself count slowly to a hundred, then cautiously headed towards the lodge. She had taken a few steps when she saw a bulky silhouette cutting through the trees towards her.

'Lady Ellen,' a deep voice rumbled, 'It is I, Theodore.'

Ellen raised her hand as she recognised the ursine para-human, 'Theodore, it is so good to see you.'

Theodore sniffed the air. 'They have gone. It is safe. Come this way.'

Theodore held his recurved bow in one hand, a quiver of long arrows slung across his great shoulders. As before, he wore nothing but a harness of leather straps and a simple breechclout. He gestured for Ellen to get behind him, peered through the trees, then turned to face her. 'It is very dangerous. We will take you to the lodge.'

There was a sudden pad of light footsteps and the wolf woman Gretel stood beside Theodore, a clutch of metal javelins in her hand. Today, like Theodore, she wore only a breechclout. Gretel's amber eyes burned like fire. 'My darling sister is dead.'

'Hilda saved my life,' Ellen said. 'I am sorry.'

Gretel lashed her tail. 'Her death was useful but it has made me angry. I will slay ten for their one.'

Muscles bunched in Theodore's long, brown-furred arm. He struck his chest with his fist. 'I will match you.'

Gretel reached up to touch Theodore's face with her long, furred fingers. Theodore's chest swelled enormously. He looked down at Gretel and she bared her teeth.

Ellen did not fully understand the para-humans but they made her feel safe. 'Who are these men?'

'Our enemy,' Theodore said. He pushed on Ellen's shoulder, forcing her to take a step, 'No more words, Lady Ellen. Move quick, move quiet. We will protect you.'

The wind had died, the forest was silent. Ellen looked around. Gretel had vanished. Theodore paced ahead, bow in hand. He looked back at Ellen and beckoned her forwards.

'Lady Ellen, follow me.'

- 55 -

The further they went into Crane's vast forested estate the more Wilson worried about Halifax. The big city man was more nervous with every minute that passed, with every step they took. They had been on the move through most of the night when Wilson decided to call a halt.

'What's wrong?' Shoulders hunched, Halifax turned full circle.

'Nothing. I just thought we could use a break. Take five and chill.'

Halifax wiped his mouth and looked nervously around. 'I'm good. Let's push on.'

A scuffing noise came from deep in the shadows of a holly thicket.

Halifax drew his gun and dropped to a half-crouch.

Wilson put his hand on Halifax's arm. 'It's just a bird.'

'You're sure?'

'It's looking for bugs.'

Halifax let out his breath. 'It sounded real stealthy.'

Wilson kicked at the mossy trunk of a long fallen tree. It fell apart under the blow, the wet black bark collapsing to reveal pithy white fibres. He moved down the trunk, tried again, then sat down. He swung his pack off his shoulders and opened a packet of dried fruit.

Halifax stepped over the trunk and sat facing the other way.

'There's nothing here, Halifax.'

'How do you know that?'

'The birds are scratching around, nothing smells bad, there are no tracks. We're alone. Gould is up ahead.'

Halifax scowled uneasily, 'I'm from the urban jungle, Wilson. These wild places full of wolves and bear spook me out.'

Wilson offered some dried fruit and nuts to Halifax, who declined.

'You eat a lot of brown rice?' Wilson said.

'No. Why's that?'

'A diet of exclusively brown rice will send you mad. It's common knowledge. That's why all the hippies went loopy back in the Cold War.'

'That so?'

Wilson chewed on the dried fruit, 'Nothing more dangerous than a pissed-off hippy.'

'What about a pissed-off wolf?'

Wilson swung his legs over the trunk so he sat on the same side as Halifax. 'Wolves are scared of folk. They're smart, they know we've got guns.'

'And bear?'

Wilson scratched his head and grinned. 'How fast do you think I can run?'

'Nobody can outrun bear, man.'

Wilson looked Halifax in the eye. 'I don't have to.'

Halifax laughed and the muscles in his shoulders finally began to relax. 'I'm heavier than you, you're older than me. I wouldn't like to call it.'

'If you can't get away from a bear you don't have much chance. You've got to stand tall, look as big as you can, show no fear. You put your back to a tree and hope he tries to maul you. That way the bear rakes the tree with his claws instead of your back. All you got to do is keep away from his teeth. Meanwhile you get busy with your knife.'

Halifax's face had a waxy sheen.

'You do have a knife?' Wilson said.

'No problemo.' Halifax showed Wilson one of the biggest knives he'd ever seen.

After another hour walking they both felt the change in the woods, a growing silence that slid into a brittle emptiness. Ten minutes later they came across Andriewiscz's forward supply dump and the scatter of dead soldiers.

'Gould didn't do this on his own,' Wilson said.

Wordlessly Halifax took an assault rifle from one of the dead soldiers, a handgun from another. He began stuffing his bag with ammunition.

A large dugout was close by, roofed with corrugated sheeting covered by a foot of earth. The entrance stepped down into the dark, a black void that gaped like an empty eye socket. Wilson shone a flashlight inside, gave a choked cry and turned aside. Halifax looked at him quizzically. Grim faced, Wilson shook his head and walked away.

The main dump was a short distance beyond the bodies, three zig-zag cuttings with side walls reinforced with heavy corrugated plastic and covered in thermally neutral netting. The largest of the three was a fuel dump, the next was stacked with low calibre ammunition, grenades, uniforms, clothing and field medicine kits. The third held heavy ordnance – tank and artillery shells, RPG and mortar rounds. Alone at the far end was a bulky silver-grey insulated case three metres long. Wilson unclipped the case tags and raised the lid. Inside were two slim missiles with four-finned tails. Beside them in the foam were the red-painted nose cones – the warheads. Black and red wires ran from each warhead to heavy-duty solid-state batteries. All of a sudden Wilson felt cold. He wanted to sit down, he needed to piss. To his own amazement he felt the hairs on the back of his neck rise up.

Halifax tramped up to Wilson. 'What the hell are those?' he said. 'Anti-aircraft missiles?'

'I wish.' Wilson pointed to the radiation decals.

'Holy shit, these are nukes?' Halifax let out a low whistle then folded his arms and studied the slender warheads. 'I thought they'd be bigger.'

'Nukes would be,' Wilson whispered. 'These are A/M. Anti-matter.'

'No way,' Halifax laughed nervously. 'There's no such thing. They're more illegal than… Shit, they don't even exist.'

'So everyone keeps saying. Now we've found two.'

Wilson traced the air above the wires with his finger. 'Half a gram of super-cooled liquid anti-hydrogen suspended in vacuum inside a miniaturised superconducting magnetic torus. This battery's a long-term assist for the warhead's on-board power supply. It's good for years, maybe decades.'

'We can't just leave them. What if a racoon took one? We should turn them off.'

'It's the power that's keeping them safe. Out here we daren't touch them. It's like having your own shake-n-bake Tunguska. We do something stupid they'll hear it all the way to Cincinnati.'

Halifax tugged at Wilson's sleeve, 'Just leave them, for Christ's sake.'

By now Wilson was about as freaked as Halifax. 'We'll hide them.'

'Yeah, hide them. Bury them deep.'

Wilson secured the lid and they carried the case out of the dugout. Then he went back to the small arms cache. Among the stacks Wilson found a dozen cases of ammo for his FaF gun. As he reloaded and put spare clips into his backpack he thought about the differences in capability of his own and Masters' weapons, the gun Gould had used to destroy the Mall. No matter, now he had an assault rifle of his own.

A few minutes later they were ready to go. Halifax had rifles slung over each shoulder and two pistols in his waistband. Grenades swung from webbing across his chest and his backpack was stuffed full of spare clips. Although he was weighed down with weapons, the big man looked more relaxed.

'You sure you got enough?' Wilson said.

Halifax thought about it, then put the guns down, removed the webbing and his jacket and taped two semi-automatic pistols to his chest. 'Can't be too careful.'

They moved out, taking the case with them. After a mile they came to a gully where a fast-flowing stream cut down through a fissure in the rocks. At one point the water leapt ten feet out over a ledge into a cold black pool.

'Down there,' Wilson said, and they manoeuvred the big box down into the shadows behind the falling water.

As they climbed out the far side of the gully they heard faint shouts. A moment later came the report of a distant gunshot. Stashing the spare weapons, they crept forwards.

War – What is it good for?

Quite a few things, actually. Starting a war can stimulate the economy, divert attention from bankrupt policies (or bankruptcy itself), improve national self-esteem, and impress the neighbours. Plus you get to play with all your expensive toys.

Victory or defeat, nationally speaking, war has been a win-win game for the developed world since the beginning of the twentieth century.

Lose and the rest of the world will rush to reconstruct your infrastructure, rebuild your industry and re-educate the population. It's probably cheaper, simpler, and quicker than balanced taxation, realistic fiscal policies and parliamentary democracy.

Personally you'll be hung upside down by your ankles and garrotted with piano wire, but who thinks of post-loyal scenarios like that in the heady days of first strike? Defeat is your final precious gift to an ungrateful nation.

If you win, well cool dude, you've won! High-five the man with more scrambled egg on his shoulder than an epileptic breakfast chef.

Free Your Inner Tyrant
(Pragmatic Advice for the Bitter and Twisted.)

- 56 -

LeBlanc's men moved in pairs, spread across a mile wide front. Still inside Andriewiscz's comms black spot they used low-power laser pens to communicate, the red lights flickering brief pre-arranged codes. As they left the army camp they traversed open, deciduous woodlands. The ground began to rise and waist-high bracken spread across the hillsides between thickets of birch and holly.

'Those army boys talked about dogs, LeBlanc,' Gould said as they jogged through the bracken. 'They must have robo-canines running around, how are we going to deal with them?'

'They are smart and fast, though some people say they are unreliable. I say they have mini-guns and they are here. We have infra-red decoys, magnetic grenades and these,' LeBlanc tapped the side of his head. 'Let us hope we do not meet them, eh?'

Gould looked across to Ayesha, who pulled a worried face, then winked and grinned. She moved easily, without any sign of tiredness. Two of LeBlanc's men were to the left, the Old-fashioned Boys trailed a few yards behind on the right.

'Morgan, Black, stay on the pace,' Gould ordered. 'Ayesha's got a hot ass, I want your eyes elsewhere.'

'I need to walk this far, I'd get a cab,' Morgan grumbled. Beside him Black was too breathless to speak.

Ayesha turned and jogged backwards, 'Time to quit smoking, guys.' Her eyes went wide, she groped for her handgun. 'Get down. Behind you.'

Morgan and Black pulled their guns and broke left and right. A silver javelin hummed out of the trees, skimmed Morgan's head and lanced into the ground between Gould and Ayesha. Morgan cried out, clutched his scalp, and dropped.

Gould stared at Morgan's bloody hat, pinned by the javelin to the soil.

'Where?' Black shouted. 'Where?'

Gould drew his own weapon. 'Cover the flank,' he told Ayesha. Something flashed in the corner of his eye. One of LeBlanc's men grunted and lurched forwards, an arrow through his backpack. All around, men went to ground under fast, accurate bow fire.

Gould was in a half crouch, turning. 'LeBlanc,' he yelled.

'Hold them,' LeBlanc said calmly. 'Help will come.' He unslung his rifle, fired twice, darted behind a tree and fired again.

Gould swept his gun in an arc, unable to locate the attackers. Black knelt beside Morgan curled on the ground, his gun in a two-handed grip.

'Black,' Gould shouted as he saw a grey figure in the fir trees. Another javelin arced out of the firs and Black flung himself aside.

Gould fired at fleeting grey shapes. Movement flickered in a new direction, Gould span round. A lupine para-human rose from the bracken and cast his spear straight at Gould's chest. He watched it come, saw the flat arc of its trajectory, knew it was going to hit him.

Ayesha snatched the spear out of the air, planted her foot and flung it back. But the wolf man was gone.

'Where the hell did you learn that?' Gould exclaimed.

Ayesha grinned and punched the air. A grey-furred shape bowled her over. Human and para-human struggled across the ground. The wolf man locked his elbow round her throat. Ayesha broke free. The wolf man kicked her stomach, Ayesha drove her fingers against his neck. The wolf man snarled and snapped at her arm.

Gould waited for a clear shot. There. His finger squeezed the trigger. His gun was struck away, a second wolf man was on him.

The para-human gripped Gould's wrists and forced his arms apart. Gould was strong, the wolf man's sinewy power irresistible. The para-human twisted, kicked the back of Gould's knee and threw him down. Gould rolled, snatched out his knife and slashed wildly. The wolf man barked laughter and kicked Gould in the head. Stunned, Gould staggered blindly backwards. Claws raked his stab vest, a blow numbed his arm, the knife span from his fingers. Somewhere Gould heard shouts and gunfire.

The wolf man attacked again, a series of sharp, fast blows that slammed into Gould's midriff. Gould twisted and kicked, punched at the grey-furred muzzle. He struck aside more attacks, grappled the creature and flung him off. Where was the knife? Gunmetal glinted in the crushed bracken. Gould hurled himself through the air, snatched up the weapon and fired point-blank into the leaping para-human's body.

Gould pushed himself to his feet. The other wolf man crouched over Ayesha's limp body, his back to Gould. Gould shot the creature and it collapsed across her. Gould staggered through the bracken and heaved the corpse away. Two great claw marks raked the left side of her face. One ran from just under her eye to her mouth, splitting her upper lip. The other opened her cheek from temple to jaw. He could see her teeth in the wound. Ayesha tried to speak, she tried to get up. Gould held her down.

'Stay here,' he said.

The wounds began to bleed, Ayesha's mouth filled with blood, it poured across her cheek and down her neck. She swallowed, tasted the blood and swallowed again, her eye wide, near to panic.

Gould gripped her shoulders, 'You're all right. Your cheek is cut through. It's not dangerous, but it's bloody. Do you understand?'

Ayesha swallowed, nodded, and swallowed again.

Gould looked around. Morgan sat against a tree his arms loose at his sides, feebly moving his legs. A gun in each hand, Black crashed through underbrush, firing wildly. Where were LeBlanc and his men?

Gunfire and bellows of fear came from behind a thicket of hemlock. Gould reloaded and ran around the saplings.

One of LeBlanc's men was transfixed to a tree, an arrow through his throat. Another limped towards LeBlanc, struck through the shoulder and thigh. Eight feet tall, an ursine para-human burst from the trees. He snatched up the wounded man, tore off his arm and flung the parts aside. Rifle at his shoulder, LeBlanc fired and backed away. The bear man roared, shook his head, dropped to all-fours and charged. LeBlanc fired, retreated and fired, retreated and fired again. The bear man kept coming.

Gould emptied his own weapon into the creature's flank. The bear-man's shoulder collapsed, he toppled sideways, heaved half upright, and died.

LeBlanc looked at Gould, wall-eyed with shock. 'Merde,' he said, and reloaded his gun with shaking hands.

Moments later the forest was full of LeBlanc's men.

Gould went back to Ayesha. She was on her feet, the front of her jacket wet with blood, a sopping red rag pressed against her cheek. Gould helped her to the medic who sealed her wounds with cyanoacrylate, and applied a dressing.

Gould and Black discussed the situation with LeBlanc.

'I lose two men here, a third by the river,' LeBlanc said. 'These are not Dawkins Dogs. They discover where our head is,' he chopped at the air with his hand, 'they try to cut it off.'

Some of LeBlanc's men had set up a perimeter. Others studied the para-humans and their weapons. One of the biggest tried to draw the ursine's bow.

'At least Crane didn't give them guns,' Gould said.

'Perhaps they have not yet made any they can hold,' LeBlanc said.

Black spat on the ground, 'That's just dandy. Morgan is blind, you can see his brain through the top of his head.'

Gould's voice was flat and hard. 'Say your goodbyes.'

'Yeah, right,' Black muttered as he walked away. 'I get to do them both.'

'So, Mr. Gould, now we must decide,' LeBlanc said. 'Do we stay or do we go? I have lost three and that is OK. Three more and people start to think "How do I get out of this alive?" At the moment the decission is still your choice.'

LeBlanc's assessment was reasonable but it made Gould angry. He had just saved LeBlanc's life, Morgan was dying and Ayesha mutilated. LeBlanc was supposed to ensure things like these did not happen, instead, he was blackmailing him with warnings of mutiny.

Gould glared at LeBlanc, 'You earn your money.'

LeBlanc looked up at Gould, his round face placid, his grey eyes mild and steady. 'Very well. We are less than three kilometres from Crane's lodge. As we have discovered, his defences are very adequate. From here, we go as two units of twelve, formations that will reduce the enemy effectiveness. We maintain close contact, each group to support the other if attacked. We strike Crane from the south east, exit north west and rendezvous with transport.'

Gould forced himself to think. He could find no fault with LeBlanc's revised plan. 'Agreed.'

'We go fast, and the devil take the hindmost. LeBlanc briefly looked towards Ayesha, drinking awkwardly from a water bottle, 'We cannot wait for stragglers.'

'There's nobody here I give a damn about, except you and me,' Gould said.

LeBlanc dipped his head in acknowledgement and moved away to brief his men.

Black sat with Morgan, both of them smoking cigarettes.

Gould went to speak to Ayesha.

'Thanks for saving me,' she said.

Gould gave a lopsided grimace. 'Now we're quits.'

Ayesha touched the dressing on her face, 'You'll have to turn the lights out from now on.'

There was a single shot from Black's gun. Morgan's chin slumped onto his chest.

'Looks aren't everything,' Gould heard himself say. 'Let's go earn that two hundred Ozzie owes us.'

- 57 -

'Mr. Crane.' Raymond St.John stood in the doorway. He struggled to form his information into words. 'Ellen. There are gunmen.'

Whisky tumblers in their hands, Crane, Novik, Marytha and Benny paused in their light-hearted conversation.

Crane spoke in a tight voice, 'Raymond, tell me exactly what has happened.'

St.John clasped his hands together. 'A man tried to shoot Ellen. He was killed by a para-human, a wolf woman-' St.John looked close to tears, 'She died too.'

Novik pushed his glass into St.John's hand.

St.John gratefully swallowed the drink in a gulp and took a deep breath. 'Ellen is heading back to the lodge, but she saw two more gunmen.'

'That bitch trog, Snarlow,' Crane said with cold fury, 'I thought she might try something, but not this. Not my daughter. By God she is going to be sorry.'

'Palfinger,' Novik shook Crane's shoulder, 'listen to St.John.'

Crane turned his icy stare on Raymond St.John.

'Mr Crane, I said we would go and meet her,' St.John said.

For a moment Crane's teeth showed like a dog's. Then his eyes cleared, he pushed his hand through his hair. 'Yes, of course. Well done, Raymond. As always, you do the right things while I stamp my feet. Open the vault, bring jackets and guns. We leave in two minutes.'

'I'm with you.' This was a plan that suited Novik's mood, a chance to hit back, to hurt the hurters.

Benny and Marytha stood behind Novik, 'Then so are we.'

'Can you shoot?' Crane said, then checked himself, 'Of course you can. You're Americans.'

St.John led them to where the wide stairs descended from the upper story. At his touch, a section of panelling slid away to reveal a reinforced door in a recessed metal frame. St.John pressed his hand against a sensor pane which glowed pale blue under his palm.

St.John took a step back. 'Mary had a little lamb.' The door sunk back, then swung aside to reveal a room with a gun rack on the right wall and a fitted cabinet to the left. An open archway in the rear wall led to a descending concrete stairwell.

'Help yourselves,' Crane said and pulled a rifle from the rack.

Novik slung the rifle over his shoulder and pulled a pistol-grip pump shotgun from the rack. As he took the weapon, he had a sudden vivid flashback of Josie firing the Dude's shotgun as they raced from Halifax and his crew, a blurry snapshot from long ago:

Josie intense, controlled, focused, the wind in her hair, swaying with the speeding car as she had fired the gun straight up into the air. She couldn't hurt anyone.

He thumbed cartridges into the magazine, and wondered how different he was.

Marytha had armed herself similarly. 'Still the best for close quarters.'

Novik gave a tight smile. 'Just feeling sentimental.'

'Then I'd hate to see you pissed off,' Crane said.

Benny gleefully stuffed a satchel with light ordnance. 'Sonic grenades, photonic disruptors, Tesla sprays, you got the lot.'

'I also have these,' Crane took down long reddish- grey coats from a high compartment. 'Thermally neutral, knife and bullet proof.'

Novik put one on. Although heavy, it was supple and easy to wear. A pocket in the collar contained a hood and facemask. Lining the fabric, a close weave of silver mesh twinkled like mica.

'Spider silk, titanium alloys and spun diamond thread. It's ridiculously expensive.' Crane gave a wry smile, 'We call it mithril.'

Novik held a second coat out to Benny, 'Put this on.'

'I'll be fine,' Benny said.

Novik pushed it at him. 'Put it on,' he growled.

'I don't need it.'

Novik's face tightened, he grabbed Benny's arm and shoved it into one of the sleeves. 'Some people are a liability, and some people are a pain in the backside. You're both. Put on the coat.'

Benny suffered Novik to dress him, then straightened his thin shoulders and tightened the belt. 'You're wrong about me.'

'I don't want you getting shot again.' Novik saw the hurt in Benny's eyes, he gripped Benny's collar and pulled him close, 'I don't want to leave anyone else behind.'

'Are we ready?' Crane said, and saw they were. 'Whoever is out there means me harm. First things first, I want my daughter safe. Getting even comes later.' Crane looked straight at Novik, 'Right?'

'All right,' Novik said.

Crane put his hand on Novik's shoulder, 'Don't worry, you just watch me do getting even. Now, let's go find Ellen.'

Dressed in their long duster-like coats, Novik felt like they were in a posse from long ago. Outside, the air was cool and fresh, the trees dark and silent. Somewhere in the forests of Million Pines were bad people. Perhaps they were involved in Josie's death, perhaps not. Either way Novik was ready to confront them.

'We'll get her back,' Novik said.

Crane looked stricken, 'By God, I hope so. All this-' Crane's simple gesture managed to take in Million Pines, his vast commercial empire, wealth and possessions, 'Ellen's all I've got.' He turned to St.John, 'Where is she, Raymond?'

'Somewhere along the river trail. I can't tell exactly, comms are failing.'

'That's Andriewiscz down on the border. He'll sit there till this is over, pass on by and deny everything. Meanwhile, we can't get out, and we can't ask for help.'

Crane led them into the forest, St.John at his side. Novik took the left flank, Benny and Marytha the right. They kept to this formation until they came to the place where the path died away.

'Over here,' Novik said. A set of deep, over-sized footprints led straight ahead.

St.John checked his map, 'Ellen said the gunmen approached from upstream, that is, south and to our left. I am sure she would cut to the north before making for the lodge. I suggest we angle to the right.'

'Ellen knows the estate well,' Crane said.

'Something is coming,' Benny said.

A hundred and fifty yards away, a robo-canine cantered through the trees. The mini-gun swivelled from side to side, the machine creature halted, turned, and trotted towards them.

'Facemasks and hoods, quickly. And stand still,' Crane said. 'Our coats will conceal us.'

The robo-canine halted. The mini-gun swung in an arc in front of the party, the barrels rotating at half speed.

Crane whispered, at the edge of audibility, 'These things work on infra-red and motion sensors. As long as we don't trigger both, we're invisible. If we wait, it will go away.'

The robo-canine shuffled its feet and obstinately remained where it was.

Novik studied the flat platform and jointed metal legs of the robot with cold loathing. Where were its weaknesses, where were the blind spots? The mini-gun was mounted on a black metal platform like a deep table top. Armoured power cables and the ammunition belt fed up to the mini-gun from a housing slung below. The bullets had punched through the armoured Lexus, it was unlikely Crane's costly mithril coats would protect them.

'Why doesn't it go?' Crane gave a short, hysteria-tinged giggle. 'Go on, shoo.'

'Get a grip,' Novik hissed.

'It can sense the carbon dioxide in our breath,' Benny said. 'It can't see us but it knows something is here.'

'Christ,' Marytha hissed, 'what do we do?'

'Shoot it,' Crane said. He settled the grip on his gun, 'Everyone get ready, on my count-'

'No,' Novik cut in, 'let me try something.' He took a slow step forwards, then another. The robo-canine shifted uneasily and Novik froze. After a few seconds he moved again. The slowly spinning gun snapped round, aimed directly at him. Sweat trickled under Novik's face mask, he hardly dared breathe. After an eternity the gun resumed its slow sweep.

Behind him Novik heard exhalations of relief. With a soft whine of servos the robo-canine trotted forwards. Now the mini-gun was aimed straight at Crane and the others.

It's the extra CO2, Novik realised. His companion's exhalations had distracted the machine. Not daring to talk he prayed that someone would realise what had happened. The robo-canine was still twenty feet away. Novik's legs trembled with tension, cautiously he edged forwards, one slow step at a time. Finally, he was alongside the machine. The ugly six-barrelled gun traversed at chest height, Novik's stomach muscles tensed at the thought of it firing. One more step took him past the arc of the gun, another brought him to the back of the machine. Drenched in sweat Novik turned to face his companions.

Attached to the rear of the gun was the feeder mechanism for the ammunition belt. Two quick-release catches secured the lid. Novik reached out, his hands shook so badly he nearly hit the spinning barrels. Novik clenched his fists, air trickled between his lips, he tried again.

All at once he was calm, a remote and dispassionate observer. The robo-canine stood before him, pure in purpose and design, his companions held in the arc of its deadly gun. In turn, they were determined, fearful yet resolute. Together humans and machine formed an intense montage, a tableau that could transform instantly into new phases, of violence and death.

Novik pushed his surreal thoughts aside. He eased open the catches on the feeder housing, lifted out the ammo belt and laid it on the robo-canine's back.

'It's safe,' Novik said. The facemask muffled his words, he pulled it down. 'It's safe.'

Instantly the robo-canine scrambled round to face him, the mini-gun whirred at full speed, targeting dead on Novik. Through the forest came Marytha's shriek of horror.

The gun's empty feeder sprockets rattled and clacked, hammers struck against empty chambers. Novik gave a savage laugh and sprang forwards. The robo-canine backed away, empty gun mechanism still clattering. Novik seized a corner of the platform, he lifted one leg clear of the ground. The robo-canine scrabbled for purchase. Novik heaved and strained, gave a great shout, and flung the machine onto its side.

'My God,' Crane ran over, 'Talk about Grandmother's Footsteps.' He clapped Novik on the shoulder, 'My God.'

St.John shook Novik's hand, 'Well done, sir.'

'Way to go,' Benny grinned. 'And you think I'm crazy.'

Marytha took Novik's face in her hands and looked deep into his eyes. 'You,' she said, and flung her arms round him.

They looked down at the robo-canine as it futilely pushed itself round and round cutting circles in the dirt.

'You must hate these things,' Crane said.

Novik's eyes were dark hollows, 'I hate the people who sent them here.'

They pushed on, dropping into a shallow, steep-sided cutting that bottomed out in mud and deep leaf mould. On the far side, flat slabs of limestone pushed out of the soil between sparse pine and larch.

'How far?' Novik said.

'The river is a couple of miles away,' Crane replied. 'We should see Ellen soon.'

A few minutes later they encountered a fast moving group of armed men coming up from the south. Torn between intercepting them, and finding Ellen, Crane hesitated. He was spotted and shots were exchanged. Novik lead them clear, then encountered cross-fire from another group. St.John proved an excellent shot and downed two combatants from the second group.

A lull ensued and Novik led them in a new direction. Accurate small-arms fire struck at them immediately. Marytha and Crane were hit. Their mithril coats set instantly hard for a microsecond, bruised but otherwise unharmed, they staggered on. A high-calibre round struck Novik in the chest and he was knocked flying.

Amongst a scatter of low rocks and shallow depressions the five companions went to ground under increasing fire.

The Grey Ghost - Positive ID

Oh boy. We got him, we got an eye-witness. There's no sound, so while you watch listen to Billy Spartacus, live from Cannon Beach, OR.

'I was just down from the Haystack, around sunset when I saw a large car out on the sand. I went over because sometimes tourists get stuck and need a tow. Some days the tide just sort of slides in, there's no real waves, it's deceptive.

'The car was empty, the beach deserted. I tried the door but there were no handles or pads. It was smooth as silk, a dark metallic grey and very clean, not a speck of dirt. I put my hand on the bonnet and it was cold.

'I saw tyre tracks but no footprints except mine. Then I saw the roof was segmented like an armadillo and I knew it was that mystery car everyone was talking about - The Grey Ghost of the Highway. That's when I started filming.

'Seawater lapped at my feet and I backed away. As the sea touched the front tyres, the headlights came on.

'The sun was half under the horizon, the sea a rich, silvery blue. A line of crimson-gold sunlight crossed the water from sun to car. The Grey Ghost just sat there, its headlights blazing out across the sea towards the sun. It was weird, like they were communing or something.

'Then the car rolled backwards, swung round, and drove away. It didn't make a sound, just tyres on the sand.

'A minute later I saw it high up on the Overlook, silhouetted against the sky. It rounded the curve and its headlights swung out and round, like lonely searchlights. Then it was gone.'

Viral post,
reposted in BFBM magazine

Theodore held up his hand and halted. The faint sound of distant gunfire crackled through the forest.

'Who is it?' Ellen said.

Theodore listened intently, 'It is not us. Two groups with guns are fighting.'

'The Americans?' Had Andriewiscz sent his soldiers to help them? It sounded wrong as she said it.

Theodore moved forwards, 'We will find out.'

He led Ellen north, keeping behind the shelter of an east-west ridge, then turned towards the sounds of fighting. Tension grew in Ellen, she had no weapon. Venture too close and once again she could become a target. As they went on, the gunfire died away, then rose to a steady crescendo.

Bounding shapes flickered between the trees.

'Theodore,' Ellen cried.

He turned, a war arrow already nocked to his bow.

It was Gretel and another lupine, this one male. Both breathed deeply, eyes bright, jaws agape.

'Palfinger Crane fights the enemy,' Gretel pranced with excitement, 'He stands at bay in his rocky redoubt.'

'Does he hold?' Theodore rumbled.

'For now. He is outnumbered and surrounded.'

'Is he hurt?' Ellen begged, 'Is he alone?'

Gretel and the wolf man went to their knees, 'Lady Ellen, your father is protected by a magic coat. He fights with courage, accompanied by two men, a woman, and one another.'

'Save them,' Ellen said.

Theodore struck his chest, 'We will. Our brothers and sisters rally round.'

Gretel turned her gaze on Theodore, her mouth showed a toothy grin. She yapped once, and both lupines raced off, barely seeming touch the ground.

'Now is the time for haste,' Theodore slung his bow and dropped to all fours. Ellen ran beside him, her exoframe just able to match his pace.

Gunfire crackled and spat from the far side of the ridge. Theodore's brown-furred body rippled with energy. 'I go to fight,' he told Ellen. 'Stay here. You are watched. You will be safe.'

Ellen touched his massive, furred arm, 'Be careful.'

Theodore flexed his huge black-nailed hands, 'No, Lady Ellen, I will be wild.'

And he was gone.

Alone, Ellen felt very exposed. A mature yew grew nearby, the springy branches high and spreading. Ellen tore off a thick bough, using the exoframe's strength and her prodigious weight. She stripped off the side branches and broke away the tip, to form a heavy club, four feet long.

Club in hand, she paced back and forth. No doubt lupines guarded her, perhaps an ursine archer. Nevertheless she felt isolated, impotent and vulnerable.

On the far side of the ridge a fan of brilliant red beams swept back and forth, then blinked out. Among shouted orders came the rapid fire of assault rifles, a shotgun boomed again and again.

Ellen crept to the top of the ridge and peered over.

The far slope dropped steeply to open ground fifty feet below. A hundred yards further on, Ellen saw her father and four companions in a jumble of flat boulders. Surrounding them, two-dozen gunmen fired in on them.

As Ellen watched, attackers took aim, fired and zig-zagged forwards. Something flew from Crane's position and burst in a blue-white flash. Forks of electricity lanced in all directions, gunmen writhed in agony and crawled back, the advance temporarily halted.

Far to Ellen's left, one of the attackers cried out, flung up his arms and fell, slain by an ursine bowman. Other gunmen returned fire. Javelins flew from another direction, rattled through the trees, and second man was struck. Her heart in her mouth, Ellen watched half a dozen lupines burst from cover and hurl themselves forwards.

Nearby, a blond man crouched with a woman and a man incongruously dressed in a city hat and overcoat. The blond man dropped his rifle, drew a handgun and fired at the lupines. A huge explosion rocked the forest, the lupine attack was destroyed in a blast of flame.

The blond man fired into Crane's position. Another concussive explosion shook the ground. Shrapnel buzzed through the air and Ellen was forced back. When she looked again, Crane's position was a scatter of stunned and crawling shapes. The blond man, the woman, and several others ran forwards, firing as they went.

A ragged fire began from her father's position and the blond man's group took cover. Where was the man in the city coat? Ellen scanned the ground and saw he ducked and darted towards Crane's flank, accompanied by three men with assault rifles. The main attack had been a diversion.

In that moment Ellen knew her moment of destiny was upon her. In the heart of the forest, her father had come to rescue her. Now he was about to be killed.

What was a life for, if not to spend as you wished?

Ellen settled the club in her hand, fear and adrenalin trembled through her massive body. Blood pressure and heart rate alarms sounded, warning lights flashed. An incoming call chimed – Dr Chandra Smith on ultra priority, his urgent voice fractured and distorted by interference.

'Mute all, divert all,' Ellen commanded and the alarms died. Chandra himself had admitted her ultimate fate. Days or months, what did that matter? Life, like good whisky, was not for keeping.

Down in the valley bullets flew. Ellen knew she was just a very fat girl with a big stick. She felt incredibly alive.

'Freiheit!' she cried, and charged down the slope.

She was running at over fifty miles an hour when she leapt across her father's position. One and a quarter tonnes of hurtling flesh and metal.

Arms spread wide, Ellen looked down at the attackers with gimlet eyes. Under her shadow, they looked up in apocalyptic amazement. She smashed down the first man before he could move. The remaining gunmen raised their weapons. Ellen lashed out with her long club and the nearest folded over with an explosive wet snap.

The second shot her twice in the chest with his rifle. She punched him as hard as she could and he burst.

The man in the coat and suit held a semi-automatic in each hand. 'You ugly fat bitch,' he spat, his face twisted with fear and hate. He emptied half a clip from each gun before Ellen snatched him up by his leg and whirled him shrieking over her head. She snapped her arm forwards and he cartwheeled away, high over the trees. Ellen realised his shoe was still in her hand. She glanced down at it and flung it away. His foot was in the shoe.

Ellen's appearance was decisive. The remaining attackers tried to fall back, lupine and ursine warriors decimated them with bow and javelin. The blond man blasted his way clear with his handgun. One other small group broke free, the rest were overrun.

Human and para-human bodies lay scattered across the forest floor.

Anxiously Ellen scanned the field until she found Theodore, alive and in the company of Gretel and two other lupines.

Novik emerged from cover. Bruised and battered, deafened and hoarse, he was amazed to be alive. Though the outer fabric of his coat was torn, scorched by fire and scarred with bullet holes, the inner fabric was intact. It had saved his life a dozen times, though he ached all over.

Marytha sat wearily on a stone nearby, hood and mask pulled from her face, her coat similarly ragged.

'Are you all right?' Novik said. It felt like such a little thing to say.

'Yes.' Marytha gave him a wan smile, 'Hello.'

Mithril fabric could not save everyone. St.John lay dead, shot through an eye. Novik straightened St.John's limbs, took off his coat and covered the body.

Benny had survived unscathed.

'I don't know which is strangest, seeing the para-humans, or simply being alive,' Marytha said.

Benny looked across the battleground and the sad scatter of bodies. 'Being alive takes a lot of getting used to.'

Ellen found her father. He stared aghast at her gore-covered body. 'Oh, Ellen, dear God,' Crane cried. He had seen her fight, seen her unbelievable power, her astonishing violence. He knew much of the blood was not her own, but there were wounds all over her chest, her stomach, bullet scars on the exoframe. That last man had fired his guns so many times.

'Daddy, I saved you,' Ellen gasped.

'I saw you,' Crane tried to smile, 'my wonderful, brave daughter.' Saving Ellen was the one thing he had ever wanted to do.

Ellen gave a puzzled laugh, 'They shot me, but I feel all right. It doesn't hurt.'

Crane knew she was in shock. 'We must get you back to the lodge, the medical wing.'

'Yes.' Ellen winced. She looked down at herself and registered the extent of her injuries.

'Reactivate your monitoring,' Crane said.

Pain erupted in Ellen before she could move, 'It hurts now,' she wailed, 'very much.'

Every warning light pulsed red: trauma, shock, blood loss, emergency. The exoframe administered a powerful analgesic, Ellen's head lolled and the frame locked itself in position.

Novik, Marytha and Benny gathered round. 'What can we do?' Novik said.

Despondently Crane shook his head, 'Very little. The exoframe contains a medical AI and pharmacopoeia. It will look after her far better than we can.'

'We need to move her,' Novik said.

'Yes.' Crane regarded his massive, blood-soaked daughter, his face crumpled and he wept in helpless choking sobs.

'Oh, mercy,' Marytha said.

Crane pushed away his tears, 'This won't do.' He pressed his thumb against a small plate on the exoframe. 'This is Palfinger Crane,' he said, 'Mary had a little lamb.'

'Confirmed,' the exoframe said.

'Return to Million Pines,' Crane said. 'Administer to Ellen's needs.'

'Confirmed.' The exoframe walked slowly towards the lodge.

Crane watched the machine carry his unconscious daughter away. 'Chandra Smith will be here soon.'

Crane looked so forlorn Novik wanted to hug him. 'Palfinger, we all did our best. You have a very brave daughter.'

'Indeed I do,' Crane said. 'Where is Raymond?'

'Palfinger, St.John is dead.' Novik didn't know what else to say, 'I'm sorry.'

It was almost too much. Crane's mind became blank. Apart from Ellen, St.John was the closest he had to a confidante. Crane had known Raymond St.John for two decades, and were the same age. Overwhelmed, he struggled to understand St.John was gone.

'Pallfinger?'

'What a terrible day,' Crane said. He moved away slowly, carefully, like an old man. Accompanied by Benny and Marytha, he followed Ellen's exoframe to Million Pines.

About to follow, Novik found his path blocked by an enormous ursine para-human and two lupines.

'Warrior, a moment,' the bear man said.

Novik studied the eight-foot tall bear-man's slope-shouldered muscularity with some trepidation.

The female lupine paced forwards, 'You fight the machine dogs. They are drones, they lack souls, you cannot defeat them. First, you must slay the Queen.'

Novik laughed wearily at their naivety, 'Impossible.'

The ursine bent down to look into Novik's eyes. 'No. Very difficult.' He held out his huge hand, 'I am Theodore.'

'Novik.' He griped Theodore's wrist, the ursine's hand covered Novik's arm almost to the elbow.

'We are the guardians of the fallen,' the wolf-woman said. Novik took what she proffered and the para-humans departed.

Marytha had seen the encounter and hung back, 'What was that all about?'

Novik showed her the white-fletched arrow the wolf-woman had given him, identical to the one they found beside Josie.

Side by side, Novik and Marytha made their way back to Million Pines.

- 59 -

Bad things come out of the blue. That was why Guinevere Snarlow did her best to cover all the bases, to make sure everything was under control. For that you had to rely on other people. People whose gifts and skills were, despite their assurances, often sadly lacking. It led to unpleasant surprises, such as the telephone conversation she was having right now.

'Palfinger, honey, I give you my word. I know absolutely nothing about it, the government of the USA knows absolutely nothing about it. This is terrorism plain and simple. Honestly, how could you believe I was involved?'

Guinevere rolled her eyes and made extravagant gestures of frustration as she talked to Crane.

'No, I did not threaten her. I'm sorry, but you're wrong. No, I'm not saying you're lying, I think you are misremembering. It's not what? Yes, of course it's a real word, that's beside the point. Ellen's a lovely child, I wouldn't dream of involving her. Yes, I agree it's a shocking thing, unbelievable. Scum, absolutely. They deserve whatever's coming. Palfinger, listen to me, this is precisely why we're going into Canada. These attacks have to be terminated at source.'

'I, ah, going for the planetary albedo?' Snarlow mutely appealed for help. Lobotnov chopped at a potted orchid with his pen. 'Yes, of course we're there for the trees. Not yours, obviously. We are only interested in managing the far north, the boreal fringe. Andriewiscz has strict orders to avoid your estate.'

Snarlow dropped her voice to a sympathetic whisper. 'Palfinger, if you can bear it, tell me, how is Ellen?' As she listened she bared her teeth. Fuck it, she mouthed. Fuck it. Fuck it.

Cheswold Lobotnov and Oscar Gordano exchanged alarmed looks.

'Looks like your brilliant plan just blew its own tits off,' Lobotnov muttered to Gordano.

It dawned on Gordano that Lobotnov was right. A dreadful sick hollow filled his stomach.

'Poor child,' gushed Snarlow, 'such a dreadful experience. How wonderful that she has that amazing machine to care for her. Palfinger, listen to me, it's Guinevere you're talking to now, not the President. Right now I've taken that hat off and I'm just your friend, I'm here for you. I share your pain, I really do. I-' Snarlow's eyes lit up, her face twisted into a savage grin. 'Palfinger, I know exactly what we're going to do. Andriewiscz is on the border, forty, maybe fifty klicks away. He's got a combat support hospital. I'm going to send them to you.'

Gordano immediately picked up his phone. When he saw the look on the President's face he put it down with exaggerated care.

'I know you've got your own people,' Snarlow said. 'Are they experienced in treating gunshot wounds? A unit of army surgeons are on their way right this minute and... And so am I! Palfinger, I'm coming to you, and I'm going to make sure everything turns out all right.'

Snarlow slowly put down the phone. 'Well, that was absolutely fucking dreadful.'

This had been an important lesson. From now on, she would make all the decisions herself.

Across the table Lobotnov regarded her with relaxed curiosity, Gordano with nauseous fear.

She slapped the table hard, 'Oscar Gordano, I hope you haven't paid that incompetent gangster idiot of yours. If you have, you've wasted your money. Twice. If Mitchell-fucking-useless-Gould isn't dead now, he soon will be.'

'What happened? What went wrong?' Gordano gulped. He felt sick, guilty, grimy, he wanted this never to have happened.

Snarlow's voice was sweet sarcasm, 'Well, as you have probably gathered, Palfinger Crane is alive and well and Ellen is badly hurt. Somehow a middle-aged man managed to fight off thirty professional mercenaries assisted only by his revolting blimp of a daughter, the butler and some trained pets.'

'They're para-humans, don't underestimate them,' Lobotnov said.

'Well, some moron did, didn't they?' Snarlow spat. 'You're through here, Gordano. You tried to be a player, I respect you for that, but you failed. Do what you can, but this administration washes its hands of you. The executive must be protected.'

Desperately Gordano tried to salvage some dignity. He felt about seven years old, he tried not to cry. 'Of course. I wouldn't have it any other way. I knew the risks when I signed on.'

Lobotnov managed to turn his involuntary guffaw into a cough. 'Anything I can do, ma'am?'

'I need two or three agents to accompany me immediately. They need to look like army doctors and have appropriate equipment. Any genuine medical experience will be a bonus.'

Lobotnov typed on his keyboard as Guinevere spoke. 'A moment,' he said, read the screen, made another entry and looked up. 'That's done. Anything else?'

'Just keep being that dependable, loyal, intelligent man I know you to be.' Guinevere moistened her lips, 'As soon as I'm back, we'll meet again in private session.'

Lobotnov's groin stirred, his face was unreadable, 'I'll look forwards to it.'

Guinevere closed down her console. 'I'm going to Million Pines. If Ellen dies before her father, Palfinger Crane ends up very sad, very vengeful, and we end up with a mutinous army owed half a year's back pay.' She tugged down the hem of her jacket, 'On the other hand, one bullet and we're back on track.'

She turned at the door and looked back at Gordano slumped hopelessly in his chair. 'Never send a boy to do a woman's job,' she sneered, and stalked out.

Gordano buried his head in his hands and wailed, 'Oh, Christ, I'm going to be impeached. I'm going to be arrested and go to jail.'

Lobotnov handed Gordano a tissue. 'You didn't really pay him, did you?'

'I've been such a fool. Always too eager to please, I know I am. My childhood. I was bullied.'

'That's why Ginny picked you for her VeeP,' Lobotnov said. 'You're such a dork, Oscar. Natch.'

As soon as Guinevere was in the air she called Andriewiscz, max crypto. "General, I'm inbound to you with F35b air escorts. I'll need surgical equipment from your CSH, uniforms, and a chopper to Crane's lodge in Million Pines.'

'All in hand, ma'am. I'm in receipt of Lobotnov's memorandum.'

'If Crane wants his medical people that's fine. Let them in and keep them there.'

The aeroplane climbed fast, banked hard then settled into level flight. Guinevere felt both relaxed and excited. Shit happened, you dealt with it, you moved on. The best way to resolve issues was to confront them head on. This was still going to work and they were still going to win. It was time to up the game.

'General, operation Pencil Head launches as soon as I am in Million

Pines airspace. I want Canada clear-felled from coast to coast.'

'Absolutely. Yes, ma'am.'

She thought she could hear the excitement in Andriewiscz's voice. Mexico had been the aperitif, Canada was the entrée. She knew what really turned Andriewiscz on was the thought of the main - Europe.

'Ma'am?' Andriewiscz sounded uncharacteristically hesitant. 'I'd like to be able to give the men and women some good news about pay. They're loyal, I guarantee it. Soldiers like to complain, but it's been more than six months.'

'Just make sure you get me to Crane.'

'We'll do that, no problem.'

It hadn't been excitement, Andriewiscz had been nervous. No politician, he had inadvertently given her a warning that the forces were with him, behind him, not her. When he said jump, the Pentagon said 'How high?', if she said the same thing, they'd look to him first before moving. Guinevere knew her history, it wasn't the loyalty of the troops she needed to worry about. Right now, Andriewiscz needed a big distraction, some new toys to play with. She kept her voice light, her tone relaxed:

'Oh yes, one other thing, Richard. Do you think we should nuke Ottawa or just ignore them?'

Andriewiscz considered the suggestion. 'Strategically it's irrelevant. Propaganda-wise it depends how serious we are about planetary albedo. Even a low-yield ground-burst will push a substantial dust aerosol into the stratosphere. As I understand it, that would help cool the northern hemisphere.'

'What a great suggestion. Pre-emptive nukes are highly unpopular, this will let us put a green spin on it. America: the new Eco-warrior. What's good for the USA is good for Gaia, that's sort of thing.'

'Saving soldiers' lives and saving the planet. I've decided – I may as well nuke it, what the heck.'

'Your call again, general. Happy gardening, speak to you soon.'

We live in a time of control, surveillance, doubt, fear and insecurity. Such times propagate cultural myths. The Grey Ghost of the Highway is part of the quest for freedom that sent the Pilgrim Fathers across the Atlantic. It was the pioneer's dream that just over the next hill was a better world. A place to call home.

Where can you go today, when the edge of the wilderness is the far side of a cultural event horizon called Global Catastrophe? Where can the pioneer spirit find expression when borders are closed and everyone is everywhere? The open road has become the last frontier, a journey without a destination.

In the end, we all know where we're going. It's still how you get there that counts.

The trip is all that's left, folks. Maybe it's all there ever was. For those of us who have had enough, who think the main thing wrong with the print edition of BFBM is the pages are not absorbent enough, then that trip will have to do.

So keep dreaming of a better world. Perhaps one morning you'll find the Grey Ghost waiting at the curb, a misty plume rising from the tailpipes, ready to take you away from all this.

I say the Grey Ghost exists because I want it to. The hell with reality, what's reality ever done for me?

T. Hank Yousomuch,
guest blog – BFBM Magazine

- 60 -

Andriewiscz opened a secure channel to Chandra Smith and offered a safe air corridor to Million Pines for him, and him alone, no team, no support. It wasn't lost on Crane that was all he did.

Supported and maintained by her exoframe, Ellen stood in the examination room of the medical wing, sedated and barely conscious. The room, a fully equipped surgical lab, was dedicated to Ellen's particular needs. Monitors, instrumentation and diagnostic equipment lined one wall. Overhead, a set of jointed steel armatures hung over an outsize surgical table, adaptable to either a human or auto-surgeon operator. Another room at the rear housed a whole-body scanner, with a recovery suite to one side. A scrub room, autoclaves and other facilities were across the corridor.

While Crane spoke to President Snarlow, Novik, Benny and Marytha stripped away Ellen's clothes and cleaned her mottled, bruised and wounded body with antiseptic swabs. Novik still carried the lupine woman's arrow, he put it down on the table.

The gunshot wounds looked terrible, each one a saucer-sized purple haematoma around a black-rimmed bullet hole oozing blood and serum. Novik counted six in Ellen's chest, three in her stomach, two in her right forearm. Apart from the wounds in her arm, there were no exit wounds.

When they were done, the exoframe lay itself on the table. Data links self-connected to external diagnostics, servo-driven arms attached intravenous and intramuscular implants, saline and antibiotic fluids began to flow.

Marytha found a sheet and covered Ellen's vast body, 'Poor great thing.'

Up on the data wall, displays showed heart rate, blood pressure, oxygen saturation and other information. Ellen's chest rose and fell in a slow rhythm, assisted by the rods cemented to her ribs, operated by exoframe servos. Across her shoulders the cooling fans of her subdermal heat exchangers hummed steadily. As they watched, her breath began to rasp. The exoframe adjusted the position of her head to keep her windpipe open, and she became quiet again.

'We shouldn't be sorry for her,' Benny said. 'She was magnificent when she needed to be.'

They watched her for a while longer before joining Crane in the study.

The moment bandwidth was available, the exoframe transmitted consolidated data to Chandra Smith, flying high over south-western Europe. Fifteen minutes later, Smith called Crane. Novik, Benny and Marytha listened to the exchange.

'Ellen is not in immediate danger,' Chandra told a relieved Crane. 'As hard as it may be to believe, I am certain there is no organ damage.'

'Thank God. So she going to be all right?'

'For the immediate future, yes.'

'Then we can move her to hospital, to surgery?'

'Palfinger, it is not that simple. Ellen's very bigness stopped the bullets before they reached her vital organs. Each round is lodged deep inside her body. To remove one bullet would require extraordinary surgery, each operation a significant trauma in itself. Remember, Ellen's heart is already under enormous strain.'

Crane digested the news, 'What do you suggest?'

'I'll know more when I can examine her. Tonight, I would hope to remove two, maybe three, bullets.

'And leave the others inside her? What about septicaemia, in Ellen's condition I know what that means.'

'Many people live for years with bullets inside them.'

Crane closed his eyes. A muscle jumped in his temple. Finally, he ground out four words, 'What do you want.'

'What do you mean?'

'What does Hyderabad need?' Crane's face grew congested, 'How much will it cost to save Ellen?'

'Palfinger, no,' Chandra Smith exclaimed, 'That's not-'

'Ten billion rupees? Twenty? Just tell me, Chandra. I will transfer the money now.'

'Listen to me, Palfinger,' Chandra said urgently, 'I am doing my absolute best to help Ellen. You are my esteemed friend, she is your daughter, I want-'

'One hundred billion,' Crane said bitterly.

On the screen Chandra stared open mouthed, 'That is an outrageous amount of money.'

'I agree. What else do you suggest I spend it on?'

'Wait for me to arrive,' Chandra implored, 'This is not necessary, it is irrelevant.'

'Hurry up, Chandra. Guinevere Snarlow is inbound with an army medical team. I don't like her and I don't want her here, but her army surgeons have great experience with gunshot trauma. She might play political hard-ball but at least she's honest about what she wants.'

Chandra stared in shock, 'Don't let them do anything. They don't understand Ellen's metabolism. The exoframe will maintain her until-'

'Don't worry. You'll still get paid.' Crane cut the connection and leaned heavily on the desk, head hanging. 'Am I doing the right thing? Was that a mistake? I don't know.'

Yes it is, Novik thought, it's a gigantic mistake. If Guinevere Snarlow really is coming in person at least her physical presence might offer some real security. Or she could simply be a new form of threat.

'Come and see Ellen,' Marytha urged Crane, 'Then you can get some rest'

On the verge of agreeing, Crane shook his head, 'St. John's family have to be told. I never once told him how much he meant to me.'

'I'm sure he knew,' Marytha said. 'You didn't need to ask for his help today.'

'He was very fond of Ellen.'

There would be no communication with the outside world unless General Andriewiscz initiated contact. Crane let out a deep, sad, sigh, 'I'll write a letter. Later. Come on, let's go see Ellen.'

The moment Marytha and Crane had left the room Benny accosted Novik. 'Are you happy with all this?'

'Crane's distraught, no wonder his judgement is skewed. What can I do?'

'Something, anything. Time is running out. If you've got any kind of scheme, go with it.'

Novik recalled his odd thoughts while they drank Crane's remarkable whisky. Reluctantly, he explained his ideas.

Benny was not over-impressed, 'It sounds crazy. No, actually it *is* crazy.'

'You're right, forget it.'

Benny gripped Novik's shoulders, 'You've absolutely nothing to lose. Mention it, see what Crane thinks.' He removed a pearl-headed pin from his lapel and attached it to Novik's jacket. 'Wear this, just in case it pisses him off.'

'What's is it?'

'A standing-wave resonator from my force field.'

Too tired to object, Novik felt a burst of affection for his awkward, obsessed, young friend. 'You never give up, do you?'

Benny's eyes glittered, 'Same as you then, aren't I?'

Whether Benny was right or not, Novik knew he couldn't stop now, there was too much at stake, too much had gone down. There had been too many –

He couldn't complete his own thoughts, stunned by the realisation he had ended up in a world where such things were true.

There had been too many deaths.

Crazy or not, that made it easier to go on. Novik fingered the lapel pin. 'Maybe we're both mad.'

They found Crane just as he was coming out of the medical room.

'Ellen looks very peaceful,' Crane looked and sounded much calmer than before. 'Thank you for helping her, thank you for everything. Snarlow's got me over a barrel with Ellen, and she knows it. She threatened us once, now she's going to save Ellen's life. It's just politics for people like her. I'll do what she wants, of course - I just wish I could get through to St.John's family.'

'The para-humans said they would look after him,' Novik said.

'Good, that's a comfort. Tell me, what do you make of them?'

Novik recalled his conversation with Theodore, and the lupine woman's advice, the feel of the white-fletched arrow between his fingers, 'Strange, disconcerting. Like dangerous, wise children.'

Crane held up the white-fletched arrow, 'I found this in the lab.'

Novik took the arrow back, 'They left another with Josie.'

Crane said, 'I brought them into being, yet their rituals and beliefs are their own. It's as if their mythologies were already contained within them.'

'I liked them,' Novik realised he admired, even envied the powerful, capable para-humans and their straightforward, bold opinions, 'I'm glad they're on our side.'

'They are not like us,' Crane tapped his head with a finger, 'Not in here. We humans stand in one place and see the world from that perspective. They stand somewhere else and see things differently, things we are incapable of seeing. I'm worried about what people will make of them. Without me they wouldn't exist, I'm responsible, I created them.'

'Like a father, or-'

'A God? If so, a small and imperfect one,' Crane said, with a haunted look. 'I made sure they had partners, companions, husbands and wives. I wasn't going to make *that* mistake.'

'Ellen-'

'Yes, of course. Bianca should be here, Ellen's mother. My daughter needs her, she always has.'

The moment arrived, Novik found he had cold feet.

'Mr. Crane, Palfinger, about Ellen-'

'Yes?' With that last word he immediately had Crane's full attention.

'Chandra Smith said Ellen is too big to operate on. When she lost weight, you may remember, it happened twice.'

'That's right. What's your idea?'

He had to say it now. He could hear the words in his head before he spoke them, and knew they were going to sound ridiculous, stupid. 'Each time it happened. Just before it did, you gave away some money.'

Crane didn't laugh, he didn't mock, he didn't tell Novik he'd gone soft in the head. When he spoke, it was with unbearable disappointment, 'Oh, Novik, not you too. I suppose it was too much to ask.'

Crane walked slowly away. Novik made to go after him but Marytha held him back. 'That's enough,' she said, 'Leave him be.'

'How small are the real wants of human nature, which we Europeans have increased to an excess... Nor shall we cease to increase them as long as Luxuries can be invented and riches found for the purchase of them; and how soon these Luxuries degenerate into necessaries...'

Joseph Banks, August 1770,
aboard the Endeavour

- 61 -

Manalito existed in two worlds, easily able to reconcile his orders from Mitchell Gould with Tanoata's spiritual summons. In both he was a killer, in both Bianca his victim. Destiny, fate, kismet; call it what you will, it had brought them together.

The heat from a high, silver-white sun fell like a dull weight, Bianca lay in a stupor of apathy in her shelter under the coconut trees. The waterless atoll was no place for life, or hope. The rising sea had drowned the reef, eroded the beech, and now the palms were dying. Of the dozens of fallen coconuts only one was germinating, a sickly thing with a single yellowing frond. The next typhoon would scour the island away.

Rousing herself, Bianca carried a coconut to the shore and flung it artlessly into the low surf. Perhaps one living thing would escape this forlorn spot.

A steady breeze pushed the coconut out to sea, far beyond the seaplane. Bianca watched it until it was gone from sight, then returned to the palms and carried armloads of coconuts to the shore. There, she threw them into the water with a flat, one-armed technique that sent them far across the water. After a few throws her arm grew tired and she changed to a two handed overarm throw. Driven by the breeze, a small flotilla of the fibrous husked nuts bobbed away in the water.

Tiger sharks began to circle, attracted by the splashes. Bianca's anger at her own impotence grew, she aimed at their dorsal fins and questing snouts.

Her two-handed style was powerful and accurate. One shot struck a tiger shark on the head, sending it into an angry spasm. She struck another on the body, and then a third. Agitated, the sharks churned the water, surging and buffeting each other. Bianca rained more coconuts down on them.

'Stop that now!' Manalito's shout carried across the water. He hung with one arm from a wing strut, his bare feet on one of the seaplane's floats.

Bianca glared at him, and pointedly threw a coconut towards him.

'You will stop that immediately,' Manalito bellowed.

Anxiety tinged Manalito's shouted commands, suddenly Bianca felt very powerful. What could Manalito do beyond his already vicious plans?

'Make me,' she screamed, and hurled another coconut into the sea. 'Come and make me.'

Manalito swung from the wing strut and slid into the water. Bianca threw another coconut at the sharks, then turned to watch him. At first he angled away from the roil of sharks, then cut towards the beach with a long, powerful crawl. With cold certainty Bianca knew that when he arrived, he would kill her.

Filled with frantic energy, Bianca flung the remaining coconuts up the beach, ran forwards and threw again. Now she stood where Manalito would land, a pile of coconuts heaped at her feet. He was twenty feet from shore when her second throw caught him on the buttocks. The next cracked his head.

Manalito choked, jerked his head, and looked about. Another coconut splashed beside him and he located Bianca. He deflected her next throw with his forearm, his teeth flashed white, and he sank beneath the surface.

Bianca scanned the choppy waves, filled with an anxiety approaching terror. She had hurt him, but only enough to make him angry.

Manalito surfaced low in the water and sculled towards the shore.

Bianca stood watchful on the beach, a coconut raised above her head. Finally she saw Manalito's dark hair, a few feet from shore. She threw wildly and missed.

Manalito took another breath and submerged.

Bianca threw the remaining coconuts inland. The world turned with deadly sloth, every breath became an eternity, loose, dry sand hindered every step. Bianca felt each fibre on the coconuts with a hyper-real clarity, the soft splash of collapsing waves came supernaturally loud.

Simultaneously, in her mind's eye, she bobbed in the water as Nei-Teakea, just before the shark took her. With crushing certainty she knew her own Doom approached. In just a few moments Manalito would stand on the island, a shark in human form. Once on dry land, her missiles would no longer be effective, he would catch her easily. Momentum deserted Bianca, her arms hung limp by her side. She had made a dreadful mistake.

Manalito errupted from the surf. Knife in hand, he charged across the coarse white sand, a force of nature.

Bianca burst back into life. Her arms jerked up, she threw one of the remaining coconuts. The throw was weak, her aim poor, Manalito dodged aside and sprinted forwards.

Coconuts lay strewn across the beach where Bianca had thrown them.

As he ran, Manalito turned his ankle on one and fell hard. He regained his feet in an instant but his ankle would not bear his weight.

Head low, Manalito glared at Bianca. His mouth hung open, veins bulged in his neck. Clenched in his fist, his knife pointed steadily at Bianca's stomach. 'Come here,' he said thickly. Wincing with pain, he limped forwards.

Bianca took a step back. Manalito limped forwards again, and once more Bianca retreated.

'You throw well,' Manalito said in a more normal voice. 'I enjoyed the game, but I was worried the sharks would damage the seaplane.'

'That would have been nice.' Bianca said.

Manalito glowered at Bianca then laughed, 'You misunderstand me completely. Mitchell Gould hired me to assassinate you, but I would never hurt a woman.' He brushed wet hair from his face and gave Bianca a rueful smile, 'The pain from my ankle made me angry, I admit it. A simple accident, caused by my own haste. The situation is simple, we will stay here for a few more days, and I will set you free.'

'Of course.' Heart thumping, Bianca took two steps back.

'This knife?' Manalito tested his weight on his ankle, 'A defence against the tiger sharks.'

'Throw it down,' Bianca said.

'Yes, certainly,' Manalito paced forwards.

'No further,' Bianca ordered.

'As you wish. I obey–' Manalito sprang through the air with a roar.

Bianca flung herself aside. Manalito landed on hands and knees where she stood, the knife rammed deep in the sand. Bianca ran behind him and kicked him between his legs. Manalito gargled with pain and curled into a ball. Bianca grabbed a coconut and brought it down onto Manalito's temple. Manalito swung blindly with his knife and rolled aside. Bianca flung the coconut two handed onto his face.

Manalito lay stunned, blood poured from his broken nose. Bianca snatched up the coconut again, she raised it over her head. Manalito's arm flicked out, his knife struck through her knee.

Bianca felt the blow but there was no pain. She looked down and saw the hilt jammed against the outside of her knee. Three inches of the thick blade protruded on the far side. It looked dreadful. Manalito still lived.

Bianca pounded Manalito in a wild frenzy. To survive she had to kill. To kill she had to become the killer, become Manalito.

'Die!' she howled into his face, up at the sky, the world. 'Die, die, die.'

Manalito twisted and rolled beneath her blows. His cheekbone cracked, another blow smashed against his eye, a third crushed his mouth. Bianca hammered at his forehead and the coconut shattered. Shrieking with frustration she pushed handfuls of sand into Manalito's mouth.

Finally, Manalito seized Bianca's wrists and flung her away. As she fell, something parted in her knee with appalling pain. Her leg no longer worked, the knife grated agonisingly inside the joint, black blood sheeted from the wounds. Sprawled on the sand, Bianca tried to pull the knife free, the blade was stuck, the pain unbelievable.

Scant feet away, Manalito rolled onto his hands and knees. He wiped red sand from his eyes, snorted, and spat blood, sand, teeth. The expression on his ruined face, the promise in his eyes lay far beyond simple murder. He drew his other knife and crawled forwards.

Manalito would not die. Bianca wailed in terror and crabbed backwards, then rolled and scrambled away on her good leg and both hands.

Manalito swayed upright and staggered after her like a drunken man.

Spray broke against Bianca's face. She had blundered into the surf and there was nowhere left to go. Out in the ocean the seaplane floated. Ahead were the tiger sharks, behind was Manalito.

Bianca moaned with fear. As soon as the sharks scented blood they would attack. Around her feet the surf was already crimson. Bianca flung herself into the water and flailed away from the shore. Compared to Manalito sharks were beautiful and kind.

Gasping with renewed pain, Bianca gained deeper water. Inside her knee the knife blazed cold agonies. Unable to swim further, she reached down. The hilt felt loose, she pulled the blade free, choked on seawater and sank beneath the waves.

The knife fell from her grip, Bianca clawed her way up to the surface. Behind her, a dark plume of blood spread through the ocean. A pressure waved pushed her aside as something huge surged close by. Bianca's heart pounded madly, a black ring fringed her vision as if she looked along a dark tunnel. Where was the seaplane? Working her arms she lifted her head clear of the water and saw where it floated, a tiny, distant thing.

Nearby, a brutal equilateral fin cut the water. The sea around Bianca was black, she floated in a cloud of her own blood. Forget the sharks, she told herself, soon you will bleed to death. Legs trailing behind, Bianca swam with her arms towards the seaplane.

Time passed, ocean swells lifted and dropped her in their peaks and troughs. Bianca grew cold, her arms heavy, the muscles stiff and sluggish. Swimming became harder and harder, her efforts more feeble, mechanically, she moved her limbs and turned her head. Why bother? The water was velvet soft, warm as silk, it would be easier to drift, to let breath trickle between her lips and sink down, down into the blue-black depths.

Face down, Bianca relaxed and drifted with the waves. The urge to breathe grew, then became irresistible. Primitive instincts compelled her body onwards.

Something hard and hollow bumped against her head. Bianca blinked and roused from her exhausted reverie. The sky was blue, the sun bright, immediately in front of her, water slapped and splashed against a brilliant white float. Bianca dragged herself forward and hauled herself through the seaplane's hatch.

Sprawled on the cabin floor, Bianca peeled off her clothes with soggy fingers and wrapped herself in a towel. She began to shiver violently. Her knee was swollen and rigid, the edges of the wounds blue-white. Bianca watched watery blood trickle down her shin and pool between her toes. A first aid kit was under the passenger seat, she sprayed analgesic and antiseptic sprays and applied gauze bandages. Then she forced herself to look through the hatch.

Manalito stood on the beach. Between them the sharks raced back and forth, thrilled by her blood scent. Bianca shuddered, locked the hatch and closed her eyes.

When she looked again, Manalito was still there. He paced from side to side, kicked at the surf and flung his arms into the air. Incoherent shouts came across the water.

Still weak, Bianca laughed at his impotence. Now their roles were reversed, she had food, shelter, and medicine, he was marooned on the waterless island. The container fed by the solar still was full of cool, sweet water. Bianca drank her fill and a surge of joy filled her - she was alive! She opened the hatch and yelled, 'Hey, Manalito, shark god, *rokea*, listen to me. You did not kill me, I escaped, I beat you.'

Manalito bellowed an unintelligible response, tore off his shirt and flung it into the sea.

'I am stronger than you,' Bianca cried. 'Stronger than your gods. You, the big man.'

Manalito roared and beat at his chest. He strode waist deep into the surf and spread his arms wide. Suddenly he gave a great shout and sank down to his shoulders. Then he surged forwards, the water parting against his bare torso in a foaming bow wave.

Horrified, Bianca watch him churn through the sea far faster than any man could swim. Now Manalito rose up, his chest and shoulders clear of the water. Once more he raised his arms, turned towards the seaplane and rushed forwards, a great wake churning behind.

Utter fear paralysed Bianca. Manalito truly was *rokea*, a death-god of the oceans, and now he came for his revenge. She could see his face, bloodied, broken and wild-eyed with insane rage. Spume flew from Manalito's body, spittle from his mouth, red tears streamed from his eyes. He reached out for her, his fingers bent like claws, and gave vent to an appalling scream.

Manalito jerked down into the water. He screamed again and blood gushed from his mouth. Then he was dragged beneath the surface and Bianca saw the giant tiger shark swimming below and knew that it had dragged him there with his legs in its jaws.

The shark descended under the seaplane. Manalito lay over the shark's back, eyes and mouth wide with astonishment, his arms trailing behind.

Slowly shock abated. Manalito really was dead, the dreadful nightmare was over.

It was time to leave, but first she must warn Palfinger and Ellen. With a pang of fear she wondered if she would be too late.

Bianca struggled into the pilot's chair and stared at the console in dismay. Even from the grave it seemed Manalito could still reach out and hurt her. He had been careful and thorough with his plans, the communications circuit boards had been removed, worse still, the main controls were keyed to Manalito's thumb print. Without him the seaplane would not fly. Ghoulishly Bianca wondered if any of his body parts would surface.

The sun set. Bianca wrapped herself in blankets and slept uneasily.

The next day was bright and hot. Her knee burned, she changed the bandages and swabbed it again with antiseptic, then took more painkillers and anti-inflammatories. The wound looked horrible, she hated to look at it, could barely bring herself to touch it. Weak and listless, she forced herself to search the seaplane for the missing circuit boards. All she found were tinned food and Manalito's spare clothes.

She told herself people were looking for her, that it was only a matter of time. The solar still continued to operate, desalinating and cooling sea water, even without food she could survive for weeks. Medicine was more limited, sepsis or gangrene inevitable if her leg became infected. Bianca made herself another promise: she would clean and care for herself, she would live, she would defeat Manalito one final time.

Days passed. Bianca burned with fever, her knee a remorseless drumbeat of pain. Her appetite died before the food was exhausted, all she could manage was to drink water and relieve herself. Hour after hour, her mind wandered through her life, the early years with Palfinger, carrying Ellen, her daughter's birth.

Half way between memory and dream, she finally understood that Ellen was a stranger, Tekirei was dead and Tanoata, if she still lived, hated her. All over the world she had sponsored communities of strangers and moved on. Her wish to live in an idealised world had led her to reject her own daughter, the one person who needed her most. She had failed her own family and destroyed another with her own selfishness.

It came to her that Palfinger had always been kind because he still loved her.

The seaplane swung at its anchor. Bianca sat beside the water spigot in a semi-trance. Each morning she changed her bandages, rinsing the old ones in the sea and hanging them to dry. Flesh melted from her body, the time approached when she would be too weak to crawl over the side.

One day she thought she was back on Ujelang, standing at the end of the Shadowed Path beside the graveyard. The sun shone, but she was freezing cold.

When she woke, she saw a black dot far out in the ocean. Over time it resolved itself into a canoe.

Bianca realised she was dying, and that it was Tekirei in the canoe, come to be her spirit guide. It would be good to see him again, though she felt sad that she would never again see Palfinger and Ellen.

She was wrong. The canoe held Mautake and his father. Together, they had navigated the wind, stars and ocean currents as their ancestors had once done, and had come to take her home.

- 62 -

President Snarlow laughed gaily as she climbed down the steps of the army helicopter. The rotors were still slowing as she disembarked onto clear ground between the lodge and the lake shore. Her hair was tied back in a simple pony-tail, she wore a western-style blouse with a burgundy check, tan slacks and riding boots.

As soon as the engines stopped the pilot and co-pilot joined her, athletic young men in dark blue overalls with snub-nosed auto-pistols in their holsters. A tubby man and a slight woman with mousey hair followed. Both wore white lab coats over army fatigues and manhandled medical cases onto a tracked electric cart. Overhead, the F38b escorts flashed past with a crackling roar, broke left and right and returned south.

Everyone at Million Pines gathered at the entrance to watch the President land. Crane advanced down the stone steps. 'Good news, I hope,' he said as he took President Snarlow's hand.

'The best. The European Union has just declared war, Ahmed Hirsch told me himself.'

'Surely, that's terrible?' Crane said.

Guinevere trilled with laughter, 'What have they got? No armies, no air force, certainly no ballistic deterrents. What a joke. They picked this fight, we're going to finish it.'

Crane stepped aside to let the two doctors with the electric cart up the step, 'This has nothing to do with Ellen.'

Guinevere looked at Benny, Novik and Marytha, 'Who are they?'

'Guests,' Crane said. Complex emotions vied within him as he considered Novik. 'Friends.'

Guinevere snapped her fingers, 'Check them.' The two dark-suited men started forwards. She kissed the air each side of Palfinger's cheeks, 'We'll go straight to your daughter.'

Palfinger, Guinevere and the doctors hurried to the medical room.

'She's pretty damned big,' the male doctor said when he saw Ellen. 'Jeez, is she fat.'

'Ellen's sedated and stable,' Crane said. 'The exoframe maintains homeostasis and provides biomechanical assists.'

'Whatever. We'll make our own assessment and get back to you.'

'The equipment is specialised, tuned to Ellen's needs, medical AIs and expert systems have minute by minute data-'

Guinevere took hold of Crane's elbow. 'Let them do their job, Palfinger.'

Crane reluctantly allowed Snarlow to lead him back to the study. There, he found Novik, Benny and Marytha standing uneasily in front of the hearth. Across the room, the President's guards covered them with their auto-pistols.

Crane halted in the doorway. 'What the hell's all this about?'

Guinevere shoved Crane hard in the back, 'Go keep your friends company, Palfinger.'

One of the guards held out Marytha's 68-calibre pistol. 'This is all they had, ma'am.'

'Sweet Jesus, that's all they'd need,' Guinevere took the gun and stood between them.

'If it's just a question of-' Crane appealed.

Guinevere stepped forwards and backhanded him across the face.

'Hey,' Novik protested.

The guards aimed their weapons. Novik put his hands in the air and stepped back, 'Let's everyone keep cool.' He took Crane's arm, 'You OK?'

'Yes.' Crane gingerly touched his face. Blood streaked his cheek, a cut from Guinevere's ring. 'What do you want, Guinevere? I thought you were here to help.'

'The war has reached a critical stage, Palfinger. America is broke, I need to pay my troops. The reconstruction of Europe, Africa and South America will require gigantic investments. Your investments.'

'You think I'll help you now, at gunpoint?'

'We've been through that. You had your chance to be on the winning team. All you need to do now is die before your daughter.' Guinevere hefted Marytha's gun, 'Christ, this is heavy.' She held out her hand to one of the guards, 'Give me your weapon.'

'I'm afraid the firearm is uniquely keyed to me, ma'am,' the guard said.

'Then this will have to do. Gentlemen, on my mark.' Guinevere and the two guards raised their weapons. 'Mark.'

'Wait,' Crane appealed, 'Stop.'

Across the room Guinevere's expression was one of blank-eyed glee.

They opened fire.

It happened so fast there was no time to think, no time for any kind of plan. Benny threw his arms round Crane and turned his back on the guns. Novik pushed himself in front of Marytha, eyes screwed shut, arms flung wide.

For a long moment the room was filled with sound and fury.

In the silence that followed Benny released his grip on Palfinger. 'OK, Mr. Crane?'

Crane shook like a leaf, 'I think so.'

Novik felt nothing. He remembered how Ellen had reacted to bullet wounds. Dreading what he would see he looked down at his own body. There was not a mark on him. Wide-eyed in disbelief, he turned to Marytha, 'You all right?'

'Yes.' She gave a shaky smile, 'Hello again.'

Novik's knees shook like reeds in a gale. 'We've got to stop doing this.'

Across the room the two guards sprawled against bullet-riddled oak panelling. Guinevere Snarlow sat splay-legged among the splintered wreckage of Crane's drinks cabinet, a single heavy calibre bullet wound low in her chest.

Novik checked the guards. Each was dead from multiple gunshot wounds. Marytha's pistol lay in Guinevere's open palm. Novik lifted it clear and pushed it through his belt.

Guinevere's eyes followed him. 'Help me,' she gasped, 'I'm your President.'

Novik picked up an unbroken bottle from the wreckage of splintered wood and broken glass, it was the Bowmore 42, still one third full. He hefted it thoughtfully and turned away.

'How?' Novik asked Benny.

'Ricochet armour.' Benny flicked the pin on Novik's lapel, 'Told you.'

Novik drank deep. Five hundred dollars a swallow, and he didn't care. None of this was real. All he could think about was the Canadian crossing, that he could have waited like Benny had wanted. Waited one more day, and Josie-

He couldn't think it.

He'd thought he was right, and he hadn't listened. When it came to Benny, had he ever listened?

They could have waited. Josie had believed him, she trusted him. She had wanted to go. Novik snarled with self-disgust and wiped that last thought away. It had been his decision alone, his responsibility. They had gone when he had wanted to.

If only they had waited-

Then Ellen would have been killed in the woods, Crane would be dead in this room. Right now, this very moment, Snarlow would have won.

Novik clutched his head and groaned. Was that the price? Was that what the big picture demanded? If they had waited, then they wouldn't have been here, today. It had all been about spending, about money, but the consequences of his decision had been beyond value, beyond cost, far, far beyond price.

Wild-eyed, Crane pulled the bottle from Novik's hand, gulped whisky, and wiped his mouth, 'Ellen.'

Novik stared at him blankly.

'Ellen's still under guard.'

Novik touched his lapel pin, 'Benny, what's the range on this?'

'I'll come with you.'

Outside the medical room the two army doctors stood on guard. Novik hurried forwards, gun in hand, Benny close beside him, 'Come quickly. The President's been hurt,'

The overweight doctor drew and aimed his pistol in a single fluid movement, 'Final warning. Drop your weapon.'

Novik laughed coldy, 'Go on, shoot me. See what happens.'

'Don't do it,' Benny said hastily.

The doctor fired. He cried out and staggered back, fired again and collapsed.

The female doctor had her hands in the air, her voice high and thin, 'I'm unarmed.'

Novik pointed his gun, 'What have you done to Ellen?'

'Nothing.' Her hands went higher. 'I promise, we haven't touched her. Our orders. I'm just an orderly. He's some soldier.'

Novik and Benny hurried into the medical room.

Ellen was still comatose, her bulk rising and falling beneath the cover. As far as Novik could tell the monitors and instrument readings looked stable. Most lights and colour bars were green, a few showed amber. The equipment cases the army doctors had brought were still stacked on the electric cart. Nothing had been unloaded. Novik opened one of the insulated cases and found it was packed with ice. Embedded in the ice were six bottles of champagne.

Crane hurried into the room. 'Palfinger Crane,' he said breathlessly. 'Mary had a little lamb. Summarise.'

'Confirmed,' the exoframe's synthetic voice spoke in even tones. 'Blood pressure low and falling. Cardiac assist ninety-two percent. Oxygenated haemoglobin levels falling. Core temperature rising. Oedema increasing in extremities-'

Crane walked out the room before the exoframe finished speaking, Novik followed behind.

Out in the hallway the orderly crouched beside the soldier. She looked up at Novik, 'He's dead.'

'Fetch the cart and come with me.'

Guinevere Snarlow still sat where she had fallen. Now she held an open bottle of vodka, alternately drinking and sloshing spirits over her blood soaked chest.

'I'm the President,' she slurred. 'Get me to the hospital. Push Ellen off the table and put me on it.'

Crane looked down at her dispassionately. 'I can't decide whether I'd rather kill you or just watch you die.'

Guinevere slurped more vodka, 'You do either and you're in an even bigger shit storm than you are now.'

As hard as it was to imagine, she was almost certainly right.

Novik and the orderly brought the cart into the room, together with Marytha they lifted the dead airmen onto the platform.

Crane turned to Benny, 'That thing you did with the guns?'

'I'm an observer,' Benny said. 'I'm not supposed to get shot. It happened once and I didn't like it.'

'An observer for who? Where are you from?'

'South America,' Marytha said. 'Acapulco.'

'Achernar,' Benny corrected.

Marytha frowned, 'I thought you said you'd come across the gulf?'

'The black gulf,' Benny said patiently. 'Of space.'

It was more than Crane was able to cope with. 'Whatever. Get those corpses off the cart. We'll take Snarlow to the medical wing.' He glared at the army orderly, she wilted under his hostile gaze. 'Chandra will be here soon. Then we'll have a real doctor.'

11. Choice

How did we get here? I mean, how the HELL did we end up where we are today?

I'll tell you.

Each and every time we made a choice we went ahead and did what we chose to do. Countries, organisations, combines, industries, and individuals.

Don't tell me some of those choices were tough, quit whining. The choices some people still have to make you forgot existed long ago. Thirsty? Which ditch do you want to drink from - the brown one, or the green one?

Well, yes, OF COURSE they should do something about it. But they're poor aren't they? And isn't poverty a choice? Some people think so. And all these opinions, aren't they choices too?

OK, so some decisions actually are really hard, life-and-death. I'll let you have that one. Many are so tough we let other people make them for us. These people are called Leaders. Sometimes letting them decide is a good thing, but only sometimes. After all, they have their own choices to make.

Eat another burger / don't eat a burger. Eat it and a cow dies, poor cow, but the owner has sold a cow to the burger factory. Lucky owner, he can buy more cows. Lucky you, you eat the burger, you put on some more weight.

Don't eat the burger and the cow's still alive. Lucky you – a little more time before that obesity related heart condition kicks in. Lucky cow, a few more days in the sun eating grass, or more likely a few more days in the barn eating grain.

Cows aren't meant to eat grain, they're meant to eat grass. We started farming cows because they turn something we can't eat - the grass - into something we can – the cow. We'd get ten times the food value if we ate the grain but we want to eat burger. We made a choice.

Still want a burger? Of course you do, but now you know a bit more.

So you go into hospital for a bariatric frame. The surgeon doesn't explain the procedure, there's a problem, and you sue their ass off. Quite right too. It's called informed consent. How can you properly choose if you don't understand the choices?

Whose job is it to keep you informed? That would be you. You're an adult, a free agent and in the eyes of the law a responsible one. Ignorance is no excuse.

Lots of people make choices on your behalf and don't tell you. Be aware. Or go stick your head in a Meeja console and let your ego tell you everything is fine and dandy.

What's my point here? Choices. We all got to make them, we all live with the consequences. Seriously, quit whining. Make better choices.

T. Hank Yousomuch
If You're So Damned Happy Why Did You Buy This Book?

- 63 -

General Andriewiscz pulled the EnRel goggles off his face and handed them back to the young technician. All around him his senior staff were doing the same. In front of them, the coniferous forests of Canada stretched into the far distance. 'These are no use, son,' he said gently, 'I can't use them.'

The young technical infantryman stood ramrod straight, his gaze fixed on a point just to one side of the general's shoulder. 'Sir, Enhanced Reality proved very useful in Mexico, sir.'

Andriewiscz gestured at the spreading forest. 'Mexico was full of buildings. They had walls. Being able to see behind the walls was a big help. I already know what's behind all these trees - another tree.'

'Sir, EnRel will let you visualise the landscape without the trees, sir.'

'When we're done I won't need to visualise it. I'll be able to see it.'

The soldier frowned. 'Sir, you could compare the views and see if they were the same. That would be interesting.'

Andriewiscz tried to look the soldier in the eye. The soldier's gaze flicked across to his other shoulder.

'Look at me, son,' Andriewiscz said.

'Sir, you no longer have the right to make that request.'

'My apologies, soldier. In the right context, your special nature is a genuine asset.'

'Sir, I already know that, sir.'

'I expect you'd rather be back with your computers and data.'

'Sir, I'd rather have a chainsaw, sir. My daddy was a lumberjack and put me through my grades. I can strip, service and reassemble any model blindfold, sir.'

Andriewiscz scribbled a note and gave it to the soldier. 'You're reassigned.'

'Sir, thank you, sir.'

Andriewiscz rubbed his jaw. 'There's no need to say "sir" all the time, soldier. Really.'

'Sir, yes sir. That's no more sir, yes sir, sir. Just yes sir, sir.'

'Just-', Andriewiscz suppressed a sigh and saluted. 'Dismissed.'

'Yes, sir.'

Andriewiscz was an old-fashioned man in several ways. He drank his scotch neat, he thought a man should be able to darn his own socks, and thought porn was good for team spirit. He chewed the ass off his officers if they screwed up, but never in public. He knew discipline was based on loyalty and loyalty swung both ways. Success was based on sweat, and attention to detail.

His staff were ready, his troops were ready. Men and materiel, ordnance and transport lay along the border for thirty miles in each direction. Flanked east and west by divisions of heavy infantry and armour, with skirmish lines of robo-canines ready to deploy, operation Pencil Head was ready to roll.

Andriewiscz faced his senior officers. 'Ladies and gentlemen, we are America and we're the world's policeman. We're here to save the planet and right now that requires a fifty-mile-wide corridor through this forest, clear-felled all the way to Norman Wells. We got some Europeans to piss off.'

As one they snapped to attention and presented quivering salutes. 'Sir, yes sir!' they bellowed.

Andriewiscz chewed down on his smile. 'Get to it.'

Soon all that could be heard was the roar of diesel tractors and the groan and crash of falling trees. The air was blue from the smoke of 20,000 chainsaws as far as the eye could see. The invasion of Canada had begun.

An hour after the rear echelons had pulled north of the border, a scattered swarm of dragonfly-like creatures flew over the army at a height of around twenty feet. Darting back and forth, they passed almost unnoticed until a cook swatted one that dipped low above his canteen. When he saw the hair-fine wires running the length of its body he took it to his officer. It was soon with Andriewiscz. By then it was far too late. Minutes later, all clothing, all cotton, linen, and wool, all gun webbing, belts and shoe leather had begun to disintegrate.

Soon afterwards the chainsaws began to splutter and die as their fuel turned to gummy gel. Vehicles ground to a halt, generators died. The communications blackout enveloping Crane's estate ended.

- 64 -

'What's your name?' Novik said to the orderly as they lifted the drunk and rambling President onto the bed.

'Janis.' She hesitated, then held out her hand.

Novik didn't take it. 'Well, Janis, can I trust you?'

'Would you believe me?'

'With President Snarlow, yes.'

'I'm just a triage nurse. I fit them up with saline and clean the wounds.'

'You do that here. And Janis, there are real monsters in the woods. If you run away, they will kill you.'

She was so frightened she started to fold over. 'I just did what I was told. The President—'

'You always do what you're told?'

She couldn't meet his eye. Novik hissed with contempt and left her to it.

Marytha and Benny took the cart back and moved the bodies of the airmen out of the study.

In the medical room, Crane called up screen after screen of data on the consoles, moving from keyboard to keyboard.

'That orderly can't do much for Snarlow,' Novik said.

'I couldn't care less,' Crane's complexion was grey, his face lined and pouchy, 'Snarlow fooled me twice, never again. I'm not prepared to spend a single second away from Ellen.'

'We've got to make the very best of this. Snarlow alive might help Ellen.'

Crane rested his hands on the instrument console. 'You're right. Very well, connect her to the secondary instrumentation in the recovery room. It will stabilise her until Chandra arrives.'

'How do I do that?' Novik said.

Crane raised his voice, 'This is Palfinger Crane. Attend.'

'Attending,' a synthesised voice said.

'Mary had a little lamb.'

451

'Confirmed.'

'Authorize Novik.'

Crane showed Novik where to press his thumb, then Novik spoke his name and the recognition phrase.

'The medical AI will now obey your reasonable requests,' Crane said.

Novik returned to the side room. Snarlow sprawled untidily on the bed, Janis sat on a chair beside her. Janis stood as soon as Novik opened the door, 'I think she has a punctured lung.'

'Fucking outstanding,' Guinevere slurred. 'I'll give myself a Purple Heart.'

Novik looked down at Snarlow and knew he hated her, and that he was going to help keep her alive.

Novik confirmed his identity to the AI and ordered it to care for Guinevere. Armatures emerged from the bedframe, sensors and probes descended from the ceiling gantry and attached themselves to her body.

Swearing and grumbling Guinevere drunkenly tried to fend them off. A nozzle puffed mist into her face and she became drowsy. A cuff clamped itself to her left bicep, measurements and assays were taken, her condition began to stabilise.

Out in the main room Crane sat beside his daughter. Novik pulled over a chair, 'Snarlow's OK, I think.'

'This life,' Crane shook his head in wonder. 'She tried to kill us all, now we're looking after her.'

'Palfinger,' Novik said cautiously, 'Back before all this, I was trying to help.'

Crane sat very still. A little of the tension left his eyes, 'I know.'

Together they watched the displays from the systems tending Ellen's vast and terribly damaged body. All across the monitors and readouts trend curves imperceptibly flattened, numbers and percentages moved further from optimal, histogram bars and status lights phased from green to amber, amber to red. What was happening was obvious to them both. Ellen was dying.

'When will Chandra arrive?' Novik said.

Crane checked his hand-held and spoke in monotone. 'He's landing at Vancouver in an hour. Door to door from there, two hours.'

'That's not too long.'

The exoframe worked its valves and pistons. Ellen's chest rose and fell in a slow cycle, her breath sounded like the slow retreat of the tide on a distant shore.

Crane looked across Ellen's body to Guinevere Snarlow, relaxed and comfortable in the side room. 'It's not fair,' he said.

That somebody like Crane should even think like that felt grotesque, yet Ellen did not deserve this, and neither did St.John. Novik thought of Josie again, the hundredth time that day, the high place where he had left her, and felt his heart change. Where was his own comfort? Perhaps, instead, he could offer some to Crane. 'Few things are. Maybe what we see as natural justice, or fate, is just chance and luck.'

Crane slowly collapsed in on himself, reducing down to a huddle of elbows and knees, the rest of him, his height, his posture, dissipating as if they were only borrowed things. He recalled the conversation he had with Ellen back on the island, under the calabash trees. As ever she had been the realist, he the ever-hopeful optimist, the denier. Underneath, he had known she was right, that one day he would have to confront the inevitable. Now, that day was here.

The urge to speak grew in Novik. 'I don't want any more of your money.'

Crane gave him a look that had stilled CEOs, Presidents, Kings and Prime Ministers, 'Tell me you came here by chance.'

'Josie and I… We thought if we had enough money we could change the world.'

The same old same old, Crane thought. Except Novik's partner had been killed, and still he'd come. Then Novik and his friends had put their lives on the line for Ellen, and for him. Single-handed, Novik had thrown down that killing-machine, the least he could do was listen to what he had to say. 'Just how were you going to do that?'

'We thought we might persuade you to give us yours.'

'And then what?'

'We'd buy everything there was, and give it away.'

'Sounds crazy.'

Looking back, of course it was. Josie must have known that, she'd been waiting for him to catch up. 'I thought it was worth trying.'

Beneath her eyelids, Ellen's eyes twitched from side to side and she mumbled incoherently. A light on the autosurgeon's ceiling array blinked amber, then burned steady red. Ellen's head lolled, she fell silent. Somewhere behind the far wall came the low thump of a compressor.

Finally Crane stirred. He stood up, leaned forwards and kissed Ellen's brow. 'Come on,' he said to Novik, 'Let's give that other idea of yours a go. What have I got to lose except my credit rating?'

Back in the study, Crane activated his desk and made some calls. Some of the people he spoke to raised their voices, others spoke at some length. Crane listened to them all and repeated his instructions.

'I've just transferred my controlling holdings in large-scale co-operative agriculture and managed forestry in Africa, Indonesia, Paraguay and Pakistan to the local collectives.'

They were on the way back to Ellen when the phone rang. Crane held it in his hand, rooted to the spot.

Novik plucked it from Crane's fingers, 'Hello?'

'This is Chandra Smith. Who is this? Where is Mr Crane?'

Novik handed the phone over, 'It's the doctor.'

'Chandra, it's me, Palfinger.'

Crane adjusted the phone, Chandra's voice filled the room: 'What's happened? The data feed opened up, I can see Ellen's information.'

Crane's voice flattened with disappointment, 'That's why you called? Information access?'

'Yes, indeed. This is excellent, I can see her condition, poor child. Is Snarlow there? Did she open a data tunnel?'

Ellen lay on the table, around her instrument lights winked or pulsed steadily, nothing appeared to have changed.

'What can you tell?' Crane glanced at Novik, 'Has Ellen lost any more weight?'

Chandra spoke slowly as he studied the flow of medical data, 'This is very complicated. Ellen is bleeding, the exoframe is replacing fluids and also trying to drain several oedema. You're expecting more weight loss? How so?'

'Chandra, please, just tell me how my daughter is doing.'

'Better, just a little. Or rather, no worse. She is less unstable, her heart is a fraction stronger, blood pressure – perhaps. It's not clear. As for weight, some, maybe. I really can't tell.'

'If she did lose weight, substantial amounts, would the operations to remove the bullets be easier?' Crane said.

'Yes, of course, much safer. Unfortunately, impossible. Palfinger, remember, we have already tried – everything.' Chandra took a breath, 'Is that it? There's something new?'

Crane checked the time, 'Perhaps. This is all rather radical, nothing's for certain-'

'We? Don't listen to those army doctors, this sounds like charlatan's advice.'

Crane checked the time again, 'I have to go.' He ended the call. 'Novik, you probably want me to try again, I agree. One data point isn't a curve. I've set up two more sets of instructions, the first will activate-' Crane held up his finger, '-now.'

Gigantic economic earthquakes, financial tsunamis and hurricanes were about to sweep the globe, all to try and save one girl. Some people would probably die. Others would be set free.

'Wait,' Novik said.

'What for?'

'I'm not sure we should,' Novik struggled to find the words, the sheer improbable strangeness of what they were about to do.

Crane stared at him incredulously, 'You doubt your own advice? Now?'

'Yes, I do.'

'Even though this is what you want?'

Novik nodded mutely.

'Good,' Crane said decisively. 'Because it's a crazy plan.' He laid his hand on Ellen's motionless shoulder, 'I'm going to do it anyway. What else would you have me do?'

There was an endless ache inside Novik where Josie used to be, 'I'd try everything.'

A tone sounded on the phone, Crane checked the screen, 'There goes WalMart-Lockheed.' Soon afterwards the phone rang persistently. Crane didn't answer. Instead, he studied the displays around Ellen's comatose body.

Something strange was building, Novik could feel it, a weird pressure, a kind of psychic charge.

Crane muttered something, pressed a key, rotated a joystick and flipped through a series of data summaries. Another timer rang, 'And that's most of Australasian pharma,' he said under his breath.

Crane studied the data flow like a hawk hovering over prey. 'See here,' he pointed to one of the screens, 'and here.'

Less than a minute later they were certain. They watched and waited for a while longer. Crane's phone rang, again and again.

Inside, Crane thought he might burst. Much to his own surprise, when he spoke, his voice sounded deep and serene. 'That's it. We've done it.'

Novik was temporarily beyond words. Something very strange, very wonderful had happened.

The phone rang again. Crane answered straight away, 'Chandra.'

Chandra Smith's breathless voice filled the room, the beat of rotors loud in the background. 'Palfinger, I'm waiting for clearance to take off. I've been calling you. Ellen's weight - down four kilos.'

Crane couldn't keep the smile off his face, 'I know.'

'How is she?'

'Everything is fine, Chandra. I can see all parameters are holding steady except for mass. You can see that too, nothing is retrograde, it's all stable or improving. Ellen's going to lose weight fast, everything is ready, you'll be able to operate as soon as you arrive.'

'What was it, how did you do it?'
'We found the cure.'
'Yes, thank God, but what? How?'
'It's the money.'

Emerald Union IS the NFC

"Sure, that was us." Ahmed Hirsch, President of the European Union announced in a press conference following extraordinary satellite pictures of General Andriewiscz's Northern Expeditionary Force.

"Just who are the NFC?"

"Natural Forces Combine are some very talented men and women whose hearts are in the right place."

"But who, exactly?"

"Typical scientists, clever and modest. Unlike insecure egoist politicians like me."

"Why did you fund them?"

"Are these real questions? We needed a way of testing our delivery systems, obviously. Brussels and the NFC discovered we had similar concerns about where things were going. We are always happy to work with creative innovators, they had the talent, we had the resources. It is a partnership that works very well. We've reinvented War."

KUWjones.org, syndicated feed.

- 65 -

Theodore drew and fired his arrow in a single fluid motion. LeBlanc twitched to one side and the arrow pinned him to the tree by his jacket.

LeBlanc slipped free of the garment, drew his hunting blade and braced himself against the tree. 'Come to me, friend,' he waved Theodore forwards with his knife, 'I know how to behave around bear.'

Down by LeBlanc's feet, Gretel's slim, grey-furred arm looped round the tree trunk. Her knife cut through both LeBlanc's Achilles tendons. LeBlanc cried out, staggered and sprawled face down in the needle-covered loam. Theodore's second arrow pinned him to the ground between his shoulders.

Gretel kicked away LeBlanc's knife. His cheek pressed against the ground, LeBlanc looked up into her amber eyes as he died.

'He's no bear,' Gretel said. 'And I'm no wolf.'

Theodore looked away into the forest towards the south. 'Two to go,' he growled.

Wilson and Halifax lay low while the gun battle raged. Finally they heard two great concussions, the distant flashes bright through the trees, and the sounds of fighting died away. They drew their own weapons and cautiously moved forwards.

'We got an army behind us and a war in front. May as well go on as go back,' Halifax muttered.

'Keep quiet,' Wilson said, and led them on.

Now the forest was truly silent, no bird song, no scurrying in the branches or undergrowth broke the uneasy calm. Only their footfalls, soft on the leaf litter, the sweep of their clothing across foliage.

'Who do you think won?' Halifax whispered as he held back a low branch.

It bore thinking about. Gould had brought a big unit. Chances were he had done what he had come to do and was regrouping before he pushed on to some pre-arranged extraction point. To stand any chance they would have to get close. A confrontation like that, with those odds, you got only one chance.

Wilson stopped walking. 'Look, Halifax, I'm only here for one thing. I get that done and everything else is all right with me.'

Halifax nervously scanned the surrounding woods. 'Thought I heard something.'

Motionless, they listened, and heard nothing.

'I'm just saying,' Wilson continued. 'If there's some other stuff you got to do, any plans, you don't need to hang around.'

'And here's me just getting used to the great outdoors.'

Wilson was suddenly weary. All his life since Mandy, every passing day had brought him to this place, this moment. 'It's a hell of a long walk to get out of some woods.'

Halifax let the branch swing down behind Wilson with the finality of a closing door. 'So we'll walk through them together.'

A few minutes later Wilson felt Halifax's hand push down hard on his shoulder. They took to cover fast and quiet.

'Something's coming,' Halifax whispered.

'You always think—'

Halifax raised a finger to his lips. Then Wilson heard it too, a steady beat, like a muffled drum – running feet.

Wilson motioned for Halifax to stay put, then belly crawled a few yards through the trees. He knew it was Gould as soon as he saw the distant silhouettes. Gould, and the woman who had killed Masters at the shopping mall.

Gould and the woman ran towards them through the darkening forest. Each had a rifle over their shoulder, strapped tight for running. They moved fast but warily, alert and cautious. As the passed by Wilson he saw the ugly wound on the woman's face and felt a cruel joy that whatever Gould had set out to do, he had failed and fled from the consequences.

Filled with elation, Wilson surged to his feet. 'Mitchell Gould,' he called, and shot Gould in the leg. Gould twisted, and fell to the ground.

The woman was fast but Halifax was already there, his gun aimed dead centre on her chest.

'Drop it,' he told her. 'Get down on your knees. Do anything but breathe and this is your grave.'

She recognised him and knew he would be true to his word. She let her pistol fall and knelt on the ground.

Wilson looked down at Gould spread-eagled on the forest floor. Gould's left arm angled down by his side, his right lay high over his head, the gun in his hand pointed directly away from Wilson. Blood stained Gould's left thigh, the wound was not fatal, it wasn't even dangerous. Wilson didn't mind. 'After all these years, I catch up with you,' he said.

Gould lifted his head, his teeth clenched in pain. 'Who the fuck are you?'

Wilson laughed out loud, Gould had no idea who he was. In its own way this was perfect. Now it would all come to an end, his life would start again. Perfect.

'This is for Mandy,' Wilson raised his gun.

Gould's eyes swam with pain, 'No, wait, don't.'

'Goodbye.'

Gould looked up at Wilson and long seconds crawled by. 'Get on with it, damn you.'

Wilson found he couldn't pull the trigger. Mandy wouldn't let him.

All the years, all the encounters and risks he'd taken, going up against armed and dangerous fugitives without a lethal weapon of his own. He hadn't wanted to kill Gould at all, he had wanted the person who killed Mandy to die. That person wasn't Gould, it was himself.

'Kill him,' Halifax said.

Wilson gave a chuckle of dry amusement. 'Move your hand away from the gun, Gould. I'm bringing you in.'

'No.' Halifax clubbed Ayesha savagely and she fell without a sound. His gun swung towards Gould. 'Merlotta, Xiong, you didn't see what Gould did.'

Wilson stepped between Halifax and Gould. 'I'm taking him back. It's what I do.'

All emotion dropped from Halifax's voice, 'Wilson, I'm telling you. Step aside.'

'Halifax, listen-'

Halifax barged past Wilson and aimed his gun. Gould crabbed sideways, his eyes fixed on Halifax. His hand found the FaF gun. He pulled the trigger. The bullet buzzed through the leaf litter, arced back on itself and slammed into Halifax's chest.

Gould screwed his eyes shut against the blast. Heat rolled over him. He heard Wilson's short, high scream, the crash of branches, then the slower, ponderous creak of falling timber. Half blinded by the flash, Gould scrambled away.

A sparse litter of twigs, needles and leaves pattered to the ground. Gould listened intently and waited for his vision to recover. Nothing stirred.

Urgency grew in him. When it became unbearable, he rose to his feet and looked around.

Halifax was smoking boots, his torso an empty cavity of splayed ribs and spattered gore. Ayesha lay where she had fallen, Gould helped her to her feet. She groaned and opened her eyes.

She saw what was left of Halifax and shuddered. 'Where's his friend?'

Gould pointed to a pair of legs pinned under a fallen tree. Alive or dead, he was going nowhere.

'They followed us up from Salem,' Ayesha said. 'This is one epic clusterfuck.'

'Time to go,' Gould said through gritted teeth. His wound burned with pain but his fear was greater. LeBlanc had vanished and the para-humans still hunted them through the forest. Hurriedly, Gould bandaged his wound while Ayesha found a stick for him to use as a crutch. Keeping to cover, watching each other's backs, they fled through the silent trees.

An hour later they found the vehicles. By morning they were in a motel on the outskirts of Vancouver. They cleaned up, shared a hot shower and screwed just to get warm. No oral, no finesse, just straight, energetic sex.

On the edge of orgasm, Gould said, 'We've still got the three hundred.'

Ayesha bucked her hips, locked eyes with Gould and came like a woman having an earthquake. Deep inside, she understood what Gould meant when he said 'We'.

Afterwards, Gould dozed and woke feeling refreshed. Naked, Ayesha walked across the room and fixed coffee. He watched her, enjoyed the sight of her clean brown skin, the muscles and tendons moving on her flanks, the way her sleek black hair slid across her skin.

Realising he was watching, Ayesha turned her back, spread her legs, bent over and shook her ass. As she straightened, she made sure her hair fell over her damaged cheek.

'So,' she said as she carried the coffees back to the bed, 'Who the fuck is Mandy?'

- 66 -

Crane had achieved some truly amazing feats in his life but there was still one significant thing left to do. Right now, standing in the study of the lodge at Million Pines, a home that was remarkably modest considering his near unimaginable wealth, he thought about that final task and realised how simple it would be to achieve. The main reason it was going to be so easy was that he wanted to do it.

'How do you want to do this?' Crane said. 'I can set up a trust, create a new over-holding, or just sign it over.'

Novik rolled the shaft of the lupine woman's white-fletched arrow between finger and thumb. Slowly, it dawned on him what Crane was on about, 'You're going to give it to me?'

'That's what you want, isn't it?' Crane said calmly.

'Yes,' Novik said. It was what Josie would want, their wildest dream come true.

Marytha and Benny sprawled on the settees beside the open hearth. Benny looked less than happy.

'Ellen's waiting, I want to do it now, and I want to do it quickly. So what's it going to be?' The corners of Crane's mouth twitched up, 'Just don't say cash.'

Novik couldn't imagine what it would be like to have the near infinite resources at Crane's disposal. He would be able to do just about anything he wanted, people, possessions, islands, houses, industries, even countries would be at his beck and call. Everyone would want to be his friend, he could have anything he wanted, any time of the day. It was a wonder that Crane led such an ordinary life. Compared to people less wealthy than he, which frankly was everyone who had ever lived, he lived like a monk.

Now Novik would be able to finish the job he and Josie had started together. He could buy everything that had ever been made, and give it away. In fact, he wouldn't even have to buy it, because he owned it all anyway.

He'd bring the global economy grinding to a halt. Shut it all down in Josie's name.

Save the world, or die trying. It would be her legacy.

Except it didn't feel right.

It sounded dreadful.

It was the sort of plan that only sounded good when it was unachievable. Josie had known that too, right from the outset. She had gone along with it, with Novik, because she loved him, so she could be there when it was over. Together, for the rest of their lives. Now there was the chance to do it properly, to change things once and for all, there had to be a better way.

Deciding what that was wasn't going to be easy. In the past, whenever there was a serious decision to be made, he'd always had Josie. Now he had one chance to get it right, to use all this power and wealth like an enormous global hoist, a financial sky-hook. To lift the entire world up to a better place, place human destiny onto a new road with a shining destination.

Benny, that skinny, mop-haired drifter from another world, watched him intently. Novik recalled something Benny had said when they first met.

'You said we were butterflies, right?' Novik said.

'Yes, indeed,' Benny grinned.

Novik felt more like they were all caterpillars, forever consuming. It was time to stop hoarding, time for the monkey to open his fist, let go of the peanut and take his hand out the bottle. Then, just maybe, things might change. One person couldn't be trusted with this, it was too big, too vast even for governments, for countries, for anything partisan. It had to be everyone, all in it together. He could only think of one answer.

It felt right.

'I don't want it. I've had a better idea,' Novik said.

'Then hurry up and tell me,' Crane said.

Novik told him.

Silently, exuberantly, Benny punched the air.

'I agree.' Palfinger Crane went to his desk. A projection of the United Nations Logo appeared, followed a few moments later by the exhausted grey face of Mikhail Lobachevsky, the Secretary-General.

'Hello Mikhail,' Crane said.

'Palfinger, a pleasure as always. My friend, if this is a social call I must cut you short. Permanent Larry has just passed over northern Cuba. This office has the atmosphere of a certain grain silo on the Volga.'

Crane absorbed the sombre news, 'Where's Larry headed?'

'Louisiana.'

'I have some important information,' Crane said.

Lobachevsky gave a weary smile, 'I hope it is also good news.'

'Yes, it is,' Crane said. 'I want to make a donation.'

'That's nice,' Lobachevsky said in a monotone, 'As ever, it is much appreciated. How much can you spare today?'

'The lot.'

Lobachevsky squeezed his eyes shut, he rubbed the bridge of his nose. 'I, ah- I beg your pardon?'

'I'm going to give it all to you, Mikhail.'

'All?' Lobachevsky quavered.

'Everything.'

Only Crane could give that word its full meaning. It carried its own echo.

Everything.

Everything.

Everything.

Everything.

Lobachevsky stared back from the screen. 'What do you want?' he whispered.

'Nothing.' Crane spread his hands, 'I already have it.'

'Haha, you are making fun of me,' Lobachevsky clasped his hands slowly. 'Great joke, bad timing.'

'Mikhail, I'm serious.'

'No you're not.'

'Yes I am. For goodness sake, how hard can this be?'

Lobachevsky stared, open-mouthed, 'You mean it?'

'I do.'

'Really?'

'Mikhail!'

Lobachevsky frowned ferociously, he picked up his handset and put it down again, he tidied the papers on his desk and rearranged his pens. When he looked up, he seemed to be surprised to see Crane still on his screen.

'Mikhail, I haven't got all day,' Crane said patiently, pleading.

'Whew!' Lobachevsky placed his palms on his desk and blew out his cheeks, 'What can I say? Thank you. I'm humbled, words do not exist-' Overcome by emotion, Lobachevsky wept as only stout middle-aged hard-drinking Russian men burdened by great responsibilities can. 'Tovarisch,' he sobbed incoherently, and blew his nose, 'spasibo, tovarisch, spasibo.'

'Mikhail, listen, it will take some time,' Crane said. 'I've gifted my personal possessions to the position of Secretary-General with immediate effect, but you have to accept. Once you do, it will initiate fiscal and legal cascades that will propagate around the world.'

Seated behind his desk, Mikhail Lobachevsky looked very small. 'All right. Good.' He blew out his cheeks then grinned like a child, an expression of pure joy. 'Incredible. Wow. Today the world changes forever. Finally we will be able to do... all we ever dreamed... I will inform the secretariat. Then, I think I shall drink some vodka. A lot of vodka.'

The UN logo replaced Lobachevsky. Faintly in the background The Girl from Ipanema played.

'I don't feel any different,' Crane frowned, then laughed, 'I thought I would. Bianca is going to be surprised. No more hand-outs for her, she'll have to get a job,' Crane laughed, 'I suppose I will too.'

Moments later every phone in the lodge began to ring. Guinevere Snarlow's sounded inside her jacket over the back of a chair in the medical wing, the phones of the dead airmen rang in the hallway. The UN logo flickered, froze, broke into multi-coloured blocks and was replaced by Cheswold Lobotnov, Secretary of State of the United States of America.

Lobotnov sat at a leather-topped desk in a dimly-lit office. Fingers steepled he gazed intently from the screen with an aura of supreme intellectual authority.

A large insect crashed into the desk lamp and fell on its back. Lobotnov flicked the madly buzzing creature away with his pencil and resumed his brooding pose. 'You fool, Crane,' he said darkly. 'What do you think you're playing at?'

Crane told him.

'Gah!' Lobotnov slammed his small fist down on the desk. The sudden movement started a fit of sneezing. 'Fuck it,' he said as he groped for a tissue. 'And fuck you too.'

The screen blurred, the speakers squawked and General Andriewiscz glared into the room. He appeared to be naked. 'ANDRIEWISCZ' was stencilled in black pen on his muscular, grey-haired chest, drawn on his shoulder were four stars.

'Give me the President,' Andriewiscz growled.

Crane discovered he was in an elevated mood somewhat above that caused by drinking champagne yet below actual euphoria.

'I'm afraid I'm busy right now,' Crane said. 'Can you call back later?'

'It's not a request.'

'Where's Chandra Smith?'

'Sitting on the runway at Vancouver until I tell him otherwise.'

Crane paled at the news, 'President Snarlow made a promise. I expect you to keep it.'

'Put her on.'

'Andriewiscz, I can't. She's been hurt, she's sedated.'

Andriewiscz's eyes narrowed, 'What happened?'

'There was a shoot-out. I'm sure you know what I mean.'

'Put her in the chopper. Send her here.'

'You'd be better off allowing Chandra's flight. I have a comprehensive medical facility, he is one of the best trauma surgeons in the world.'

Andriewiscz knew when to make a tactical retreat. 'Deal.'

And so the future became inevitable. Andriewiscz would retrieve Snarlow, she would recover and return to the White House. And it would start all over again.

Nobody noticed Novik slip out of the room.

On screen, the General turned to one side and spoke to a naked man wearing a section of tarpaulin as a kilt. 'Clear airspace. Fighters engage on my explicit command only. There will be absolutely no mistakes.'

'Yes, sir.' The man saluted and turned away.

Now everyone could see Andriewiscz wore a piece of green plastic sheeting round his waist. In the background a squad of naked men swatted and stamped at flying insects.

'General, if you don't mind me asking, what happened?' Benny said.

'Those puking tree-huggers in Europe. Gutless lesbian hippy liberal pussies don't have the balls to fight a normal war, they get bugs and creep-crawlies to do it for them.' Andriewiscz's already angry face congested with rage, 'We're not through.'

'It can get pretty cold at night,' Crane said.

Marytha watched the naked soldiers run and leap. 'It looks pretty cold right now.'

Andriewiscz stared out of the screen. 'Don't you worry, we'll re-equip, we'll refuel. Until then, there's plenty of wood for some damned big fires. We'll keep things warm. Right now, the whole damned world looks like a marshmallow. I got my orders, we're still coming.'

'Who we got on the lines, Rik?'

'Let's find out. Hello port… nineteen. Who's waiting on port nineteen?'

'Hello Rik, hello Ralf. Can I say that I'm a big fan of your show?'

'You just did, and you either have highly refined tastes or you want something. Share your name, my friend.'

<pause>

'I'd rather not say.'

'Ralf, we got a shy one. My friend on port nineteen, as a regular listener you'll know we not only respect, we also guarantee, your privacy. I can see from your connection socket you're… Actually I can't see anything. That's like – hang on – that's totally secure. I'm in awe.'

'I didn't think you could do that, Rik.'

'Ralf, our caller's doing it, so you must be. Whereabouts are you, port nineteen?'

'I'm on the road.'

'And what can we do for a mysterioso stealth gypsy tonight?'

'I'm lonely, Rik. And I'm looking for some advice.'

'We're full of advice, aren't we, Ralf.'

'We're full of something. Spit it out and we'll see what we can do.'

'Well, I got this friend–'

'And who hasn't got a friend like that? I know Ralf has.'

'Rik, I know him like I know myself. What kind of trouble has this friend got himself into?'

'He's going to die.'

<pause>

'Woah. Right. I'm damned sorry to hear that. Is it the big C?'

'It's OK, Ralf. And it's sunshine. The sunshine is killing him.'

'This might be a silly question, but why not stay indoors?'

'Oh no, I just got to be outside, under the sky and on the open road. Wait, I mean, HE has. That's what he wants.'

'It's all right, we understand. Look, we chew the fat and play music, I don't know what decent advice we can give you.'

'What - what HE wants to know is what should he do? He's got a year to make sense of things, understand who he is, what life is all about.'

'Rik?'

'Well… I think your friend should live for the day. Have fun, see the sights. He should find a good woman, better still, a bad woman, a dirty, open-minded woman–'

'Um – a woman?'

'Yeah. Maybe two.'

'But, um– My body isn't–' <pause> 'I just realised something.'
'Yes, my friend?'
'You've really helped. I got to go.'
<pause>
'What was that, Ralf?'
'Damned if I know, Rik. Let's have some music.'
<fade>

Rik'n'Ralf's Podneck Redcast

- 67 -

The medical rooms were silent except for the soft hum of instrumentation and Ellen's slow, frame-assisted breathing. Novik watched her vast chest rise and fall, and wondered if he actually had the balls to do what he had come to do.

Ellen was visibly smaller. She was still huge but you could see some differences. Her face had begun to emerge from the puddingy folds and slabs of surrounding flesh, her hands and wrists were less cuffed and dimpled. She gave a long, heavy sigh, opened her eyes and squinted at Novik.

'Hello, Ellen,' Novik said.

'Hi.' Ellen's voice was high and thin, she tried to sit up but the exoframe wouldn't let her. 'I remember you. You helped my father.'

'My name's Novik. Don't try to move.'

She frowned. 'I feel funny.'

'You've been sedated.'

Ellen screwed her eyes shut, 'It's something else.'

'You're losing weight. Your father discovered a cure.'

Ellen became very still. A tear glistened in her eye, 'Am I still going to die?'

'Chandra Singh is on his way. He thinks you'll be all right.'

'This cure, is it expensive?'

Novik smiled, 'Yes and no.'

Weary again, Ellen closed her eyes. 'Being normal…' She slept.

The painkillers had taken the edge off Guinevere's injury, and her hangover. It wasn't so bad, and the oxygen tube compensated well for her collapsed lung. Andriewiscz would get her out, get her into surgery in his CSH and they'd move to plan B, or C. Or whatever. She'd think of something. There was only one way out of this, and that was forwards.

The door opened. Novik stood in the entrance.

'Why so serious?' Snarlow said. 'Come on in, son.'

'How are you feeling?' Novik said.

'A lot better, thank you.'

'Don't thank me,' Novik said, 'You tried to kill us.'

'It's nothing to do with you. It's not exactly personal.'

'That's nice to know.'

'Where are you from, son?'

'Here and there. Oregon.'

'When you love your homeland, when you devote your life to its service, sometimes you have to make sacrifices, no matter how personal and painful.'

Novik gripped the shaft of the white arrow, 'I know that.'

'I can use people prepared to do that. Pragmatists. Realists.' She gave him her campaign smile, it was hypnotic, incandescent, 'People like you.'

Novik felt the muscles of his own face involuntarily respond. That power of hers, the betrayal of his own body, gave him the strength he needed, the conviction. He spoke out loud:

'This is Novik. Mary had a little lamb. Full sedation.'

'Don't you dare,' Guinevere struggled to push herself upright, briefly blacked out with the pain and slumped back. She clawed at the tubes attached to her veins, Novik grabbed her wrists and held her down. She tried to summon the Voice, her Look, the Face that was worth five percent in a swing state. 'Stop this immediately.'

'You've lost,' Novik said. 'It's over. I'm not like you.'

'It's never over. I get what I want.'

She fought it all the way down, struggled against the vast, oceanic drowsiness, the blank concrete emptiness that seeped through her blood and into her brain. And she failed.

When Guinevere was completely still, Novik pressed a pillow over her face. She did not struggle. It seemed to Novik that lying there, she was complicit in his own actions, both accepting and participating in her own death.

When every monitor showed flat lines, he took the pillow away. 'I'm not like you,' he whispered, broke the arrow in two and placed the pieces on her chest.

Back in the study, Andriewiscz was still on-screen and making demands.

'I want your medical data patched through to my surgeons. You got full comms, even if I wanted to block you I can't, the generators are down.'

Novik walked back into the study, 'There's no point. She's dead.'

'You're lying,' Andriewiscz snapped automatically.

'I just killed her.'

Andriewiscz's brow furrowed, his mouth twitched, his eyes lost focus. He tried to imagine life without Guinevere Snarlow, tried to imagine the Executive and the United States without her at the helm. Then he thought about the future with the new President, Oscar Gordano.

Jesus Christ Almighty.

'Son, you're going to fry,' Andriewiscz said. 'Hell, I don't think you'll make it to trial alive. Comes to that, I think you'll have trouble lying on a feather mattress without breaking your legs in five different places.'

'You've lost,' Novik said. 'It's over. There's nothing here for you.'

'We'll see about that. I've got all the keys to all the launch codes I need. Three minutes from now you're going to be nothing but black shadows and molten glass. So is Paris, London, Berlin, Athens and any other God-damned city I can think of east of Lisbon. Oh yeah, Lisbon. This is war. Only the survivors get to say what happened.'

The screen went blank.

Novik turned to Benny, 'If you're really who you say you are, do something now.'

'You mean break the Prime Directive, violate every principal of my training and intervene in the destiny of an advanced, intelligent species?'

Novik felt dizzy, breathless. He thought he might be having a heart attack, 'If that's what it takes, then, yes.'

'There's no such rule. Anyway, you and Palfinger have saved yourselves. You did it, Novik. Andriewiscz isn't a threat, he's just lost a war and doesn't even realise. However, he's a nasty man, and seeing as you asked so nicely, we'll be very happy to help tidy up any reactionary factions.' Benny spread his hands. 'Interfering is what we do, and we do it very well.'

Purple lightning flickered across the southern sky as, down by the 49th parallel, a dozen spider-legs of violet light hammered down from the stratosphere and stalked through Andriewiscz's HQ. Moments later a teeth-jarring vibration came through the ground. Crockery rattled, furniture juddered across the floor, bottles jumped across the table. Benny reached out and snagged the Bowmore. Upstairs, something smashed. Slowly the grinding vibration died away.

Despite Benny's scruffy attire, he radiated poise and dignity, 'My name is Bennjeffre the Spoke, Ambassador to Earth from the Commonwealth of the Galactic Arm. Congratulations! Palfinger Crane, thank you for your donation, and welcome to the future. I guarantee it will include your daughter.'

Crane felt a gigantic weight lift from his shoulders, 'You don't much look like an Ambassador, and I've met a few.'

'By necessity I was travelling incognito.'

'I still have trouble,' Novik said.

'I'm used to doubt. It doesn't matter what you believe, we're coming anyway,' Benny said.

Silver light swung ponderously through the woods, each tree had many shadows. Together, they went to the window. Everywhere they looked, the sky was filled with falling cities of light.

'But I... We...' Marytha was lost for words. 'Lord have mercy, I bonked an alien.'

Benny gave her a big hug, 'Hey, me too.'

Later, Novik and Marytha walked out onto the veranda. The new lights in the sky were extremely big and very far away. They shone down over Vancouver in the west, formed a scattered line south along I5 to Seattle and beyond. Great bands of luminescence rotated like spokes, strings of titanic pearls hung over cities like gigantic fairy lights. They were all over the world. Even Calgary.

A second helicopter now stood beside the Presidential aircraft, Chandra Singh was with Ellen. Visibly thinner, Ellen was awake and stable. Chandra was preparing to operate using the special instruments and equipment he had designed for Ellen, when Benny offered to translate them to the hospital deck of one of the capital ships orbiting the planet. After a brief discussion including Palfinger, it was agreed. Benny, Chandra and Ellen would leave within minutes.

Marytha and Novik leaned on the stone balustrade of the veranda.

'I wish Josie could have seen this,' Novik said.

Marytha put her hand on his.

Out of the darkness at the edge of the lawn strode the ursine bowman, Theodore. In his arms he carried a human form wrapped in a ground sheet, beside him limped a bruised and battered man, heavy-set and middle-aged, his clothes were torn and covered in dirt.

Novik and Marytha hurried down the steps.

'Theodore, bring him inside. We have doctors,' Novik said.

Theodore lowered the body he carried to the ground and stepped back, 'This man is beyond help. He was a stranger, yet he fought the enemy.'

The man with Theodore wiped his hands on the seat of his trousers, 'I'm Jericho Wilson, I've been hunting Mitchel Gould and he led us here. Gould killed my partner, then this man's crew. We teamed up, I don't know much about him, his name was Bernard Halifax.'

'I knew him,' Marytha's voice shook, 'Let me see.'

'No, ma'am,' Wilson said. 'If you knew him, you don't want to see him now.'

'What happened out there?' Marytha said.

'Mitchel Gould.'

'That's not enough.'

Wilson gave a weary sigh, 'Can we sit down? It's been a long day.'

'Go inside, both of you,' Novik said. 'Get a drink, get cleaned up.'

'Thanks,' Wilson said gratefully. 'What's with the giant lights?'

'Spaceships. The aliens have landed.'

'You don't say?' Wilson took it in his stride. 'It's sure been one of those weeks.'

After they had gone to the lodge, Theodore said, 'Novik, will you take this warrior back to his people?'

'Wilson said they're gone. If Halifax was here, it was because he wanted to be.'

Theodore scooped up Halifax's remains, 'I will lay him with St.John. Their spirits will become guardians of this land.'

'The Queen is dead, Theodore,' Novik said.

Theodore dipped his head, 'That is good news.'

'I don't know. Yes, I am. I'm just not sure how I feel about what I did.'

'And that is it should be.' Theodore sniffed the air, 'Rain, I think. Farewell, Novik. We may meet again.'

Theodore walked away into the gloom. Novik stood alone in the night.

Wilson and Marytha talked late into the night. He told her some of what had happened, some of what he knew about Mitchell Gould. More about himself.

'You're a cop?' Marytha said.

'Kind of.'

'Halifax hated cops.'

'We got along all right.'

'It happens.' A nostalgic half-smile grew on Marytha's face, 'Lord, it happens.'

Wilson also told her about the anti-matter missile cases hidden behind the waterfall in the woods.

'Where do you think Gould is now?' she said.

'Heading back to New Orleans.'

Marytha thought it over. 'I think we've both got reason to make a house call.'

At sun up they were gone.

Age of Wonders

We're not alone and we're not in charge. Now I think about it, we never were, not truly. When unmanageable emergent phenomena like Permanent Larry come into being, the result of things we shouldn't have been doing anyway, Masters of Destiny is not the phrase that best describes the human race.

Maybe now. Now that we have some help.

Strange things are happening all over. Some of them might even be true. One that does seem to be is Spontaneous Human Combustion. All across the world, mostly in North America, some in Europe, a few in China, Africa, people have been bursting into flames.

They've been seen in vehicles, found in apartments, filmed in parks and malls. Every single one of them was a young adult, smartly dressed and well-groomed. They all fell over at the same time, everywhere, and burned with a flame many describe as 'like a white flower'.

Slobodan Jones,
KUWjones.org

- 69 -

Deep in a subterranean command and control centre far beneath the near infinite corn and soya fields of Nebraska, Oscar Gordano slunk from one empty chamber to another. As soon as news of Guinevere's death reached him, his security team had insisted he transfer immediately to this gigantic, silent bunker, an underground city for the entire administration.

President Gordano. How he had once dreamed of this moment.

Guinevere was dead, Lobotnov was missing, and, if reports were to be believed, Andriewiscz had been turned to a pillar of salt. As far as anyone knew, Gordano was the last surviving member of the executive. Soon after he arrived, his bowels turned to water and he locked himself in the can.

'Sir, Are you all right?' a voice called, then sneezed explosively.

'Motion sickness,' Gordano gasped, then giggled hysterically, 'Motion sickness – geddit?'

'I'm just going to check the perimeter, sir.'

Gordano never saw him again.

They had promised him an administration, engineers, scientists, a gathering army. One by one his people had slipped away on some pretext or another. The last, his Adam's apple bobbing up and down with wordless fear, had simply fled.

'Go on, you pussy,' Gordano shrieked at the receding footsteps. 'You run like a girl.'

Lobotnov should be here. He had promised he would be as he shook Gordano's hand beside the big USAAF helicopter.

'You go on ahead, Oscar,' Lobotnov said. 'I've got some tidying up to do. Room service.'

Utterly alone, Gordano tried to raise the outside world. For a few minutes he watched the external view of mown grass, tarmac and perimeter fence.

Strange insects like fat-bodied dragonflies swarmed outside. Fascinated, he watched them fly past and crawl over the lenses. In the middle distance was a running figure. Gordano manipulated the controls and zoomed in. It was a naked man.

At night he was unable to sleep, his head thick with cold. Outside, high overhead, enormous clusters of lights tumbled through the sky. They awed and frightened him, he wanted to go outside but was too scared. In the morning when he tried to call Jazmin his phone fell apart, spongy with black mildew. Back in the security room the consoles and monitors had burst open, masses of tiny, long-stalked mushrooms had forced their way through the seams and joints of the electronic equipment. Outside, all the insects were dead.

One by one the monitors stopped working. Gordano didn't know what to do, he was running a fever, it was so hard to think. He was frightened.

Three levels down Gordano located a standby security office in working order. He called everyone he knew on open channel. He used all the passwords and access codes in the envelopes he had been given when they told him he was President. He even tried to call Shirleen.

'The bitch is probably blowing her new houseboy,' he muttered. What he really wanted was for her to tie him up and beat him.

He put the entire site into lockdown and sealed the upper levels. He took a double dose of cold cure.

The Presidential suite was large, luxurious and silent. Gordano lay on the bed and drank bourbon. He swam naked in the pool, he watched porn and masturbated. Sinuses throbbing, he fell asleep. When he woke he felt terrible, burning up with thirst. As he fixed himself a glass of soda, he noticed the Meeja console in the corner. He put on the headphones and turned it on.

Immediately he felt better, healthier than he had for days. This time he read the note that had appeared beside the console, then sat back to enjoy a fresh glass of cognac and the hand-rolled Havana cigar he found in a previously empty drawer.

After a few minutes' peaceful enjoyment there was a rap on the door and a busty young blonde intern hurried in. She must have just come from cheerleader practice because she was dressed in a short pleated skirt and a tight sweater. Two large bright yellow pom-poms were clutched in one hand. Beneath the thin sweater her ample and obviously natural breasts heaved with excitement.

'Sir, wonderful news. We've won!'

'Why don't you come in?' Gordano said.

She gave him an impish smile, 'Can I use your pool?'

'Sure. Call me Ozzie.'
'I don't have a costume, Ozzie.'
Gordano felt his terrors slip away.

Oh my God, oh my God. Oh my God.

Oh.

My.

God.

    I don't know how I'm going to say this so I'm just going to say it. No spin, no angle, no bias - just the facts.

    I don't believe I just said that. And you are not going to believe what I am going to say next, I shit you not.

    Oh my God.

    That's not it. I haven't said it yet, don't go away. Yes, they've landed. Yes, they walk among us. Weird shit all over, people catching fire, big flappy bugs melt your underwear, but this!

    Listen.

    Somebody has detonated an antimatter warhead inside Permanent Larry.

    I did just say that, didn't I? You heard me right. In this New World Order of ours crazy-ass shit still happens.

    Now for the good news.

    Compared to an average hurricane, a tactical nuke or equivalent is about 0.1% of total stored energy. The likely environmental effect – zip, and Larry ain't average. On the other hand his eye was right over Nu-Orleans.

    Why is that good news? Well, if you're into geo-engineering, Lake Pontchartrain is now big enough to qualify as in inland sea, and there's a storm surge pushing up the Mississippi powerful enough to kick start the great mid-western ocean.

    But most important, that worthless scumbag, that trader in human misery Mitchell Gould is almost certainly dead. If he isn't, then his organisation most definitely is, because Nu Orleans, Big Easy 2.0, whatever you want to call it, is no more. Whoever did this got all strategic, just like our former Glorious Administration always denied they did in Mexico.

    They got biblical, folks. They smote the Big Easy and she died. The fused glass wastelands at the heart of Mexico City and Ottawa look like the Garden of Eden compared to this.

    So, well done good buddy, whoever you were. If you were after revenge you got it. If you wanted to be remembered, you got that too. Just one thing - next time, send a postcard and tell us who the hell you are.

    And why.

    You complete NUTTER.

- 70 -

It was over.

The lodge at Million Pines was near deserted. Benny and Ellen were in space, Palfinger already on his way to meet Bianca in Micronesia.

Novik spent the rest of the day at the lodge. First he walked down to the lake and sat on the lonely shore. After an hour he returned to the lodge and wandered through the deserted rooms. Echoes of action and conversation still hung in the air, laughter and screams, the sounds of gunfire. The bullet holes in the study panelling already looked like the fossil remains of some ancient conflict. As the afternoon wore on, the prospect of a night in the company of ghosts and memories felt increasingly unappealing. Novik loaded his backpack with spare clothes, a knife, a blanket and other useful equipment. He took a fresh bottle of the Bowmore from the cellar. He opened up the armoury and put on one of Crane's armoured coats. Ready to leave, he stood in the entrance hall and listened to the house. Then he pulled the wide doors shut behind him and walked away.

The blacktop ran in a series of long rises and dips east and west, the flanking forest darkly green. At the bottom of Novik's backpack were the last few thousand dollars of Gould's stash, he tightened the straps and looked along the road. One direction seemed the same as the other, Novik turned left and started walking.

He had gone several miles when he heard the sound of a car coming up behind him and stuck out his thumb. Sleek and charcoal grey, a lobsterback Cadillac AFC-16 rolled along beside him. The nearside windows rolled down and Novik saw the passenger compartment was empty. He stopped walking, the car drew to a halt.

'Where are you headed?' the car said.

Novik stuffed his hands in his pockets and kicked at the road with the toe of his boot. Despite everything he grinned, 'How's it going, Mr Car?'

'I needed to find myself.'

The answer surprised Novik, 'Did you?'

'Yes.'

'Good for you,' Novik resumed walking.

The Cadillac rolled quietly beside him, 'I'm sorry I wasn't there.'

Novik remembered the madness of the border crossing. The speed, the gunfire and screams. So much blood. 'There was nothing you could have done.'

'If I had been-'

'No.' Novik faced the car. 'I've replayed what I did a hundred times and Josie's still dead. Don't think like that, Mr. Car, it hurts too much.'

Novik had been wrong about a lot of things but he knew he was right about this. He'd been wrong about Benny, wrong in Spades, a world-class kind of wrong. And he'd been wrong about Mr. Car too. Machines never came back to say sorry.

A diamond squadron of white lights silently tumbled across the sky.

'All right,' the Cadillac said. 'There's one other thing you need to know. About me.'

'What is it?' Whatever was coming Novik knew he deserved it.

'It's Ms. Carr.'

Novik fought an intense, lethal battle with his smile, and won. 'You think you're a-?'

'I *know* I am,' Ms. Carr said forcefully. 'Trapped inside this crude metal body.'

'Well, OK,' Novik said slowly. 'If that's what you are, then that's cool. But what difference does it make? What can you do about it?'

'You'd be surprised,' Ms. Carr's engine purred, the passenger compartment lights dimmed and soft music began to play. 'Why don't you climb in and find out?'

The heck, Novik thought, I'm being come on to by an automobile. 'So where are we going?'

Ms. Carr looked up at the stars. 'Anywhere we want.'

Far over Novik's head Ellen Crane was currently being translated into a new, more slender form in one of Ambassador Spoke's starships. Even though she would still retain her remarkable exoframe, whatever her final appearance, it would still be her own body.

Ms. Carr wasn't the Cadillac. Her body didn't define who she was in the same way it did Ellen, or Novik. Ms. Carr could radically change her form, yet remain the same person.

She sounded her horn, 'Are you going to get in or what?'
'Are we cool?' Novik said.
'Dude, we are completely and awesomely cool.'
Novik opened the door, 'Are you still going to call me sir?'
Ms. Carr laughed, 'You have a lot to learn about girls.'
Novik settled himself into the passenger seat. 'Let's go.'
They got. And the going was good.

Menu

2. Main Characters

Novik	A drifter, idealist
Josie	A drifter, realist
Benny	Their hitcher
Mr. Car	A car.
Palfinger Crane	The cash machine
Ellen Hutzenreiter-Crane	His daughter
Bianca Hutzenreiter	His wife
Guinevere Snarlow	President of the USA
Oscar Gordano	Her bitch
Cheswold Lobotnov	A weird little smart guy
General Andriewiscz	A boy with his toys.
Mitchell Gould	King of New Orleans
Ayesha	His consort
Manalito	His right-hand man
Black	An Old-fashioned Boy
Morgan	Likewise
Bernard Halifax	A performance artist
Jericho Wilson	A burned out, deadbeat loser
Masters	A special agent
Johnson	A special agent

And

Introducing Carmichael Donovan
As
'Marytha'

(Bernard Halifax is currently appearing in Blythe Spirit at Drury Lane Theatre.)

Menu

3. Set-up and Language Options

3.1 Set-up

Sample Text:

This way up.

Instructions:

a)   Rotate book until the sample text is in correct orientation for comfortable reading.
b)   Your book is now set up for reading.

3.2 Languages

a)   This edition is only available in English. If you are able to read English you should be able to read this book.
b)   In the unlikely event you encounter an unfamiliar word please consult a dictionary*.

*Dictionary: An authoritative collection of word definitions and spellings.

Menu

4. Credits

The quotations at the beginning of chapters 4 and 21 are taken from James Burke's book Connections, with kind permission.

The calling of the dolphins in chapter 30 is inspired by Arthur Grimble's account in his autobiography, 'A Pattern of Islands'.

Menu

5. Special Features

http://davidgullen.com/

BRANCH	DATE
	11/13

Lightning Source UK Ltd.
Milton Keynes UK
UKOW05f1846061113

220582UK00002B/68/P

9 781909 016200